ROAR
OF THE
TIDES

ROAR OF THE TIDES

VERONICA ROSSI

Roar of the Tides

For information about this title or to order other books and/or electronic media, contact the publisher:

Pathos Books
questions@pathosbooks.com

ISBNs:
979-8-9872305-0-3 (hardcover)
979-8-9872305-1-0 (softcover)
979-8-9872305-2-7 (eBook)

Printed in the United States of America

Cover and Interior design: 1106 Design

For my readers who wanted this story.
Thanks for showing me I wanted it, too.

~ 1 ~

ROAR

Roar cut through the water like a blade, his strokes quick and relentless. He couldn't feel a thing—not the cool water, nor the sting in his lungs, nor the competitive fire that had burned in him once, before everything had changed.

He was in a race, but he couldn't care less whether he won or lost. What he cared about was getting it over with. Even more so, he cared about appearing like he was fine, still his usual self, so he pushed harder, slicing through the waves and churning his legs for speed.

When he felt sand under his feet, he popped up and saw what he'd hoped for: a perfectly empty beach. Nothing but white sand, palm trees, and sandpipers in sight.

Good. Alone, there was no need to pretend or to feel guilty.

Rubbing his salt-stung eyes, he jogged across the beach to the trail, where the palm trees swayed overhead. There, he rummaged through the rushes for the bottle he'd stashed earlier.

Dropping down, he uncorked it and took a long drink, the luster burning a path down his throat. The day was bright and hot, his skin drying right before his eyes. Squinting, he looked out toward the surf.

Perry and Talon were just coming in, both of them swimming hard to catch a wave. Roar took another sip, then quickly hid the bottle before Perry could see it.

"Roar!" Talon's shout broke above the crashing surf. "You cheated!"

Even from a distance, Roar could easily tell them apart. His best friend Perry was the fairer head, obviously blond even soaked. Perry's nephew, Talon, was the darker one, shaking his fist in the air even as he swam the rest of the way in. Beyond them, the black rock that Roar should've rounded before heading back to the beach jutted from the water.

"Roar!" Talon yelled louder, wading through the shallows. "That wasn't fair!"

Roar sighed, shaking his head. *Fair.* What a word.

Lying back on his elbows, he watched Perry and Talon roughhouse their way over—a familiar cycle of lunges and takedowns, wrestling, escapes, then the whole thing starting again. With the luster finding its way into his veins, the tight feeling around his heart eased slightly. Not enough to go unnoticed by the approaching Scires, though, so he went about lifting his mood through sheer force of will, drawing deep breaths and trying to clear his mind.

It wasn't their fault he found paradise tedious, so why ruin it for them?

Not a year ago, they'd been hundreds of miles away, their tribe, the Tides, sheltering in a cave as the Aether devastated their homes, their land. Everything.

They had survived somehow and made it here, to the safety of a new land.

No, not *somehow*. It'd been Perry's leadership and refusal to accept defeat. Aria's bravery and her gift for turning mortal enemies into allies. Marron's organizational brilliance and kindness. Cinder's life. Reef's life. The lives of so many others. So much had been given so that he could sit there, surrounded by undeniable beauty, and find it wanting.

By the time they finally reached him, Perry and Talon were basted in sand and panting.

"So?" Perry flipped his hair out of his eyes. "Did I win, or did he lose?"

Talon's head snapped up. "*What?*" he said. "*I* won*!*"

"Winner's obvious." Roar shook the sand out of his shirt and shrugged it on. "Sorry, Per."

"Yes!" Talon threw his skinny arms up. "I won!"

At nine, he already reached Perry's shoulders and was comically gangly. He'd be a giant someday. Bigger than Perry. Bigger, even, than his father had been.

Perry smirked at the boy. "No way you won. Not with these things slowing you down." He tugged on one of Talon's ears. "They're like sea anchors."

"Look at that thing! You look like a swordfish that ran into a wall!" Talon jumped up, swiping for Perry's nose. Perry lunged for him, but Talon dodged aside deftly, agile in spite of his coltish limbs. Laughing, he flipped his hair out of his eyes exactly like Perry had moments ago. "I'm hungry," he declared, suddenly serious, like he'd just received orders from his stomach. With that, he spun and dashed up the trail, disappearing into the trees.

Perry's smile faded as he watched him go. "He's becoming so much like Vale."

Vale was Perry's deceased older brother and Talon's father, who Perry had supplanted as the Tide's Blood Lord in a brutal confrontation.

"In looks?" Roar tossed Perry his shirt, then grabbed his knife belt and hopped up. "No doubt about that." In appearance, Talon was his father through and through: strong jaw, leaf-green eyes, and brown skin a shade lighter than mahogany.

"Well, yes. But I meant he's merciless." Perry tipped his chin toward the waves. "I had to push to stay with him out there."

Roar looked up from buckling his belt and snorted. "And you think he gets that from *Vale?*"

Vale had been calculating, underhanded, and paranoid, but mercilessness was a quality that ran through their entire bloodline. With Perry, it just took a lot to get him there.

Perry smirked. "Fair enough," he conceded, and they started for home.

The trail cut through lush foliage that softened the relentless sun and made the sand feel cool under Roar's bare feet. The tunnel of greenery stirred with gentle breezes and light fell through it, dappled and dreamlike. From all directions, he heard the chirring of insects and the twittering of birds. It was never quiet here, never even close to it.

It hadn't been at home, either. But there, it hadn't bothered him.

Nature was such a vivid thing here. The birds and flowers. The fruits and fish. Everything was saturated with colors that shouted at him. This place—once called the Still Blue, but now called Cinder—looked pretty, it *was* pretty, he *knew* it was, yet he found it grating. Like someone tapping incessantly on his shoulder that he didn't want to speak to. It was a problem he'd tried to fix for a while, until he'd realized the solution was beyond him.

"Where'd you hide the bottle?" Perry glanced back. "In the rushes?"

"Bottle? I don't know what you mean," Roar replied, keeping his voice neutral, for all it would help. Perry was a Scire, the rarest Marked, possessing an enhanced sense of smell. The keenest Scires, like Perry, could detect people's moods and know when they were lying—or when they had luster on their breath even from a distance of several paces away.

Perry ducked under a branch. "Didn't we just clear this a few weeks ago?"

"It's jungle, Per," Roar said, relieved by the change of subject.

Perry reached a hand back. "Knife."

"To *hack brush* with?"

"Roar."

"Fine." He slipped one from the sheaths at his belt and offered the handle with a quick flip. "But this demeans it."

Perry dove right in and attacked the more obtrusive branches. Roar could hardly watch. He had very few possessions, but they mattered to him, his father's knives more than any of them. Soon enough, though, guilt set in. He drew the twin blade from his belt and took care of whatever Perry missed, which wasn't much.

Our relationship encapsulated, he thought. Some people led. Others followed. He did neither by nature, preferring instead the freedom of independence. It was only because of Perry that he fell into the latter group. Sometimes he wondered where he'd be if their lives hadn't intersected a decade ago. Not just where he'd be, but *who* he'd be. Would he have turned into a hustler and brawler, like his father? A smooth-tongued liar and opportunist like his mother?

Perry wheeled sharply. "Do I remind you of her—is that it?"

Roar's heart gave a lurch, but he kept walking.

Perry stepped to the side, blocking his path. "Do you see her in me?" His eyes were wide and direct. Rarely did Roar receive such a challenging look from him. "Liv?"

"I know who you meant," Roar snapped. In his mind, *her* was always Liv. Perry's sister. The girl he'd loved and lost. And still loved. "And no, I don't." He shoved past Perry. "No more in you than in everything."

"She's gone, Roar. She's been gone for over a year. I'm trying to understand where *you* are."

Roar kept slicing branches. "Right here, obviously. And you're sharpening these for me later. And show some respect for your sister."

"My sister's memory," Perry said behind him. "Liv isn't here."

"You keep saying that. You think I don't know she's gone?"

"I know you do. I think you could stand to forget it from time to time."

Roar reached for a branch, then pushed past it. "We're not having this conversation," he said, and kept walking. He'd known this moment would come eventually. How could it not with a Scire for his closest friend? Even if the depth of his pain weren't what it was, he couldn't have hidden it from someone who scented emotions every time he breathed. But it didn't mean he had to listen to this.

He'd only taken a few steps when Perry shoved him in the back.

Roar spun, suddenly coolly furious. "What are you doing, Peregrine?"

Angry determination stared right back at him. "I'm asking questions that you're not answering. I'm tired of pretending I don't see what's going on. I know you're not good. Things can't stay like this. How do we stop this?"

Without making any conscious decision to do so, Roar laid the blade against his throat. "I can think of a way."

Perry settled into perfect stillness, like drying mortar. "You're serious?" His voice was low and hurt. "You'd do that to me? To *yourself*?"

The pressure of tears built behind Roar's eyes. Then shame hit him, making his face burn. What the hell was he doing? "No." He slammed his knife back in its sheath and turned away, blinking fast. "It's not—it's not like that." But maybe it wasn't far off.

On one or two occasions, when he'd remembered Liv, remembered the night she'd been murdered by Sable of the Horns right in front of him, maybe he'd heard the call of darkness beyond regular darkness. Maybe he'd come close to exhaustion so heinous it turned life itself into a burden.

"Then tell me . . ." Perry said quietly. "What *is* it like?"

Roar let out a slow breath through his teeth. Perry wasn't going to back down. This wasn't his friend anymore—it was Peregrine of the Tides. Slayer of tyrants. Savior of the lost and forsaken. Roar had no fight left, anyway. That was rather the point, wasn't it?

Resigned, he turned and searched for a Perry-less place to rest his eyes. He settled on a bird with a bright orange chest and beady eyes. It cocked its head sharply left and right, looking determined to hear his answer, too. Answers, then. As quick and bloodless as he could make them.

"You're not wrong. Liv *is* part of it. I don't know how to forget her. But I don't want to. She keeps me company. She reminds me of other times, better ones, and I need those memories. But there's more to it. There's another piece." He tapped his temple. "Something in here doesn't seem to be working right. I don't think I'm seeing the same world you do, Per. All this brightness . . ." He opened a hand and caught a spot of sunlight in his palm. "I don't feel it. Want to. But don't." He shrugged. "It's like I'm separate from everything. Like this isn't my world anymore." He did a quick mental review of what he'd said and nodded. "That's it. I can't explain it any better than that."

Perry stirred, a statue coming to life. "This is worse than I thought," he said, his brow furrowing.

For reasons utterly beyond him, that made Roar laugh. He slumped against a tree, noticing the bottomless fatigue in his body. The luster had settled poorly, too, and he felt the beginnings of a headache. Not for the first time, he wondered how Perry had come through grief and violence worn and scarred but stronger, while he'd come through with part of himself deadened. A big part. Head to toe. Why were some people more resilient than others?

Roar looked at his best friend. "What, no advice?"

Perry shook his head. "I'm out of my depth."

"You should have sent Aria." Roar would've accepted anyone Perry loved, but he genuinely loved Aria, too.

"Agreed," Perry said. "I'm terrible at this."

"It's true. You actually look like the depressed one now."

Perry smiled. "I think I might be."

"No, no. None of that." He had to let Perry off the hook. "This is my hole to crawl out of. There's nothing you or anyone else can do. I think I just need . . ." He wished he knew what he needed. He'd give almost anything to feel like himself again. "Look, don't worry. I'll figure something—"

The distant blare of a horn had him straightening and turning to the sound. It was the signal used to muster Cinder's citizens in times of emergency. Roar had only ever heard it in practice drills; no practice drill was scheduled today.

"What is it?" Perry demanded.

Before he could answer, the horn sounded again. This time whoever was blowing it got the full measure of the instrument, issuing a resounding moan loud enough that Perry heard it, too.

They locked eyes for a split moment, then they ran with the speed of fear.

Minutes later, they sprinted into Cinder's central square and made a direct path to Aria, who was waiting for them. Thanks to his acute hearing, Roar already knew there was no fire or injury. From the small group that had already gathered, he didn't even detect any real sense of urgency in the pitch of their voices.

"What's going on—you alright?" he asked, first to reach her.

"Yes." She turned to Perry, who thundered up seconds after, his stare severe and assessing. "I'm fine. Talon, too." Talon was actually a short distance away, chomping on an apple and playing a game with other kids. The square was in the midst of being paved and only the larger stones were laid down, which made for a good leaping course. "Everything's fine, Perry. Really." Aria stepped closer, her voice gentling. "Sorry. I didn't mean to alarm you."

"We heard the horn," Perry said. "I don't understand."

"Because we needed to convene the Council quickly," she explained. "We received a distress call. There are people out there who really need help. Come on. You should both be there."

Roar's mind churned as they walked to the common house. A distress call? In the year they'd been in Cinder, they hadn't received a single comm from anyone. They'd left the rest of the world behind when they'd made the Crossing. A burning, war-torn world. It wasn't a stretch to call it apocalyptic. He was almost surprised to learn that there was anyone left.

Inside, most of Cinder's nine governing representatives were already present. As he walked to the large table where they sat, Roar was struck by the hodgepodge of distinct societies that had melded seamlessly: members of the Tides, his and Perry's tribe; a few members of the Horn tribe; Dwellers; members of Marron's remote mountain society, Delphi. They had all come together surprisingly smoothly, in large part because of the work of the Council.

He spotted Soren's burly figure splayed over a chair and headed over to him. A Dweller like Aria, Soren had once lived in an enclosed Pod, a highly advanced biosphere, and had seemed more like an alien species than a fellow human. Now, Soren was one of the few people who'd grown on him over the past year.

Roar dropped into the chair beside him and nearly fell over backwards.

Soren grinned, the long scar on his jaw deepening. "That chair's rickety."

"I noticed." Though he really should've known. The carpenters' priority over the past year had been the construction of essentials: homes, animal pens, tools. The era of chairs was still young.

Soren's gaze fell to his neck. "What happened to you?"

Roar touched it and his fingers came away with blood. Wonderful. He'd nicked himself. "Tried to cut my throat."

Soren scowled. "Moron." He crossed his thick arms. "So, a distress message. Exciting, right?"

"I don't know, Soren. Is it?"

"I don't know, Roar. Yes?"

Roar's eyes flicked to the comm equipment on the table in front of them. It *was* exciting, actually, especially considering that over the past year the word had lost its meaning.

Talon fell out of a tree and needed his knee stitched up? Not exciting. Discovery of a source of limestone? Incredibly not exciting. First anniversary of Cinder's founding? Still not.

But a call for help?

Yes. That *did* spark his interest. And it was taking his mind off the uncomfortable exchange he'd just had with Perry.

Aria called them to order as the last Council member arrived. Silence fell, an air of gravity settling over them. Because of the mild climate, the common room had shuttered walls to allow for breezes to pass through it. Open now, they made inside and outside seem like different worlds: one sunny and noisy with swaying trees, flittering birds, and laughing children; the other dim and still. Tense.

In brief and clear terms, Aria explained the distress call. Roar listened, admiring her poise, something she'd always had, but that had increased when she took a seat in the Council. While he felt like he had faded this past year, she'd polished to a shine. Love, family, a sense of purpose. She had them all and it showed.

"It came in about an hour ago," she was saying. "We'll play it in just a moment. We've been trying to establish communication, but so far we've had no luck. There's no sign any of our messages have gone through. We've received no additional message from them, either. All we have is this." She tucked her glossy black hair behind an ear and nodded. "Go ahead, Soren."

"On it." Soren sat up, his chair cracking against the floorboards. As he swiped through commands on the comm screen, the day dimmed dramatically, like a light switching off, and a hard rain began in that sudden way Roar could never get used to. The kids squealed and went running for cover. The ceiling droned a low threatening sound as rain battered it.

"All right, we're set," Soren said, looking up.

Roar heard the rumble of thunder in the distance, then a voice came crackling through the speaker.

2

TEMPEST

Tempest tapped her finger on the comm device, wrestling with remorse.

She'd been careful not to give away her identity, but still. Should she have done it? Was it reckless to send that message? Would it have been more reckless *not* to send it, considering their precarious situation?

She sighed. There was simply no way to know, and it was done now. No point regretting it.

"That was good," Daisy said over her shoulder. "Hopefully someone will hear it."

Tempest looked up into her sweet, freckled face and saw compassion and nearly a decade of memories. Daisy was officially Tempest's attendant, but she'd always felt more like an aunt and, more recently, like an older sister.

"Hopefully the *right* someone," Tempest replied. *My brother,* she silently pleaded. *Please let him be the one who hears it.*

"It's a shot in the dark." The deep baritone came from the shadowy figure in the dim recesses of the communications room. "It'll hit whatever it hits. But we'll be ready."

It was a typical comment from Ventus, the captain of her guard. Realistic. Reassuring.

"We *are* ready," added Calista, the sole guard Ventus captained. She stood beside him holding the flashlight that provided the only source of illumination in the chamber. "Can we get out of here now?" She swept the beam over the destroyed space. "This place makes my skin crawl."

It made Tempest jumpy, too. Most of it was undamaged with the exception of the western wall, which had caved in entirely. In the weak light, it looked like a concrete tsunami suspended in time, pieces of chairs and desks and circuitry protruding in places. A blanket of dust covered every surface, but the worst part was the lingering smell of decay.

They had moved the bodies away months ago, when the four of them had first taken shelter in this crushed Dweller Pod, but Tempest still smelled it with her sensitive nose. Being a Scire had advantages and disadvantages.

She glanced at the comm device one last time, hoping for some confirmation her message had been heard. There wasn't any. "Sure," she said, standing. "Let's go home."

Together, they made their way back through a maze of dark corridors and chambers, chaos that had become familiar to them over time. This part of the Pod had taken the worst damage in last year's intense Aether storms, so they slowed often, taking care not to trip or twist ankles. Sometimes when Tempest looked at the broken girders, snapped pipes, and endless shrapnel, she could imagine she'd been devoured by a mechanical leviathan. Jonah, swallowed by a whale.

"Sweet relief," Cal said when they stepped through a thick steel door and made it home. She blew over the flashlight as she clicked it off—an old joke worn into habit.

Tempest stopped and let the others flow past her.

Living in a demolished Dweller Pod wasn't ideal by any stretch, but it wasn't terrible, either, and they'd been lucky to find this area within the larger complex. A onetime station for emergency personnel, it offered everything they needed: a comfortable meeting room connected to a full kitchen, ample food, water and medical stores, and offices they'd turned into bedrooms, all connected by the wide corridor where she now stood.

The wing also ran on its own backup generator, which had given them power for the last year, but the lights flickering overhead reminded her that that would end soon. When she'd checked that morning, the generator was down to 3 percent remaining power. That would only give them a few weeks more, at best. But their waning power supply was only one of the reasons they had to leave this place.

Part of the distress call she'd just sent had been a lie. A necessary one. But the important part—that they needed help—was absolutely true.

We've been lucky, she thought. *But luck doesn't last forever.*

Down the corridor, Daisy turned and noticed her standing there. "You all right, Temp?"

Cal and Ventus stopped, too, Cal reaching over to dust concrete powder off Daisy's shoulder. Tempest smiled at the unconscious gesture, her gaze roaming over their faces: Daisy's, fair and freckled and so easy to smile; Cal's, gorgeously smooth and dark and anchored by those steady eyes; Ventus's, cragged by time and experience.

Her subjects. Her saviors. Her family.

It was her duty to keep them safe. She was no longer sure how she'd manage it after they left the shelter of this broken Pod, but she knew better than to let that show. She remembered her brother's advice: *Some people say it takes strength to show vulnerability, but that's a lie; it takes strength to show strength.*

Tempest forced a bit more brightness into her smile. "I'm fine, Daisy. I was just thinking about dinner. Who's hungry? I'm cooking."

That sent them all into a frenzy, just as she'd known it would. She hid her amusement as they worked together to divert her away from food preparation of any kind. Cal went outside to collect fresh herbs. Daisy pulled a few of the Dweller ready-meal-kits from their storage cabinet and set them in the warmer. Ventus sat her down at their dining table and gave the same report she'd heard for the past five days.

"Here's where we are." He pointed to a dent on the stainless steel with a blunt finger. "The Wolf River's this scratch here. The tracks I found were here and ran south, along this valley. Five people, spread out evenly in a search formation." He tapped his thumb in front of Cal's usual spot. "Same tracks I saw three weeks ago over at Devil's Back range. I haven't a doubt in my mind they're a search party. They're moving too methodically to be anything else." His hazel eyes lifted to hers, his gaze steady in spite of the fizzing anxiousness she scented in his temper. "They're Banyan's men, Tempest. He's still looking for you and he's narrowed on this territory. If we don't leave here soon, it'll be too late."

It was a worrisome report, no matter that she'd already heard it a few times, nor that it came from a man she'd trusted completely since she was seven. Ventus—and Daisy—had gone south with her to the Night tribe when she became their hostage, Cal joining more recently. For nine years, she had lived with that tribe, her life serving as surety, holding together an agreement between two Blood Lords. One, her older brother Sable of the Horns. The other, Banyan of the Night.

After a rough beginning, she'd settled in, growing close to Banyan's children in particular. Sable was so much older than her, more a father. But Ash and Raven had been a couple of years on either side of her. It had all fallen apart a year ago, though, on the night she'd left in secret and fled for her life. She'd been hiding from Banyan ever since.

Tempest reached across the table, patting Ventus's big warrior's hand. "Let's give the message a day," she said, pretending not to see his disappointment. "It's going to work."

If it didn't, they'd be forced into the open, where they'd be vulnerable to any number of dangers.

They ate together, as always. Daisy had selected Tempest's favorite meal-kit, savory rice with vegetables, and added a bit of the venison Cal had provided by hunting. A treat—and a perfect representation of how they complemented each other. If they had to be in hiding, she was glad that at least Cal and Daisy had found love.

Tempest always read a bit before they began. Sometimes a poem. Sometimes pages from one of the ancient books they'd found over the past year. She varied it to keep their minds engaged. You had to do these sorts of things when your entire world consisted of four people, including yourself. Tonight, she chose *Beowulf*, Ventus's and Cal's favorite for its extremes of honor and courage. Daisy's favorite because it was Cal's. Hers, for the beauty of the old language.

After, she took the book to her room, but her mind kept wandering back to the message she'd sent out. Would Sable hear it? Part of the problem of evading Banyan was that she'd had to all but disappear, concealing her identity whenever they came across the rare stranger. She couldn't trust anyone. For all she knew, her brother had been searching for her for the past year, too.

Unable to settle into the book, she retrieved a bundle of letters from her satchel. They were from her brother, and her most valuable possessions. She took them to bed and brought the packet to her nose, breathing in the paper and ink. She used to be able to scent Sable, too, but his scent had faded.

Usually she liked reading them outside, under the Aether. For centuries, it had wrought so much damage and human suffering; but when she was under its dancing light, she felt more connected to Sable, like the blue veins above ran with the blood they shared, the last remaining members of their family line. She wasn't going out there now, though. Not with Banyan's men circling like hawks. Her room would have to do.

There were twenty-two letters, all of which she knew by heart. Untying the twine that bound them, she opened the first one. It was the oldest, worn with soft creases from all her readings. She'd been a little girl when she received it. Just seven years old and already parentless for three years by then. Her older brother had meant everything to her. When he'd told her she was going to live someplace far away, she couldn't understand it, no matter how many times he explained the word "hostage."

When this letter arrived, she'd already been with the Night tribe for a few weeks. They'd still been strangers to her who treated her either with false kindness or barely suppressed dislike. It was one of the worst times in her life.

Unfolding the paper carefully, she read.

My dear Little Storm,

The halls are too quiet without you. No one skips through them singing from the top of their lungs and swinging books in each hand. No one pouts at me because I haven't made time for them, nor has anyone begged me to gallop them around the fortress. I have a surplus of apples I know not what to do with. I do miss you.

I trust they are giving you apples there. It was one of my demands. You asked for forty-three per day. If Banyan is giving you less than that number, raise hell!

Tempest, you are surely unhappy with me now, but one day you will understand: You are valuable and that which is valuable must serve a purpose. Because of you, there can be peace between Horn and Night. There is alliance now where before there was bloodshed and enmity. By being where you are, you are doing a great service to our people, to me, and to our forbearers. Never forget this is your duty.

Banyan will foster you with care and respect. If he fails to give you either, demand them. Remember what I taught you, the Horn way: Observe the entire field, then lower your head and take it.

I will come for you one day. Do not lose faith.

Your loving brother,
Sable

She refolded it, her heart filled. Her confidence renewed.

Smiling, she lay back on her bed, remembering how he'd playfully chuck her chin and wink at her with the pale blue eyes she also had. She remembered his particular scent, a blend of fixed things—stones and roots and confidence. She remembered, too, that he always did what he promised.

I will come for you one day.

He *would* do it. He'd hear her message and come for her. Together they'd go to Rim, the true home that awaited her in the north.

She would not lose faith.

~ 3 ~

ROAR

Roar sat up and listened.

The quality of the recording was poor, the message broken and half-buried in static, but he had no equal when it came to hearing. He could cast a wide net and haul in sounds in bulk, or target his hearing like a spear singing through sunshine to pierce a single target.

He did this now, isolating on the girl's voice and discarding the static like dirt he could brush away with his hands.

"If anyone is out there—forty-three of us are stuck inside the Dweller Pod called Resolute in the Wolf Valley west of—anyone out there? We've been sheltering here since—food stores already low when the rubble shifted. We're trapped—forty-three—no way out of here and—please help us—if you—how much longer we can survive—"

It ended abruptly.

He looked immediately across the table at Aria. She was a strong Audile, too—the only other one present. Only she had heard what he had: the message beyond the words. The fingerprint of the voice. The girl was young, educated, and spoke with controlled urgency. There was a light roll in her r's, typical of southerners, and a general crispness in her enunciation, typical of tribes in the north. She was well-traveled, intelligent, and cool-headed in dire situations—and this *was* a dire situation.

Her fear was genuine.

Being on the farthest side of the hearing-sensitivity spectrum, it hit him like a dousing of icy water. He suddenly felt more alert than he had in months.

Aria nodded, understanding. "Play it one more time, Soren," she said.

"Sure," he said, complying.

The recording ended and a long silence followed, the rain hissing outside.

Roar gleaned nothing more from the second listen. His hearing was perfect every time. But listening to it again enhanced what he felt. Sharp. Awake. Like some window in his mind had been propped open to let in fresh air.

Marron was the first one to break the silence. "Forty-three people," he said, his plump hand fluttering to his heart. "My *word*."

Marron served on Cinder's council with Aria. Before the Crossing, he'd governed a peaceful mountain settlement where Roar had spent a winter healing from a knife wound to the leg. A little over a year ago, Marron and his people had been ousted by the united Rose and Night tribes and come to Perry as refugees. As a group, they were compassionate and intelligent: Cinder's doctors, teachers, and civil servants.

Perry sat up. “We have to help them.”

“Absolutely,” Aria agreed. “That’s why we’re here. Let’s figure this out. Soren, can we get anything more out of that comm? Is there a way to sharpen it?”

“Already did that,” Soren said. “It’s maxed.”

“Are we running a constant recording? If another message comes through, I’d hate to miss it because no one’s around to hear it.”

“Done. And I also programmed an ‘S.O.S. acknowledged’ message to blast on the hour around the clock. Maybe something’ll get through.”

“Great thinking.”

Soren lifted his burly shoulders. “I thought so.”

Roar settled back as Aria continued going through a list of action items. Sometimes he could hardly remember the skitty Dweller girl who’d only met the real world for the first time a couple years ago after she’d been exiled from her domed city. She wore confidence like skin now.

Soon enough, the discussion grew impassioned. Everyone there remembered the Aether bearing down on them. The fires the storms had caused, vast stretches of fields and hills and mountains, burning. Charred. The Dweller Pods crumbling. Villages and cities razed. The Aether storms had cornered them. Then it had driven them away—which had led them here.

All Council meetings were open to anyone, and people began to enter from outside, drawn to the first truly unusual happening in Cinder. Old Will, bent as a willow tree. Molly and Bear. Twig and Brooke. Caleb and Jupiter. They crowded around, turning the room muggy. Aria's father, Loran, took a seat to her left and she quickly filled him in on what he'd missed.

Rune, a tiny Dweller with a surprisingly deep voice, interrupted her. "Hold on. Before we keep discussing this, shouldn't we figure out if we can even get back there?"

A fair question. *Back there* made it sound like what they'd left behind was across town, but it was the question on every mind, his included.

"How can we without Cinder?" asked Lyric, another council member.

They had made the Crossing through the Aether barrier because of Cinder, the boy the city had been named after. It was thanks to his extraordinary ability to channel the Aether, and his sacrifice, that they'd survived. He'd cleared a safe path for their hovers. Without him, none of them would be alive.

"Marron?" Aria turned to him. "What can you tell us?"

"Actually, I believe it may be possible," he said, his clear eyes widening, like he couldn't believe his own words. "Soren has the hover running flawlessly. We've been using it to survey the surrounding islands, as most of you know. I have no reason to think it couldn't make the trip back if a passage can be found."

There was a stir of excitement. Chairs scraping. Whispers flying low.

Soren's eyes slid over to Roar. "Flawlessly," he mouthed.

Roar rolled his eyes.

"I guess that's the real issue," Aria said, leaning forward on her elbows. "*If* we find a passage. Can we?"

"Well . . . ." Marron absently smoothed the colorful silk over his stomach. "*Perhaps.* I've been monitoring the Aether barrier closely to see how it responds to magnetism. I believe the Aether is repelled by this little piece of sand we've made our home because we're in a pocket of reverse polarity, somewhat like oil and vinegar. I've been thinking for some time that if there's *one* pocket, then there must be more, perhaps even within the barrier itself. If we found one, that might give us a navigable channel. It would be a way to get across."

"How do we find one?" asked Lyric.

"Unfortunately, our equipment is too limited," Marron replied. "The only way would be to go to the barrier and trust in luck—both in my theory and in locating a gap. But that's only the beginning of the journey. The situation on the other side of the barrier is . . . well, it's quite frankly a terrific unknown. We all know what we left behind. It could be even worse now. Freeing the trapped people is another concern. A structurally compromised Pod is a huge danger in itself. Can it even be done? Then there's the return trip home, which would mean crossing the barrier again." He shook his head slowly. "Many, many layers to this. Any of which could have devastating consequences."

Aria let out a little laugh. "You seemed so optimistic at first."

He returned her smile. "It *is* doable."

"But dangerous," Loran said. "Possibly deadly."

Marron nodded. "Yes. Quite possibly."

Outside, there was an ominous rumble of thunder that stretched into silence.

"I'll go," Roar said. Dozens of heads turned to him, staring liked he'd just appeared from thin air. "I'll go," he said again.

He'd made the decision the instant he heard the girl's voice. This rescue meant purpose. A distraction. Who cared if it was deadly? *Life* was deadly. *He* was deadly. So was love and truth and hate and silence. Really, almost anything could be.

"He needs a pilot." Soren raised his hand. "That's me."

"*No*," Lyric said sharply. "They can't just decide to head off. We hardly know anything!"

Suddenly it was mayhem, people protesting and shouting over each other.

"Exactly! It's mad! Didn't they just hear what Marron said?"

"I heard him say there was a chance to help them—that's what *I* heard!"

"I won't vote for it! I won't condemn us to death!"

"Neither will I. I'm sorry for that girl, but I won't turn our citizens into martyrs."

"What if it was us? Hell, it *was* us just a year ago!"

"All right, everyone. All right." Aria's hand came up. "Quiet down, please. You'll all have a chance to speak, but can we discuss this calmly?"

Apparently not; this had struck too close to home for too many of them. The shouting only intensified, filling Roar's ears. He drummed his fingers on the table and tried to relax the tension in his jaw.

Every person mattered in Cinder. Even him, though he often wondered why. He didn't serve on the Council like Aria. He didn't help raise walls like Perry. He didn't teach or work in the gardens or the orchards. Once or twice a week, he went spearfishing and added whatever he caught to the common good. On occasion, he played guitar and sang. Sometimes he chased the kids or let them blindfold him so he could prove yet again that he could navigate by sound. That was it—the scope of his role.

Games. Songs. The work of a jester.

Which was why the concern flurrying around him was embarrassing.

He curled his hands into fists. What *was* the problem here?

Lyric still led the charge. "They're complete strangers. How can we justify risking our lives for theirs?"

Easy, Roar thought. He saw no risk at all. He didn't fear for his life. If anything, he wanted to bash his life's teeth in.

The noise was getting to him. Time to get out of there before he did something he'd regret.

He stood. Then he saw Perry rise and he sank back down.

Now he was interested. Roar hadn't seen this is in quite some time.

The heated arguments died instantly, snuffed like a flame between fingertips. The attention of the room swung to Perry, who absorbed it like a hard wind, bowing his head, his gaze boring into some point on the table. He was a good leader—a great one—but it wasn't something he loved doing.

In moments like this, Roar saw him the way others did: far beyond his nineteen years in wisdom, misfortune, and accomplishment. And *theirs*. Though he'd relinquished his role as Blood Lord after the Crossing, he still belonged to them. Roar saw it in their eyes; he would always belong to everyone.

Perry lifted his gaze to Aria's. Whatever he saw in her expression—pride, approval, encouragement—was apparently what he needed to begin.

"I admire what we do here," he said. "Giving everyone a voice. Ensuring we're equals. We share the responsibilities of being citizens of Cinder, and the rewards." His speech, always unhurried, was even more measured than usual. "It's the way it should be. I'm amazed by it every day. Thankful for it. But I don't think we're looking at this rescue mission the right way."

He scraped a hand down his jaw. It was the hand with the badly burned knuckles; Roar knew he wasn't the only one who noticed. It'd grown very quiet. No rain or thunder anymore.

"I've been warned against a lot of things," he continued. "My brother told me leaving the Tides would spell doom. The opposite turned out to be true. I was told we could never coexist with Dwellers because our cultures were too different, our prejudices too ingrained. Wrong. When Marron and his people needed asylum, I was counseled against giving it because there wasn't enough food. We found a way. Sometimes the right decision is the hardest one, the one that seems doomed to fail. But that doesn't make it any less right.

"As for who makes this one, I don't think it should be all of us. Apart from approving the use of the hover, which is Cinder's collective property, I see no reason for a Council vote. If Soren and Roar want to go, they should. We shouldn't have the authority to stop them—or even to allow them, for that matter. We have to be able to make our way within this society as individuals when we need to."

Roar took a look around the table and felt his mouth curve. Just like that, he'd swung them.

"We have to be able to choose for ourselves," Perry went on. "Roar and Soren should go if they want to. It's their choice. Just as it's my choice to go with them."

Roar cringed as the room erupted again, even more intensely. This time, there was no argument; everyone was of the same opinion.

"That can't happen!" cried Bear.

"Damn right," Molly said. "You *can't* leave us."

On they went. He and Soren might be spared, but never Perry.

Roar had heard more than enough. He slipped outside before he became furious. Perry was idolized, cherished, and it was unfair. They expected too much from him, demanded too much.

It's the opposite, he thought, *of what they expect from me.*

A short while later, Roar had the moonlit beach and the rest of the bottle of luster all to himself.

He finished it and lay back, crossing his arms behind his head as he waited to feel it.

He hated that he was starting to lean on drink like his father used to. It was one of many traits he'd spent his life fearing would eventually surface. But it was the only time he could numb the numbness—the only hope of brushing against the real and vivid feelings that were normally out of his reach. He restrained himself to a couple of times a week, at least. Any more, and Perry or Aria would've noticed.

Well, they'd noticed anyway, hadn't they?

He sighed and gazed up at the stars, listening to the palm trees rustling. The waves rushing up and back. Usually, he thought of Liv on nights like this, going over his favorite memories of her first, then the harder ones, the ones that cut down to the bone. But tonight was different.

Tonight, the girl's distressed voice echoed in his mind. Just remembering her message made his heart thump faster.

He was going on this mission. Forty-three people needed help, but he knew himself. That was only part of what drew him. He needed this for *himself.* He needed a change. A mission. Something to do that might possibly hold some meaning. Anything besides spending another day feeling more alive in his memories than in his life.

Is anyone out there? the girl had asked.

"Me," he said to the stars. "I am."

The following afternoon, he stood in the clearing that served as the hover's landing zone. After he'd left yesterday, the Council came around and approved the mission—or rather, approved that they didn't need to approve it. That morning, the hover had been provisioned and made ready. Now, it was time to go.

After endless months of inertia, he felt like he was finally moving again.

There were seven members on the rescue squad: Soren, to fly the hover; Rune, to copilot and argue with Soren, standing in for Brooke, Soren's sometimes partner who was staying behind with the little sister she couldn't bear to part with; Hyde, Hayden, and Straggler, the tall Seer brothers who were expert archers, and who had never, not for a day, stopped viewing Perry as their Blood Lord. Rounding out the team were Peregrine and himself.

Roar put on a smile and headed into his goodbyes like he had to get through them in one breath. He pulled Talon close and frisked his hair. "See you."

Talon swatted him away, grinning. "Watch out for my uncle, Roar."

Under the light comment was an unmistakable note of command, his confidence effortless, innate. Someday, the kid would be unstoppable.

"That's what I do best," Roar replied. Then he turned to Aria and waved. "Bye."

She caught his wrist as he was turning to go. "Nice try. Come here." She threw her arms around him, squeezing tight.

Roar patted her back awkwardly. "All right, then. This was great. You can let go now."

"Not until you hug me back," she said, her voice muffled against his chest.

Roar had a complicated relationship with farewells. They made him feel edgy and wild—and she knew it, the little witch. Hence, the entrapment. He drew a few breaths, shedding the strain with every exhale, like he was heaving sacks of grain off a wagon, until he felt lighter, calmer. Enough to draw her in closer.

“He’d stay if you asked him,” he said, dropping his voice. “Or you could come with us.”

Her gray eyes flicked up. “Perry knows where he needs to be—and so do I.” She looked to Talon, who was with Perry. “Talon loves three people in this world and two of them are already going. I won’t let him lose everyone. Neither of us will.”

“I didn’t realize Talon and Soren were so close,” he said.

“Fool,” she said, poking him in the ribs.

Grinning, he dropped a kiss on her forehead and stepped back. He understood her need to stay back for Talon. Like her, he’d been orphaned, too. Along with being Auds, it was one of the big things they shared in common. “Leave some things for us to do when we get back.”

“I will. And Roar . . .” her eyes narrowed, softening, “you’re not still holding out hope, are you?”

Hope. Hope of finding Liv alive. Hope she’d miraculously survived a crossbow bolt fired into her heart from eight paces away.

“You were there,” he said, hoarsely. Aria had been on that balcony with him when Sable had murdered Liv in cold blood. But of course he was holding out hope. They both knew it.

Roar winked at her, seeing that Perry was heading over. “See you soon.” Roar tugged on his Aud cap, pulling the thick flaps down over his ears, and made for the hover. They didn’t drown out all sound, but they helped and he had no interest in hearing their parting.

Would Perry be going on this mission if *he* weren’t?

Not a question he wanted to ponder.

He strode up the ramp into the sleek craft's main hold, pulling down one of the jump seats and strapping himself in. He'd slept poorly last night and tiredness soon swamped over him. He was only half-awake as Perry sat beside him, as Soren ran through the launch protocol in the cockpit.

"Roar." He opened his eyes. Perry was holding his knife out, hilt first. They were already in flight. He had dozed through liftoff. "Sharpened."

Roar took the elk horn handle, his fingers sliding perfectly into the ridges worn through years of use. He tested the blade with his thumb. "Not bad." With a practiced flick, he spun the blade above his fingers. Spun it again and kept going. Toss, reverse grip, toss, reverse again. Meaningless tricks. No real purpose except that they made him feel steadier. His ears and his knives were two things—well, *four* things—he could always count on.

He hadn't grown up with physical abuse like Perry, but neglect was its own form of abuse. In his mind, his childhood was like a moth-eaten blanket, riddled with his parents' absences. Some long, some short. They were always leaving to chase some scheme or another. His father, Rush, had wanted land, power, and wealth. Anything that had the shine of prestige, respectability—which, ironically, he'd sought through the dirtiest of means.

His mother, Dawn—who'd been as beautiful as she'd been emotional, volatile—had taken longer for him to understand. What she'd wanted, he eventually saw, was to be the center of her husband's life. A doomed proposition. His father only wanted things he didn't have.

Neither of them had ever hesitated to let Roar know he'd been a mistake.

He'd learned early not to cry, that it was shameful and weak, that it irritated them. He'd learned not to be noisy, to never ask for help, to never play until the house was spotless and there was food on the table, and even then, not to go outside.

What if they needed him for something?

He had to be there and not be there, at the same time.

The best thing he could do, he came to see, was to disappear inside their small house, so he found its shadows, its corners and hiding places. He taught himself how to be utterly silent.

A ghost child, quiet as fog.

Never had anyone been given a less befitting name.

When his parents left him alone and went off to seek their fortunes, he'd move his tattered pillow beneath the window that faced the road. It was too high for him to look through, but he could lay there and listen to the chatter outside: the market hawkers, the birds, the kids playing. His parents, both strong Auds, had given him one thing of value: hearing so sharp it could approximate sight.

He sat alone under that window for days, weeks, months. He listened with his body, then his soul. Sounds sustained him when food did not, when love did not. With his parents gone, he could've ventured out for more than just market errands, but by then he'd had no idea where to begin. How were you supposed to meet the world?

He was around five years old when he discovered the twin blades his father had left behind. Rush appeared to be gone for good and Roar's mother had begun to search intensely for a replacement.

Roar recalled how the knives seemed enormous, longer than his arm from his elbow to his fingertip. Holding one of the blades, he had felt less helpless and alone. It wasn't a real friend, but he believed he could trust it. He had passed it from hand to hand as he listened to the world outside. Those first months, he'd cut himself often. But by the time his grandmother came for him a few months later and explained that both his parents had been killed by one of their enemies, the knives weren't even knives anymore. They had become part of him.

"You going to brood the entire voyage?" Perry muttered at his side.

Roar looked up, leaving behind his unhappy memories. "Depends how long the trip is." He had both knives going now and the Seer brothers were watching him with annoyed expressions, like he did this for show. "If it bothers you, shove your sleeves up your nostrils."

Perry snorted.

"You know, Per," Roar ventured, "if this works and we make it across the barrier, we could go home to the Tides. We could just go see it. Aren't you the least bit curious?"

"No," Perry said firmly. "I just left home." He leaned back against the seat, shutting his eyes.

His curt reply was no surprise. It had been terrible leaving the Tide's land. Traumatic for all of them, but it had actually been *Perry's land*. His responsibility. His birthright.

Still, Roar decided he'd keep working on him. He was determined to get there. Maybe it had to do with that *hope* Aria had mentioned. All he knew was that he *hadn't* just left home. The last—and only—time he'd felt at home was at the Tides.

"Comin' up on the barrier," Soren called from the cockpit.

Roar jumped up, sheathing his blades. He joined Perry and the brothers in the cockpit, all of them jamming into the narrow space behind Soren's and Rune's seats and staring through the canopy windshield in collective awe.

It'd been over a year since he'd seen the Aether. Long enough ago that he was dumbstruck by it. On every possible level—the sheer scale, the iridescence; the way it moved—it was awesome. Like the sea around Cinder—that bright, blue-green water—had been spun into veils that dropped straight down from the heavens, disappearing into the sea. In some places, it ran in thick currents, in others, it billowed in sheer swaths, but everywhere it looked *alive*. More alive than a squalling baby or a galloping horse or a lush flowering tree—or anything he'd ever seen.

"Wow, right?" Soren said.

"Yes," Rune agreed. "*Wow.*"

Since the Dwellers had come into their lives, Roar had learned the scientific cause of the Aether's appearance in the world some centuries back. A solar flare had scorched the upper atmosphere, and admitted this alien substance—part energy field, part weather system, part organic intelligence. A mystery in too many ways still, but the Dwellers had made progress in their studies of it. In harnessing and weaponizing it, more like, as humans tended to do. Cinder—Cinder, the surly boy who Roar had found and who Perry had all but adopted—had been a product of that research, which the Dwellers had been conducting inside their Pods.

In truth, Roar liked it better before he knew what the Dwellers had learned. He still preferred to think of it as something *other,* something magical. Worthy of intimate worship, instead of close scrutiny. It could be horrible, the Aether—he knew that as well as anyone—but he'd missed it. Until a year ago, he'd never known life without it.

"Uh," Rune said, "am I the only who sees that?"

"No," replied all four Seers.

Roar squinted his average eyes and finally saw what they did: Far to the north, there were two thick currents. Between them . . . *nothing?*

Soren spun the hover and accelerated so fast, the brothers went flying. "Oh—hold on, you guys," he said. "I'm taking us in for a closer look."

"Thanks for the warning," Hayden said, smashed against the bulwark.

As they came closer, Roar's heart started thudding. It hadn't been a trick of the eye. There was a break in the barrier, a slender gap between the curtains.

"It's *clear,*" Rune said, wonderingly.

"Sort of," said Straggler, the youngest of the brothers.

They were both right. It *was* clear. The problem was the curtains of Aether on either side weren't static. They billowed like a heavy wind was blowing them, making the width of the gap fluctuate wildly. One brush against the Aether and the hover would be in serious trouble, circuits frying, power shutting off, all hell breaking loose.

"We're going through," Soren declared. "We're doing this!"

Again, he accelerated boldly, giving no one a chance to argue with him. Roar's back thudded against the bulwark behind him even as his grip dug into Soren's pilot seat.

Memories flashed before his eyes of the Crossing. Perry's craft had crashed into the sea and he'd spent harrowing days adrift; Roar had no desire to experience that. He was telling himself that Soren's approach might be a good one (speed and certainty were assets, weren't they, when he went spearfishing?) when suddenly the Aether barrier wasn't *ahead* anymore.

The hover had soared through; they were safely on the other side.

It seemed like something he'd imagined. A daydream.

Shouts of celebration boomed all around him, filling the small space, and everyone piled on Soren, shaking him and thumping him on the back.

Perry laughed. "How about that, Ro?" he shouted, shoving him. "No problem!"

Roar's mouthed twitched into a smile. "Yeah, no problem," he repeated, under the triumphant hoots. After all that argument and apprehension, it had wound up being a breeze.

He should've felt better about it, but all he could think was: *too easy.*

He wondered . . . what lay ahead?

As the hover soared on, they grew quiet again. They were *under* the Aether now, the barrier curving over them, shooting so high it was almost hard to tell they were enclosed in a kind of massive bubble. The light was different here. Cooler. Bluer. The difference somehow both subtle and obvious.

Roar gazed at the glowing billows above, a sight as familiar as his own hands. This was *true* beauty. Terrible and terrifying. *This* was what Cinder lacked.

"It's different," Hyde said.

Roar saw that, too. The flows moved in veils that looked downright tame compared to the fierce veins they'd fled a year earlier. As the minutes passed, he saw no change in it.

They'd left behind a scream; this was a lullaby.

"Per . . . ?" He couldn't even formulate the question. He knew what they'd experienced—the betrayals, the hunger, the fear and deaths. But seeing the Aether this way made the past feel imagined, like some nightmare they'd all shared.

Perry just shook his head, a strange look in his eyes. "Let's just get this mission done."

~ 4 ~

TEMPEST

Nothing.

No one had replied to her distress call.

Tempest had given it a full day, but now she was forced to accept it: Her brother hadn't heard her call for help. Sable wasn't coming—but Banyan's men were. Ventus's daily reports had made that clear enough.

She rubbed her tired eyes. "Daisy? I'm ready. It's time for us to leave."

Beside her, Daisy set down the pants she was mending. Cal liked to fire her bow from her knees and wore through them regularly. "I thought you might say that," she said, gently. "You look like you didn't sleep at all."

"I managed a bit." Tempest toed the dirt with her boot. Mixed in were bits of plastic and rusted nails. Pieces of the home she had to walk away from. But they would find someplace else. She already had some ideas in mind.

Going to her birthplace, Rim, was out of the question. Sable had left to search for the Still Blue and someone else would be in power—someone who might welcome her, then stab her in the back to ensure she didn't try to claim the territory that had always been ruled by her family. She couldn't go there, but if she got close enough, maybe she could learn something about Sable's whereabouts. Surely, there'd be news, or gossip. Something. All she needed was a direction. Reunited with her brother, her troubles with Banyan would vanish and she and her little troop would be safe again.

She looked up as Ventus fell with a grunt, Cal pinning him with a knee to the back. Ventus yielded. Cal hauled him up and they reset, pacing and ready to attack again. They were among the best fighters in the entire Horn army, according to Sable. Tempest didn't doubt it.

"Maybe we can find another Pod," she mused. "Reverie or Elysium." This was her back-up plan if she failed to find Sable.

She looked to the destroyed Resolute a short distance away and wondered if she'd spend the rest of her life in hiding, running from one broken Pod to another. Never settled. Even during her time with the Night tribe, she never forgot she was a hostage. When she thought about it, she hadn't had a real home since she'd left Rim.

"Ventus and Cal will be relieved," Daisy said.

As she watched, Ventus spun away from Cal's attack, his silvery ponytail flying wide. He was nearly old enough to be her grandfather, but so graceful. And fit as Cal, which was saying something. "Should they be?"

Leaving Resolute, they'd be exposed to attacks from roving bands. Dispersed, lawless criminals who had no tribe affiliation. Croven, who saw flesh as meat regardless of the source—human or animal. Or they might meet with the search party that was after her. The second they left, they would become hunted.

"We'll figure it out," Daisy said. "What matters is that we go before it's too late."

They decided to leave in the morning and spent the afternoon gathering supplies and packing their satchels. Tempest shoved a blanket into her leather bag and a change of clothes, then set her brother's letters on top. She cast a longing look at the books she had to leave behind. *Emma. Endurance. The Count of Monte Cristo. Man's Search for Meaning. Frankenstein. The Art of War.* All tattered. Brittle with age and rumpled with use. They were too heavy to bring on a long trek, but she was thankful for her strong memory, at least. She could reread them in her mind.

She cinched her satchel and set it by the door. Grabbing her flashlight and butterfly knife, she headed to the common room. Cal was fletching arrows at the table. The room smelled strongly of the cedar arrow shafts spread out before her. "I'm going outside for a bit."

Cal looked up, concentration still on her face. "I'll come with you. I can finish this later."

"It's all right. I won't go far, I promise. I just want a breath of fresh air."

"Did you charge your flashlight?" Cal called as she strode down the corridor.

"Of course!" Tempest called back, though she probably could've charged it longer.

She clicked it on as she left their home base and ventured into the dark wreckage. The way out had seemed labyrinthine to her once. Now, she navigated without a thought, turning right, then right again, ducking below a beam, squeezing through a pinch point, then a clean stretch, and so on.

Her emotions had been all over the place today—worried, nostalgic, impatient—but now she felt surprisingly at peace with her decision to leave, and excited to surprise Cal, Ventus, and Daisy with a small going-away celebration tonight. Earlier, she'd set aside candles and gone for a bottle of wine from the crumbling old cellar. Flowers were hard to find nearby, but she decided she'd clip some willow branches, which were pretty enough.

She reached the destroyed auditorium and was almost outside when she heard a quiet rumble. It quickly grew louder, making the floor hum under her feet. She threw herself between the rows of seats and tucked into a ball. Fear hammered in her chest as broken concrete hailed around her, pelting her back and clacking against the floor. Was the entire thing coming down?

After what felt like a lifetime, the noise softened to the hiss of falling dust, a sound like grease sizzling in a pan, finally fading to silence.

Blinking the grit from her eyes, she stood on shaky legs and laughed. "Really?" she said to the heavy darkness. "On our last day here?" It had been months since the Pod had settled this way. She swatted the dust from her hair and clothes. "Be Resolute for one more night, will you?"

She picked up the flashlight and started back to check on Cal, stopping almost immediately at the sound of a male voice.

"Hello? Anyone here?"

Her head whipped to the crumbled corridor at the top of the aisle, a fresh wave of adrenaline shooting down her spine. The voice was muffled and indistinct, but she knew without a doubt it wasn't Ventus.

"Can anyone hear me? If you're in there, hang on. We're coming for you." The man's voice—a smooth baritone—grew clearer as the speaker came closer, navigating wreckage.

Tempest's legs tensed, ready to run. Was it Sable? Would she even recognize her brother's voice? Or was it one of the men in Banyan's search party? Saved or trapped? Hide or stand firm? She couldn't decide. Then there he was, a shadowed figure a dozen paces away.

She turned the beam on him. "Who are you?" she demanded.

"Your . . . rescuer?" He winced, a hand coming up. "That's bright. Can you point it away?"

Before she did, she quickly assessed him. On the tall side. Rangy. Dark hair powdered with dust. Knives at his hips. "Rescuer?"

"Yes?"

Dust moved through the air between them. Through it, his scent reached her. A puzzling mixture of iron and woodsmoke, solid and immaterial. Darkness in two kinds. Was he one of her brother's men? She couldn't ask without giving herself away.

He lowered his hand. "You *did* call for help?"

"Yes."

His dusty eyebrows drew together. "Doesn't feel like it." He stiffened suddenly, his attention shifting beyond her. A moment later, bright light filled the auditorium as a flare bounced into the aisle. Cal ran up with her bow drawn. Ventus and Daisy came behind her, both armed with Dweller guns. "Now it really doesn't feel like it."

"Who are you?" Cal demanded.

In the next instant, another stranger came through the corridor. In four bounding steps, taken in a blink, he joined the first stranger, a massive drawn bow in his arms. "What's going on, Roar?" he asked with surprising calm as he swung the arrow from Ventus to Daisy to Cal. He was enormous, long and muscular.

"The people we're here to save want to kill us," said the first stranger, his tone bemused.

"Why?"

"Great question."

"Save?" Cal said in disbelief. "They heard the distress call?"

"We did," said the big one. "Now if you don't mind, could you put your weapons away?"

They were polite enough words, but they were said with bite.

Tempest looked to Ventus and Cal. "It's all right. Put them away."

They complied reluctantly. Tempest had never seen the expression on Ventus's face before. He looked wary and fearsome.

"I'm Roar," said the first stranger. "This is Perry. The message said forty-three people were trapped. Where are the others? Have you freed them?"

Tempest suppressed the urge to cringe. Of all the scenarios she'd imagined, she had not once considered this one. Captured by Banyan or saved by her brother? Yes. But rescued by random strangers? No. She needed time to gather her wits.

"Follow me," she said.

As she led them back to their home base, she grappled with her options. She avoided looking at Cal and Ventus as she wove through the winding wreckage. They had both been opposed to the distress message to begin with.

The number, forty-three, had been a sort of code. She couldn't announce herself on an open frequency, so she'd hoped it would be a signal to her brother. Forty-three apples. As a child, she used to claim she could eat that many in a day. It was a silly thing, the largest number she could imagine at that age, and it had become a running joke between them. They'd passed it back and forth a few times over years of correspondence.

Still eating forty-three apples per day, Little Storm? he'd write.

I certainly am, she'd write back. *Every day without fail.*

She'd thought if Sable heard that particular number, he'd recognized that it was *her* broadcasting that message. It had seemed a lot smarter than shouting her exact position to the entire world. She couldn't explain this to the two strangers behind her, though. Not without revealing who she was—and she was *not* going to do that. She had no idea who they were. Maybe they'd heard that Banyan was searching for Tempest of the Horns. Probably, there was some reward for bringing her back. It wasn't a risk she was going to take.

She was going to have to tell them *something*, however.

In the common room, they gathered around the table. No one sat, including her. She stood behind her chair like it was a shield. Her heart had been racing since the rubble had shifted and it showed no sign of slowing down. These were the first new people she'd seen in a full year and awareness buzzed all the way to her fingertips.

The one named Roar stared at her coolly, dark brown eyes glinting with challenge. He was younger than she'd first thought. Near her age. "I still only see four people."

"It's just us now," she said, forcing herself to hold his gaze. "We were forty-three once, but when we got free of the rubble, most of them left. They didn't want to stay here and risk getting trapped again." It was the best lie she could come up with. She prayed it would work.

Roar sent a questioning glance to Perry, who watched her with oddly bright green eyes.

He shook his head.

Roar smirked. "How about the truth this time?"

Tempest's cheeks reddened as recognition rang through her. She studied those green eyes again. Perry was a Scire, like her. He'd caught her lie. Scented it in her temper. She could only own it now.

"All right, it's only us," she admitted. "We may not look trapped, but . . . we are. We can't stay here any longer and we have nowhere else to go. And does it matter how many of us are here? Would you not have helped just four people?"

Roar crossed his arms. "If they were four decent people."

That stung. She'd never had her character called into question before. Yes, she had lied, but she wasn't a liar. She'd had to do it. Her back was against a wall.

"Careful," Ventus murmured, low and dangerous.

The crimson scent of anger was pooling on her side of the table.

"Roast in hell," Roar said, as lightly as someone might say, "Nice to meet you." He looked at Perry. "I need some air," he said, and left.

Tempest expected Perry to go, too, but he stayed where he was, his attention broad but engaged, like he was listening to music only he could hear. She knew that look. He was scenting tempers. She knew she got that way herself—probably had a similar expression on her face now.

"This place isn't going to last," he said, tartly. "If you stay, you *will* be buried eventually."

"I'm well aware," she snapped, before she could catch herself. She hadn't expected strangers, but perhaps this was still a solution. She should be trying to smooth things over. Or, at least, not make things worse.

He stared at her, his temper like a breaking dawn, all crisp wariness and simmering frustration. "We have transportation. If there's somewhere else you can go, we can take you there."

"Like I said, we don't have anywhere to go." She shifted her weight, her mind galloping ahead. She needed to find them a new home. That was her priority. Worth anything. Even her pride. She swallowed. "Can . . . can we go with you?"

Perry looked like was going to speak, then he seemed to think the better of it.

"Seems I've failed some sort of test. Haven't I?" she asked. His size was downright intimidating. He was nearly as tall as the door behind him. As wide, too.

He shifted the longbow across his chest. "We risked our lives to come here."

"Because you wanted to be a hero and save forty-three people."

An odd expression crossed his face. Not a smile, exactly. Something darker. "You deceived us. Maybe you can understand why I'm not ready to invite you to my home."

A crashing silence followed. The space to place an apology. Tempest felt like she was drowning. She *had* deceived them. But if there was anything her brother had taught her, it was to never apologize. Perry was a Scire, though. She couldn't hide her regret, nor her pride and shame. Whether she spoke or not, he'd scent all of that.

"There are materials here that could be useful to us," he said after a moment, his gaze roaming slowly over the supply cupboards before returning to her. There was an unhurried quality in the way he moved now, so dramatically different than when he'd bounded out of the corridor, bow swinging. "We'll need some time to search for them. A day or two. That'll give us a chance to figure out what's next."

"We know this place inside-out," she said. "We can help you find what you need. It'll go faster, and I'm—" No apologies.

Ever. *Strength is strength.* "I'm afraid we started off poorly. That's my fault, not theirs." She glanced to either side of her. The veins stood out on Ventus's temple. Cal looked bored, which meant she was rabidly angry, and Daisy had flushed so red her freckles had disappeared.

To their credit, they held their tongues. The lines between them had blurred a long time ago, but they served her, were sworn to follow her command. When it mattered, they never forgot that. "Whatever you decide, I hope you keep that in mind."

Perry dipped his chin. "I will."

There were seven of them in total in their party. Perry, Roar, and five others—who were just as irked to discover there was no big rescue to perform.

Tempest ignored their grumbles—it was getting ridiculous, like they *wanted* forty-three people to be in peril—and made good on her word. They spent the afternoon helping the rescue crew locate items within Resolute. Medical supplies, computer equipment, construction materials, and more. They knew precisely where to find everything, and it went quickly. Working together for hours smoothed over the sore feelings.

By that night, they all gathered for dinner outside Resolute.

The newcomers had brought plenty of food to share and she indulged herself. It had been a long time since she'd enjoyed fresh fruits and vegetables, soft cheeses and crusty breads. They even had fruits she'd rarely eaten in her life, like pineapple and banana. It was all so full of flavor, her dulled tastebuds rejoiced.

As darkness fell, they sat around a fire talking in careful words, Ventus watching the plume of smoke rising into the sky with a worried frown. They'd avoided fires for a year, not wanting to betray their location.

Tempest told them she was from the north, but said nothing about Rim. She told them she'd been separated from her brother, carefully avoiding naming him as Sable, Blood Lord of the Horns. Daisy, Cal and Ventus protected her identity as well, of course.

She sensed the strangers holding back, too, but she still learned a few things about their party. Five of them—Perry, Roar, and the three brothers—were from the western territories. Where exactly, they didn't specify. The other two were Dwellers, which shocked her. She'd always believed they couldn't survive outside of Pods. That notion had hung over her for the past year: the idea that she was in a sort of cocoon, where vulnerable beings had lived until it'd been damaged, but apparently they'd received a special inoculation to allow them to survive outside. And their presence in the group explained why they had a hover and how they'd had equipment sophisticated enough to hear her message.

Perry was the decision-maker; that was as clear as it was subtle. He didn't command so much as answer questions the others put to him.

From Hyde, one of the three brothers: "You want us on watch tonight, Per?"

From the Dweller named Soren: "Should I find a better place to park our ride?"

From the Dweller named Rune: "Want me to try to send word home again?"

From Roar: nothing.

He'd been the first one to arrive, the first one to speak to her. Now he was physically present, but otherwise gone. He stared into the fire intently, a furrow between his dark brows. Or he watched the Aether, his mouth pressed into a grim line. Going by his temper—an ocean of smoke, crashing and turbulent—the thoughts that occupied him weren't good ones. In the tense initial moments of his arrival, she'd noted distantly that he was attractive. Now she saw he was exceptionally so.

Most people had a great feature, like Daisy's charming freckles and Cal's proud forehead, but Roar had a great everything: arched eyebrows and honed cheekbones; bronzed skin and waves of nearly black hair; eyes that sparkled darkly, mirroring the churning emotions she scented. He was being unsociable, leaning against a tree away from the main group and hiding under a dark hood, yet she couldn't stop her eyes from drifting over to him over and over. It was like she was on the end of a fishing line, reeled in whether she resisted or not.

Banyan's son Ash, beautiful in a different way, had used attractiveness as a form of currency, flirting and dallying to get anything he wanted. *You've got a good brain,* he'd told her once. *I've got an exceptional body* and *a good brain. We trade with what we're given. You never dumb yourself down, do you?*

She was dumbing herself down right now, wasn't she, fixating on a stranger's looks when their survival was at stake?

But she forgave herself. She was seventeen and human, and it had been a year since she'd seen any male other than Ventus. The kick in her pulse when she looked at Roar was normal. She'd felt it around Ash for a while, too.

With thoughts of Ash came a wave of regret. She had grown close to both of Banyan's children—Ash and his little sister, Raven—and the hardest part about how she'd left on that storming night a year ago was not saying goodbye to them. She knew she'd hurt them, and that hurt her. She only hoped they understood she'd had to flee.

As night fell, Cal and Ventus left with the three brothers, Hyde, Hayden and Straggler, to set up a perimeter watch to protect them and to guard the invaluable hover. With a solid defense established around them, Tempest realized she could sleep outside without fear, something she'd longed to do for months. She and Daisy went back inside the Pod to gather blankets. As they were heading back out, Tempest decided she needed a few moments to gather herself.

"Go on ahead," she told Daisy. "I'll be right behind you," she promised.

Daisy nodded like she wasn't surprised. "Got your flashlight?"

Tempest held it up. "Right here."

After she left, Tempest sat on her bed and let herself feel the disappointment she'd been suppressing for hours. Someone had heard her message. Just not the *right* someone. Then she slipped one of her brother's letters out of her backpack, craving the only closeness she could have with him. The letter she chose had been one of her favorites for many months. And then that had changed, and reading it began to tear her heart apart.

Tempest,

I have great news to share. I am to be married! Yes, you read that right. Her name is Olivia of the Tides. She is from a strong line of Scires. Her brother Vale is Blood Lord and it is a good allegiance. The Tides are a small tribe, but their territory is well-positioned on the coast, particularly as the latest reports from my scouts suggest the land of the still blue skies lies seaward, to the west. If this is indeed true, and if the Aether storms continue to worsen, we will have ready access to it.

Though it is a decision of the mind as all our decisions must be, I am taken with Olivia. She is intelligent and beautiful. She has fire.

Be happy today. You are gaining a sister. Once we are married, I will bring her to meet you.

We've been apart a great long while now. Keep strong. It will be over soon,

Sable

Her eyes always filled when she came to the line: *She has fire.*

He really *had* fallen for her. Sable never complimented anyone unless he meant it. To think he'd seen Olivia murdered right before his eyes on the eve of their wedding by her jealous ex-lover . . . it was almost too hard to bear. Her poor brother had found love and then lost it in the most horrific way.

"Excuse me?"

Her head snapped up, her heart leaping in her chest.

Roar leaned casually against the doorjamb, one hand tucked in a pocket. A wine bottle dangled from the other. A dark lock had escaped the messy knot at the back of his head. It cascaded down to his jaw, shadowing one eye.

"Sorry," he said. "Didn't mean to startle you."

"It's fine," she said, quickly refolding the letter. She wondered how long he'd been there. Had he been *watching* her? She zipped up her backpack and stood. "I was just heading back outside."

"Bad news?"

She shrugged, trying to be casual. She knew she still had tears in her eyes. "Old bad news."

"Must have been pretty bad if it still hurts."

It was an observation, not compassion. She pulled her backpack over her shoulder, blinking away the last of the blurriness. "You could say that." She wanted to leave, but he was standing in the doorway.

He lifted the bottle. "Found this in the kitchen and helped myself."

Was that a soft slur she heard? "It's only fair. You fed us dinner." She'd noticed he hadn't eaten much, though. He was pure muscle and bone. Not emaciated but spare. Considering the familiar way he held that bottle, his flinty stare, and the smoky darkness in his temper, she had no doubt he was as haunted as he was handsome.

"Still a bit thirsty," he said, an eyebrow rising sardonically. "Any idea where I can find more?"

Her first instinct was not to help him. He already seemed pretty glazed. But she'd lost favor with him and Perry earlier and she had to play this right. They were her shot at a new home. What she *wanted* mattered less than what was *needed*.

"Sure," she said. "There's a cellar on the way out."

~ 5 ~

ROAR

The girl, Tempest, led the way through the broken corridors, illuminating cracks in broken walls to climb through and beams to duck beneath unerringly with her flashlight.

Roar followed her, quietly clearing his throat. It had been aching all day, like a bone was lodged in there, but he knew what it really was: a name.

Liv.

Aria was right: he *had* wanted to find her alive. He had wanted to say her name just once more and have it mean her, and not her memory. That hadn't happened and now it was stuck right above his Adam's apple, an unmoving ache halfway between his heart and his mind.

At least the wine he'd found had knocked the sharpness back some, and the little liar in front of him claimed she could take him to more, so there was still hope for tonight. There was no chance he'd sleep. He hadn't found Liv and there had been no rescue. He'd wanted something to change—and nothing had. If he was going to face yet another long night ahead, why not ease the agony a little by blurring his mind?

Time heals all wounds, people said.

"People are idiots," he muttered.

Tempest swung around, training the flashlight on him. "What?"

He cringed under the glare. "Are you not aware that's painful?"

"I guess I've gotten used to it. I thought I heard you say something."

"I might have." He frowned. "Interesting."

"What is?"

"The, uh, the light." She'd lowered the beam to his groin.

She made a strangled sound and the light shot away, moving crazily over the rubble. "I was looking at your *knives*."

"*Were* you?"

"*Yes*," she said firmly. She whirled and walked on, her pace brisker. "Do you always wear them?"

Roar smirked. She was sticking to her story, at least. "Almost always." She'd seemed unflappable all day, cool and a little superior. The inexplicable urge to keep prodding her came over him. "They can be a hindrance in certain situations, as you might imagine."

She scoffed. "You're pretty full of yourself, aren't you?"

I used to be, he thought. He was more empty-of-himself now. "Just being honest. You should try it sometime." That came out sharper than he'd intended. This morning was in the past, and she *was* helping him now.

"I'll think about it," she said lightly.

As they continued on, he thought about the flimsy excuses she'd given that morning. This girl was hiding something. "Why did you lie in your message?"

"Why does anyone lie?"

"Why does anyone answer a question with a question?"

She lifted a shoulder. "Why do you think?"

"To avoid answering when they're asked why they lied?"

"Perhaps. We're here." She aimed the beam at what had once been a short corridor. Now, the cement walls resembled crumpled paper, the way through a slim and jagged darkness. He could hear the space open on the other side, some eight feet away. A faint odor of wine drifted out on a damp draft. "It might be a tight squeeze for you," she said.

"I'll be fine." He wasn't sure, though. He'd dropped weight over the past year, but he still had the same bones, and they didn't bend. It didn't matter, though. Wine was on the other side.

Pain now, pain later. It was all just moving pain around.

"I'll go first. Here, take this." She handed him the flashlight.

Unable to resist, he aimed the light at her face. "Whoops." He drew the beam slowly down her body. "Whoops again. What's wrong with this thing?"

"Very funny," she said. Then she climbed into the opening, leaving him frowning over what he'd just seen: A heart-shaped face. Large eyes of such a pale blue they were like mist, framed by thick lashes. Dark auburn hair partly pulled up, the rest spilling over one shoulder. Dusty gray pants and ratty sweater over a slight figure with pert curves—whoa, *pert?*

"Tempest? Just out of curiosity . . . how old are you?"

"You know, I've never understood that phrase," she replied as she wedged herself through. He could only see her left leg now. "Can a question come from anything else?"

"Yes, but that's not important." His question had come from a square punch of attraction. A surprise. How long had it been? Easy answer. More than a year.

"I'm seventeen," she said.

That seemed young, but not too young. For what, he couldn't begin to fathom.

Actually, it seemed he *could* begin to fathom. The image of her wasn't fading away.

Served him right for trying to be clever.

"I'm through," she said. "Pass me the flashlight. And just out of curiosity, how old are you?"

He reached his arm deep inside and felt her take it. He'd never liked this question—answering it felt too revealing, like announcing he'd had a terrible childhood—but he'd walked himself right into it. "Best guess, nineteen or twenty," he said. "My parents weren't much for details."

"Twenty-one was my guess. Or twenty-two."

Did she think he was old? He shook himself, irked at his own thoughts, and began contorting through the tight space.

About halfway through, his shoulders slid into a concrete groove, snug as a key fitting into a lock. He tried to shift and swore as something sharp—a piece of steel rebar, he suspected—dug into his collarbone. "Tempest? I'm stuck."

"Hold on, I'm coming." She climbed back in from the cellar side, her face appearing between crumbling slabs. After some wriggling, her arm came through with the dreaded flashlight.

"Do you want me to pull you through?"

He squinted. "Tempest—" He wanted to explain that darkness was home, that he found comfort in shadows and night and any circumstance that kept him unseen, invisible. He wanted her to know that light gave him nowhere to hide. But he didn't actually want to have to explain anything. What he wanted was just to be understood without saying a word.

"No," he said, suddenly tired. "Please don't." If she pulled, the rusty bar jabbing into his collarbone would skewer him. He let his head fall back on the wall behind him. "Well, not bad. I made it to the ancient age of possibly twenty-one or twenty-two." She smiled and it was like seeing her for the first time. Like she'd dropped a cloak of poise and carefulness, revealing the wit and warmth beneath. Desire flashed through him again, quick as the sun on a blade.

"It's not over yet, old man. There has to be something we can do."

"There is. Grab one of those bottles in there, pop it open, and pull up a chair."

"How about if I try shifting some of this rubble instead?"

"Sure. Sounds like a great way for me to lose an arm."

"Good thing you've got another." She shone the light on the area around his arm, examining it. "If I can find a way to—" Her words died in her throat as the flashlight winked twice and went out. "No!" she cried.

"Yes," he said, as darkness fell, cool and sweet.

"*Yes?* This is not a *yes* situation!"

For a little while, she engaged in a desperate battle with the flashlight, smacking the barrel, frantically clicking the power button, shaking it, and so on.

He watched her do these things with his hearing. Another good thing about the dark: His ears reigned supreme. They became his sole connection to the world, which was what they always wanted to be.

"How are we going to get out of here now?" A quaver had come into her voice.

"We'll be fine."

"Great! I'm so comforted!"

"I can still see, Tempest. Sort of."

She stopped assaulting the flashlight. "What do you mean?"

"I'm an Aud. A pretty decent one. If I concentrate, the way sounds move can give me a sort of mental image. It's kind of like seeing but, I don't know, more spatial-feeling. Hard to explain. Anyway, if we go slowly, I can navigate us out of here. And I can't move forward, but if I sacrifice a shoulder, I might be able to move backward."

He tried it. The bar scraped his skin and tore his shirt. "It worked. I'm out." He touched his collarbone and felt blood.

"You cut yourself. Are you all right?"

Roar smirked at the darkness. Of course she was a Scire. Rare as they were, he always managed to find them. He needed a second to mentally adjust to that little revelation. A few moments ago, he'd bared a piece of himself by sharing that he had no idea how old he actually was, but this was a whole other level. Like Perry and Talon, like Liv when she'd been alive, Tempest would know his temper. His shifting moods. He started to backtrack in his mind, recalling what he'd been feeling around her, but he quickly stopped himself. If she'd scented the no-man's-land that was his emotional landscape, then so be it. He couldn't change that.

"It's nothing. Just a scratch. Your turn to come through." He noticed her breathing was going shallow and quick. "Tempest?"

"I don't think I can. I can't even see what I'm supposed to crawl through. What if *I* get stuck?" There was a thin, rising note in her voice.

"Did you double in size in the past ten minutes?"

"No?"

"Then you'll be fine. Reach your arm out. I'll guide you through."

Her hand brushed past his twice, then closed like a vise. Instantly, her inner voice came through, her anxiety like a chant.

Please don't let go, please don't let go, please don't let go.

He cleared his throat. The right thing to do would be to tell her that he could hear her thoughts—another neat feature of his strong hearing. Privacy and all that. But she hadn't exactly told him upfront she was a Scire, had she? And why get into it now? She was shaken up. The priority was getting her out of there.

"I'm right here," he said. "I won't let go."

Yes, yes—skies, thank you. Now if he just kept talking.

"You can do this, Tempest. Just take it one step at a time. Keep coming toward my voice."

Liv used to call this cheating, he remembered. He pushed the thought away and kept talking, encouraging her. When she finally came through, she didn't climb out so much as throw herself out. Roar caught her as she slammed into him.

"Whoa—you all right?" He set her down, keenly aware of the curves slipping past his hands.

"Not really, no. I'm a little dizzy. Can I hold on to you?"

She already was; her fingers were digging into his forearms. "Of course. You might feel steadier with your hand on my shoulder when we start walking."

"I'll do that. Thank you."

"But first you have to go back for the wine."

"Roar!"

"Joking. Come on. Let's get out of here." He was turning to go when her thoughts came to him again.

This is what drowning must feel like. Floating and not getting enough air.

"Whoa, Tempest." She was shaking, her fear palpable. He took a firm hold of her arms, trying to give her some feeling of stability. "You're good. Take a big breath." She drew a breath, her exhale shuddering. "How about a couple more? All the way in and out." She did that a few times. "Good. There you go. You live here, remember? It's the exact same place. You just can't see it."

"I know. My mind knows. Logically, I understand that. But I can't seem to convince my body. Everything bad in my life always seems to happen in the dark. I can't help associating it with . . . with bad memories." They must've been really bad, he thought. He was trying to work out if he should put his arm around her shoulder or if that would only terrify her more. "But it's my stupid fault for not charging the flashlight longer," she went on. "It's so stupid, right? Embarrassing. I should have outgrown this."

"Not at all. It's nothing to be embarrassed about. And the dark's not always a bad thing, is it? There's a lot to like about it."

"Like?"

"Surprises. The darkness is filled with them."

"I hate surprises—isn't that obvious?"

"Right. Predators, then. Lots of those love the dark."

"Are you serious?" she said, laughing.

It was exactly what he wanted to hear. A great sound, too. Feminine and bright, like flower petals scuttling in a breeze. "*I* love the dark," he offered.

"You already said predators."

That got a laugh out of him. "Stars, then. Can't have stars without the dark."

"I'm not seeing any stars, Roar."

"I could change that pretty quickly."

Well, look who it was. Old full-of-himself Roar, peering up from the grave.

He hadn't known he was going to say that. He couldn't remember the last time he'd remotely felt the urge to flirt. But this wasn't the time for that kind of banter, not when she was genuinely scared. "Forget I said that."

"If you mean what I think you do," she said carefully, "then that's a hell of a claim."

For a few seconds, his heart beat an irregular rhythm, like the first raindrops in a downpour. "Well, I'm a hell of a person."

"*Stars*, Roar?"

"Stars, Tempest. Doubt me all you want. It's the truth."

"Prove it."

Prove it. A bright heat sped through his body, shorting out his ability to think. She *had* actually said that—it wasn't his imagination. He made a halfhearted attempt to evaluate the situation objectively. This was a bad idea, probably, for many reasons. Whatever. He stepped closer to her, smoothing his hands up her shoulders, then lightly framing her face. Her skin was as soft as down.

"All right, then," he said. "Let's go for a whole galaxy."

6

TEMPEST

She had lost her mind. It was the only way she could explain why she'd said what she had.

Prove it.

What was she *thinking?*

She wasn't thinking; the darkness had pushed her beyond all reason.

In the ringing silence, she heard Roar exhale softly. "All right, then." He stepped closer, his hands drifting up her arms, then framing her face. His scent, cedar smoke tangling with ocean, was everywhere. "Let's go for a whole galaxy."

His lips brushed over hers, feather soft. Exploringly and with such tenderness she felt everything curl inside her. This wasn't stars. This was a spell. It was magic. She didn't know what she'd expected, but it hadn't been this . . . this *sweetness.* She took hold of his wrists. She wanted it to go on forever. Just like this. His lips dancing over hers. But at the same time, it wasn't enough.

His mouth curved into a smile. "Ready?" he whispered.

A hot thrill zipped through her. Was this bliss really only the beginning? She made a sound she hoped resembled assent.

Roar bent lower, his fingers sliding into her hair, his scent crisp as a winter fire. Then his tongue swept over hers, a searing sweep, and she did, in fact, see stars. He tasted like fire, or like what she imagined fire would taste like. Hot and lithe and light. And somehow, he brought that light into this darkness. Into *her.*

She came up on her toes, wanting to be closer to him. In her eagerness, their teeth scraped softly together, and he laughed a little, a low husky sound, dazzling and real. Proof this was really, actually *happening.*

As their kiss deepened, she sensed the desire emanating from him and shivered. This wasn't sweet anymore—they'd left *sweet* behind. In the corner of her mind that was still working, she wondered how far this could go, their want pinging back and forth, their connection as clear and solid as a diamond.

Too soon, his arms loosened and he drew back.

She stood for a moment, trying to locate herself in the world. To find even a hint of balance. She felt like she'd just woken from a dream—was still half in it. Not even an hour ago, she'd been on her bed reading her brother's letters. Now *this.*

This was so far from anything she'd ever experienced.

"Your hound's coming," Roar said quietly. "Another minute or so."

"My hound? You mean . . . Ventus?"

"Yes." A rough finger drifted over her cheek. "So? Verdict? Any stars?"

"As a matter of fact, yes." She was too rattled to be coy. That was unquestionably the best kiss of her life. "Who *are* you?" she heard herself ask.

"No one you need to bother with." He cupped the back of her head and pressed a kiss right between her eyes. "For what it's worth, I saw them, too. A whole lot." Then he stepped back, keeping hold of her elbow.

A faint glow fuzzed through the darkness up ahead, growing brighter by the moment. Slowly, Resolute's broken walls filtered back into focus and Roar took shape beside her. His hair had come loose in chunks that he'd tucked behind his ears. There was a tear in his shirt at the collarbone, a spot of blood staining the fabric. His features looked sculpted—high cheekbones, that perfectly straight nose and full mouth. A master work.

Had she really just kissed *that?*

"You should answer him." His eyes darted to her. "He sounds worried."

Tempest heard Ventus now, calling out to her. She cleared her throat and answered.

That night, she lay awake on her bedroll watching the Aether as she went over every moment of what had happened. First, regretting it. Had she jeopardized their chances to leave with this group by falling for what was probably a well-worn trap? Surely, Roar was no stranger to spontaneous interludes. Then, wishing she could go back in time to experience it again. Then looping back to start the cycle over again.

The entire event confounded her. She wasn't impulsive or rash, yet she'd behaved that way. And Roar had surprised her, too. He didn't kiss like someone who looked like him should kiss—selfishly, greedily. Like he was used to being worshipped. He'd been giving and sweet. *Tender* was the word that kept coming to her. He was a stranger, but he hadn't kissed like one at all. Almost as fascinating was the change she'd seen in him once the flashlight had gone out. The surly façade had fallen away, and he'd been funny and charming. Considerate.

She rolled over and shut her eyes. She was turning what had happened into something monumental when he hadn't said a word to her since.

"What's going on, Temp?" Daisy whispered. "You've been flopping around like a fish."

Tempest wanted nothing more than to tell her everything. But Roar was somewhere on the other side of the glowing embers, and he was a strong Aud. "Later," she whispered back.

"Okay," Daisy said. She scooted closer and ran her fingers through Tempest's hair as she hummed a ballad from the north called the "Wind's Wisdom"—her favorite song.

At last, Tempest finally drifted to sleep and dreamed she was an owl, soaring soundlessly through the night.

7

ROAR

"I'm thinking about inviting them to come back with us," Perry said.

The sun had just come up. They'd spent the past hour hunting, rising at the same time without having planned it, like they'd always done growing up together. They'd been lucky, spotting a wild pig soon after leaving their campsite. With the fat animal swinging on a long branch between them, the crisp temperature and cool blue tint over the woods, he could almost convince himself he was back in better days, that Liv might pat her stomach as she saw them coming and call out, *nice kill, boys, but what are you two eating?*

"What do you think, Roar?" Perry continued. "About bringing them? Tempest and the others?"

"Makes no difference to me," he replied with a shrug, though Perry was ahead of him and wouldn't see. He wasn't surprised. This was what Perry did: He gathered the strays of the world and gave them a place to belong.

"Really? No thoughts on the subject at all?" Perry glanced over his shoulder, suspicion flashing in his eyes. This was the trouble with Scires: They were inherently nosy in every sense of the word. Roar was fairly sure Perry had picked up on some shift in his temper. He raised his eyebrows, sending Perry a *we're not talking about this* look. In his gut, he felt a tangled ball of emotions, but he wasn't about to unravel it now—or ever.

Perry smirked and turned back around.

They walked in silence for a while, then came around a bend and the smoke from their camp appeared over the trees ahead. Up on the ridge, he could just see the top curve of the hover. A sudden urge to drop the branch and head the other way came over him.

He didn't want to go back to Cinder yet. Aside from Aria and Talon, there was nothing drawing him there. What he wanted was to go to the Tides, to see the compound, the gentle hills surrounding it to the east and the rugged beach, with its coves and craggy cliffs, to the west. And though he'd said he didn't mind just moments ago, Roar wasn't at all sure how he felt about Tempest coming back with them.

What had happened between them had been fun, surprisingly so, but he was in no place to pursue anything further. If she came to Cinder, he was afraid he'd have to have an awkward conversation with her. He was even more worried that she'd already discarded him from her mind. Yes, it had meant nothing. But rejection was never pleasant, was it?

Perhaps worst of all was the idea that if she came to Cinder, she'd see just how adrift he was in life. Roar, with the sad story. Roar, who used to have some spark, before it all fell apart when Liv was murdered. Roar, who spent his nights alone on the beach with a bottle.

Maybe she'd look back on their kiss and wonder what had gotten into her.

The entire thing, wondering about all the possibilities of what might come next, annoyed him to no end. He had no energy for it.

"Soren wants to stay," Perry said, interrupting his thoughts. They were almost back to camp. "He wants to take the hover to the east. He thinks there may be Pods that are still intact, undamaged by last year's storms. Apparently, there's one called Valhalla. It's the largest one. The headquarters for their central government."

Roar asked the question that was expected of him. "Why does he want to do that?"

"The Aether. He's been fixated on it since we came through the barrier." Roar knew Perry's voice better than anyone's. He could hear the forced casualness in his drawl. "It doesn't make sense how it became intense so quickly, then settled down just as fast. Unnatural. He thinks if he finds Valhalla, he might get some answers. I think he's got it in his head that there's something we don't know. Something that's been kept hidden. He wants an explanation."

Roar's pulse began to beat hard. He looked up at the blue currents dancing in the sky. Since they'd crossed the barrier yesterday morning, nothing had changed. It was still so tame-looking, so unlike what had driven them to Cinder.

"You're making it sound like he suspects . . ." He couldn't even finish the sentence. If there were Dwellers somewhere who'd had a hand in causing the hell-storms they'd survived, that people had endured for centuries . . . the ramifications were too vast, too horrifying. "Soren's just being paranoid."

"Then maybe I am, too."

Roar froze.

Perry lurched to a stop and turned, shifting the branch on his shoulder. "Can you blame me?"

Roar couldn't. His gaze fell to the pig's lolling head and wide, dead eyes. Over and over again, the Dwellers had proven that they could do terrible things and keep them secret. "So what are you saying? That you want to chase down a conspiracy theory on Soren's whim? That you'd rather do that than go to your birthplace and lifelong home?"

Perry scowled. "I don't know, Roar," he snapped. "I'm trying not to care about any of it. We came here to help people in trouble. That's all I wanted to do."

"Then stop getting involved in these massive trouble campaigns! Haven't you had enough? You don't have to *save* everyone, and *fix* everything! Just let the damn Aether be strange and beyond understanding! You're not going to learn anything good—I can tell you that right now. My *god*. Can't you just let this one go?"

Roar was surprised by his own vehemence. If there was work to do, a mystery to solve, people who needed him, Perry charged in. He pretended reluctance sometimes, but he couldn't help himself. He was made for bold and grand actions. His sense of duty had been big enough for the both of them once, the strength of it sweeping Roar along like an undertow. Roar had never envied it before. He was shocked to discover that he did envy it now. It just seemed so easy for him to *care* about things.

A grin was working its way onto Perry's face. "*Trouble* campaigns? Never say that around Aria."

"Where do you think I heard it first?" Roar grumbled, adjusting the branch. "And keep walking, you oaf. This is getting heavy."

"Aww," Perry said, in a syrupy voice, "are your feet hurting? I could carry it all by myself. If you hop on top, I could probably even carry you, too."

"Oh, shut up."

"But I want *to save* you, Roar. And I can't let it go."

"One more word, Peregrine. One more."

~ 8 ~

TEMPEST

When Perry found her the following morning, Tempest was by the creek splashing water on her face, trying to wake up. Hours of missed sleep had left her tired and with a tinge of a sore throat. The newcomers had prepared another feast—eggs, rashers, fruit, and cheesy-bread—but she'd only picked at it, too preoccupied by her thoughts.

"Got a minute?" he asked.

Tempest dried her face with her sleeves and stood. "Sure."

"You're welcome to come with us to our home," he said without preamble. "If you're still interested."

Tempest's breath caught. "We are. Thank you, Perry. Very much." The morning suddenly seemed brighter.

"There's a few things we should talk about, though. Get straight between us beforehand." His green eyes narrowed, like he could see every minute of her lost sleep. "I understand what it's like to be in situations that have no good way out. Whatever it is that made you lie in your distress call, it's your business. But I need to feel confident you won't lie to us again."

She nodded. "I won't."

"Good. And there's something you should know before you decide if you want to come. Home for us is . . . well, it's far. You might have heard of the Still Blue?"

Her legs wobbled, the world turning watery for a second. She forced herself to draw a slow breath. "I have." The Still Blue—lands safe from the Aether—had been her brother's quest for a decade. His obsession. "Did you find it?"

"About a year ago." Pride sparkled in his eyes, but there was a tinge of something dark there, too. "Wasn't easy to get there, but it's been worth it."

He explained that they'd crossed an Aether barrier and found islands under Aether-less skies. There, they had created a new society in a place they called Cinder.

"That's incredible," Tempest said, when he'd finished. A sharp ringing had begun in her ears, and she couldn't move a muscle. She felt like her blood had frozen. Like she'd topple over if someone shoved her. But somehow, words were still coming out of her mouth. "I remember hearing that the Horns were trying to find it. Something about an alliance with Dwellers."

It was a risk to say this, but she had to know if he'd heard of her brother. It had been so long since Sable had written. Maybe Perry had some news? Maybe their paths crossed at some point?

He shifted his weight, sunlight dancing on his broad shoulders, a cold look coming into his green eyes. "There was no alliance. Sable, the Horn's Blood Lord, blackmailed the Dwellers, then he betrayed them. He did the same to us."

Paradoxically, her own brother's name struck her ears like a foreign word—one that sounded unfamiliar, but that she intuitively understood. A moment ago, she couldn't move. Now an earthquake was rumbling inside her. She crossed her arms, needing to hold herself together. "I think I remember hearing something about that. I take it Sable of the Horns isn't in Cinder?"

Perry shrugged tightly. "You could say he is and isn't. He's buried on a hill not far away from our settlement—so Roar tells me. Like I said, it was a rocky start, but we found our way. Cinder's a good place. Lush and green and warm. There's ample food and fresh water, timber and . . . well, it's abundant in all ways except Aether," he added, with a smile. "Most of us are from the Tides, but there are a few Dwellers from Bliss, like Soren, people from Delphi, a few people from the Horns."

The Horns. Tempest couldn't help it; she had to lay a hand on a tree to steady herself.

Perry noticed, frowning. "Everything okay?"

She dredged up what she hoped was a smile. "Yes. Just a little shaken up." Inside her, forests were going up in flame and mountainsides were crumbling, but she had to cover it up. She grasped for an excuse a Scire would buy. "I've been living inside a shell for a long time. I want to leave, but I'm also scared to. I've gotten attached to Resolute. It's been home, and change for me is difficult." Her voice sounded like it came through a tunnel. "That probably doesn't make any sense."

"It does. Believe me."

"Thank you, Perry. Cinder sounds like quite a place," she said.

"It is." His expression eased. "Leave in an hour?"

"That sounds perfect."

As soon as he walked away, she crouched behind the tree and groped through her satchel, tears threatening, her breath rising in ragged gasps.

This was a mistake. A misunderstanding. He couldn't have meant Sable.

She found her brother's letters and snapped two open before she found the right one.

Her hands shook so badly, she could barely read it.

Tempest,

I grieve, sister. My betrothed, Olivia of the Tides, was murdered in cold blood by a spurned former lover on the eve of our wedding. The madman took her life because he could not take mine—though he tried, sister. He tried.

Tempest, I fear this man is unstable and intent on destroying all I hold dear. I have written to Banyan to increase your guard. With that addition, and Calista and Ventus, I can give you no better protection short of sending my entire army. Stay close to them. Until I write again with news that I've ended this murderer's life, consider yourself in danger.

Strength is strength, Tempest. And revenge is the only solace,

Sable of the Horns

Pain tore through her chest, like a hook dragging down her sternum. She muffled a sob with a hand, waiting for the urge to pass. Then she folded the letter and pushed down the screams inside her, pushed down, down, down, stopping a raging storm before it could begin.

She stood, empty as a husk, nothing but quiet inside her, and shouldered her satchel. She knew she couldn't hold the pain at bay forever. One day, her emotions would rise up—grief, rage, despair and more. She would shed oceans of tears when that happened. But not yet.

She remembered this same detachment when she'd first been sent to Banyan: this loss of inner feeling, everything duty and logic now. Black and white and gray.

And soon: red.

She wouldn't rest until that color spilled.

The next hours passed in flashes: She carried boxes into the hover; the Aether danced across the sky; Daisy beamed with the excitement to fly; then gravity pressed her down in her jump seat and she was airborne, soaring above the Earth.

Tempest linked her fingers in her lap and swallowed the mysterious taste of blood in her mouth. Roar sat directly across the hold, his distinctive scent—iron and woodsmoke—making her dizzy. She made herself breathe shallowly and turned her mind to organizing what she had learned and what she still needed to discover.

Her brother was dead—that was known. He had gone to the Still Blue, now called Cinder, and died there. With that followed other knowns: She'd never see him again; she had no family anymore; her future no longer had shape.

Those revelations led to still others. There were questions she'd need to answer and fears she could no longer avoid, some of them the worst, the hardest and ugliest. But for now, she kept her attention on the first stab, which was also the killing blow: her brother, lost to her forever.

Perry's words surfaced in her mind. *He's buried on a hill not far away from our settlement—so Roar tells me.*

Roar, whose boots were in her field of view, was . . . Olivia's former lover?

Was . . . her brother's *murderer?*

Nausea swirled up, along with the urge to rub her lips until there was no skin left.

Could it be?

It seemed to fit. She'd seen a dark edge in him, glimpsed the wounded soul in his eyes. He lived with demons—she'd sensed that intuitively.

Her eyes lifted, moving to Perry, who was dozing beside Roar. Gossip had been a favorite topic in Banyan's dinner hall. *Peregrine of the Tides* was a name she'd heard before, but she hadn't made the connection. Hearing the stories of what he'd done—killed his brother and taken over as Blood Lord—she'd imagined someone older, a man. For all of Perry's size and quiet confidence, he was still young, the scruff on his cheeks thin, his build still filling out with muscle. Both he and Roar looked like they couldn't put on weight if they ate cake for a solid month.

Soren's voice came through cabin's speakers, cutting into Tempest's thoughts and startling Daisy beside her. "Good afternoon, ladies and gents. This is your captain speaking. I have good news and bad news. Mostly bad, so let's go with that first. I'm going to have to make an emergency landing in the very near future. The good news is we probably won't crash, but brace yourselves just in case. Thanks for flying Soren Airlines. Hope you'll come soarin' with us again soon."

Roar and Perry leapt out their seats and collided at the cockpit entrance. Suddenly, they were all shouting—Soren, Rune, Roar, Perry.

Tempest felt an absurd urge to laugh build inside her. A moment ago, she thought she'd hit the bedrock of tragedy. Now she saw life's game, how it always had a better trick. A nastier one.

Oh, you think this is bad? Try this on.

"Wh—why are you smiling?" Daisy said breathlessly. "Soren wasn't joking—was he?"

Cal grabbed Daisy's hand. "If he was, I'm going to bury my ax so far between his—"

The hover dipped sharply, the seat restraints digging into Tempest's shoulders. Bags flew up, boxes toppled. Perry and Roar hit the ceiling. Chaos erupted, clattering and clanging. Then everything came down at once, smashing to the floor, but the hover was angled steeply, the nose tilted far higher than the tail.

Clinging to a seat with one hand, Roar caught Perry's shirt with the other, stopping him from sliding to the back.

Everything loose—boxes, arrows, bottles—bounced and careened downslope, where Ventus and the brothers ducked, covering their heads.

"*Soren, do something!*" Cal yelled.

"Working on it!" he yelled back.

The cabin's lights flashed, and an alarm was blaring.

Roar's dark gaze flicked to her as he and Perry climbed back into their seats. He didn't look frightened, but then, she wasn't scared, either.

A kind of euphoria had washed over her. Death was an ugly answer, but it was an answer. She wouldn't have to grieve her beloved brother, or search for a new purpose in life, or grapple with blinding fury or terrible loneliness, or any number of other problems. It was the coward's way out, and her brother would have loathed it, but life had become terrifying. So much more terrifying than this.

As the hover went into another stomach-dropping plunge, shouts erupted from everywhere.

"Hold on!" Soren yelled. Then the hover struck down with a bone-bending jolt and a metallic scream. A second later, or a minute, the alarm shut off and steady white light flooded the cabin.

A thundering silence crashed over them, punctuated by the topple of random items in the back. Aside from the gear strewn everywhere, and the enormous, shocked eyes all around, everything seemed normal.

Soren emerged from the cockpit, pale as the moon, and leaned against the bulwark. "Everyone all right?" He swept an unfocused look over the hold.

There was a general grumbling—curses and grunts of agreement—but she knew she wasn't the only one with whiplash and new bruises.

"Good." Soren swallowed visibly. "That was much—much closer than you probably—'scuse me." He tapped the control panel by the bay door. Dusky light spilled in, mellow as the glow of a campfire. Soren jumped outside as soon as it parted.

She heard him fall clumsily, like he'd splayed out on the dirt, then a sound unlike anything she'd ever heard: retching through sobs, through gasps for breath, all happening at once.

Roar threw off his seat restraints and went after him.

"Come on, man," he said, his voice carrying on a breeze. "Let's walk it off. Get up. There you go."

"I th—thought that was it," Soren sputtered.

"Yeah, me too. It was a close one."

"You have no idea how close, Roar."

"No. I guess I don't. But we're still here. Soren Airlines lives to see another day."

For a long while afterward, no one said anything. They stood in the open field where Soren had put down the hover, letting the night fold in around them. A wind was kicking up from the west. On the edges of the field, trees bent and swayed restlessly.

Tempest's legs were shaking, her body finally registering the tragedy they'd narrowly avoided.

"We know what went wrong," Soren said. "It was the—the—" He made an abstract gesture with his hand. "You tell

’em, Rune.” He wandered away with his hands on his hips, still struggling to regain his composure.

“It’s the circuit board that controls the fuel injector,” Rune said. “We can’t fix it. It’s fried to a crisp. We’ll have to replace it. That means trekking back to Resolute and hoping we can pull one from another craft.”

Perry crossed his arms. “How far is Resolute?”

Soren turned to them. “One hundred miles or so.” He stared into the gathering darkness. “If I run parts of it and go with someone who knows the way, it’d take four-ish days, maybe. Depends on the terrain. And other things.”

“Cal?” Tempest said. “Can you get him there?”

Cal’s chin jerked down. “Yes.”

Tempest felt a surge of pride at her ready confidence.

“I’ll go, too,” Rune said. “This is my knowledge-base more than Soren’s.”

With that decided, they headed back to the hover to gather their packs. Adrenaline was still coursing through them; they’d planned to take advantage of it and leave immediately.

“We’re a little over a day from Tide Land, Perry,” Roar said. He tipped his head to the silhouetted hills to the west. “Escape trail’s right over that ridge.”

“Escape trail?” Perry said.

“Liv used to call it that. We came out this way a few times to get away from Vale. What do you say? No reason not to go now. We could take a look and still get back here before they’re back from Resolute.”

The world began to rotate on the name *Liv.* Tempest almost had to kneel.

There it was. Confirmation.

Roar was the one. He had killed her brother and his fiancée—and destroyed her life.

"I don't want to sit here for a week," she heard herself say. "Can we come?" Her mind felt sharp as an arrow; she knew what she needed to do now. The hover would attract the attention of any parties nearby, drawing Banyan's men if they were around. But the real reason she wanted to go with Roar and Perry came down to a word: revenge.

Revenge is the only solace.

Perry was watching her closely. He didn't miss much. He was a strong Scire, maybe as strong as her.

She gestured at the hover. "I don't want to go anywhere near that thing anytime soon. Just looking at it is making me skitty." If he was scenting her roiling feelings, she hoped that would explain them.

"Come on, Perry," Roar pressed him. "It's *home.*"

"It was."

"It *is.*"

Perry was quiet for a long moment. "Fine. Let's go."

They left barely minutes later, leaving the brothers—Hyde, Hayden and Straggler—to guard the hover. Roar and Perry took the lead. Tempest walked with Ventus and Daisy a little way behind them. She had never felt keener or more awake. As the night deepened, the wind died down and new scents filled her nose—the briny smells of the sea. Mustard flowers and healthy ryegrass. The musk of foxes and the dusty smell of field mice.

Because Roar was an Aud, she would need to be careful about telling Ventus what she wanted from him. She decided the safest thing would be to write out her command.

When they stopped by a creek at dawn to sleep for a few hours, Tempest removed one of her brother's letters. It was the last one he'd written her, only four short sentences—four sentences that had sent her fleeing in the middle of the night a year ago.

Tempest,

I have struck a deal with Dwellers to travel to the Still Blue, breaching my treaty with the Night tribe. You must leave immediately. Banyan has just cause to end your life. Take shelter. When the time is right, I will find you. We will begin again in a new place.

Sable

Short as it was, there was plenty of room on the paper to write her own message. She dug to the bottom of her satchel for the Dweller pen she'd stashed there and wrote:

Roar killed my brother and his betrothed. I order you to bring me justice. He must pay with his—

Life.

Her hand hovered over the paper, her knuckles going white. Birds squabbled in a high branch above her. *Come on,* she urged herself. *It's just one more word! Strength is strength! Revenge is the only solace!*

Her vision blurred. Still, she couldn't bring herself to write it.

She crossed out the half-written sentence and wrote another after it.

He has scarred me deeply and deserves the same.
I want him to remember how he's hurt me for the rest of his life.

She handed it to Ventus a few hours later, as they were walking.

He looked markedly older to her in that moment, his lips dry and cracking, his eyes reddened from the sun. But he read it quickly and handed it back with a nod.

"I'll see it done," he said with his typical unflappable confidence.

Tempest stared at the paper, waiting for regret to kick in. Or relief. *Something.*

Perry and Roar were some distance ahead of them, the flaxen grass rippling around them in waves. The sky was a pale, washed-out blue. Perry turned sharply then, like she'd called his name, his eyes locking on her. Her heart gave a stutter-step in her chest. She pushed the letter back into her pack—she'd burn it as soon as she had the chance—and kept walking.

It didn't feel like she was walking, though. Her feet seemed to be hovering above the Earth.

She felt weightless as a cloud, drifting on the whims of the wind.

~ 9 ~

ROAR

"Remind me why we're doing this again?" Perry said, as they followed the old trail to the Tide's territory.

"Because it's your land," Roar said. He understood Perry's misgivings, but he couldn't remember the last time he'd felt this sure about anything. He *had* to go back. He'd spent ten years there with Perry and Liv. The best times of his life. Over the past year, he'd leaned on those memories, but the images were starting to fade, growing worn as old leather. He needed to fix it all in his mind again, crisp and solid. "Aren't you even curious?"

"I guess." Perry glanced over, humor flashing in his eyes. "You didn't sabotage the hover to make this happen, did you?"

Roar smirked. "If I'd thought of it, I might have."

They came to the top of a crest, and a broad vista spread out before them, rolling hills dotted by trees, the sun sinking into the sea in the far distance. Perry stopped, a lion grin spreading over his face. "Smells like home."

Roar shook his head. "And you didn't want to come." Even *he* smelled it—that soft, damp breath of the sea. A challenging look flickered over Perry's face—his eyes narrowing, his mouth tugging up—and that was all it took.

They broke into a sprint, tearing down the hill like they were twelve again.

Roar pulled ahead. He was faster, and Perry had his bow and quiver to contend with. The tension in his body peeled away with the dusky air and his speed, a feeling of dead skin sloughing off. He stopped only when he'd reached the edge of Tide Land.

Lungs burning healthily, he stared at the gentle rises and falls of earth as the last of the daylight faded, wishing he could run his hand over them. The Aether storms had laid waste to much of it, but stretches were still thriving, and others were already coming back, plant life pushing vibrantly through scorched dirt.

There's a lesson in this, he thought absently. Something about resilience, or new beginnings. Or maybe the lesson was that life and death weren't opposites, but partners. Each strengthening the other, and that nothing was ever really lost.

He wanted to feel those green shoots inside himself. He wanted some sense the scorched blackness had had its time, that he was on the path to something better. *Come on*, he thought. *I'm ready.* Even in his thoughts, he sounded like he was trying to convince himself.

He turned as Perry thundered up, and saw the tight set of Perry's jaw. The flare of his nostrils. "What's up, Per?"

"Scent trails," Perry replied coolly. "Fresh ones. People have been through here recently."

Roar tensed. They were only five, a problem if they were confronted by a hostile band of any size. And out here, theft was the kindest thing that could happen to them.

"Wait here for the others," Roar said. "I'll go take a listen." Perry had excellent night sight, but Roar's hearing still had the edge in the dark. He vaulted up to the top of a rocky outcrop, turning his full concentration on the sounds drifting on the breezes. He didn't like what he heard.

Perry appeared at his side a couple of minutes later. "Anything?"

"Voices. Two of them. Sounds like they're on the split oak lookout. They're men—that's all I can tell. The wind's shifting too much. I'll have to get closer to hear what they're saying."

"I'll send Ventus around from the south. Between the two of you, we should be able to hear something."

Roar looked at him, surprised to learn Ventus was an Aud. He could usually spot his own kind. For a split second, his thoughts cast back to two nights ago, when he and Tempest had kissed, the question of what Ventus might have heard rising up, but he shook his head, pushing it back. "No, Per. Better if I go it alone. Less risk."

A steely look settled in Perry's eyes. "We left the compound a year ago in ruins. There shouldn't be anyone here. I need to know who they are."

"And I'll tell you."

"I'm sending Ventus, Roar. It's my land. This is my call."

This was exactly what Roar had been saying all along, but this was no time to point that out. "Do it, then. Or try. The old man never leaves Tempest's side." Again, his thoughts backtracked to those heated moments with her in the darkness. *Why now, of all times?* he thought bitterly, and was speaking before he could stop himself. "Have you picked anything up from her? Scents that are out of the ordinary?"

"I've been wondering when you'd ask me that. What happened between you two?"

"It's none of your business."

"You just asked me about her."

"So I did." Roar sighed. "Nothing. Nothing happened. Nothing that was anything."

"That's a lot of nothing. Going by her temper, and yours, it was definitely something. She's been all over the place since we left Resolute. Big swings of anger and distress. Sorrow. I can't get a firm read on her."

Roar couldn't believe it. "And you think it's got to do with *me?*" All that over a kiss? It had been a hell of a kiss, granted. And, yes, he'd been ignoring her since, like a cad. But was that enough for anger, distress, sorrow?

He swore under his breath. Why had he done that? He'd known then it was a mistake. Now, he felt like he'd used her. He didn't know the first thing about her, and he didn't *want* to—and that was as much for her sake as anything. The last thing he wanted was to drag an innocent into the miserable bog of his psyche.

But there was more to this, wasn't there? He was afraid he'd tampered with something sacred. He'd never kissed anyone but Liv, and now there was this meaningless thing that had happened with another girl, and he couldn't say Liv was the *only* anymore and she deserved that. And probably—no, definitely—part of his manic need to go to the Tides came from that fear, too. Liv's memory was all he had. His lifeline. It needed to be preserved, protected.

Put on a pedestal all by itself.

Perry was shaking his head. "Something happened with you two, all right. I'm not sure if it's just you, though. I don't think she likes me very much. I'll look at it more closely. See if I can figure it out when we're all together again."

"When *you* are," Roar said. "From now on, I'll be keeping my distance." He glanced back, spotting the three figures on the trail behind them, shadows against the blue grass. He could just hear Daisy's voice. "I'll be back by daybreak."

As he jogged away, his mind was still in turmoil. He had never envied Perry's sense. To know what others felt constantly? To be bombarded with their sorrows and anxieties, their delights and desires? No, thanks. He had no interest in that at all. But as he worked toward the sentry knoll, he actually found himself wishing he could scent tempers.

He wanted to know: Just how angry was Tempest with him? And what did she expect, that they'd share a random kiss, then start a relationship? It had been a few minutes of pleasure. But it was *nothing.* It had meant *nothing.* And if he ever felt the urge to touch another girl again, he was throwing himself into a pit before he could.

With his thoughts churning, propelling his legs, he came within hearing distance of the lookout much faster than he'd anticipated. It was the same spot they'd used in the Tides, a small hill with a thick oak trunk that lightning had split down the middle, the two toppled halves providing plenty of great perches from which to observe the surrounding terrain. Knowing it well, he also knew its blind spot—a row of shrubs that followed a drainage depression that provided cover from both sight and sound lines.

He crept toward it, his mind clearing of all noise. He came to a knee amid the branches and laid a hand on the cool grass. One of the men was humming on the knoll. Every once in a while, the other one coughed.

Carefully, he picked his way closer. They could be Auds themselves, or perhaps Seers, given the brightness of the Aether tonight. The odds were low they were Scires, those being rare, but Roar knew he was playing with fire by getting this close. With the wind shifting from the offshore flows, a strong Aud might be able to hear him. His heart thudded with the possibility. He had missed this intensity, all instinct, no room for thought. Finally, the men began to speak, picking up what sounded like an ongoing debate.

"The entire thing is on Banyan's shoulders, you know. He's the one who screwed up. He got comfortable with the girl and let his guard down. If Ash had been in charge, she'd never have gotten away. We'd still have that leverage."

"Ash is a clever fox, for sure. But he's young and arrogant and thinks himself invincible. If he comes to power, first thing he'll do is split with Rose tribe."

"You say that like it's a bad thing."

"It's not, but it's *how* you do things as much as—hoy, d'you hear that?"

Roar held his breath, listening. He didn't know what they'd heard; he hadn't made a sound.

"Just a possum or something," said the deeper voice. After a beat, he went on. "If Ash splits off Night tribe from Rose, it won't be bad, it'll be terrible. Scar's just about raised the lad. You think he won't take that personal?"

Roar caught on to the conversation easily enough. Blood Lords of large tribes were widely known, but Banyan of the Night and Scar of the Rose held a special place of hate in his heart. Just over a year ago, the two lords had united their southern tribes into one, Nightrose. Together, they'd traveled north and seized Marron's mountaintop stronghold, Delphi. They'd slaughtered most of Marron's people and turned the rest out in the midst of the worst Aether storms anyone had ever known. Roar didn't know who Ash was, but he had to be Banyan's son or whoever was next in line to rule Night tribe after Banyan.

Roar had heard these sorts of conversations his entire life. Power plays within and between tribes were constant. He suddenly became aware of just how much work Aria, Marron, and the rest of the Council had done over the past year to create a stable society in Cinder. He also wondered why these two sentries were talking so passionately about Rose and Night, when Delphi was hundreds of miles away.

After listening for another couple of hours, he gleaned nothing new. Still, he'd confirmed that someone else had taken up in the Tide compound: These two were without a doubt sentries on watch duty.

He stood and began his silent retreat, grinding his teeth in anger. They had abandoned the village and this land, but the thought of strangers living here infuriated him nonetheless, and it would surely be harder for Perry to bear.

He was trying to remember how many generations back the Tides had been in Perry's family when he heard footsteps thudding over the dirt behind him.

Roar spun and drew his knives, but the dark figure was shockingly close, only a few feet upslope. Seeing he'd been spotted, the man took the rest of the way in thundering strides and leapt. Roar threw himself sideways, trying to dodge, but the man had anticipated this and adjusted. He slammed into Roar's shoulder, throwing him back.

Roar was aware even as he fell through the air that this would hurt; he was falling *down* the hill and gravity wouldn't be kind. He crashed on his back, taking the full weight of his attacker square on his chest. The impact stunned him, his breath exploding out, and then they were tumbling together. Fighting for control. Grabbing, punching, the world spinning, rocks flying by. Everything a mad confusion.

He needed air *badly*—his lungs had become a vacuum—but the man seemed to know this. He hooked an arm around Roar's neck even as they twisted and crashed downslope, compressing his windpipe. Roar threw his hand up to gouge the eyes, aware he was fighting dirty, fighting for his life, but a shrub snagged his sleeve and he missed.

The angle of the slope lessened, the speed of their tumble slowing. He was ready for it. Faster than he'd ever done anything, he unsheathed his blade and impaled the man's leg, immediately slicing hard across. He wanted the femoral artery, wanted it severed clean. This man was skilled, ruthless, and *very* motivated to kill him. In the same instant as he pulled his blade through his attacker's thigh muscle, he felt two smacks on his chest, quick as snakebites.

Then the man grunted and released him, and they rolled apart, finally stopping in a puff of dirt. Roar was gulping for air and sucking in grit instead. He began coughing, the dust offending his desperate lungs. He forced himself to his feet; if he stayed down, it was over. His eyes were streaming with tears, but through them he saw that dawn was breaking, the flat black hills taking dimension. He watched his attacker pull himself up on one leg and recognized him.

"Ventus," he gasped, unable to conceal his shock. Ventus held a knife in one hand. He stood bent to one side, his other hand pressed to his thigh. Blood was gushing darkly through his fingers. "I guess you're not here to help me do recon."

"I'm here to end your miserable life," the man replied, his voice rough and out of breath.

You may have managed it, Roar thought. He didn't want to look down, didn't want to see the damage, but he could feel blood fast soaking his shirt. He didn't feel pain, just a strong pulsing where the hot torrent sprang. An extreme sense of detachment had washed over him. He was fairly sure he had a deep hole over his heart. Maybe in it. "You're surprisingly quick for an old man. That was a fine effort."

Ventus's determined scowl deepened. "I'm not done yet."

"That's the spirit."

Ventus hobbled a step closer. "You sicken me."

"Yes, that part's clear." Roar noticed his left arm was going numb. He firmed his grip on his knives. "What I'm trying to understand is how I've wronged you."

"You hurt her, you hurt me. Haven't you done enough damage?"

"*Damage*." He suddenly thought of Tempest. But . . . this was ridiculous. His life could *not* hang in the balance because he'd spurned her—which he hadn't even really done. "You're not serious?"

"You've wronged us all, murderer."

Murderer. The word seemed to hang in the air, suspended like a dark star. He swayed in place, still trying to understand. He was no innocent. He had killed before. He'd taken life when there was no alternative. When he'd had to protect himself or the people he loved. But he was not cold-blooded. There was only one man he'd have slain with pleasure, and Perry had taken that honor.

Ventus was shaking his head, disgust twisting his features. "You *dare* pretend ignorance?"

"I pretend nothing. I have no idea what you mean."

"Sable wrote to Tempest. He told her what you did in his letters."

Sable. The name threw his mind into total darkness. For the briefest instant, he thought this might be a nightmare, which would explain the interjection of something so horrifying and nonsensical. That name. *Sable.*

"Do you truly not know?" Ventus said. "Sable is her brother—was, no thanks to you."

The world seemed to fly apart and rejoin again in a form he didn't recognize. A sound began in his ears, high as a hawk's cry. "Are you—" Words were hard to find. He still hadn't caught his breath. "Are you telling me Tempest is *Sable of the Horn's* sister?"

There was a flicker in the older man's gaze, a question or confusion, like the possibility of Roar's cluelessness was registering. "Yes. Yes, she is. She's younger by some years. Did you truly not—"

Ventus never finished the question; he turned sharply, his eyes flaring wide.

Both sentries were hustling down the hill toward them with nocked bows.

Roar had already spotted them. He couldn't bring himself to care.

In the rising light, he could now see Ventus's ashen face, and the scarlet red that covered his hand and darkened his leather pants. He was bleeding badly, soaking the dirt.

Ventus turned back to him and spoke through gritted teeth. "I'll find you again. And I *will* kill you."

"Ex—excellent," Roar said. "I love a good comeback. And I've still got a lot of—a lot of questions."

With a final snarling look, the old warrior hobbled away. He could barely put weight on the wounded leg—he looked like he was on death's door—but Roar didn't even bother to attempt a getaway. He was panting just standing there. A cold feeling was creeping over him, and he felt like he'd been rained on, but it was his blood that soaked him, chest to boots. The world was fading behind a dense fog. The cut on his chest—not good. He really was going to die.

"Throw down your blades!" shouted one of the sentries as he ran up.

"You don't have to yell," Roar heard himself say. "I'm an Aud."

"Your knives!"

Roar winced. Too loud. The man's voice, the shrieking in his ears. The fog over the world had become aggressive, blotting out his vision. "Can I set them down? Bad for the blades to drop them and my friend just sharp—sharp—sharpened them."

"Set them down, then back up."

Set them down, then pick them up? That made no sense. Then he understood. The man meant set the blades down, then for *him* to back up.

He smiled, proud he'd figured that out, and bent down to lay down his knives. Next thing he knew, the dirt was rushing up to smash against his face.

He had a final fleeting thought as darkness slammed down like a door shutting in a gale.

More.

He still wanted more life.

10

TEMPEST

"If you're going to pace, I'll do it with you," Daisy said. She set down Tempest's backpack and the needle and thread she'd been using to mend a hole in it, and rose from her spot by the campfire. Her arm was warm as she looped it through Tempest's. "Maybe it'll look like we're strolling instead of worrying the tread of our soles down to nothing."

Tempest glanced at Perry, who was sitting in the shade of a tree. He looked up from the willow branch he was stripping with a knife. "Thanks, but I think he's been suspicious for hours."

"All the more reason we should actually go for a walk and get away from here, Temp," she lowered her voice, "will you *please* tell me what's going on?"

"Not now. I can't leave. I need to be here when Vent—" a sob came up, almost escaping, "Ventus gets back." She'd been worried about him since the moment he'd left. Now he was hours late.

Was he hurt?

Had he succeeded?

She winced. How could any mission to do harm ever be called a *success?*

Daisy's frown deepened. "Come on. I'm not taking 'no' for an answer." They left the small campsite where they'd slept—or not slept, in Tempest's case—following a game trail to smooth granite boulders that cascaded down a slope.

Tempest fell against the first one and pressed her hands to her stomach. "I feel like I need to be sick, but I've got nothing in my stomach."

"Start talking. Maybe that will help. Tell me what's going on."

Tempest's mouth wobbled. "You'll hate me."

"Impossible and you know that. I'm listening."

"Ventus is taking so long. He's late, and I think I've just made the hugest mistake of my life; but my brother's dead, he's dead, and I didn't know what else to do or how to make it right—I mean I *did* know. I knew what my brother would have wanted, but I couldn't do it." Now that she was going, she couldn't seem to stop rambling. "Daisy, I thought I'd be merciful, but I don't feel better. I feel *worse* now, so much *worse*. I don't know what I've done. What have I done?"

Her control broke and the tears spilled over—the first tears she'd shed for Sable.

Daisy pulled her close and Tempest let herself cry—but only enough to relieve the intense pressure of grief. The instinct to protect herself, to protect Daisy, was too strong even now. She could bend, but she could not break. She stepped back and wiped her face.

Daisy had tears in her own eyes. "Sable's really gone?"

"Yes."

Daisy's hand fluttered up to her mouth. "Oh, Temp. Oh, sweetie. I am so sorry."

"I know. Thank you."

"But . . . I don't understand. You said you made a mistake?"

"I did. I ordered Ventus to—to—" Tempest's eyes filled with fresh tears; she breathed until they faded back. "I ordered him to do something I can't even bring myself to *say*. It's Roar, Daisy." An image appeared in her mind: Roar, leaping out of the hover to comfort Soren.

"It's okay." Tempest didn't realize she was hugging herself until Daisy took her hands, peeling them away and squeezing them firmly. "What about Roar? Give me the whole thing, Tempest."

"Roar killed my brother. He's from the Tides. The tribe my brother's wife—*intended* wife—was from. Olivia of the Tides. I guess Roar and Olivia were together before it was arranged for her to marry my brother. Roar became mad with jealousy. He came to Rim to kill my brother, but he took her life instead. My brother knew Roar would come for him again. Last night, Perry said that Roar had—" Here was another thing she couldn't seem to say. But she had to. She had to get the whole thing out of her. "He said Roar *buried* my brother."

Patches of red were working up Daisy's fair neck, spreading over her jaw. "Oh, Tempest . . . I don't know what to say."

"You don't have to say anything." Tempest let out a shuddering breath. "My brother would have wanted revenge.

Anything else he'd see as weakness. When I gave Ventus the order, I wanted Roar dead myself. He took everything from me, Daisy. My only family. All I ever wanted . . . But I couldn't do it. I told Ventus to hurt him instead. To scar him, as he's scarred me. I thought it was a mercy . . . . So why do I feel sick? Why do I feel evil? Have I let my brother down? I don't understand anything anymore. It's like I can't even see—"

She broke off. Perry was heading toward them on the trail, his strides long and purposeful. "Oh, skies no . . ." She saw the packet of her brother's letters in his hand. Her blood iced, and the hair on her arms stood up. The order she'd written to Ventus! She hadn't found a good window yet to burn it! "Go back to camp, Daisy," she said as calmly as she could. "I'll see you there."

Daisy hesitated but seemed to understand: She had to face this alone. "I'll be close."

Perry strode up and tossed the letters at her feet. They landed with a dead thud. "Tempest of the Horns." His voice was hard, but nothing compared to his temper. The power of his rage knocked her back on her heels. "I thought there was something familiar about you."

"Familiar? You knew my brother?"

"Yes. I knew him."

Her mouth went dry. She swallowed thickly. "Because . . . Olivia was your sister? I didn't know. That you knew Sable, I mean.

"There's a lot you don't know." His green eyes blazed into her, twin emeralds with flames inside. "Tell me you didn't really send Ventus after Roar."

She didn't understand. "That's exactly what I did. He killed *my brother!* He killed *your* sister!" She waited for his shock; there was no way he could know this and still count Roar a friend. "My brother wrote me. See for yourself. Roar killed your—"

"I read them! Your brother *lied* to you! Roar didn't kill Liv! That's the last thing he'd *ever* have done! *Your brother* killed Liv when she was trying to leave him! He shot her with a crossbow from eight paces away. Roar was there to witness it. *Sable* took my sister's life."

For an instant, she was blinded. Literally blinded, a white wall falling over her vision. Then it whipped away, but the world was too bright. Too painfully, starkly bright.

"No—he didn't," she said. Unconsciously, she'd spread her hands and widened her stance. "He wouldn't. My brother wouldn't do something like that." But she scented no deception in Perry's temper, just clear rage. Rage like a comet. Rage like a burning spear.

"He did that and worse," Perry returned. "Sable tortured a child. *Sacrificed* him. Why do you think we named our city Cinder?"

"No! That can't be true. You're—"

"Lying? You know I'm not. And here's more truth you won't like: Your brother's dead because I killed him. *I* did it. Not because he destroyed the lives of people I love. Not because he took pleasure in causing me pain. I did it because he wouldn't have stopped otherwise. Sable was a plague. A demon. I did the world a *favor.* I *know* I did, and I still feel lucky if I sleep through the night. But

Roar?" He shook his head. "People don't come any better than him. If he dies, this whole world dims, and that's on *you*."

"I didn't order him killed!"

"Of course you did," he spat. "You just don't see it yet. *Think*. Ventus is Sable's sworn man, isn't he? Because of you, Ventus thinks Roar killed his Blood Lord. He has his own reason to see Roar dead at his feet."

He was right, and it landed like a slap. "I wanted justice!" She was coming apart. Nothing felt real. How was this real? "I still want it!"

"Have it, then." Perry unsheathed the knife at his belt and held it out. She took it on pure reflex. "Here, I'll make it easier for you." Turning, he knelt before her and tilted his head. "Don't slice or saw. Put the point here." He tapped the vein that disappeared under his jaw. "Drive deep, then slash out through the esophagus and gullet. It's tougher than you think, so be vicious."

She stared at the thick vein pulsing with life, like a river after a hard rain, as tears brimmed in her eyes. She couldn't breathe. She looked at the knife in her hand. She was not a killer. My god, she was not *this*.

"I hate you." She tossed the weapon down on the grass, disgusted at her own weakness. "This isn't over yet."

Perry swept it up and stood. "You're damn right it's not. If Roar dies," he said, pointing the blade at her face, "I'll teach you what true hate is."

Somehow, she located the strength to give him her smile. "And what do you think you can teach the sister of a demon?"

It was hours before the rage left her. When it did, she felt hollowed out. Empty as a robbed grave. That morning, she hadn't recognized her life. Now she didn't even recognize herself.

She had never hated anyone. Not even the cruel maid in Night tribe, who'd whispered in her ear every morning that she was a worthless Horn tribe slut when she braided Tempest's hair. Not even the Night tribe boys, who used to heckle her, to speak to her like she was their property. To her knowledge, she'd never been the object of true hate before, either.

It was all new, this jagged, poisonous inner landscape.

More than ever, she needed the confidence her brother alone gave her. She wanted to know he was out there somewhere: a solution, a goal, a comfort. But she'd thrown all his letters in the fire in a fit of confusion and hurt. All the words she used to lean on were gone.

He was gone.

"Am I horrible person and I've just never known it, Daisy?" she asked, breaking her silence. "What have I set in motion?"

They were sitting together, breaking pine needles into tiny pieces and throwing them in the fire. Perry had left immediately after their fight, presumably to go find Roar, his bow thumping at his back as he ran off. Now the sun was melting into the horizon, blazing and red. A full day gone. Ventus still hadn't returned. Perry and Roar hadn't returned. She stared into the dancing, hungry flames. Everything was destroyed. Even time seemed to be losing shape.

"We don't know yet what's in motion," Daisy replied. She sounded and looked exhausted. "Let's try not to jump to conclusions until we do. And you're the opposite of a horrible person, Tempest."

She drew in a deep breath, scenting the simple, straightforward note of Daisy's temper, so like the flower whose name she bore. "You're telling the truth."

"I always tell you the truth." Daisy glanced over with a light smile. "What point is there in lying to you?"

"Maybe I've fooled you. Maybe you don't know me at all. The real me. What if I'm not even a Scire and I've been tricking you all this time?" She didn't know what she was saying. She was lost in an endless darkness, and there was no way out.

"It's certainly possible I've missed something in the decade I've spent by your side."

"What about my brother? Was he . . . ?"

Daisy picked up a stick and poked at the fire. "A horrible person?"

Tempest nodded, swallowing the lump in her throat. Perry had accused Sable of atrocities so heinous she couldn't look at them squarely. Now, scenting the bruised sourness that was melting into Daisy's temper, overshadowing that light simplicity, she couldn't deny it anymore: The brother she loved wasn't the same person she'd always believed him to be. She swallowed again. The raw knuckle in her throat wasn't going away. "You're stalling. That's a bad sign."

Daisy's smile was sorrowful. "I'm trying to decide whether the oath I swore to Sable still takes precedent over my duty to you now that he's passed on. I don't think so. Anyway, I can't deceive you about this any longer." She looked over, meeting Tempest's gaze. There was something apologetic and pained in her expression. Something determined, too. "Sable of the Horns was charismatic, deceitful, handsome, unrelenting, manipulative, remorseless . . . brilliant. Every room he entered became his room. You couldn't look away from him. He was an exceptional Blood Lord for these reasons, and more. The Horns prospered under him. We never feared outside hostility or political instability the way other tribes do. At least not while I was still there." Her hand settled over Tempest's. "But as a person, he was very, very dangerous."

"To his enemies?"

"To everyone."

Tempest sighed. "I see." *A plague*, she recalled Perry saying. *A demon*. "Could he have . . . done what Perry says?"

Daisy nodded. "Yes. And . . ." The apology in her expression came forward, her eyes tightening into a wince. "There were rumors, Temp. There were rumors when it happened."

"It?"

"Olivia's death. Her murder."

"By my brother?"

"Yes. Cal, Ventus, and I—we went to lengths to protect you from them. We weren't going to let you suffer unless we were certain it was true. It was chaos in those days, the Aether worsening every day. And at the same time, everyone was talking about the Still Blue, saying that Sable had the edge on finding it. We thought the rumors might just be vitriol directed at him because of that—because he was closest to the answer. The Horns were going to find it and survive, and to hell with everyone else. People were terrified. They were angry. Then when we left the Seven Hills and merged with Rose tribe, that was stressful on another level. We were all so scared and then the rumors faded away—and we let them. Do you hate me?"

"Never. You did the right thing," she said, without letting herself question whether that was true or not. Daisy and the others had done what they *felt* was right. It would have been an agonizing decision for them, and regardless, it was in the past. "Do you know what's worse than losing someone you love? Loving someone who never existed. That's what I've done, isn't it? All this time, I've loved a phantom. I've loved someone I imagined." She shook her head, staring into the ashes. Her brother's letters had long since burned to nothing, but she could feel them in there. His words. His lies. "I can't believe this."

"I'm so sorry, Temp. I've broken your heart."

"It was already broken. That happened yesterday. Today what's left is getting pulverized."

Daisy wrapped an arm around her. "The pieces are all still here. I'll hold them together until they're steady again."

She rested her head on Daisy's shoulder. "I have nowhere to go now. Not that I want to go anywhere. I just want to hide." The irony hit her. "Can you believe it? For a whole year, we hid. I thought it was so bad. I couldn't wait for it to end. Now that's all I want to do. I want to hide from myself. From reality. From everything."

Daisy was quiet a moment. "You've been in hiding because you've had no other option. It's not your style. It never has been. The world's come down on your shoulders, but you'll rise up. Life wants you to reach. It wants you to stretch up to a higher shelf. There's a version of you that will emerge from this stronger and wiser. All this means is it's time for you to stretch."

"Or get a ladder if you're short like I am."

Daisy smiled. "And that's how I know you'll be fine. You're resourceful. You're smart and resilient and tenacious. And you're incredibly unhorrible."

Tempest found a shaky smile. "And incredibly lucky to have *you* in my life." Then a thought occurred to her. "Daisy, you're free of me. You're released from your duty. You were sworn to Sable." The revelations kept coming. "The Horns have no Blood Lord anymore. Our tribe is part of history now."

"It's not. You're still here and I'm staying with you. If you won't let me stay as your servant, then I'll stay as your friend. Either way, I'm not going—" She looked up, her eyes flying wide. "Ventus!"

He had just come through the trees. He shambled towards them like a walking corpse, pale and ungainly, his face twisted in pain. Almost beyond recognition.

They leapt up and ran over, helping to ease him down by the fire.

"It's all right. We've got you now," Tempest said, but she blanched at the gash visible through the tear in his soaked pants. Wide, gaping. Muscle showing beneath. The smell of blood hit her hard, both fresh and clotted. Rancid. There was so much of it. She had no idea how he'd managed to take a step, much less trek from wherever he'd come.

Daisy ran for her satchel. They'd packed Dweller medicines—sprays that stopped bleeding and knitted flesh—but Tempest had a crashing feeling none of it would help. His eyes looked sunken; his lips were pale blue. Life was leaving him.

What have I done? she thought, her eyes burning. Ten years ago, he had left Rim to protect her. He'd given up a life with his children and friends, with grandchildren he'd never met. For ten years, he'd been faithful to her—and *this* was how she repaid him?

"I've failed you," he said thinly, his eyes rolling back. "Roar . . . I can't be sure he's dead."

Dead. She didn't react, though inside she was withering. Perry had been right. Ventus had either acted on his own need for vengeance, or he'd assumed she'd been too soft to give the order she truly wanted and taken the initiative himself.

Either way, it was done. Either way, now wasn't the time to discuss it.

She took his hand. It was cold and rough as rock. "You can't fail me. That's impossible."

"Nightrose tribe's taken the Tide compound," he continued, his voice so soft she had to lean in to hear him. "Aldred's men were on sentry duty. They heard our fight and captured Roar. They'll be searching the area for you by now. Go, Tempest. Run. Run, before it's too late."

He shut his eyes and exhaled a long breath, like he'd just set down a heavy burden.

Aldred was one of Banyan's lackeys. It should've worried her, but it didn't. She only wanted to comfort Ventus. She squeezed his hand. "I'm not abandoning you," she said, but she could no longer tell if he heard her.

She held his hand as Daisy treated his leg. She stayed with him overnight and willed him to keep breathing, pushing back hard against her fear of the dark. She could feel all the unseen evils that hid inside it, and memories skirted along her consciousness of other terrible nights.

Leaving Rim, at age seven. Sable had picked her up while she'd slept and placed her in a carriage. She'd understood what was happening and begged him to change his mind. She didn't want to leave, she wanted to stay with him.

Stop this, he'd said gruffly, prying her arms off his neck. *Be strong, Tempest! Don't be sentimental! You are a Horn, and this is your duty!*

After that night, so many more of them, crying silently in her new "home" amongst strangers.

The night Banyan's nephews had surrounded her in the orchard, then thrown her down amongst fallen apples, worm-eaten and half-rotten. Cal had run up, her sword swinging wide, flashing in the Aetherlight, her expression bland, almost sleepy. *If this ever happens again, if I even see one of you* near *her, I will force-feed you your genitals.*

Since that night, just a whiff of apples made Tempest feel sick.

Not this night, she prayed, stroking Ventus's big hand. *Please, not him. Not this.*

By dawn, he was still hanging on, but it was time for her to leave his side. She had thought it over for the past hours and knew what she had to do. This time, she felt utterly calm and confident.

Quietly, she packed her backpack, then roused Daisy. "I'm going to the Tide compound to find out if Roar is alive. If there's anything I can do to help him, I have to do it. I need you to stay with Ventus. Will you do that?"

Daisy rubbed the sleepiness from her eyes and sat for a moment, considering. "I heard Ventus earlier. He said they're Banyan's men."

"Yes. Aldred." Tempest thought of the greedy, slimy man. Aldred had a son a little older than her who'd been there that night in the orchard.

"Aldred will send you back to Banyan." A frown line had appeared between Daisy's pale eyebrows. "Are you really going to forfeit your life for a stranger?"

Tempest almost said that Roar wasn't a stranger, but he was. And he wasn't. And he was. She simply couldn't grasp what he was, truth be told. Though barely days old, their relationship had followed no pattern that was remotely familiar. They'd kissed. They'd ignored each other. And now, she had possibly condemned him to death. She dug around in her tired mind and found an answer for Daisy. "Banyan has no reason to kill me now that my brother is dead."

"No reason except pride. You embarrassed him. You defied him. Sable still betrayed him. He might do it because he's raving mad."

Tempest shook her head. Banyan wasn't an emotional man—that was Scar, Blood Lord of Rose tribe. She'd only met him a few times, but he was without a doubt unstable, violent. With the two tribes united, though, it was possible that Scar would influence Banyan. Maybe by turning herself in, she *was* sacrificing her life. She didn't know. She only knew there was no other path ahead that seemed possible or right.

"I can't run anymore, Daisy. I can't hide anymore. I can't close my eyes anymore or let my fears about how others might react be what guides me. I did an unforgivable thing. If I can make it right somehow, then I will. That's the higher shelf, remember? I'm going to reach for it."

She hugged Daisy and planted a kiss on Ventus's forehead. "I know I'll see you again," she whispered. Then she swept her backpack over her shoulder and headed off, alone.

~ 11 ~

ROAR

I'm dead, Roar thought.

There was no other way to explain it. Why else would he be in Liv's home? In Perry's home? He'd bled out and died and this was heaven. This home that he'd made his own. In these walls, where he'd wrestled with Perry, and where he'd kissed Liv, and where he'd learned, day by day, what it meant to have a family.

But if he was really dead, he wouldn't feel pain—and pain was *all* he felt.

He slumped forward in a chair, his head lolling, the rope around his shoulders the only thing keeping him from toppling over. Blood-soaked gauze was wrapped tight around his chest.

Someone grabbed his hair and yanked his head up. Roar stared into the eyes of a red-haired young man near his age.

"Who are you?" he demanded. He had a soft, childish face that made his sneer especially disturbing.

"Your biggest regret," Roar croaked.

Red Hair backfisted him. Roar's head whipped to the side. "Who are you?" he repeated.

Blood surged into Roar's parched mouth. He leaned over and spat. "I'm quite thirsty," he rasped. "So it would help if you heard me the first time."

Red Hair snorted and turned to an older man—his father, judging by the porcine resemblance. "Can I kill him now?"

"Not until he talks," said the father.

"If that's what you want, then let me see to his wounds," said the woman who stepped around his chair. "He'll not survive to answer questions otherwise. Out, both of you. *Out.*" She herded them to the door. Warm light cut into the house as it swung open. Roar had no idea if it was dawn or dusk, but inside him, night was coming again, closing in fast.

He had a vague impression of the woman and her daughter moving him to a bed—Vale's bed, a place he'd never thought he'd ever be—then cutting through the bindings that were keeping his heart inside his chest. He felt them loosen and hissed, desperately pressing his palm over the wound. Blood was flowing again.

Was she trying to kill him?

"Easy now, lad. It's all right." She cut his shirt away with shears and gave it, sopping and red as a skinned animal, to the girl.

Roar was suddenly freezing down to his bones. He began to shiver violently. He glanced down and saw two ugly, weeping lacerations on his chest. They made a perfect X over his heart. That seemed too ridiculous to be true, so probably he was imagining things.

"Deep cuts," said the woman, Sage, clucking her tongue. Somewhere along the way he'd learned her name. "But you might live if we cauterize them."

Cauterize. A kinder word for burned.

He passed out then, quick as lightning. When he came around again, the girl, Morgan, was wiping the blood off his chest with a sponge. Seeing he'd woken, she ducked her head and blushed all the way to the tips of her ears. The absurdity filled him with aimless rage. How could the forces of attraction be present in this hellish moment?

I'm dying, he wanted to say. *I'm practically a cold corpse.*

The girl bolted away when Sage entered the room.

"I'm all set," said the woman. She stood over him with an iron rod that glowed sun-bright where the end bent back. Even a few feet away, he could already feel its wicked heat. "This will hurt more than anything you've ever felt."

"No, it won't," he said. "Do it."

When she touched the neon metal to his skin, he heard—and saw and smelled—his skin sizzle. He bucked hard, his vision swimming, his mouth gaping open to beg for mercy, for death, for anything.

This will hurt more than anything you've ever felt, Sage had said.

And he'd thought of Liv, of course. But as it happened, Sage was right. What he felt went beyond words. It went beyond comprehension or sense.

Once again, unconsciousness came swiftly, covering him like a blanket. Saving him.

He drifted in and out. Feverish. Thirsty. Tears leaking out of him, his heart still sizzling. Still burning. Still smelling of scored meat.

When he finally woke fully, it was to darkness.

His head throbbed. His tongue felt like rough burlap. His ears rang terribly, but he could hear voices in the outer room.

"He's been having fever dreams," Sage was saying. "He's been talking in his delirium. Much of it's rambling nonsense, but he keeps mentioning Peregrine. Vale. Liv. He's been recalling things that happened in this very house. He's a Tider, Aldred. I couldn't be surer of it."

"He can't be. They all left."

Roar recognized the older man's voice. Aldred. It was the redhead's father.

"They did leave," Sage returned, "but the Aether's gentling. What if they're wanting their land back? What if he's a scout and there's more of them coming?"

Aldred heaved a tense sigh. "How long till he comes around?"

"Given the amount of blood he lost, he might never. But the earliest I'd say is tomorrow."

"We have to assume the worst, then," said Aldred. "The Tides gave this land up. I'm not giving it back. Double the sentry watch. Make sure everyone's prepared for a raid."

"Yes, sir," replied the son.

They kept talking through their defense strategy as they left the house. Roar heard the front door open and close, then quiet descended. He stared at the knots in the ceiling timbers, forcing himself to think. They hadn't tied him up or left him under guard, thinking him incapacitated. It was an advantage that wouldn't last. He had to escape tonight.

Somehow, he had to find the strength to move.

Somehow.

He shut his eyes. His chest throbbed, the pain radiating out to every part of him. Constant. Relentless. A madness he couldn't escape.

He'd suffered a serious injury in the past when he, Perry, and Aria had been ambushed while leaving Delphi. It'd taken him months to recover from the gash to his leg. He hurt so much worse now, the pain writhing and evil. Exhausting just to bear.

The deep sleep was coming again, his body spent. He fought it off. Fought to make sense of his situation.

An image of Tempest appeared in his mind. Small, lithe. Deep red-brown hair, falling in tumbles. Eyes the gray of herons' feathers at times, bright silver at others. From the start, he'd liked how she held herself, alert and contained, a bright look in her gaze, a smile always close.

He'd *kissed* her.

The girl whose brother had killed Liv.

The girl who'd lied to him, who'd sent Ventus to assassinate him.

Murderer, Ventus had accused him.

Of Liv.

It simply defied comprehension.

Someone had deceived her. Given her false information. In the swamp of his pain-addled mind, Roar saw the shape of a possible truth for an instant—Sable had lied to his sister about Liv's death and pinned it on him—then it darted away.

He allowed himself another moment of laying there, then he pushed his legs over the side of the bed and stood. Stars exploded before his eyes and the world tilted wildly to one side. He crashed against the wall—which was good, a solid place to lean—and stood there, catching his breath. Waiting for the stars to fade. Sage had said he'd lost a lot of blood and he actually *felt* the emptiness in his veins.

Keeping one hand on the wall, he moved toward the door, testing the handle. It was unlocked. He already knew the house was empty, so he staggered out to the main room, where the kitchen, kitchen table, and sitting area all blended into one space.

It was messier than it ought to be, crammed with boxes and bags. It didn't smell right, either. The floorboards where he'd bled had been scrubbed, sanded and oiled, the wood there too pale and smooth. A fire was winking in the hearth, the iron rod resting nearby, innocuous-looking. Seeing it, pain flared in his chest and a desire to burn the place down seized him. It shouldn't belong to thieves. Squatters.

He made himself keep moving. He pushed through the front door and was pleased to see no one guarding it outside. He couldn't have fought a day-old duckling at that moment with any hope of winning. Step by careful step, he walked to the center of the clearing.

A light mist was falling, cool on his face. Torchlight wavered around him, illuminating the heart of the compound and the homes encircling him in a soft glow. Across the way, the cookhouse thrummed with the voices of hundreds of people gathered for dinner.

Such a familiar, nostalgic sound. So wrong now.

He knew he should keep moving before he was spotted, but he couldn't seem to make himself. So much *good* had happened here. Molly's carrot cakes. Bear's soundless laughter. Mila's clay-stained clothes and Old Will's comically unfunny jokes.

The memories kept coming, each of them rich and real. An ache began to build in his throat. He'd been an idiot this past year. He'd shortchanged the past by making it all about Liv when there was so much more, so many things he'd left behind that mattered. So many people he loved.

Why, he wondered, *do I pretend that* everything *is about her?* Why did he keep his life so lean? As slim as what he could fit on the edge of one of his blades?

If he survived this, he vowed he'd find a way to miss her with his entire being, and still allow room for other things. It wouldn't mean he loved her any less.

"Roar."

He turned to the sound of his name, sure he'd imagined Perry's voice, but there he was striding up, his blond waves resembling a Medusa's snarl under the Aetherlight. He was flanked by guards, big muscular men as tall as Perry but broader. One of them was in possession of Perry's bow and quiver.

Unexpectedly, Perry hauled him into a hug.

"Chest—my chest," Roar hissed through his teeth.

Perry stepped back, swearing darkly. "You look like a corpse."

"Could be worse, I guess. I could look how I feel." He drew a measured breath, edging around the pain. "Are you rescuing me?"

Perry shrugged apologetically. "I heard and just started running."

"Well. Good effort, anyway." He was digging around for a smile, but that liminal darkness was threatening again, the pulse growing louder in his head, consciousness no longer a sure thing.

Aldred's men were talking. Something about orders to bring them to the cookhouse.

Perry pulled one of Roar's arm over his shoulders, ignoring Roar's curses. Bearing most of his weight, Perry guided him into the cookhouse, a long structure the Tides had used for all large gatherings, from nightly suppers to important meetings.

The hall was crowded, thrumming with heat and noise. Perry lowered him into a chair and took the one beside Roar, then turned to the person behind him and demanded water. When a cup arrived, he handed it to Roar, who took it down in one tilt, like he was dumping it into another vessel.

"You all right?" Perry asked.

"Definitely. I feel great." Roar had never felt so depleted in his entire life.

"Keep your mouth shut. I'll handle this."

"*You're* doing the talking? We're doomed."

"That bastard's in my seat," Perry muttered. His level stare went across the table.

Aldred was on the other end wearing a patient, scheming smile. His son sat beside him. Every chair down the length of the table was occupied and people stood around it, three and four deep. A hum of anticipation hung in the air, like an audience hungry for a performance to begin.

"Pere-grine of. The *Tides*," Aldred said, in a grating sing-songy voice. "What brings you to your *former* home?"

"Isn't it obvious?" Perry let a long beat of silence stretch out. Aldred glanced nervously at the men standing around him. *Clever*, Roar thought. Perry was letting Aldred's imagination run. "You captured my friend."

"Ah, yes. Your man who got a good carving by Ventus of the Horns." Aldred spoke like Roar wasn't even there. The sentries who'd found Roar stood behind him. Apparently, they'd overheard the words he and Ventus had traded. "Give me one good reason why I should release a man who was spying on land I hold by right of Nightrose."

"Roar is no spy," Perry said, a steely note in his voice, "and this is not your land, or theirs."

"You think it's yours?" Aldred's forced laugh sounded like a cough. "You abandoned it."

"It was unlivable," Perry said, his tone growing even cooler. "I did *not* abandon my home."

Roar couldn't believe his ears. Had Perry made a complete turnaround, or was he bluffing?

Aldred's round cheeks were going red. "We will discuss your spy later, and the matter of this land. There are other matters to discuss first." He waved a hand impatiently. A few servants snapped to, hurrying over with wine cups. One was set down in front of Perry. He lifted it to his nose, then set it down in front of Roar, who drank it down as greedily as the water.

He'd have preferred water again, but he was in no position to be picky. He needed anything he could get into his body. The wine hit within seconds, making the room rotate slowly, like a flower to the sun. His splitting headache, at least, lessened slightly.

"Tell me, did you reach the Still Blue?" Aldred asked.

Perry nodded. "We did."

Aldred's eyes sparkled with bewilderment. "And you've been there for the past year?"

"Yes."

"So the rumors were true."

Perry didn't reply to that. Another cup of wine appeared in front of him, delivered by a haggard, sweating servant. Again, Perry sniffed it.

Aldred snorted. "You're unarmed and surrounded by my men. Do you really think I'd resort to poison if I wanted you dead?"

"The thought crossed my mind. Poison is a coward's weapon."

"I'm no coward, Peregrine. But I am tempted to kill you. A sure way to become a legend is to slay one. You've proven that. I know you challenged your brother. Killed him in his prime, and you just out of boyhood. Very impressive." He paused, waiting for a reaction. Perry gave none. "But I can understand your *paranoia*. You'd have no claim to this land if I killed you. Simple solution for me. You can see the appeal of the idea, I'm sure."

"If you spilled my blood here," Perry said, "I'd have an eternal claim to it. You'd *never* be rid of me. I would haunt you, Aldred. And your children, and your children's children."

Roar roused himself from his pain. "You wouldn't live long enough to be haunted," he croaked. "You have no idea how many people would come for your head. I'd be first in line."

Aldred's eyes lost focus, like he was imagining being chased by angry hordes. Then a sneer spread over his sweaty face. "Then I'll make you swear an oath to me."

"Never going to happen," Perry said easily.

"What if I kill your friend here—or lover?"

"Brother. Roar would have married my sister."

Aldred glanced briefly at Roar, vague recognition filtering in. "Ah, right. News of what Sable did traveled fast. And now you've found his sister, Tempest." Roar had no doubt now that he and Ventus had been overheard. "I know she's nearby. My men are searching for her now. Was revenge your plan, Peregrine? An eye for an eye? A sister for a sister? Hurt him how he's hurt you?"

Liv was the love of my *life*, Roar wanted to shout. He was completely invisible to this idiot.

"There's a steep bounty for her, you know," Aldred continued. "Such a purse might have tempted even you."

Perry's laugh was a dark, chilling sound Roar seldom ever heard. "You think I want to hurt Sable for killing my sister?" He reached into his collar and pulled two heavy-linked chains from beneath his shirt. Roar recognized them both. Vale had worn the plain silver one—the Tide's chain—before Perry. The other one—richly jeweled with emeralds, rubies, and sapphires, some as large as quail eggs—had belonged to Sable.

Roar hadn't seen either of them in over a year. Perry had stopped wearing them in Cinder when he'd all but stepped away from leadership in favor of being an uncle—a foster father, really—partner, and friend. But here—here in the old world they'd left behind, here under the blue and shifting light of the Aether—they meant something.

They meant a whole hell of a lot.

Aldred's eyes rounded to the whites and shock erupted around the room.

"Silence!" Aldred barked. "Silence!" The room quieted. "Is that . . . his?"

"Was," Perry replied. "Sable died by my hand."

There was another uproar around the room. Aldred's guards shouted for quiet this time. He waited for it to come before he spoke again, his beady eyes shining and intent. "You are truly peerless, Peregrine. First your own brother, Vale of the Tides, then Sable of the Horns . . . *and* you led your people to the Still Blue?" He whistled low. "My, my."

Perry stared at the oily-faced man, as unmoved as ever. Aldred's expression, on the other hand, had become worshipful. Roar saw the same look on every face around the table. It was like they didn't even see Perry anymore but some glowing aura around him.

"Well, this certainly changes things!" Aldred's scheming smile returned. "This changes *everything*." Roar could practically see the ideas building in the little man's mind. He was sitting up in his seat now, inflating under the power of his own thoughts. "I shall sow the seeds of my legacy in the graveyard of your sins, Peregrine," he said fanatically, ornately. "I shall rise upon fiery wings from the ashes of your destruction." In the span of a few breaths, he had become a caricature, some garish blend of statesman, poet, and visionary.

"With Sable dead," he continued, "Tempest is now next in line to rule the Horns. She is the key to *everything.*" He turned his feverish gaze on his son. "You will marry the girl, Garen. You will become Blood Lord of the Horns. With you as their ruler, I will forswear my oath to Nightrose and lay claim to this land as Blood Lord. Allied to the Horns, I'll be untouchable! No one will dare challenge me with the might of such a tribe behind me!"

"Yes, Father," said Garen breathlessly, the zeal in his eyes matching his father's.

Aldred turned back to Perry. "And *you*, my dear young prince of the Tides! Tomorrow, you will kneel and swear fealty to me, then hand over the Tides' chain, or you will watch your beloved brother there draw his final breaths." He jutted a flabby chin to indicate Roar, then surged to his feet so quickly, the men behind him had to catch his chair. "Take them away! Take them away and bring wine for everyone! Tonight, we celebrate!" He swept up his cup, wine spilling over. "By this time tomorrow, my son and I shall both be lords of our own realms, and rulers in our own right!"

They were taken back to Perry's home and thrown into Vale's room.

This time, the door was locked behind them.

Roar lowered himself onto the bed carefully, lying back. A sense of euphoria washed over him as the ferocious pain began to recede. Slowly, the blood returned to his heart and his mind. The room stopped spinning. The simple act of holding himself upright had nearly wiped out all his strength.

He'd been no help at all to Perry back there, and though he was scouring the foundation of his energy for scraps, he was still disappointed in himself. Roar had gotten him into this mess.

Perry wouldn't be there if it weren't for him.

Whatever it takes, he vowed silently. *I'll get him out of this.*

He peered through his lashes.

Perry was still by the door, frowning like he had no idea where he was. "I have no good memories in this room," he said, quietly. "Talon and Mila were both sick here. This is where Aria was poisoned. Where my father would haul me so he could thrash me without Liv trying to stop him." He looked at Roar. "How is it possible it feels good to be here?"

"Maybe because these walls are part of the whole house, where good things did happen."

"Maybe." He blinked slowly. "They burned you."

What would it be like, Roar wondered, *to scent your best friend's scorched flesh?* "Yes."

"How bad is it?"

"Not sure yet." Gingerly, he reached up and rested his head on his right arm. His left arm, shoulder to wrist, was numb when he held still, but when he moved the wrong way, which was almost every way, pain pushed him to the edge of blacking out. "Why did this happen? Why are we here?"

"You're the color of ice. Are you sure you want to do this right now?"

"Yes. I need to know why my heart's nearly carved out." He had a hunch, but he needed to know for sure.

Perry sighed, then came to the bed and sat. Shafts of moonlight spilled through the shutters, painting lines on his back. He turned, peering at Roar over his shoulder. "You heard Tempest is Sable's sister?"

"I did. Funny, isn't it? Life?"

"No," Perry replied flatly. "Sable sent her to the Night tribe as a hostage when she was younger. He wrote to her over the years. I saw the letters. He lied to her. He told her you were mad with jealousy and that . . . you killed Liv and were coming for him, too."

"So she sent Ventus after me to avenge her brother."

Perry nodded solemnly and turned forward again. "And maybe Liv, too."

"Funny, isn't it? Life?" he said again. A random tear spilled out, running down his temple toward his ear. He brushed it away and pressed his eyes shut, sealing them tight. For the past hour, he'd fought to control the pain, to stay conscious, but he was too tired now. He wasn't sure he could hold back anything for much longer. "Did Ventus survive?"

"I don't know. If he did, it's temporary."

"No. I want him dead, believe me. But this death spiral, this spiral of bad information and killing, it has to stop. My dear young prince has to live for a long time."

Perry scowled over his shoulder. "What the hell *was* that?"

"Adulation. Idolatry. You're the real prize. More than Tempest."

"Come on. The man never laid eyes on me until today."

"That's the *point*, Perry. He worshipped you before he even met you. You're so blind to this stuff, it's maddening. And I'm too tired to talk about this right now."

"Darn. I was hoping we could dig into it."

"Sorry, my lord. We can't."

Perry stretched out beside him, the bedframe creaking in protest. "How long until you can fight?"

"A week. Maybe two." *Could be three*, he added silently. *Or could be never.*

"And you were trying to escape? Idiot."

"I know, I know." Roar scratched his cheek. "I was trying to take initiative."

"You're better off staying passive."

"If you say so. You really read Sable's letters? That had to have been a struggle." For a number of reasons, not the least of which was his trouble reading.

"Skimmed. Most were short." Perry fell quiet for a moment, lost in his own memories. "Made me feel sick, the things he wrote. He manipulated her like he did everyone."

"You don't actually think I'm going to feel sorry for the girl who ordered my death, do you?"

"She didn't. She only wanted you scarred. She wrote her order to Ventus. I saw it myself."

"He came to kill."

"His own decision, then. He was Sable's man. He had his own motivation to see you dead. I'm not defending her,

Roar. I'm just telling you what I know. It's like you said. Too many people have gotten hurt because of misinformation."

"Well, I disagree with me now. What she did was evil. She's as blackhearted as her brother was." He loathed himself for feeling even the briefest attraction toward her. For bringing her into his memories, where Olivia lived. He would give anything to purge Tempest completely from his thoughts, but that would never be possible now.

She'd wanted him scarred, did she?

Well, goal accomplished.

They fell quiet for a time. Roar lay there, silently fuming. Hurting and raw. He was fairly sure Perry had dozed off when he heard voices outside. A raucous group of young men was walking past the house.

"Almost burst out laughing!" said one. "All I could think about was the time in the grove when she spurned you! Didn't she call you a simpleminded twit?"

"That and worse," Aldred's son, Garen, replied. "The little bitch'll regret every word. I'll bring her to heel, see if I don't."

Roar's fists curled at that ugliness. But on second thought, maybe they deserved each other. Ogre and witch. Boar and snake. He glared at the ceiling, trying to focus his mind on finding a way out of their situation.

Escape wasn't an option. Perry was the only capable fighter, and they were weaponless and well-guarded.

On the positive side, Perry's life wasn't in danger. He was too valuable, his reputation too powerful as the slayer of Blood Lords to be dispensed with trivially. What Aldred hadn't even mentioned was that, having killed Sable and taken his chain, Perry technically had a shot at usurping the Horn tribe. It was the Old Way of claiming a territory, brutal and bloody. He'd never do it, of course. But the fact stood that his legend—it really wasn't too strong a word—protected him.

The howling pain in Roar's chest was testament enough to the sort of retribution a Blood Lord's death could instigate. If Perry were killed, all of Cinder would mobilize. Between that looming threat and Aldred's obvious obsession, the odds were that Perry would remain a captive in his own territory, far away from Aria and Talon and the good life he'd earned.

As positive sides went, it was a terrible one.

His own fate was much clearer and straightforward. Whether Perry bent the knee to Aldred or not, Roar knew he wouldn't be allowed to live. He had nothing to offer. He was a pure liability. A threat to Aldred as long as he was alive.

"I know what you're thinking," Perry said, his voice graveled with sleep. "But you're wrong. There's a way out of this for both of us."

"Good attitude, Per. But just in case, I'd rather it be you than a stranger. Your hand, one of my father's knives. A sea burial if it can be negotiated." He felt lightheaded as he spoke, like he was already casting about in waves.

Perry's green eyes flashed. "If you ever ask me that again, I *will* kill you."

"Now you've confused me. Is that a yes or—"

"Shut up for a second? I'm trying to tell you I've got an idea. You're going to hate it. Maybe worse than death."

"Sounds great so far. Does it get you out of this alive?"

Perry nodded. "Me and you."

"I'll do it, then."

"Don't you want to hear it?"

"Sure, but I don't need to. Whatever it is, count me in."

12

TEMPEST

Tempest walked through the night, trying not to jump at every sound.

Everything was too loud: her footsteps, the hiss of the wind through the trees, the animals scurrying through the undergrowth. Though her Sense was blade-sharp, how much help could her nose really be? By the time she scented danger—a stranger, a predator—it would probably be too late for her to do anything about it.

Had she ever truly been *alone* like this, surrounded by no one she knew and nothing but darkness?

Yes. There was that night she left Rim in the carriage. Those endless lonely nights when she'd first arrived at Night tribe. That night in the orchard. But this was different. She'd be fine.

To calm her anxious thoughts, she called up old lessons. Knowledge she'd never needed to rely on before. Cal had taught her to follow depressions in the earth or animal trails when she could—the better to hide her scents and sounds from roving bands. Ventus had taught her to veer off paths occasionally to confuse anyone who might be following her. From Daisy she'd learned never to pass a water source without refilling her water skin. From all of them: Confidence and *pretending* confidence looked the same. *Were*, in fact, the same.

In the background, she sensed her subconscious picking through the debris of her life for the pieces worth saving.

It was all a mess—a terrible one—but she had hope now. She had a firm hold on what was right—for now, that meant undoing wrongs. She was on that path.

And she had a full skin of water.

With the first blush of sunlight touching the sky, two men approached her from the west. Tempest knew them by sight if not by name. They were Aldred's men, and the irony wasn't lost on her: After a long year of hiding, she was walking right up to the people she'd been hiding from.

"You're to come with us," they said when they reached her.

"Lead on," she said, waving a hand. She asked a few questions as they walked, confirming that Aldred had been sent to claim this vacated territory for Nightrose. It made sense. She remembered hearing Banyan talking to Ash once about Aldred, counseling his son. *Some ambitious men you keep close, some men you don't. Aldred is one you don't.*

It seemed Banyan had put that wisdom into practice.

Not an hour later, she was striding into the Tide's compound.

"Wait here," said one of her captors. Then he jogged off to find Aldred.

She turned in a slow circle, observing the homes around the central clearing. It was a humble place, the houses made of stone and timber. Slate roofs. She could smell the sea on the early morning breeze. A woman swung open a door, pausing in her sweeping when she saw Tempest. A dog barked somewhere, underscoring a sense of ordinariness. Everything looked a little weathered and worn, but better for it. Like a good belt that had been broken in.

She had spent a decade with the Night tribe, which numbered in the thousands. She remembered Rim, too, from her girlhood. The Horns were an even larger tribe. Thousands upon thousands. And yet this tiny seaside hamlet was the site of some of the most memorable stories of the past few years.

Betrayal. Fratricide. A Dweller girl, Tempest recalled hearing, had come to live with the Tides, forsaking her own kind. She remembered speaking about the Tides once with Ash and Raven. They'd debated whether murder—between family especially—was ever justified.

It had seemed so sensational. Peregrine of the Tides murdering his brother Vale had only been a far-fetched story, like characters invented by some daydreaming storyteller. But here she was. In the place where those far-fetched stories had happened. Searching for people who were very much real. A tiny shudder rippled down her spine as she realized that her own life, her family's, was one of these very wildfire tales that lit up the gossip rivers. Drawing a breath all the way in, she let it out slowly and centered her attention on her objective again.

"Did Peregrine arrive yesterday?" she asked, spotting a home with two guards outside.

Her captor uncrossed his arms. "He did."

"I bet Aldred was all over him."

He frowned. "I wouldn't say that."

"You don't have to."

The man who'd left in search of Aldred returned wearing a strange look. "He's out cold," he told the other man under his breath, like he didn't want Tempest to hear. "I couldn't rouse him. Sage couldn't, either."

Tempest wasn't surprised. Aldred found any reason to drink himself into a stupor. She remembered that about him.

"I tried looking for Garen, but he's worse off," the guard continued. "They'll come around in a couple of hours."

"What are we supposed to do with her until then?" asked the other.

"Take me to Roar and Perry," Tempest said. "I assume they're together?" She was inwardly amazed at the cool control in her voice. She was being taken *captive*. Captive, but not captured. This was her decision. She had walked here under her own power.

"They are," replied the man.

"Then I'll wait with them."

Some men were so trained to obey, they did so instinctively. These two were such men.

As they led her to the home with the guards out front, her pulse sped to a frantic pace and her hands went clammy. She had to do this. She had to face the consequences of her actions, and fix them if she could, but her body was screaming in resistance.

The men talked briefly to the guards at the door, then led her inside. The shutters were all drawn. In the dimness, she saw a kitchen area, a hearth, a ladder to a loft. She smelled honey and wool. The ashes of last night's fire. Stale blood, lingering in the bleached spot on the floorboards.

Roar's, more than likely.

One of the men unlocked the only door, swinging it open. "In there."

She shored up her strength and stepped inside.

The room was small. A bed. A trunk to one side. A table with an unlit candle. Above the bed, a shuttered window striped with pale morning light.

Peregrine sat on the trunk, scowling at her. Roar stood on the far side of the bed, looking like he'd seen a ghost—a ghost he might want to murder. Seeing that he was alive, relief washed over her, cool as a winter wind. Then she saw how he stood, unable to straighten fully. She noticed the bandage wound around his chest, looping around his left shoulder, and the bloodlessness of his complexion.

Maybe she didn't deserve to feel relief yet.

Going by the roiling tempers in the small room—fury and despair and more fury—she had a feeling they'd been talking about her, maybe even expecting her.

She looked at Perry again. Her brother's killer. At Roar, who she'd harmed deeply and deliberately. She had no idea how to proceed. No idea what to say. She had come here with such a feeling of intention. Now, she just felt paralyzed.

"Aldred's men found you?" Perry said, breaking the tense silence.

She had to clear her throat a few times before she found her voice. "I made it easy for them. I was almost here when they did." To her great surprise, it was easier to look at him than Roar. "You met him?"

"Aldred?" Perry nodded. "Oh, yes. Last night."

She shifted her weight; she had no idea what to do with her hands. "So you must know he'll send me to Night tribe. Banyan is more reasonable than Aldred. I'll see that he frees you both."

Perry shook his head. "Aldred's not sending you to Banyan. He's got other plans."

Her heart squeezed for a desperate beat, like a fist. Her hands felt quivery; she stuffed them in her pockets. "What other plans?"

"His son," Perry replied. "Aldred plans to marry you to Garen and claim the Horns. He'll do it today. He won't risk you slipping away again, or word getting back to Banyan."

"I see." Her voice had gone high as a flute. She saw the forces at play clearly now. With her brother no longer Blood Lord, there'd be a power grab for control of the Horns. As his sister, she had the strongest claim.

Or did she?

She knew of only two women over the centuries since the Unity who'd been tribe leaders. Both had taken the chain after achieving fame through impressive feats of territorial defense and political cunning. Furthermore, they'd both been women in their prime. And further still, Tempest hadn't been back to her birthland in a decade. She hadn't set foot in the Horns' territory since she was a *girl*. In many ways, she felt more a member of Night tribe than the Horns.

Marriage.

She swayed, feeling her blood drain to her feet. This was all wrong. She was supposed to go back with Sable, not with a *husband*. Not just a husband, but *Garen*. He'd harassed her for years, his hands finding her body when no one was looking, his mouth whispering indecencies into her ear, Cal's warning in the orchard notwithstanding.

"If—if I marry Garen," she shuddered involuntarily, "he'll let you go?"

"No," Roar said. "He'll force Perry to bend the knee and gain the Horns through your marriage to his son, but I'm nothing more than a risk. He'll dispose of me at the earliest chance. You don't seem pleased, Tempest. Isn't that what you wanted?"

It was too difficult to hold his gaze, so she focused on the bandage around his chest. "I came here to help, Roar. I know you don't care, but I've given up my freedom. I know I can't make this right, but I'm trying to make it not as awful. I'm ready to do what I can. All I can." She was rambling and tears were pushing into her eyes, but she couldn't seem to stop. "It's horrible, what I've done to you. I'd do anything if I could undo it, but I can't."

"You're right. You can't undo it," he said. "But there's a way we might still get out of this."

She blinked, needing a moment to rein in her emotions. "There is?"

"Yes," he said tightly. "Possibly. But it would require that—" He scowled at the floor. "It would require that—" He muttered a curse, shaking his head. "I can't say it." He peered up at Perry. "You say it."

Perry let out a bark of surprise. "*Me?* Hell no."

An obsidian gleam settled in Roar's eyes, so cold it was almost chilling. Perry seemed to always take the lead, but when Roar drew a line, she now saw, he drew it permanently.

"Fine." Perry rolled his eyes. "Fine, I'll say it." He brushed twists of dirty blond hair behind his ear and fixed her with a peculiar look, not bashfulness or frustration but something in between. "We've been talking and, uh, there is one way Roar lives through today."

They exchanged another glance, the meaning beyond her. They were making her feel like a foreigner in a strange land. "Well, what is it? I'm listening."

"You marry him instead of Garen," Perry said. He kept talking, not pausing for a beat. She somehow managed to keep listening, to keep standing and breathing, even as her body went totally and completely numb. "Roar would gain the protection of your tribe as your husband. A formal connection between the Horns and the Tides through marriage would also make it easier for you to extend allyship to me—that means I could walk out of here, too. Aldred won't tempt the retaliation of the Horns. In other words, by marrying Roar you could wield your political power to save his life and mine. Or you could marry Garen like Aldred wants." He shrugged. "Your choice."

Your choice. Like she was deciding on a book to read or a shirt to wear.

A terrible ringing began in her ears.

"Tempest?" Perry said.

"Just a moment," she replied. "I'm thinking." But she could see immediately that, logically, it was the best plan. At the same time, though, it also seemed utterly *illogical*. Marry the person who loathed her, who she'd wounded, who had loved a girl her brother had slain? It was absurd. Like reality had swung on some pendulum, reversing in polarity. All the things that should've been positives were negatives.

On yet another level, she was aware this wasn't a time to consider her emotions; this was life and death. And hadn't she just spent an entire night swearing to right wrongs no matter what it took? *Amazing*, she thought abstractly. *I'm deciding on my own marriage without considering how I feel.*

She hadn't looked at Roar in some minutes. She made herself now. It felt like a physical effort, like picking up a boulder with her bare arms. His expression was even more indecipherable than Perry's moments ago. His dark eyebrows were drawn in a frown, casting his eyes into shadows. His mouth was pursed tight, his full lips thinned to a line.

Instinct kicked in. She started pulling in a breath to scent his temper but stopped herself. She didn't want to scent his rage, his hatred.

Life and death, she reminded herself.

Clearing her throat, she asked, "And you'll do this? You actually . . . want this?"

~ 13 ~

ROAR

Roar watched Tempest go pale, her gray eyes locked on Perry as he finished explaining the plan. The proposed plan. Then she was thinking (*Just a moment, I'm thinking*, like the entire world needed to stop for this hallowed occurrence) and a silence stretched out and kept going. It ran on for so long that Roar questioned himself, then reality, then whatever thing was beyond that.

He ceased caring about everything in that silence.

A surprise, because he thought he'd already been there.

Finally, she turned to him and spoke, her voice reedy, barely carrying. "And you'll do this? You actually . . . want this?"

"Yes, I will." He felt an ugly smile come to his face. "And, no, I very much do not want this. What I *want* is to live and for Perry to live. Marrying you is the only way to make that happen. You're holding the only card we can play."

Another long silence followed, her eyebrows drawing slowly together, her backpack sliding off her shoulder.

"If you *think*," she said, finding the strength in her voice again, "it would make you Blood Lord to marry me, think again."

"I couldn't care less about that."

Her eyes narrowed, like she wasn't sure if she believed him. "I haven't been to Rim in a decade. I'm not even sure the Horns will want me. We could be staking everything on power that's not even mine."

"Only card," he returned coolly.

"Roar . . ." Her backpack slumped to the floor; she didn't even seem to notice. "You *despise* me."

It seemed a strong word, but maybe it was the right one. He didn't know. "That's irrelevant."

"To our *marriage?*"

"This isn't a marriage. This is survival. Either marry me or condemn me to death. Choose."

"Of course I'll do it."

"Which one?"

"*Marry you,*" she said, exasperated.

"All right," he heard himself say.

All right? No. Not even close.

He'd wanted to marry Liv. This girl was not Liv. She was almost a perfect stranger. Worse than that. She'd sent an assassin for him. Because of her, he'd bear a terrible scar for the rest of his life, at best. At worst, he'd live with a maimed arm and compromised health.

"Okay. Then let's get this done before we run out of time." Perry slid off the trunk and pulled one of the chains over his neck. It was the Horns' chain. Sable's. Roar was going to object, to ask for th Tides' chain, but Perry eyed him and shook his head. Roar understood. She was Tempest of the Horns; the smallest things might make a difference down the line.

Roar came around the bed to stand before her. He was right in front of her, but she still seemed far.

Perry handed him the chain. It felt almost too cold and heavy. He firmed his grip and lay the edge of one of the settings on his palm. The morning sun set one of the rubies on fire. His eyes dropped to the bandage around his chest; he was fairly sure he'd just stopped bleeding. *The irony*, he thought, yanking the metal across and slicing his skin freshly. A line of blood welled up parallel to lines on his palm. He handed the chain to Tempest. "Your turn."

She fumbled with it for a few moments, her hands shaking badly. The urge to help her came up, but he ignored it. Finally, she got the side of the setting turned down over her palm. She gave a vicious jerk, catching a gasp in her throat.

Roar winced. She'd made a far deeper cut than was necessary. Within seconds, blood was pooling in her palm. With a silent curse, he took her hand firmly in his, squeezing tight as much to staunch the bleeding as to get on with the ceremony, which was beginning to feel like a prolonged cut in itself.

With their skin touching, the chaos of her mind invaded his. There was so much despair roiling through her, he couldn't hear any single thing. What he heard was a chorus of dread, anger, and fear that was similar to his own inner chaos.

"Before we do this," he said, "I want to be clear that this is a temporary arrangement. We do this until the safety of the three of us is ensured. We project a front until we no longer need to."

But whether temporary or not, he knew he was about to lose part of himself and so was she; this would desecrate that inner vault of their souls where marriage was protected. Something precious. Something worth revering.

She nodded tightly. "Perfect."

"Perfect?"

"Can we just get this done, please?"

"Yes. Let's just get this done," he said, with more than a little sarcasm. He drew an unsteady breath. A sharp pain flared in his chest, just under his wound. Then words were somehow coming out of him. *The* words. Ones that would forever change him.

"Tempest of the Horns . . . with these words I, Roar of the Tides, vow to be yours in mind, body, and spirit. From this day forth, I will honor you in the light and protect you in the darkness. My blood is your blood. My heart is your heart. My life and love is yours forever."

Surprisingly, his voice was steady, as though spoken from the heart, no warble or hesitation. Not so when it came to her turn. She paused at every other word, turning a lost look from their clasped hands to his eyes—or rather, a point just above his eyes. He noticed her trembling lips. The terrified pulse at her neck.

This is wrong, he thought. *This is just* so *wrong.*

Finally, she got through her vow.

"I have witnessed your oaths," Perry said, his expression somewhere between relief and dread. And now was when a

Blood Lord usually offered congratulations. "It's done," he said instead.

"Right. Done," Roar echoed. It was customary for the bride and groom to kiss at this point, but that sure as hell wasn't happening. "You poor girl," he found himself saying. "You're stuck with me now."

Tempest yanked her hand away from his and stepped back. "*Temporarily.*" She looked around the room, blinking dazedly like she'd had no idea where she was. Then she sat heavily on the bed and buried her face in her hands, her chestnut waves spilling forward.

Was she crying already?

What did it matter? She *would* cry. Now. Later. Often. So would he, once it sank in. This went far beyond any map he'd ever imagined for his life.

What do I do now? he wondered.

He looked at Perry, needing reassurance. Some sort of lifeline.

Perry shrugged, compassion in his eyes, then a laugh burst out of him. "Sorry," he said, pressing his fist over his mouth. But a second later, he was laughing again. *Really* laughing. He dropped on the trunk, doubled over, and howled.

Roar shook his head, then started laughing, too. It *was* funny. Of all the things they'd gone through together, nothing approached this.

It hurt to laugh. It hurt to live.

It was all horrible and hilarious.

Tempest looked up. Her expression was wounded, but it was the smears of blood on her cheeks that sobered him. She might need a stitch or two on her hand. He'd never heard of a blood oath cut requiring a needle and thread afterward. That couldn't be a good omen, but really, how much more could go wrong?

She stood with a determined look, brushing her fingers under her eyes and getting more blood on her cheeks. "Let's get out of here."

He flourished a hand toward the door. "After you, darling."

The sun seemed especially bright as they stepped into the clearing. Their laughter must have been heard because people had emerged from their homes and were congregating.

"Do we keep walking?" Tempest whispered urgently.

"Yes," Perry said. "We have to get out of here before Aldred—"

"Stop!" boomed a voice behind them. Two armed men jogged over, bows and quivers clattering. Guards who should've been posted by the door, judging by their ruffled, guilty expressions. "Where do you think you're going?"

"Away," Roar said. "Tell Aldred we're leaving."

"I disagree," said Aldred, who trundled out of the cookhouse, hiking up his pants. "I gave you no such permission." Rumpled and red-eyed, his stained shirt barely covering his round stomach, he hardly looked threatening. But the dozen warriors who came behind him in a wall of muscle and weaponry did.

Aldred looked at Tempest, an oily smile spreading over his face. "Well, well. Filled out a bit, I see. Still a bit girlish for my taste, but I don't think my son will have any complaints."

He glanced at his son. Garen stepped into the clearing with a leer on his face and yet another reinforcement of warriors. "You've caused a good deal of trouble, Tempest. A good deal."

Roar's hands moved to where his knives should have been. He had just vowed to protect her. Apparently on some instinctive level, he was ready to do so. He looked at her.

Her chin came up, something sizzling behind her eyes. "Have I?" She strode toward Aldred with the swaggering authority of a hardened sea captain, not a girl he could've swept up with one arm. "Well, I'm not sorry to say I'll cause you more trouble before we're done." She gestured at Roar with the hand that was still dripping blood. "I believe you've already met my new husband, Roar of the Tides. As well as Peregrine of the Tides, who incidentally became an ally of the Horns this morning."

She paused, letting the unnatural quiet that had fallen over the compound thicken.

Aldred stood, dumbfounded and blinking very fast. "You're lying!" he managed finally. "My Scire will prove it!" His gaze flicked to an old man, bent and wizened and clear-eyed.

"I'm telling the truth," Tempest returned. They had expected this; the marriage had to be legitimate specifically for this reason, no cutting corners. Having a Scire around—and they knew Aldred did as Perry had spotted the old man last night in the cookhouse—made lies impossible to keep. "If you want to check, be my guest."

Aldred's mouth pumped like a dying fish as he realized that it was real. He and Tempest were married. Roar felt rather the same way.

"I should mention as well that the Horn traits," she continued, "which you surely remember in my brother, did *not* skip over me. I am unwaveringly loyal to the people I count as friends and allies, and extremely protective of them and their interests. Some might even say *aggressively* so. You have wronged the two people behind me, Aldred. And I won't ever forget that. If you have any brains in that thick skull of yours, you should be thinking about making amends."

When she spun, turning to him, Roar unconsciously took a step back. As the presumptive heir to the Horn tribe, she possessed far greater power than Aldred—or anyone he could think of aside from the Nightrose Blood Lords. Her message just now—delivered with steel in her spine and supreme control—had been a bold reminder of that. He was impressed. Even a little awed.

Her eyes widened, pointedly telling him *something.*

"Oh—right." He looked at Aldred. "*Amends*, Aldred. And make them snappy. Because, let me tell you, patience isn't a strength of mine. Consider that warning a . . . a warning." To drive that bit of brilliance home, he pointed. "You got it?" Then he turned and walked away.

It wasn't the best threat he'd ever made, but he hadn't expected to have to contribute. Beside him, Perry was trying not to laugh. Tempest was fighting a grimace.

They had only taken a few steps when Aldred's voice broke behind them. "*Halt!*"

They froze, trading anxious looks. The only way this plan *didn't* work was if Aldred came unhinged and lost his ability to think rationally. He had to fear the might of the Horn tribe. The retribution he might incur for wronging her and, by association, her new husband and ally. That was their leverage—their *only* leverage—but it should work.

On any sane person, it would work.

Grudgingly, they turned around. Aldred's warriors were spreading out and forming a loose circle around them, some unsheathing blades that flashed gorgeously in the bright light of morning. Roar eyed them longingly; he'd give anything to have his knives back.

"You really *married* him, Tempest?" Aldred spat. "This—this *no one?* I don't even remember his name, and I *just* heard it."

The "insignificant friend" role was really starting to chafe, but Roar didn't react.

"*Father!*" Garen stalked to his father's side, throwing his arms up in indignation. "Father, this can't be! You said she was mine!" His voice had risen to a petulant child's whine. "You promised me—"

"Not now!" Aldred barked, silencing his son with a raised hand. "This was clever, Tempest. I'll give you that. To marry—" He looked at Roar. "What was it again? A sound of some sort. Mewl or Grumble or Whimper . . . ?"

Roar knew better than to let this idiot goad him, he really did. But the silly taunt put him over the edge. "It's Roar," he said, grinning darkly. "But only to my friends. To everyone else, it's now Roar of the Tides, First King of the Horns."

Aldred choked on his tongue. "King!" he exclaimed.

"*King?*" Garen shrieked.

"There you go, you're getting it," Roar said. He almost added, "It's King-*fucking*-Roar," but his father had been vulgar, and he'd spent his life trying to avoid being the same. He had no idea what he was saying, in fact. Inside him, there'd been some explosive collision between the exhausting pain, the marriage he didn't want, and the lifetime of being overlooked. Maybe the whole Prince Perry thing had irked him more than he even realized. Who knew? He just knew that here, in this moment, he did *not* want to be some throwaway sidekick.

Garen's arms flailed. "But there isn't one! There's no *king* of the Horns!"

"Keep up, Garen. I said *First* King."

"Actually, the Horns have been ruled by monarchs before." It was Tempest, speaking in a voice that would sound casual to anyone else. He heard the tiny quaver of anger, though. "So I'm sorry to say you're not the first king, Roar. I think six is where things left off. Will you settle for being the seventh?"

"I suppose I have no choice. Fine. Seventh."

Perry shook his head in disappointment. "Your first act as king and it's a concession."

"I am not unreasonable."

Aldred had had enough. "You *fools!* You're outnumbered! I can make Tempest a widow with a single command! One arrow would do it, and she'd remarry my son and I lose nothing but *you*, Whimper! A nuisance I already wanted to be rid of!"

"And bring the wrath of the Horns down on you?" Tempest demanded. "Do you really want that?"

"You think you can rally them to you, girl? You, who've been in hiding for a year like a mouse? You, who've been raised in the south by Banyan of the Night? A *rival* tribe? No. I'm not afraid of your brother's tribe. He's *dead*. And *you* are not *him*. I'm not fooled by your posturing. I've spent more time in Rim than you have, little girl. I'll take my chances."

He motioned to one of his men, who came forward unshouldering a bow. The archer notched an arrow and drew the bowstring. For the second time in the span of two—three?—days, Roar felt the brush of death's cold whisper.

"*Don't* do this, Aldred," Tempest commanded.

Then it was Perry, speaking low and deadly. "If you kill him, you will have far worse than the Horn tribe to deal with. You don't want to see my vengeful side, I promise you."

That sent a stir around the clearing, voices murmuring about Vale and brothers and betrayal. Roar was listening wide, getting the general tenor of the gossip, when his ears tuned to a sound in the distance. A low drone that was the sweetest sound he'd ever heard.

He shot Perry a look—in ten years of friendship, they could say a lot with a glance—then he turned to Aldred, raising his right hand. "All right, Aldred. All right. I'll yield. Just promise you won't hurt them."

Aldred's black little eyes gleamed with victory. "*Idiot*, why would I hurt *them?*"

Roar's heart was thudding with hatred now. "Easy, there. No need to be a sore winner. Can I—" he winced, like he was broken up emotionally, "can I at least have a moment to say goodbye to them before you kill me?"

Aldred's gaze swept over the clearing. He pulled his back straighter. "Very well," he declared grandly, letting his voice carry. It seemed he'd just realized he had an audience. A stage. "I shall allow it. A few moments, but no more. Patience is not a strength of mine."

Roar inclined his head, recognizing his own words bandied back at him. The man was like a mirror; he had no cleverness at all. Then he fixed Perry with a grave look. "Well, Peregrine, this is goodbye for good, I guess. You've been a mediocre friend. Thank you for trying, though."

Perry's expression flickered with a mixture of confusion, trust, and humor as Roar moved in for a one-armed embrace.

"Tell me you're up to something, you fool," Perry said quietly as he thumped Roar's back.

"Of course," he returned. That was all there was time for. He stepped back and went to Tempest. He wasn't surprised to see an inkling of understanding in her eyes; she might be wicked and coldblooded and vindictive, but the girl was sharp. He took one of her hands and stepped close, bowing his head to hers. "Hello," he said.

"What are you doing?" she whispered.

He turned her palm up, frowning at what he saw. "Damn. You may bleed out before Aldred kills me. Then what would we do?"

"*Roar.*"

He brought a hand to her face, aiming for an adoring groom posture, to help conceal their conversation. "I'm stalling." Since he was already there, he tried brushing the blood off her cheek with his thumb. Blood was turning into the theme of the past days. But hopefully that was at an end.

"So you can come up with a solution?"

With her thoughts entering his mind now that he was touching her, he had to juggle his concentration for a moment. "So the solution can come to us. I hear the hover. It should be here in another minute or so. I suppose there's a slight chance it's not Soren. In that case, we *will* have to come up with a solution."

"You really hear it?" The hope in her voice matched the light in her gray eyes.

"My hearing is perfect. You can always trust it."

"What about the rest of you?"

"The rest of me is also perfect," he said, knowing full well that wasn't what she meant. But he had no idea how to answer her real question: whether she could trust him.

Trust him to do *what?* Be a *husband?* She was responsible for his pain, for the arm that hung limp at his side. He could hardly stand to be near her; he felt like cymbals were crashing in his head. It was a hell of a time to even *consider* such a question.

"Let's just get out of here," he said in reply. "We'll talk later." This was what happened when you cleaned up a mess with another mess.

"No need. That was answer enough." Her lower lip was trembling, but not with sadness. She looked livid.

"Temper—I mean *Tempest—*"

"Very funny," she said. "How much longer until it gets here?"

He wasn't the only one struggling with this "intimate goodbye." A steady stream of invectives—the arrogant, self-loving *child*—flowed through her mind.

"Two seconds." His ears were full of the hover's noise. Exactly two beats later, a few people around the clearing began to turn to the sound. These were the Auds, like him but with weaker ears. Another two seconds, and everyone else began to stir in agitation, looking for the source of the hum in the air.

Tempest stepped back. He exhaled, not sure if he'd breathed the entire time they'd stood close.

Perry turned, focusing on some faraway point over the hills. "Your chariot's here, your royal highnesses," he said, grinning. Then Roar saw it, too. *Everyone* did.

Instantly it was mayhem, like someone had tossed a bomb into the clearing. People scattered, hauling children into their arms and running for their homes. Aldred threw his head back and shouted commands at his warriors at the top of his lungs, but none of them heeded him. They disappeared into homes along with the others, drawing shutters and latching doors.

Fear of the Dwellers—the child-snatchers, the Moles, the pale ones—was deeply ingrained. They had modern medicines and weapons, and hoarded them. They had secrets; they lacked souls. Before Aria, the Tides had believed these things, too.

He had.

By the time the hover touched down, everyone had vanished.

A shame, he thought, because the craft was an awesome sight. A sleek, pristine thing, white and gleaming from nose to tail. Alien against the dusty compound.

The hatch lowered with a familiar hiss, then Soren and Hyde jogged out. Hayden and Straggler followed behind them with Cal and Daisy, all armed with Dweller weapons countless times deadlier than any bow or sword or dagger.

Soren walked over with a grin, shouldering his gun. "Did I miss anything exciting?"

Roar was genuinely happy to see him. "I almost died?"

"I said anything exciting."

"I got married? Does that count?"

Soren laughed. "Right," he said. Then his smile disappeared and his eyes darted to Perry. "He didn't really . . . ?"

"It was survival," Tempest said curtly as she strode past him, climbing into the hover.

Roar waved a hand after her. "My wife."

Soren's expression was transforming from shock to pure, maniacal joy. "Holy god, you're not kidding," he sputtered, his laughter already starting. "This may be the best day of my life!"

Roar smirked. "I'm glad someone can say that."

14

TEMPEST

Tempest collapsed into the jump seat beside Daisy, who pulled her into a firm embrace.

"What happened?" Daisy whispered. "I can tell something happened."

Tempest shook her head. "Later."

She sensed that Daisy wanted to press her. She knew she held things in, was careful about sharing her emotions, maybe even strategic about it. But now really wasn't the time, not with Roar striding into the cabin and pointedly *not* looking her way.

She sat back, sensing Cal's protectiveness reaching her from across the cabin. Knowing they worried about her was a comfort in itself, but she'd rather they didn't. She made herself smile reassuringly at them.

To her surprise, Roar took the seat on her other side. Did he think he needed to stick close to her now? Or had he sat down without any thought as to where? She leaned back against the headrest with a weary sigh, deeply uneasy with her new Roar-crammed mind. But it was her doing, wasn't it? If she hadn't sent Ventus—

She jolted upright. "Daisy, where's Ventus?"

The hover was climbing rapidly, giving her the feeling she was leaving her stomach below—or maybe what she felt was dread.

Daisy smiled at her sadly; she seemed to have been waiting for the question. "He's in the back on a cot. Rune's with him." She took Tempest's hand. "I'm so sorry to have to say this, but he's in bad shape."

"But will he l-live?" she stammered.

"No, sweet girl," Daisy said, using an old endearment. "I'm afraid it doesn't look like it."

Tempest's eyes instantly welled up. She looked to the back of the craft. Behind that bulwark, Ventus was *dying*. It was too much. She'd borne everything so far, but this . . . She couldn't fight it anymore. Tears spilled over, splashing on her cheeks. She dabbed at them with her sleeves, but they just kept coming.

Beside her, Roar quietly cleared his throat. "I was defending my life, Tempest," he said, softly. "But I am sorry."

His gaze felt like a sunburn on her cheeks. "Please, not now."

If he hadn't entered her life, none of this would have happened. But *she'd* sent the distress message. No matter how she looked at it, this was her fault. She couldn't make it *not* her fault.

Roar nodded, shifting the seat restraint so it didn't rest on the bandage over his chest.

What sort of damage was under it? She could smell scored flesh and clotted blood. As pale as he was, and as guarded as he was being with his left arm, it had to be bad.

Her gaze moved to his hands, which were in tight fists on his lap. They were covered in fine, faint scars. Dozens of them, like crosshatching in drawings.

How did a person get so many tiny scars like that?

She turned her palm up to see the gash she'd made barely an hour ago.

"Tempest, *what happened?*" Daisy said again, seeing it.

Tempest shook her head. She was out of words. She needed some time alone, time to catch up to her life. But she didn't have to explain.

Roar raised his hand. His cut—already scabbing—was a neat line across the middle of his palm, like a quick pen stroke.

Daisy gasped, covering her mouth with her hand. Everyone was staring now. The three brothers. Cal. Even Perry, who knew what had transpired. Cal cursed viciously at the ceiling, practically spitting with anger. Straggler let out a bubbly giggle. Hyde and Hayden appeared to have had some sort of wager, going by the look they exchanged.

So be it, Tempest thought, glad that bitter hurdle was behind her.

There'd be many more of them to come.

"Temp? Wake up, Tempest."

She stirred at the sound of Daisy's gentle voice, lifting out of a heavy sleep, her neck stiff and aching. She looked around blearily, no idea how long she'd slept. The hover was empty and quiet. A shaft of amber light poured through the open hatch.

Daisy's eyes were red and swollen like she'd been crying. "We've landed. We're on the edge of Horn land. Ventus is dying, Tempest. He wanted to die on our land. He's asking for you." She squeezed Tempest's shoulder. "You should go to him. He doesn't have long."

Tempest stumbled outside, her heart thumping, the sudden transition from deep slumber to intense emotion jarring.

They had landed in a field of rye. There was only one tree a little way off, a massive oak with twisting bows that reached as much to the earth as the sky. Most of the group was gathered around a fire closer by. There was no wind. The smoke lifted in an almost perfect column, but she smelled roasting meat and the coffee that was just starting to burn in the saucepan resting by the flames.

They'd been talking, had fallen silent when they saw her. All but Soren, who was sitting with his back to her and whose voice resounded for a beat, isolated and clear, the sound of it uniquely his—part biting sarcasm, part friendly teasing—before he caught himself and turned to see her.

Roar alone was standing. Against the dusky sky, a silhouette in his black pants and shirt. He'd been pacing, she realized. His hair was unbound, and he looked both unhappy and dangerous, like some sort of dark angel who'd failed in his purpose to corrupt souls.

My husband.

It was unfathomable.

She pushed the thought away. Right now, she could only think of Ventus.

"He's over there, Temp," Daisy said, pointing to the oak tree. Cal and Ventus were sitting under it, both of them mere shapes in the shadows. Daisy hugged her. "Go. It'll be all right."

Pulling in a deep breath, she went.

Cal met her halfway. To Tempest's surprise, she was smiling. "He brought you home so he's happy," she said simply. Another hug, this one firmer, quicker. "Be strong for him."

"I will be," she promised.

Ventus slumped against the thick trunk wearing a tired smile. His skin had almost no color; his lips were nearly as white as his eyes. A blanket covered his lap and the wound that was pulling him away from life.

"May I ask your forgiveness?" he said, as she approached.

She shook her head incredulously and knelt before him. "My forgiveness? What for? You've done nothing but serve me honorably. Beyond honorably."

"I disobeyed your order. The wound I gave Roar . . . it should've killed him." He spoke at a whisper, as though conserving the last dregs of his strength. "Had I merely wounded him like you'd asked, he might have fled from Aldred's men. You would not have felt compelled to help him, to marry him. And I would not be dying." He chuffed, a heartbreaking sound. "The only time I ever disobeyed you and look what a muck-up I made."

"No, stop," she pleaded. "Please. You did what you thought was right."

"It wasn't right, though."

"It doesn't matter now. It's done. And if you need to hear it then, yes, I forgive you." The tension eased around his eyes and his brow, the wrinkles smoothing slightly. "I should be asking for your forgiveness," she went on. "I believed what I read in my brother's letters. All this time, I thought I knew who he was. I've been missing a figment. I've been idolizing a mirage."

She seldom spilled her heart out to him, but when it happened, like now, she didn't hold back. Daisy was a constant source of comfort, Cal a constant source of strength, but Ventus was just constant. Like ancient ruins that never budged, never lost dignity as seasons passed and civilizations rose and fell around them. His steadiness made her feel like she could say anything.

"I feel so betrayed, Ventus," she continued. "By my own *brother.* Why did he lie to me? Why didn't he come for me? I'm never trusting anyone again."

He reached over, patting her hand. It was only then she realized someone had bandaged her palm as she slept. Daisy, probably. His hand was cold and calloused and wrinkled. She'd always loved his big, honest hands. "You are hurt, Tempest," he said. "And you have every right to be. But caution is useful. Fear is not. Don't let it rob you of a full life."

She smiled shakily. There was so much she wanted to say, and even more she wanted to hear from him. He was a treasure, a wealth of wisdom and dignity, and she'd taken it for granted that he'd always be with her. She needed more time with him—and she'd never get it.

"He came to speak to me," Ventus said after a moment, his eyes moving to the group in the distance.

Tempest's breath caught. "Roar did? I'm so sorry. I don't know how Cal let that happen."

"It's all right. I would have asked for him had he not."

She swallowed. "What did he say? What did *you* say?"

"For a long time, neither of us said a word. I think we were both trying to work out whether apologies were appropriate."

"And were they?"

He shook his head. "No. We never exchanged them, at any rate." He grimaced, a spasm of pain wracking through him. "But after a time," he continued, "we talked about . . . well, a lot of things. Some of it isn't my place to share. But he did tell me about the wrongs Sable committed against him and Olivia. Against Peregrine and their tribe. I knew your brother's character, Tempest. I knew it long ago. But the actions Roar described go beyond dishonor. They're unspeakable. Inhuman."

"If you thought Sable so evil," she blurted, "then why did you try to avenge him?" She immediately wanted to take it back—this was a man of his word if there ever was one—but it was too late.

"Because blood oaths are sacred," he replied. "To break one is to break one's sense of self." Was it her imagination, or was he staring at her bandaged hand? "And I didn't go after Roar for love of Sable. I did it for love of you. All you've ever wanted since you were a little girl was to reunite with your brother. When I learned he was dead, that he'd been taken from you and that Roar was to blame,

I lost my mind and . . . Well. You know the outcome. We're in it."

They were quiet for a time, watching the sunset. He had just told her he loved her, and she was trying to say it back. Three simple words. Slippery ones. She couldn't seem to grasp them.

"Do you truly believe those things about my brother?" she asked instead. "That he killed Perry's sister? And tor—tortured Perry? And all the rest of it?"

Why was she asking this? She already knew it was true. Her conversation with Daisy had already driven that stake into her heart. Sable was someone she wouldn't have respected. She might have loathed him and even feared him. That he was despicable was a truth. She just wanted to trust her instincts again. Banish the feeling that everyone would let her down.

"Yes," Ventus said simply. "I believe Roar. He was there, Tempest. Sable killed her right in front of him. All he did in his letters was change the roles in the story he told you. But we're here now. There's no changing the past." He returned his attention to the group by the fire. "I know he was not your choice, but you could have done worse. He has a quick mind, he's an uncommon knifeman, and an even stronger Aud." He gave her a weak smile. "Not an ugly one, either. Even I can see that. He has gone through exceptional pain, though. The kind that roots deep." His eyes were glistening. She wondered just what he and Roar had discussed. "If you were anyone else, I'd think your marriage doomed."

She laughed, a strange, forced giggle. "You may be overestimating me. Anyway, our marriage is only temporary. We agreed on it."

"I'm not underestimating you and everything is temporary."

That last part rang painfully true at the moment. His grip on her hand was growing weaker, and he had begun to sag to the side. She moved next to him so he could lean on her shoulder.

"How about some Beowulf to see me out?" he said.

Night had fallen. Under the cover of the canopy, it felt like they were in a cottage, staring out at the world through a window.

"Beowulf," she said, pretending to grumble. "Always Beowulf. So predictable." Reliable, she could have said. Steadfast and noble. Every word she'd unwittingly and wrongly ascribed to her brother, she could give to this extraordinary man who'd been by her side for a decade. A father, sometimes. A guardian, always. "But I'll indulge you, of course," she went on, "Before that, though . . ." She never had the chance to say goodbye to her brother, and that was its own pain, a tragedy that stood apart from his deception and the terrible things he'd done. She didn't want that to happen with Ventus, though. She wanted no regrets with him. She had to say what she needed to say. "You know, don't you? That I love you, too? That I always have?"

His nod was a slow shift on her shoulder. "That you do has been one of the great gifts of my life."

A tear spilled down her cheek. She brushed it away. Then there was nothing left to do but tell a story. She dug through her memory for his favorite passage and recited it, line by line. Long after his hand went slack in hers, she told him the story of a great hero lauded through the ages, never to be forgotten.

15

ROAR

Let's go back, I said. It'll be great! It'll be an *adventure*—

"You never said that, Roar," Perry interrupted.

Roar stopped pacing the cabin, turning to him.

Perry was sitting on the floor of the hover, eating a Dweller meal bar. He took another bite, speaking around it. "You came here to chase the past."

"I concur." Soren tore into his second bar with his straight white teeth, ripping the wrapper open. They'd already eaten dinner earlier, heaping quantities of venison, rice cooked with vegetables, and fresh trout they'd caught nearby. Roar hadn't managed more than a bite. "I've definitely never heard you call this mission an *adventure*."

Roar frowned. That was fair. He'd been in an especially grim place that day he'd heard Tempest's distress message; even his memory of that rainy afternoon was tinged in gray. All he'd wanted was a reprieve from the intense apathy, to feel *something.* Well, he was feeling something now, wasn't he? Though he couldn't pinpoint exactly what.

Fuming, entrapped, delirious?

"Fine, whatever." He raised his hand. "I sure as hell wasn't asking for *this*."

"If it's any consolation, I'm pretty sure marriage is one of life's biggest adventures," Soren offered. He was trying not to laugh—and Roar was two seconds away from throttling him.

"Soren," Perry said, "why don't you go somewhere else for a while?"

Soren jumped up. "Sure," he said lightly, but Roar could hear the edge in his voice. He jogged out to join the others by the campfire, his footfalls banging down the ramp.

Perry waited for the tromping to fade before he spoke. "So?" He balled up the wrapper and set it down beside him. "What are you going to do?"

"I have no idea." Roar dropped down across from him. "I can't think of any path forward that doesn't create another problem." He didn't want to be married, obviously. But the idea of forsaking a blood oath made his soul feel like it was crumbling. He'd kept his life streamlined for a reason; when he took something on, or committed to someone, he did it for good. He'd never wanted to be anything like his parents, who hadn't known the meaning of the word loyalty. Sure, he'd told Tempest their marriage was only temporary. But if he broke his vow, he had a feeling it would damage him down to his core. "The only thing that's clear to me right now is that I don't want the Tides to be in that idiot Aldred's control."

Perry brushed his hands on his pants, nodding. "I'm with you. I didn't think it would hit me the way it did to go back.

Then to see someone else there . . ." He shook his head. "You were right. It's still part of me. Always will be."

"I never wanted you to have to see it in someone else's hands."

"You couldn't have known."

"No. I guess not. What are you going to do about it?"

"Nothing right away." Perry smiled faintly. "I've been thinking about what you said a few nights ago about trouble campaigns. You were right. I can't just throw myself into retaking the Tides. I've got Talon to think about now. After what I took from him, the least I can do is be there for him as he grows up. Being reckless with my life is unfair. After all he's gone through, losing his parents and his home, being sick for so long, he has to come first." Him and Aria.

Roar nodded. "I understand." He stared through the open hatch, happy for Perry. At the same time he felt like Perry's life was moving down some path without him. Maybe he was the married one—*gods, married!*—but Perry was the one becoming settled. Aria was here to stay, no doubt about it. They were perfect together. And though Perry had been thrust into the role of father, he did it easily. He loved it.

Roar tried to think objectively of what *he* loved. He'd loved loving Liv. Still did. But it was more than her. He loved supporting Perry. Supporting anyone, or anything, he believed in. In spite of what he'd said that morning, he'd never needed to be a king figure, or hero. But then, he'd never tried to be.

Why? he wondered. Why did he always choose the shadows? Was it even a choice?

He turned to the open hatch and listened to the chirring of insects sweep in from outside.

He had come in here to avoid looking at the oak tree, where Tempest was helping ease Ventus into the next world. Though he'd been pushed to it, it was his knife that dealt the death blow. The least he figured he could do was remove himself from their view.

He considered his long conversation with Ventus earlier. They'd spoken candidly about the misunderstanding that had precipitated their fight, and then, surprisingly, they'd kept talking. Somehow, Roar had found himself sharing things he'd only ever said to Perry about his childhood and about Liv. He'd learned that Ventus was a widower; that he'd lost a daughter, too, to illness—which Tempest didn't know. Serving her for the past decade, he'd admitted, had healed his grieving heart.

You will find no one brighter or more loving than her on this Earth, he'd said.

Roar had had to hold his tongue. From where he was sitting, she was callous, vengeful and dishonest. Cut from the same cloth as her brother.

But now, all he could conclude was that Ventus was a decent old fellow who'd loved Tempest and served her honorably, and that the entire episode had the feel of an old Shakespearean play, complete with tragic misunderstandings and a forced marriage.

Gods.

Married.

Gingerly, he rolled his left shoulder back. The bandage around his chest was digging painfully. It had been since Sage wrapped it around him yesterday afternoon, and he couldn't stand it anymore. He untucked the end and began unraveling it.

Perry jogged to the supply closet and returned with fresh bandages and burn spray to help change the dressing. He didn't say anything when Roar pulled his shirt over his head with one arm and the X over his chest was laid bare—a black crust of scarring surrounded by bright red, inflamed skin—but Roar saw his jaw clench and the florid color that rose into his face.

When it was done, Roar slumped in a jump seat, exhausted from bearing the ache that boomed from his chest and spread down his arm.

"You know, Per, the Tides are Talon's legacy as much as yours. Maybe even more so. Think about it. His father and uncle, both Blood Lords. His grandfather. Great-gran. On and on, right?"

"That's exactly what I've been thinking, too. Whether I fight for the Tides or not shouldn't be my decision. It should be his. It's his birthright."

And Talon would want it. There was no doubt in Roar's mind.

"I'm going to try to get word to him back in Cinder," Perry continued. "The comm has been down since we've been here, but I'll send Soren all the way back there if I have to." A determined look was settling into his eyes. "If Talon wants the Tides, I'll take it back for him."

"We will," Roar said, his thoughts already racing ahead, sorting through possibilities.

Perry nodded. "Damn right."

16

TEMPEST

They buried Ventus under that great oak in the morning. Tempest presided over the small ceremony they held for him. She said things. She knew she did. She didn't cry. That she also knew. The rest was all a foggy, muddled blur.

She still felt disconnected from reality when it came time to decide her next move. Fortunately, it was obvious enough.

She had to go home. *Really* go home.

To Rim.

She felt it calling to her, drawing her like a magnet. Like destiny. All these years, she'd thought her only connection to home was her brother, but it wasn't. No matter how distant her memories, no matter that she sounded more like a southerner than her own people, it was her territory, too, and the only anchor left in her life.

She *was* a Horn.

In a way, the decision to go back wasn't a decision at all; she was already on her way, brought to the edge of Horn land by Ventus's dying wish. All she had to do now was keep going.

She grabbed her pack and set off on foot as soon as she finished the ceremony. There was no time to linger. She wasn't safe out in the open. News traveled fast: her marriage, her whereabouts, her brother's death. Information would reach the Nightrose tribe in Delphi in a hurry, and she could only imagine how much more Banyan—and Scar—would want to find her when they learned that her brother had died. She was a pawn to them, just as she'd been to Sable. They'd see her as a means to gain control of the Horns, just like Aldred had.

There were other threats, too, besides being captured by Scar and Banyan. Though she was technically on Horn land, it was a vast territory with unguarded borders. Even here, she was still a target for roving tribes who survived by any means necessary, be it theft, ransom, or murder.

She had to get to Rim.

Of course, she'd have a whole slew of new problems to deal with when she did, but one hurdle at a time.

Cal and Daisy fell in step with her without a word, and she felt Ventus's absence immediately. They were three now, not four. It felt like they had lost a limb.

Though she was very tempted, she didn't turn around to see what Roar was doing—or *not* doing. She concentrated on the green hills ahead of her and the purple mountains looming beyond them. *This is madness*, she thought. She had no idea if she'd just seen the last of her husband. *Temporary*, he'd said. Had he meant two days—*that* temporary?

After an hour, she couldn't resist her curiosity anymore. "Is Roar behind us?"

Cal smirked. "Yes. I'd have hog-tied him and dragged him along if he wasn't." She glanced over her shoulder. "It's him, Peregrine, and the triplets," she said, using her term for Hyde, Hayden, and Straggler. "Soren and Rune took the hover to who-knows-where."

"Back to Cinder," Daisy supplied. "They haven't been able to get messages home, and Perry had to get an important question to someone named Talon. That's his nephew, I think, but I'm not sure."

Tempest nodded absently. She'd stopped walking the instant Cal had said "yes." A feeling was spreading through her that she couldn't name, like she was lightheaded, but through her entire body. Now, she did let herself turn back and have a look.

Roar was with Perry at the base of the hill she'd just crested. The brothers were farther back. She noticed that Perry carried two satchels—his and Roar's—and that they were talking.

About her? About something that related to her?

Why did it feel presumptuous to wonder that when she was his wife?

Then again, *was* she? Moments ago she'd had no idea if he was heading in the opposite direction, their marriage already forgotten.

"Were you afraid he wouldn't come?" Daisy asked.

She nodded. "And that he would."

Cal adjusted the lay of her bow. "Brave of them, you have to admit. Perry will have every man who was loyal to your brother out for revenge as soon as they hear he killed Sable. And it can't be easy for Roar to return to where he lost his . . . friend."

"Beloved. That's what she was. Is."

"He called her that?" Cal asked.

Tempest shook her head. "He didn't have to."

As morning gave way to afternoon, they traded rolling hills for steep valleys. Burbling creeks for flowing streams. Aloof oak trees, bent and brown, for crowded pines that shot skyward like emerald spears. The scents shifted, too, from dusty notes and the tang of small game to loam and pine sap. The musk of deer, bear, and ram. They took her back to her girlhood, making her dizzy with nostalgia.

She spent hours considering what she'd encounter in Rim, sometimes in silence, sometimes bouncing questions off Cal and Daisy.

"There has to be someone ruling in my brother's stead," she said. "Any ideas who?"

"We've been thinking about that," Cal replied, like she and Daisy shared the same mind. "More than likely, it'll be your Aunt Lerra's husband, Lund. He was power-hungry. A parasite. Always hanging on your brother's words."

Aunt Lerra. A fuzzy image appeared in her mind of a lean, stork-like woman who'd worn beautiful jewelry and had an easy smile. But the name "Lund" conjured nothing. "I don't remember him."

Daisy's eyebrows furrowed. "I'm relieved to hear it. He was manipulative and petty. I kept you away from him."

"Thank you."

Daisy looked at her, her expression softening. "I would've done it anyway, but it was on your brother's orders. You should know that. I know he lied to you, but he did love you, Tempest. I have no doubt that he—"

"I can't yet, Daisy," Tempest interrupted. "I can't take that on right now. In a couple of days, we'll be in Rim and I have no idea what to expect, no idea how I'm going to show up and pretend to be a worthy leader. I have to concentrate on—"

Cal stepped in front of her, looming and furious. "I don't think you realize this, so I won't hold it against you. But you demean me, Daisy, and Ventus when you say that. For years, you have been *our* leader. Do you think we'd serve an incompetent?"

The anger in her tone put Tempest back on her heels. "Of course not. But leading three people isn't the same as leading thousands, Cal."

"Then figure it out!" Cal wheeled and strode off.

Daisy winced. "She's hurting, Temp. We all loved Ventus. It's not you." She rushed off to catch up to Cal.

For a while, Tempest could only stand there under the tall pines and watch them pull ahead, her cheeks stinging, her mistake as clear as water. With all that had happened over the past days, she'd forgotten that there were limits to what she could say to them. She had to guard her fears, tread carefully when it came to any topic that might cause them to lose faith in her. Vulnerability wasn't a luxury she could afford; she was well-versed in that part of being a leader, at least.

She vowed to be more mindful going forward.

She turned around, wondering how far back Roar was now. Her heart lurched to find him not ten paces away—*how?*

She hadn't heard a twig snap or a leaf crunch. He was alone, Perry somewhere on the trail behind them.

"Hello, Tempest," he said, somewhat formally.

To her dismay, she liked the way he said her name. Crisply. Unhurriedly. Like a story with a fantastic ending that shouldn't be rushed. There were faint purple shadows under his eyes, though the hours of walking under the sun had also given him a healthier overall color. He had the sort of skin that wouldn't easily burn, but rather deepen into warmer and warmer browns.

"Hello, Roar," she returned, and suddenly became worried that she was staring at him. She didn't think so, but she looked away just in case, finding a loose thread on Daisy's patch job on her backpack to fuss over.

She heard him sigh. "We haven't talked since . . ."

"The hover, I think," she said.

"Right. Early yesterday. And I figured we should. How is your hand?"

"My—?" She looked up. "Oh, it's fine. I mean, it hurts a bit, but . . ." Her eyes fell to the bandage around his chest. *It can't compare to whatever's under there.* "It's fine."

"But you have use of your fingers still?"

She frowned, not sure if he was joking. "It wasn't *that* deep. And what can I say? It was my first time swearing a blood oath." Why was she explaining herself?

"Mine, too," he said. "For marriage."

"Thank you for clarifying. I've been wondering if you have wives all over the place."

"Nope." An odd expression drifted across his face, like he couldn't remember how to smile. "Just you." A long silence stretched out, heavy and important. Tempest made herself not fidget, not fuss with the loose thread again. He appeared to be mustering up the courage to say something. A farewell? Best of luck and have a nice life? "Can I walk with you?" he asked, finally.

A tiny laugh escaped her.

His mouth twitched. "Was that a funny question?"

"I was expecting you to say something else."

"Which was?"

"Goodbye forever."

He blinked. "Right. How about we just walk for right now?"

"Sure." They began to walk side by side. She was very conscious of that—that he was *beside* her, a silent presence. She noticed that they were keeping pace and maintaining a perfect amount of space between them, even when they had to step over a fallen branch. It felt like some incredible thing they were accomplishing, some complicated bit of choreography. She'd never considered how intricate a process it was to simply walk with someone.

"Is that what you want, Tempest?" he asked after a while, turning to her. "Goodbye forever?"

She froze, the question somehow blindsiding her. That word he'd said so pointedly yesterday—temporary—had made *goodbye forever* seem inevitable. In her mind, she hadn't been wondering *if* but *when.*

"What I mean is," he stopped, "what do you want?"

That was an even harder question to contend with. *What did she want?* How on earth was she supposed to answer *that?*

She unslung her pack and sat on a fallen trunk, suddenly deeply tired.

It made no sense to her, none at all, but it would hurt to have their two-day marriage crumble. If she'd ever chosen to marry, she'd always hoped it would be a lasting love. A commitment to a true partner who she could be totally open with, share all her fears and insecurities with—things she'd never tell Daisy or Ventus. She'd never imagined that she'd end up married to someone who *despised* her.

As painful as that was, she had to make the best of this, and the ideas were starting to come, filtering down like the soft sunlight blurring through the canopy.

"I'm thinking," she said.

"I figured," he replied. He walked over and sat beside her, stretching out his legs and crossing them at the ankles. She had noticed that he had an elegant way of moving, with silky feline grace. When his temper was darker, though, like now, he seemed more wolflike: swift and menacing.

This conversation, this moment, had to be probing a sensitive spot for him. She wondered if he'd spent the past days thinking about Olivia, wishing he could swap Tempest for her. The thought made her heart squeeze painfully.

A breeze swept past. The trees swayed and whispered, whorls of dust circling in hazy shafts of sunlight. *This is too pretty a setting*, she thought, *for two people to hurt each other.*

She cleared her throat. "You asked me what I want, but I don't know how to answer you. I don't think I've ever been asked that before. For as long as I can remember, I've had to do what my brother told me, then what Banyan did. After I left Night tribe, I had to do what was best for Cal and Daisy and Ventus. All I've thought about for the past year is how to keep them safe and content. And now . . . now I have to do what's right for my tribe. I'm going home to Rim, Roar. And I'm going to take control of the territory."

He was staring straight ahead, like the forest was telling him something elaborate and unpleasant. "I assumed."

"I have to expect that it'll be a challenge to . . . well, to be taken seriously," she continued. "Blood Lords don't usually look like me, you may have noticed. They tend be older. Intimidating. And male."

"One out of three. Could be worse."

She had no idea what that meant, so she ignored it. "If I'm seen as a girl who married hastily, one might say irresponsibly, and who was then spurned by her husband a mere two days later . . . It wouldn't help my situation. Can you see that part of it?"

He nodded. "I can. On the other hand, as a married woman, you'd project the appearance of being older. More dependable and mature."

For a few seconds, she could only stare at his profile. Had he already given this some thought? "That's right," she went on. "I think it could be an advantage. A husband, that is."

"Meaning me."

"Yes. Meaning you. There is the issue of you being a Tider. The Horns will see you as an outsider. Then again, I'll probably be viewed that way, too. But even taking that into account it would be better, for me, if you came to Rim. Just for a while, of course," she was quick to add. "Until I secure my claim. I don't know how long that might be, but maybe a few weeks? A couple of months at most. Then we could create some explanation for why you disappear and, you know. Goodbye forever."

She let out a breath, relieved to have gotten it all out.

"Seems like a sound plan," he said agreeably, but his stare had gone unfocused and his temper was going darker, hollower and heavier, like a cave deep underground.

"That's what I want." She swallowed thickly and made herself put the same terrifying question back to him. "What do *you* want?"

17

ROAR

What did he want?

First and foremost, he wanted her to answer that very question, which she'd just artfully sidestepped. She claimed she didn't know how to want things for herself. Well, he wasn't buying that for a second. Even when he'd felt numb to the bone, even during the worst stretches this past year, he'd at least *wanted to want* things—which was a want in itself, wasn't it?

No. Her problem wasn't with want, it was with courage. She was hiding behind a cloak of duty, using it to avoid speaking from the heart.

Yesterday, they'd gotten *married*. Did she have no feelings about that at all?

Well, if she wasn't going to be straight with him, then he wasn't going to be straight with her. He made a quick mental adjustment, cutting away the conversation he'd meant to have like a tangled fishing net. What a fool. Had he actually been considering giving this union a try? Like an earnest discussion about *blood oaths* and *forgiveness* and *new beginnings* could've cast a spell over everything that was wrong between them.

This was Tempest of the Horns; it was his fault for not bearing that little nugget in mind. She was as opportunistic and ruthless as her brother had been. She didn't want to give this marriage her best. She wanted him to be an accessory to her plans. But only for *just a little while.*

She'd asked what he wanted. The answer was simple: For once, he wanted to be enough. Not a boy who was left alone for weeks at a time, nor a partner who could be abandoned without so much as a goodbye. Nor someone useful for the present time. But this was reality, and whether he liked it or not, the girl sitting next to him was his wife.

She had asked him to serve as a tool, so he would. For whatever time they had together, he'd be a better husband than his father had been—no cheating, no manipulation or insults—but he'd go further than that. He'd give her the best of himself because he'd sworn to, and because it was the right thing to do; and when the *goodbye forever* part came and he destroyed his word and dignity, he'd at least walk away knowing he'd treated her decently.

"You know, I did answer *your* question," she said.

Roar swam up out of his tumultuous thoughts, realizing he'd been quiet for a stretch. "You didn't, actually. I asked you what you wanted. You gave me a political strategy."

Her eyes flared with surprise. She shot to her feet and paced away. "That's the truth, Roar," she said, tossing the words over her shoulder. "I answered you as best I could."

He went after her, a hot urgency rising in him. "It was still a terrible answer."

She whirled to face him, her hair fanning wide. "*Excuse* me?"

"It was a terrible—"

"I heard you! You're the one who's not understanding! What I want is irrelevant to this discussion! It has *never* mattered."

"I'm part of this discussion and it matters to me. Why else do you think I asked?" She jerked back like he'd insulted her. Nearly as quickly, the shock washed out of her features. Though he'd barely known her a few days, he was beginning to recognize the appearance of Thinking Tempest. He could almost see waves of logic and sense crashing over her emotions, knocking them down like sandcastles. He couldn't have said why, but he didn't want to let her off the hook. "Come on, Tempest. Everyone wants *something*. I'm not talking about whether it's possible. I'm talking about the piece before that. Everyone lays awake at night, dreaming before they fall asleep. Wishing for things. Are you telling me you've never done that?"

"That's different. You're talking about fantasies."

"Great. Let's use that word."

"Roar—"

"I'm serious about this. Let's pretend you could build a perfect situation from this point forward. What would you change? Say anything. Say the first thing that comes to mind."

"I'd heal you," she blurted, her gaze darting to his chest. "I'd undo the wound Ventus inflicted on you because of me."

"Wish granted. It is healing, it will continue to heal." He hadn't been sure about that even an hour ago, but he was gesturing with both hands now—so wrapped up in the moment he wasn't thinking about pain or mobility—and that seemed like a good sign. "Next?"

"I would unmarry you."

"Why?"

"Because I feel trapped, and you feel trapped, and we're both miserable."

"Right. We are indeed. But as you said, there may be some advantages to staying married for a period of time. You want to secure your territory."

"I do," she said carefully. "And you want . . . ?"

"And I want something, too." The girl was perceptive, he couldn't deny. She was catching onto his idea almost as fast he was coming up with it. "I'll help you shore up your claim to the Horns by posing as your husband if, in return, you help Perry retake the Tides—if that's what he decides to do. That means you offer up whatever military is required to oust Aldred, or whoever else may be there."

"Deal."

"Really?"

"Really. Everyone should gain something in a good negotiation, and you'll be more invested in your role as husband if my ascendance benefits you, too. I think it's a great idea. You have my promise."

"Excellent," he said smoothly, though he was more than a little dazed by the speed with which that had transpired. "So if we're staying in this union for now, how do we make it tolerable?"

"That I don't know."

"You don't have to *know*. Pretend we're still in the fantasy. Nothing you say has to matter. How do we go forward?"

She stared off, thinking. "I'm going to need to feel confident that we're working together. Maybe we can agree to certain terms?"

"Sure, like what?"

"Honesty? We'll have enough to contend with without needing to parse out truth."

"Absolutely. What else?"

"We keep this arrangement secret. We tell no one who doesn't already know."

"Yes again," he said. "Keep going."

"Well, we're going to have *look* convincing."

"How?"

"We spend time together in public?"

"You're good at this."

"And treat each other with respect."

"Sorry, no."

She frowned. "*No?*"

"I hate respect."

A light sparked in her gray eyes. "Then maybe we could just yell and throw things at each other?"

"Actually, I'll take the respect. You look like you have good aim."

"Trust me, I don't." She smiled. "I've tripped before and missed the ground."

"That's something," he said, then he dropped his head and eyed the dirt between them, fighting off a smile. He wasn't sure why he felt he needed to. Everything felt tentative, like they were moving over a spiderweb and jostling it even a tiny bit could be dangerous. He also needed a second to reconcile Tempest of the Horns with the girl who could make wise-cracks and flash a gorgeous smile.

All right, he told himself. *Easy. This is nothing new.*

He already knew he found her attractive. So what? Lots of people were attractive and lots weren't and the world kept on turning indifferently, plenty of room for everyone.

He looked up as a pine needle flittered down to his shoulder. Tempest plucked it up, twirling it between her fingers.

He wanted to scratch the spot her fingers had brushed, but he resisted. "What else? How else do we appear convincingly married?" he asked, steering them back to safer footing.

"We should try to get across that we're a love match instead of—of whatever we are."

He was glad to hear that little stammer. He wasn't the only one struggling with their situation. "I think you're underestimating people. We were brought together by attempted murder, blackmail, and terrible misunderstandings. Who wouldn't find such a story romantic? But I'm fine with a charade. What's that look like to you, specifically?"

"Specifically?" She shrugged. "Holding hands? Exchanging smiles? An occasional kiss on the cheek here and there seems tolerable to me. Would it? To you?"

"It would," he said, as neutrally as he could. Their kiss that first night rushed through his mind, clear as a bell. How she'd felt, how she'd tasted, the thoughts running through her head.

She sighed, the sound echoing with his memories. “Good. We could also sleep in the same room, though of course not in the same bed.”

A muscle twitched in his hand. “Of course.”

“And you can keep your charmer routine going. I’ll laugh when you say amusing things.”

“Better not. People who laugh constantly look like imbeciles.”

She laughed—a real laugh that sent desire scattering through him like ashes lifting into darkness. “We could venture off at times, the two of us. Like we want privacy.”

“Good thinking. Newlyweds want lots of *privacy*.”

“Exactly so.” She blinked a few times, her eyelashes fluttering like butterfly wings. Her smile went wider. “Well, I feel good about this!” She clapped her hands together. “And we can always add ideas later if we have them, but we should keep walking, for now.”

He was glad to; it was beginning to feel stuffy under the trees.

They walked in silence for a while, leaving the dappled woods behind. Roar went over their conversation a few times, deciding it had been successful all in all.

If they were going to spend some weeks together in Rim, firming her place as the Horns’ ruler, he wanted it to go as smoothly as possible. And he’d been stupid to think of giving their marriage a legitimate try, but he would at least get something out of this.

He felt strongly about helping Perry reclaim the Tides, and having the Horns behind them could make all the difference in the world. The Tides and the Horns had been in league with each other once before, when Vale and Sable had negotiated Liv's hand in marriage. This was just continuing the partnership. Hopefully with a much better outcome.

He snuck a glance at Tempest when she wasn't looking. The glow of sunset burned on the tips of her eyelashes and brought out the auburn in her hair. Without warning, he saw Sable's face in his mind—saw the resemblance in their features and in the sleet-gray of their eyes—and his blood chilled.

Skies, he thought. *What am I doing?*

She'd already lied to him and caused him horrible pain. There was a saying, wasn't there, about being fooled? *Fool me once, shame on you, fool me twice, shame on me.* But what if there was a third time?

Fool me thrice, he thought, *and we all go up in flames.*

They slept that night along the banks of the Snake River, Tempest across the fire, between Daisy and Cal. Over the next days, they ascended into the mountains, occasionally passing through villages where they traded game for hot meals and other provisions.

Strangers always drew attention in remote settlements, but they revealed nothing of who they were, traveling anonymously. It was understood by all that Tempest would take the lead in making decisions, and she had decided it would be best to arrive in Rim without sending word ahead.

Not a bad strategy, he thought. Her allies would be pleased to see her, whether they learned of her return to Rim ahead of time or not, but adversaries would only plot trouble if given the time. Over and again, she demonstrated a savvy intellect, especially in political matters.

Days and nights passed. They climbed gradual slopes and then steeper ones. Uphill. Downhill. Uphill again. His chest stopped hurting constantly, flaring up only when he stretched his left arm above his head. He shed the bandage and stopped needing the burn spray. The black scabs fell away, leaving shiny, pale scarring in a ridiculously perfect letter X over his left pectoral, like on the ends of the hashed lines in old-timey treasure maps.

With each meal, he regained strength—and his old appetite. Maybe it was going without luster, or being back under the Aether, or something else entirely, but he began to eat with gusto again, which started to bring some long-lost heft back to his muscles.

After their conversation that first day under the pine trees, he and Tempest only exchanged passing words during meals or while laying camp. It was better that way, he assured himself. Easier to keep things cordial, their interactions limited.

What they had wasn't a marriage; it was a business arrangement. And though at times it could leave him feeling confused and angry, frustrated and disappointed, bitter and uneasy, he knew he'd get through it.

It was temporary, after all. Just for a little while.

18

TEMPEST

Five days after burying Ventus, Tempest reached the farms on the outskirts of Rim. Night was falling, the sky purpling over spear-like peaks in the distance that seemed to defy gravity. Aether flowed in gentle rivers above, mirrored in the glassy waters of the Snake River.

They walked toward the city, which shone like a gemstone necklace on the mountainside up ahead, winking in the gloaming. Along the narrow street, people were emerging from their homes, swinging doors open to watch them walk past like they'd been summoned by some bell she couldn't hear. She'd been careful not to let word of her coming travel ahead.

Maybe not careful enough.

A couple of days ago, some mingling scents and textures in the air—pine sap, icy peaks, tumbling waterfalls—had started her heart racing. She recognized it as the fragrance of her childhood. Her speeding pulse had never quite returned to normal since then; but now, with the quiet stares and the anticipation of the past days coming to a culmination, her pulse kicked into an all-out sprint. She felt breathless and like she was walking through a dream.

They reached a wide stone bridge bracketed by impressive ram statues. She stopped before one of them and gazed up, her memories colliding with the present. Her great-grandfather had commissioned these statues, she remembered. So many generations of her family had loved and cared for this place.

As she continued on, she noticed that Daisy and Cal drew in closer to her sides. Perry, Roar, and the brothers cinched in tighter, too, staying no more than three paces behind her.

They arrived at a street market on the other side of the bridge, bustling and noisy, people roving from carts to tents with baskets on their arms or sacks of burlap over their shoulders. She flowed into the commotion, relieved to get away from the doorway stares. Music floated on the cool evening air. Flutes and drums playing a racing melody, like playful squirrels. Vendors shouted over it, eager to sell off the last of their fish and cabbages, their walnut loafs and salted meats.

A mile ago, she'd been famished. Her appetite was nowhere to be found now.

They followed the main road, leaving the lower part of the city and the river behind and ascending the mountain. Stone homes hugged either side, laundry lines swinging between them. All was sound and movement now. Carts clattering along. Mules bobbing their heads as they trundled on. Children playing chase, weaving deftly through the heavy foot traffic.

Then she rounded a corner and there it was: the fortress. Sitting fearlessly above everything like a hawk over its hunting fields. One tower from a distance; many as she drew closer. All stalwart and timeless as only stone could be.

As absorbed as she was taking everything in, she didn't realize Daisy and Cal had fallen back until Roar appeared at her side, his deep brown eyes alert and shining with intensity. He didn't look like someone who'd been on his deathbed days ago, then trekking through the wilderness since. Apart from a shadow of scruff over his jaws and his peeling lips, he was as dashing as ever. Maybe more so. The moisture of the mountain air had brought an appealing curl to the hair that escaped the knot at the back of his head. The dramatic mountain slopes enhanced the dramatic sweep of his features, from his carved cheekbones to his heavy lashes and full lips.

It was a supremely poor time to be noticing these things, but her perception was filtered through high adrenaline, everything diamond-clear, and she couldn't help it. He was, without a doubt, the most beautiful human being she'd ever seen.

She considered her own travel-weary pants and shirt and what impression *she* might be making. She should've given more thought to her appearance; she could've at least redone her braid and wiped the road dust off her face.

Look the part, or lose the part, Sable had written in one of his letters.

An ache began in her throat. She had no idea what to do with his supposed "wisdom" anymore. He'd been a murderer and a liar, but did that make all his advice worthless?

Roar turned to her. "Something on your mind?"

"No," she lied.

"Tempest, what is it?"

"Nothing."

He pursed his lips, obviously disliking her answer.

She couldn't blame him. They had agreed on rules—or whatever those had been—for their marriage. Honesty had been one and here she was, disregarding it at the first opportunity.

"It's not anything I want to talk about," she whispered. "Especially *now*. Let's just say I'm feeling significant stress."

His eyes softened briefly. "Thank you. And me, too. We'll be fine."

They weren't really a *we*, and his temper was wary, restless and mothlike, but she dipped her chin in gratitude.

Soon, they arrived at the perimeter wall that protected the fortress. The wide iron gates were open and foot traffic passed through seamlessly. That changed as she approached.

Two sentries in the Horn red-and-black livery left their posts by the gates and came over. They were enormous, wore matching glowers, and both carried spears. She half expected them to cross the weapons in front of her with an ostentatious snap, blocking her path. They merely stopped in front of her, but the message was just as clear.

"State your name and purpose in this city," said the male guard. Olive skin and a thick black beard set off his sky-blue eyes.

Here we go, she thought, steeling herself for yet another moment that could change her life irrevocably. "My name is Tempest of the Horns. My purpose in this city, in this territory, is to rule over it well and wisely, as is my duty and birthright." She had not planned that, but it came out sounding fine to her ears. Clear and firm. But she began to question this in the seconds that followed in which the guard stared at her, a bead of sweat slowly working its way down his temple to his cheek.

She wondered if he was searching for a resemblance to her brother. She had Sable's bronze skin and pale eyes. His straight nose, too. Did the guard notice?

The sentry beside him, a stout woman with dirty blonde hair, gaped outright.

"How long's this going to take, Mattock?" Cal grumbled behind Tempest. "Because my bladder's about a minute from bursting."

The first guard's gaze darted over Tempest's shoulder and lit with recognition. "My god. Calista? Is it really you? Well, damn!" He rammed the butt of the spear down on the cobbles with a crack. "All this time I've been so happy thinking we got rid of you!"

"Never celebrate too soon," Cal drawled.

"Or too hard," Mattock bandied back. "A rule I'll have to abide tonight." His blue eyes came to Tempest again, and she saw warmth in them now. "I don't expect you'll remember me, but I'm Mattock of the Horns. You lost your first tooth under my watch. Bit into a market apple like a starving horse, and there it was."

Tempest smiled, the memory filtering up through the years. "I remember. You made me gargle with spirits to stop the bleeding. I spit all over you."

"And rightly. I should've given you saltwater instead."

Cal smirked. "Corrupter of the youth."

"Of more than just the youth, hate to admit." Mattock's gaze went to Roar and narrowed, making some calculation.

Belatedly, Tempest realized she should make introductions, but it was too late.

Mattock turned his assessing gaze briefly to Perry, then addressed her again. "I hope you understand I can't pay you proper obeisance," he said soberly. "Your uncle Lund wears the chain at present. But I welcome you, Tempest of the Horns. With the wholeness of my heart, I welcome you home." He smiled, and it transformed him from imposing guard into a man who'd been like a mischievous uncle to her once. "Give the order, Iris," he said to the female sentry at his side. "Tell them to strike the Horns' Return."

Iris made a series of signals in the direction of a lookout tower. High above, a guard acknowledged her with a signal and shouted commands beyond Tempest's hearing. It was only a few seconds before three men jogged up to the crenels, looking excitedly down at her before their soldierly composure returned. They raised horns to their mouths, and then the early evening air shook with a series of blasts. Immense sounds, full and echoing. Three short bursts, a longer note, then three again. A pattern they repeated.

By the end of the third round, other horns were taking up the call all over the city. The hair on Tempest's arms lifted. These were the sounds that used to announce her brother's homecoming. Longer ago, her parents'.

She glanced at Roar, wondering how it would sound to his ears, but he was wearing a bland expression, only the slightest tension visible around his eyes. His temper, though, was concentrating into a hard pit of bitterness and anger. Her brother had killed Liv here; Roar had seen it happen. She shook away the thoughts and pulled her shoulders back, focusing on this moment, which she'd dreamt about for a decade—and which was turning out to be nothing like what she'd ever imagined.

Mattock began to step aside, then hesitated. "Shall I escort you in?"

"Please," she said gratefully. She had no idea where to go. In her memory, the halls of the fortress wove like vines.

With another command, Mattock had the other guards formed quickly into a processional. People were pouring from taverns and homes now, and a crowd was forming around them.

Tempest took everything in. Their faces. The shapes and sounds and smells of the city. Daisy beamed with pure joy. Cal almost looked at ease.

They were *home.*

She was home.

But Ventus wasn't with them. Nor would she find her brother anywhere inside.

~ 19 ~

ROAR

For the past few days, Roar had been trying not to think about the last time he'd come to Rim, but with the fortress rising up before him, so were the memories, and he was powerless to stop them.

As they moved through the snaking corridors, he could almost imagine he'd gone back in time, that Aria was beside him—dear, headstrong Aria—and that he was dizzy with the need to find Liv. She'd run off some months before without warning, furious her brother Vale had betrothed her to Sable. But then, she'd come here to marry Sable all the same.

While he'd thought only of Liv, Aria had been on a quest for information about the Still Blue—still only a mythical place then, a hope. Not the lush green land that would become Cinder.

Walking through the cool corridors, he could hear the echoes of time, like it had all happened yesterday. When he'd found Liv here, she'd been days away from wedding Sable. She'd begged Roar to step aside, to give up on her. He'd known her for ten years by then. Had fallen in love with her from the first day, even if he hadn't realized it until later. He had convinced her, finally, to choose what *she* wanted. In her last living moments before Sable had murdered her, Liv had chosen Roar.

But if he hadn't come to Rim, she *would* have married Sable.

That fact blared through his mind now.

Other memories rushed in. Things he'd always tried to forget. Liv could plunge into moods. Often, she'd go inward, and he'd be lost. He'd be mad with the desire to help her, but she wouldn't open up. She had loathed his ability to hear her mind when they touched, which he'd wanted more than her. Having never grown up with affection, it had seemed like magic when it appeared in his life. The mere textures of her skin, her hair and lips, had been enough to drive him wild. The idea that you could make someone feel cherished by merely holding their hand or kissing their cheek? It was incredible. He'd been like a starving person, but Liv had kept them to some invisible quota he'd never understood.

I don't want you to hear every thought in my head, she used to say. *It's unnatural.*

She had often disappeared to hunt alone, leaving without a word. A hundred times, he'd asked her: *Can you at least tell me when you're going, so I don't worry?*

To which she'd always replied: *I can take care of myself, Roar.*

Roar had never doubted that for a second, but accidents could strike even the most capable people, and he had a selfish reason to want a simple word in parting from her: Leave-takings made him anxious as hell. They took him back to his boyhood and the countless times his parents left without telling him. Then the endless days he spent under that window waiting for them to return, unsure if they ever would.

He hadn't allowed himself these thoughts in a very long time, but surrounded by these stark walls, he couldn't avoid the stark truth: Maybe all this time, he'd been seeing their relationship as something stronger than it had been. Maybe it wasn't perfect. Maybe he'd only convinced himself it was.

"Steady, Roar," Perry murmured, pulling him out of his brooding thoughts. "Stick to the plan."

Tempest, walking a few paces ahead, turned her head slightly, like she was listening.

"I'm fine," he replied. *The plan* was to stay focused on helping Tempest take her place as rightful ruler of the Horns. Roar had told Perry about the bargain he'd made with her, securing her promise to help win back the Tides in exchange. After, Perry—never chatty in the best of circumstances—had dipped into a silence that lasted half a day, ending at last while they'd been gutting fish with a simple and unexpected, *Thank you, Roar.*

"Are *you* good?" Roar asked, peering at his friend. Perry had never been to Rim before, but Liv was his sister, and this was Sable's former domain. If anyone had a darker past with Sable, it was him.

Perry's green eyes gleamed. "I'm great," he said dryly.

They passed a sizable courtyard with ivy-covered walls and then the main hall: vast, soaring ceilings, low rows of tables laying in near darkness. Mattock took them up a stairwell into a large dining room that opened to the corridor, its double doors thrown wide.

Roar had dined here once before. It'd been a horrible, tense night in which he'd had to watch Sable fawn over Liv. The room was much like he remembered it. A long table ran down the length. Oil paintings of moody landscapes and seascapes hung on the dark plum walls. Doors led to balconies on the far side, beyond which there was only sky. When the wind shifted, the candles on the table danced and he could hear the rush of the Snake River far below. The horns had stopped trumpeting and now music floated up from the city.

A man and woman were the only two seated at the table, though huge platters of fragrant food crowded its surface. Enough for a feast. They set down their wine cups and looked up at the interruption, wearing matching looks of mild annoyance. Then Mattock announced Tempest's arrival and their annoyance turned to open-mouthed shock.

The man—surely the man married to Tempest's aunt who Daisy had quietly briefed him on over the past days—was older, large-boned and handsome, with a thick head of hair going from jet-black to silver. His ample girth and jowls looked wrong, like unnecessary layers of clothing piled over an athletic build. He'd either suffered a recent turn in his health, or a recent turn in his fortune.

The woman was in her forties—a decade younger than her husband, Roar guessed—with silver hair that fell over a frail shoulder in an intricate braid. She bore a passing resemblance to Tempest. It was those eyes. Roar had no idea how they could be so colorless. Eyes should be brown, green, blue, hazel. Not the color of ice.

"Aunt Lerra?" Tempest said tentatively, as Mattock stepped back.

"Tempest?" The woman snapped out of her shock and rose with a gasp. "Oh, my dear niece! Is it really you?" She rushed to embrace Tempest, her ivory gown flowing behind her slender figure. "You're back! How you've grown! Let me look at you!"

According to Daisy, Tempest had never been close with Lerra, but her eyes sparkled under her aunt's fussing, and her smile was real. As this heartfelt reunion occurred, Lund reclined in his chair and studied the group, his gaze moving right past Roar to settle on Perry.

"Who ordered the Return of the Horns?" he asked.

"I did, sir," said Mattock.

"You've grown rusty in matters of protocol, Mattock. The Return is only sounded for the ruling Lord's family. Tempest is not my blood."

Lerra's head whipped to her husband. "She is my brother's daughter. She's *my* blood."

"I wear the chain, Lerra," he said sharply.

Around his neck was a chain as gaudy as Sable's had been, full of precious stones. Sable's chain was in the satchel slung around Perry's shoulder. Thinking of it, Roar's hand closed involuntarily around the palm he'd sliced using the side of a setting.

"But you shouldn't be wearing it," Tempest said, wasting no time at all. "My brother is dead. But this territory is not yours."

This news was met with a long, tense silence. Lerra bowed her head. A threatening edge came to Lund's gaze. "*What* are you *saying?*" he said deliberately.

Roar looked at Tempest and waited for the follow-through. For her to stake her claim to the title. The territory. The chain. *Tell him how it is*, he thought. *Just like outside at the gate.*

But she only stared at the big man, seconds passing, her lower lip trembling almost imperceptibly.

Roar's gaze fell to the floor. What was *this?* She wasn't cowed by anyone—not Aldred, not Mattock. Certainly not *him!* Where was her backbone now when she needed it most?

He looked up and they locked eyes. Insight came suddenly, as though he could hear her thoughts, and he understood her struggle: She was an outsider just like him, challenging a man three times her age and over twice her size. A man who looked *very* comfortable in his chair and unwilling to give it up. The aunt wasn't helping anymore, either. She had clammed up, leaving Tempest out on a limb.

Lund seized on Tempest's hesitation and went in for the attack. "If you're as foolhardy and presumptuous as I'm beginning to suspect, allow me to clarify a few things. This is *not* your territory, Tempest. It *was* your brother's, but that doesn't mean a damn thing anymore. It certainly doesn't give *you* any standing. I'm happy to list the reasons you're unworthy of ruling, though you might want to get comfortable, as it'll take awhile. There are *many.*"

Tempest was going pale beside Roar, and he was done. This wasn't his fight—or was it? It didn't matter either way. He couldn't stand by any longer.

"Thank you, Lund," he said, stepping forward. "That's kind of you to offer." He pulled out one of the chairs. "Sit, my darling. It's been a long journey and you must be tired."

Tempest's stare widened briefly, but she sat. He took the chair beside her and picked up the decanter in front of him. "Never been happier to see wine in my life," he said cheerfully as he filled two glasses. He handed one to Tempest. "Cheers, love." He chinked his glass against hers, took a healthy sip, and sat back. Only then did he return his attention to the far side of the table. "Please, go on. We're comfortable now. You were going to list some reasons . . . ?"

Lund looked incensed. Volcanic. Roar glanced around the room. Everyone looked both confused and riveted, even the servants in the corridor. This was going better than he'd hoped.

Inspired, he reached for Tempest's hand and pressed a kiss to it. "Oh, but first—" he was pushing it now, but he couldn't resist, "I think we're going to need more wine." He smiled at one the servants attending the meal. "Would you mind?"

"No, sir!" said the man, bolting from the room.

Lund had recovered himself. He leaned forward, his elbows thudding on the table. "Who the *hell* are you?"

And now, at last, Roar heard what he'd been hoping for: Tempest's voice, smooth and assertive. "Allow me to introduce you to my husband, Uncle. Roar of the Tides."

"You're married?" Aunt Lerra squealed, hands flying to her breast. "How *wonderful!*"

Roar smiled at her. "Just days a few ago, Aunt. May I call you that?"

Lerra practically swooned. "Of course! Nothing would delight me more! This is *wonderful!*"

He was starting to get the feeling that anything positive in her life was *wonderful*. She was proving to be a rather dim candle, but she seemed sweet. Harmless. Unlike her husband. "I couldn't agree more." He raised his glass to Tempest. "I'm *very* lucky."

She raised her own. "Not as lucky as *I* am."

"Oh, come on, my little duckling. *I'm* the luckier."

"I simply can't agree with you, kitten." *Kitten?* He almost spit his wine out. "But this argument of ours will become tedious for others. Shall we pick it up after we eat?" she asked sweetly. She was swimming with the current now.

"Of course." He motioned to another servant. "Can you bring a plate for my bride, please?"

"I think we're all hungry, aren't we?" Tempest said. "Sit, everyone. I insist."

She didn't have to. Perry, Hyde, and Hayden plunked down to Roar's right, Cal and Daisy sat to Tempest's left. Straggler wedged himself into the only remaining empty chair.

"Plates and glasses for all of us." Roar was having a hard time keeping a straight face. Then Perry stuffed a roll into his mouth and Cal sank into a turkey leg, and he had to disguise a laugh with a cough. "On second thought, just the glasses will do. Seems we still have a bit of the outdoors in our manners." Across the table, Lund turned a killer stare from him to Tempest. "But I think we're settled now, right?" Roar continued, undaunted. "We're ready to hear all the reasons why this intelligent and capable young woman isn't deserving of what's rightfully hers—oh, do you hear that?" he said, turning to the open balcony doors like he'd just heard the music drifting in. "They're celebrating, Tempest. They're *dancing* out there." He draped his arm over her chair, toying with the soft curl that was right at his fingertips. "And you were worried they'd forgotten you." He smiled. "Welcome home."

Something in her eye—a wistful, searching look—had him forgetting himself for a moment. She was looking right at him, but it was like she couldn't see him.

But then he turned away as he heard the hard scrape of a chair on floorboards.

Lund rose from the table, tossing down his napkin. He had lost control of the room and he knew it. To recover it, things would need to turn ugly. He'd need to take a hard stance against Tempest's claim to power and her link to the Horn line, ousting her. From what Roar had seen, and heard, the city—and possibly also her aunt—would clearly take issue with that.

"See that they're settled tonight," Lund ordered his wife. "Tempest, we will continue this discussion tomorrow. In private."

She held his stare. "I look forward to it."

When Lund was gone, Roar drew a deep breath. He was beginning to feel his own potent anger, which he'd kept under leash since Lund had first opened his mouth.

Tempest was gripping the stem of her glass like it might scurry away. "Thank you," she said quietly.

"Of course," he replied.

They'd won this battle. It didn't feel like it, though.

Gradually, they relaxed. Perry, Cal, and the brothers turned dinner into an eating competition. Tempest's aunt almost singlehandedly kept the conversation flowing. When she learned that he and Tempest had married without a proper ceremony, it became her mission to rectify such a terrible oversight as soon as humanly possible. She seemed to have a unique gift for talking at length about things he could've wrapped up in a few words. He liked her.

Tempest said very little and only picked at her food. Her lack of appetite destroyed his own.

"Did I do anything wrong?" he whispered when the conversation was lively and carrying on without them.

She bowed her head close. "No. You saved me. *I* did wrong. I froze. I don't know what got into me."

"Tempest—" A whole host of encouragements were on the tip of his tongue, but her warm breath was drifting over his cheek and he made the mistake of looking at her mouth. "Let's talk later," he said, straightening. He pretended to join the conversation again, while privately bashing his head against an imaginary wall. *No,* he told himself. *No and no again.* He did *not* need to add temptation to the viper's nest of a marriage they were tiptoeing through.

After dinner, Mattock the Glarer escorted them to their chamber. The man hadn't stopped sending Roar cool looks since their encounter at the gate. Roar was sure they'd never be on good terms, but Tempest seemed delighted by the man. They chattered easily as Mattock led them down one long corridor and then another, catching up on lost years.

Tempest's suite—and his—were at the end of a private corridor dashed by slit windows that showed dramatic slices of the Aether and mountains. It was much quieter in that part of the fortress, remote as an island.

Mattock opened the heavy doors at the end. They were almost twice his height with brass pulls that clanked loudly as he let them go. "A guard will always be posted at the end of the hall. If you need service, there's a bell pull by the hearth. It'll summon one of the servants."

As he went on, the scar on Roar's chest began to pulse with pain, reminding him that it had been a long week. A long year, really. He entered the chamber, leaving Mattock to Tempest.

Inside, a servant was opening doors to a balcony. Another lit candles around the room. A boy slightly younger than Talon was struggling to get a fire going in the hearth, his small hands shaking, his eyes darting nervously back to Roar.

Roar went over and knelt beside him. The boy flinched like he expected to be struck. Fury flared in Roar's heart for whoever had put such a fear into him. He cleared his throat. "My grandmother used to say the fires that are hardest to start are the ones that burn the longest." He pulled a blanket off a stuffed chair and held it open, creating a windshield. "Now try."

The boy struck the flint. On the third try, a spark found the kindling. He blew on it vigorously, spitting in his enthusiasm.

Roar was tempted to make a wisecrack, but then the kid split the widest, happiest grin he'd seen in a long time.

"Thank you, my lord!"

"Well done," Roar said, smiling. "What's your name?"

"Elias?"

"Are you asking me if I want you to be named Elias?"

"No, my lord. My name is Elias." He was going red to the tips of his ears.

"I'm Roar."

"I don't think I can call you that, sir."

"Says who?"

Elias's answer was to shrink in discomfort.

"I see. That's your ruler right there," Roar said, tipping his chin in Tempest's direction. She had stopped talking to Mattock and was watching his exchange with the boy. "She will be, by week's end. Tempest, is it all right if Elias calls me 'Roar'?"

"Of course. And I insist you call me 'Tempest,' Elias."

This nearly undid the boy. He leapt to his feet, bowed twice, and darted out like he himself had caught fire.

Mattock rolled his eyes. "I'll arrange for another page."

"No," Tempest said. "Not necessary. Elias is perfect."

"Very well." Mattock frowned down at her. He seemed to want to say something, but then he looked at Roar and changed his mind. "Good night, Tempest." He pulled the doors closed with a resounding boom.

Roar poked at the fire and listened to Tempest moving around the chamber. It was the first time they'd been alone since their conversation in the woods some days ago. The only other time they'd been alone was that first night he'd gotten stuck in the rubble in Resolute. It seemed impossible, given all that had happened. He kept expecting her to say something *and* dreading what it might be. That same feeling was coming over him from the last time they'd spoken, like they were picking carefully over a web, afraid to shake things up.

He set the poker aside before he started looking like a pyromaniac.

Tempest was roaming around the chamber, exploring it. Running her finger over a lampshade. Touching the roses in the vase. Like she was moving from one memory to another.

He remembered the ostentatiousness of this place from last time, but he'd been a passing stranger then. Too consumed with getting Liv out of here to really see it.

He saw it now, though. It was the most luxurious space he'd ever seen. Gold and silk everywhere, luminous with candlelight. A soft wool rug almost as large as the chamber. A table with crystal glasses to one side, a carved wood bed the size of a large carriage half covered in fat pillows to the other. Two big stuffed chairs by the fireplace. He could hear water running from the adjoining bathroom and wasn't surprised; there were fountains all over Rim. He also heard the rushing of the Snake, the moan of the wind and snap of the fire. Tempest's shallow breaths.

Tempest turned, like she'd remembered him. "Thank you for what you did, with Lund." She moved to the fire and held her hands in front of it. She looked tired and weary; he wondered how much of that was owed to him.

"You already thanked me, remember? It was after you called me 'kitten.'" He smiled. "Can't say I minded it."

"I was only trying to match your theatrics," she said, without looking at him.

"Right," he said, sensing the awkwardness in the room sliding toward tension. So much for lightening the mood with humor. He sat on one of the plush chairs and untied his boots. "We talked about my sleeping here. Part of the necessary theatrics we decided on *together* a few days ago. I'm assuming you haven't changed your mind?"

"You assume correctly."

"Excellent. Would you like to use the bathroom first?"

She shook her head, still not looking at him.

"Would you like to use the bathroom second?" She shot him a glare. "I'll take that as a yes. I won't be long."

He stepped into the bathroom and a laugh burst out of him. There was a small . . . lagoon? He didn't know what to call the massive marble basin along the length of the far wall. Levers and pipes to one side regulated the temperature and flow of the waterfall pouring into it. Smaller, but only by comparison, were the sinks. Everything was hewn from the same gray marble that was softened by the candlelight and plush towels that sat in neat stacks. It was a display of riches beyond anything he could have imagined.

He didn't belong here. Growing up, he'd either bathed in rivers or he'd taken what his mother had called "birdbaths" using a copper tub hardly bigger than a pail. His heart started racing. A wild, criminal feeling flashed through him, like he'd broken in. Like he might be found out at any moment and tossed out.

"Come on, now," he whispered under his breath. "Relax."

He stripped down and entered the warm lagoon. He sure as hell wasn't going to get any other opportunities; why not enjoy it while he was here?

Though it was deeply relaxing, laughter kept burbling out of him. Life was downright surprising sometimes. He scrubbed his hair and examined his scar. It had improved from disfiguring to merely grotesque. He rolled his left arm, pleased to find he'd recovered full range of motion. He snorted when his eyes fell on his Naming Marking: a roaring panther that wove down his arm, its tail wrapping around his wrist. "*Kitten*."

He lay back under the waterfall, letting it massage his shoulders as he tried to empty his mind of his worries. His thoughts kept returning to the wedding ceremony Tempest's aunt was insisting upon. A "proper wedding," she'd said, to serve as both a welcoming home for Tempest and a chance to introduce him to "the families." These, he remembered from his first time in Rim, were the five dynasties that essentially controlled the territory's economy, each family dominating a particular segment, like farming, ranching, river transport.

"They'll start coming tomorrow regardless of whether we hold a wedding," Lerra had said, at dinner. "None of them will want to be the last ones to lay eyes on you. Better to get ahead of things and avoid the appearance we're playing favorites by controlling the circumstances in which they come to us. We'll just do a small thing tomorrow night. Some food, some champagne. A little music in the courtyard. Oh, the excitement! It's wonderful!"

It was *not* wonderful. He was dreading being put on display so strangers could "lay eyes" on him. He wasn't much looking forward to marrying Tempest again, either. It would only dredge up all the complicated feelings of guilt, frustration, and disappointment he was trying to put behind him. They hadn't kissed passionately, tried to kill each other, or sworn blood oaths in a few days, and he wasn't eager for more "excitement." But Lerra's argument made sense and this was what he'd agreed to do. To get the Tides back, he could play a role for a little while.

He dried off, pulled on his pants—he'd find some fresh clothes tomorrow—and combed his fingers through his hair. It was too snarled—he needed a brush or shears, and neither were laying around—so he gave up and tied it in a knot.

"You certainly weren't raised in squalor, were you?" he said as he returned to the chamber. He lurched back as he nearly ran Tempest over, his shoulder blade thudding against the doorjamb. There was only one cramped space in the entire chamber and there they were, squeezed into it. "I didn't see you," he said, by way of explaining the obvious.

She was staring at his Naming Marking like it was an actual living panther. Then her gaze moved to the scar over his heart and she blanched.

"Heinous, isn't it?" He tried to sound cavalier and failed. He wondered if she'd noticed.

"No, it isn't." She met his eyes. "But what caused it is." For a second, neither of them said anything. He was waiting for her to apologize—it seemed suddenly necessary, and like the logical follow-up—but she didn't. "And I can't help how I was raised any more than you can," she said instead, breezing past him into the bathroom.

"Yes, all this velvet and silk must have been a real hardship."

"*Excuse* me," she said, then she threw the door shut in his face.

Roar shook his head, trying to understand what had just happened. Why did *he* care if she'd grown up pampered? He certainly hadn't minded her circumstances a few moments ago.

He set up a bed by the hearth, piling up pillows, a sheepskin, a blanket. Makeshift, yet the most comfortable bed of his life, every texture supple and silky.

He lay down, but sleep was out of the question. Tempest was naked behind that door. He didn't want to think about that, but he thought about it a lot. To try to distract himself, he studied the craftsmanship all around him: the deep, coffered ceilings that soared so high the firelight barely touched them; the bronze fire screen with a leaping stag in relief; the massive four-post bed that required a set of rolling stairsteps to climb.

How could he *not* to be daunted by this opulence? He'd spent his life in lean-tos rife with holes that were filled with sunspots by day and invited in every crawler by night. Black was his color—what he'd long worn top to bottom—not just to help him blend into shadows, but because it could be sewn and patched inconspicuously, over and over and *over.* He had his father's knives—*used* to have them; they were in Aldred's possession now—and that was it, the sum total of his wealth. He'd never felt *poor* until this moment, though.

Tempest emerged from the bathroom wearing an ivory robe belted at the waist. She smelled like springtime, like flowers and fresh rain. He watched her through his lashes as she shut the balcony doors and snuffed out candles, tilting her head here, rising on her toes there. There were times she was so confident that it seemed to magnify her, make her seem taller and older than she was. But at the moment, she struck him as small, quick and light as a bird, the thoughtful, dreamy look in her eyes hinting at the girl she must've been. She'd been a hostage most of her life, which couldn't have been easy. In spite of that, she had an upbeat air about her, a positivity that usually only belonged to the naïve and innocent.

When only the crackling hearth lit the room, he watched her climb into the bed and burrow under the thick covers. A feeling of disappointment and wrongness came over him. He waited to see if it would go away, but it didn't. "Are you still awake?" he asked after a while.

He knew she was; he'd been listening to her breathe in uneven little sighs of frustration.

"Yes," she replied.

"Should we talk?" he asked, against his better judgment.

"I don't see why. You played your role earlier. You don't have to continue the farce here."

Farce. "Tempest," he said, "I was trying to help. And we both have to perform, don't we? In order for this to be believable? I thought we agreed on that."

"We did. We do." There was a beat of silence, then she kept going. "All I'm saying is you don't need to pretend to be friendly or anything when we're alone."

"Tempest, I'm not pretending—"

"Yes, Roar. You are. And I want to add an additional rule to our agreement. While we're married, pretending to be married, we should be faithful to each other. That may not be ideal for you, but I won't budge on it. I won't be made into a laughingstock. That would defeat the whole point of this—this arrangement."

Anger flooded over him, immediate and potent. He sat upright, pain flaring in his chest. "Let me see if I understand this right. Are you telling me I shouldn't sleep around while we're married?"

She was sitting up in bed, too, swimming in and out of the flickering dimness. "That's right."

"I see. And can I ask what I've done to make you think I'd do that?"

"Certainly. First, you were lying when we took our vows. I scented your insincerity, Roar. I *am* a Scire. And secondly, you're . . . *you*."

"And that means what, exactly?"

"Do you really want me to say it?"

"Yes, please."

"You're loose, Roar. You're a—a libertine. I mean, you kissed me immediately after we met, and you had all the servants going tonight, batting their eyes at you and shoving each other out of the way to see who could pour your wine."

"The *servants?*" His blood was boiling now. "I haven't got the foggiest idea what you're talking about. I treated them like human beings, Tempest. Maybe I smiled and said please and thank you—is that a crime? Was I supposed to ignore them and pretend I grew up being waited on? I *didn't.* And even if I did, I'd like to think I'd still treat them with some goddamn courtesy. And about our kiss. Let's set aside the fact that *you* also kissed *me*, too, for now. Do you think that's typical for me? 'Hello, I'm Roar. Nice to meet you. How about a snog?'"

She rolled her eyes. "Of course you're making this a joke."

"I'll gladly be serious, Tempest, if you'll stop making assumptions about me. Do you know, I haven't even *thought* about being with anyone since—" He caught himself. *Stop. Go anywhere but there.* "You know what? Never mind. Yes, I'm—whatever you said I am. A libertine. It's got a nice ring to it, so sure. Let's talk about our vows, though, shall we?

"As I recall, you weren't exactly thrilled about taking them yourself. I could hear the strain in your voice." He was tempted to tell her he could hear thoughts through touch—that as soon as they'd clasped their bloody palms together, her abject despair had filled his mind—but he decided not to. It would only cause more damage. "I took the vow, Tempest. I said the words, though they pained me. You're right. I didn't feel or believe any of it. I was furious and I didn't want to die, so I lied through that oath—and I know you did, too."

"And you also have the right to be confused and offended!"

"Confused? I'm definitely that." He scratched his jaw, bewildered. "I honestly have no idea what we're fighting about. Can you just tell me why're you're angry in simple terms? Even if you think it's obvious."

"Gladly! You hate my brother, and you hate me, and you hate this place! You ask me how I am, like you care, but I know you don't. I know you want to be anywhere else but here, and I can't escape your unhappiness. Every time I breathe, I'm reminded of it! Can you understand what it feels like to try to fall asleep knowing you're resented for everything you are?"

Roar opened his mouth to reply. Closed it. Tried again. "This feels like the right time to point out that you put out a hit on me, and that your brother killed Liv."

"That's exactly my point! That will always be between us."

"Yes."

"Yes? That's all you have to say?"

"I'm telling you the truth, Tempest. Plain and simple. I will never forget that Liv died at your brother's hands, or that you ordered a man to maim me. I don't *hate* you—that's also true. I think I might have right after, but—"

"You resent me. You're wary of me, and you don't trust me."

He let out a bitter laugh. *Scires.* She had a better grasp on his feelings than he did. "Maybe that's true, but I do have good reason, wouldn't you say? And I don't know what you expect, anyway. The things that happened *happened*. I'm not wiping out my memories to please you. I've given up enough for you already."

For a second, he thought she might launch a pillow at him. Then she said, "Yes, thank you for making the *sacrifice* of being my husband."

Ah. *Now* he saw what this was about. She thought he wasn't being grateful enough, that he was some good-for-nothing who should be giddy to marry someone so far above his level. Someone who slept on silk and bathed in a marble mausoleum. "I don't need any of this, Tempest. You, on the other hand. You need—"

He pushed a hand through his damp hair, his fingers catching in knots. He always used to feel slightly nauseous when his parents had yelling matches, and the same queasiness was coming over him now.

"Go on. What do you think I need? I can't wait to hear this."

He'd been primed to tear into her ambition. *You need to rule*, he was going to say. *You're obsessed with power and control.* But it was a ludicrous thing to criticize.

She was intelligent and driven—why shouldn't she aspire to great ends? Why shouldn't she attain what she was worthy of? She needed more than just to reclaim this territory. She needed loyal people around her, besides Cal and Daisy. She needed a home, a heart mended of grief. A life without a husband who'd been foisted upon her. He couldn't make himself say any of these things, though. Who was he to claim he understood what she needed?

"Sleep," he said at last. "I think you need sleep, and I think I need it, too." He stood, exhaling a tense breath. "I'm tired, Tempest. Aren't you?"

"Yes," she said softly. "I am."

He felt some of the anger leave the room.

"Good. We agree on something. We both need sleep and you can't sleep while I'm here, emitting my natural feelings. Thankfully, there's an easy solution to this problem." He went to the door. "Good night."

He was halfway down the hall before he regretted not grabbing his shirt and boots. Away from the chamber's fire, the cold was stark, the stone like ice under his bare feet. He came to the guard posted at the end of the corridor.

The man startled, his heels snapping together. "Is everything all right, sir?"

"No, not at all. Show me the way to Peregrine's chamber, please? And may I have your cloak?"

The guard blinked. "Yes, sir."

He unhooked the red cloak hanging off the back of his leather uniform. Roar threw it on, feeling ridiculous but warmer under the thick wool, and followed him.

Perry's room was on the other side of the world, but they got there. Roar stepped inside and was greeted with a blade to his throat. He cursed, twisting away. "It's me, you big idiot!"

"Roar?" Perry stepped back. "What are you doing here? What are you *wearing*?"

"Never mind that." In the darkness, he could only see the glint of Perry's eyes and the silver slash of the blade. "Are you really expecting to be attacked in the middle of the night?"

"Maybe. I don't have a lot of friends here." Perry pulled a curtain open, letting in the Aether light. He set the dagger down on a table. "You should be prepared for it, too."

"I think it already happened to me, actually. Just now."

"Marital troubles?"

Roar shrugged. "I know, surprising. We got off to such a good start. But love can be fickle and cruel and . . . ." he couldn't think of anything else, "lots of other bad things. We hate each other. Or, I don't know. Maybe we're trying not to hate each other and it's not working. I can't make sense of it. Anyway, I'm sleeping here."

He was about to flop down on the bed when Perry grabbed the hood of the cloak, yanking him back. "No, you're not. If you run now, you'll never fix this."

"What if I don't want to fix it?"

"You have to."

"You can't make me."

"Watch me." Perry opened the door and shoved him out. The startled guard was still outside and still looking startled. "You're better than this."

"Wrong, you're the noble one, Perry. And it really bothers me when—" For the second time that night, a door slammed shut in his face. "That wasn't very noble." He looked at the guard. "Show me the way back, please. And may I have your dagger?"

Tempest was either asleep or pretending to be asleep when he got back. Either way, a good thing. He was exhausted and had nothing left.

He tossed the cloak onto a chair, set the dagger down within reach, and climbed into his bed by the hearth. Then he listened to Tempest breathe and searched for patterns in the dancing flames until sleep finally came.

~ 20 ~

TEMPEST

Tempest sat in a chair by the fireplace, turning the glass jar in her hand and waiting for Roar to wake up. He was sleeping on his stomach, part of his face buried in a pillow, the rest draped in tousles of deep brown hair the color of rich earth. Even splayed out, his legs tangled in a blanket, there was an innate elegance in his face and long limbs.

She still couldn't get over the shock that he was her husband.

The fire had burned down to glowing embers and the first rays of sunlight fuzzed through the seam between the curtains. It was early, but she'd already been down to the kitchen for tea and then to the infirmary, remembering the way there from a childhood full of bee stings and tumbles off her pony.

It was so strange to be back—deeply comforting on one level, the winding corridors and trickling fountains so familiar—but she didn't feel safe like you should at home. Her position was precarious: Lund clearly had no intention of ceding control over to her. For all she knew, he would throw her out tomorrow and she'd be back in the wilderness, wondering where to go next.

She tapped her finger on the metal lid of the little jar. The healer in the infirmary had said the poultice would help heal burns. She prayed it would because the image of the scar on Roar's chest—pale pink and corded, the skin around it florid and inflamed—had haunted her since she saw it last night.

Really, how could he *not* resent her?

When he'd returned to their room last night, she'd been awake, agonizing over whether she should go after him. A restless night of sleep had followed.

Their fight seemed silly now. Though they did have issues to sort through, the real cause had been a coalescence of her exhaustion, fear, and overwhelm. She'd been disappointed in herself after botching her first meeting with Lund. Had she trusted Roar, it would've been a perfect chance to open up and lean on him. But they'd never gotten to that when they'd established the terms of their agreement. Truth and respect, yes. But those didn't add up to trust.

Last night, she'd wondered if there was even any point in getting to know each other. Why bother, if they were going to part ways eventually? They could put on a public display of marriage without having a private relationship of any kind. But the answer was now clear to her.

Yes, there was a point. Yes. As painful as it might be, it was the right thing to do.

Roar stirred, his visible eye fluttering open. "Have you been watching me sleep?"

His voice was gravelly, deeper than normal.

"I guess so."

"For how long?"

"Awhile."

"Were you trying to work up the nerve to kill me?"

She smiled. "Darn, it didn't occur to me." She held up the jar. "Actually, I wanted to give you this. It's a poultice. For your burn." She unscrewed the lid; a honey scent perfumed the air.

"Thank you." The blanket fell to his waist as he sat up, revealing taut skin over a grid-work of knotted muscles at his stomach, longer, fluid ones tapering down his arms. Her eyes flicked to that elaborate Naming Marking she'd seen last night. A stunning piece of art. Beautiful and dark and beguiling.

She cleared her throat. A knot was forming low in her own stomach. "You're welcome." She handed it to him. "It might sting a bit, I'm not sure. I forgot to ask."

"I can handle a bit of stinging."

As she watched him apply the poultice over the livid wheals, a sharp ache rose in her throat.

"This stuff really works." He set the jar aside. "Thanks again. You can't imagine what—" he looked up and frowned. She knew she had tears in her eyes. "Tempest . . ."

He hesitated, like he wasn't sure if he should ask what was wrong. That was her fault. She gestured to the wound. That was her fault, too. "You must have been in so much pain, Roar. You must *still* be and—and I don't know how to say this. I don't know how to say the thing I need to say."

Her brother used to yell at her when she apologized to people. He used to boast that he'd never apologized to anyone *ever.* Only the weak asked for forgiveness. She knew that wasn't true. She didn't understand why this was such a struggle. Why was there part of her that still wanted to be like him?

Roar was watching her. A stripe of sunlight slashed across his face. His eyes weren't as dark as she'd thought. Toward the center, they became amber.

"If it's what I think," he said, "then it doesn't matter how you say it. Just that you do. It'll help both of us. I think we need to clear the brush away. Otherwise, anytime we disagree will end up in wildfire like last night. Just say what you're feeling. It won't be wrong." He hesitated, then added, "And I'd very much like to hear it."

She nodded and pulled in a breath. *Here goes nothing.* "I'm sorry, Roar. I'm so sorry you were hurt because of me. I'll never forgive myself for causing you so much hurt." That was what she'd meant to say, but she was surprised to hear herself keep going. "And last night? I'm sorry I went after you for how you feel. It was unfair. This must be so hard for you, too, and I hate that I put you in this situation. I'm sorry. I really, really am."

He titled his head, moving away from the sunbeam. "You didn't start this. Neither of us did. As for regret," he scraped a hand over his jaw, "I've been down that path. I've nearly followed it to the end. It's not a good one. You should forgive yourself."

Her smile quavered. "Is it that easy?"

"No. It's not. How about this? Do you want my forgiveness?"

"More than anything."

"I'll give it to you, if you try to give it to yourself as well."

"That's not playing fair."

"What's life but a game with no rules?" he said lightly.

Though it was an offhand comment, it shot through her mind like an arrow, sinking firmly into her curiosity. She knew life hadn't treated him kindly. There was Olivia, of course. But what else had he had to bear? Would she ever know?

"Tempest, you came to the Tides for Perry and me. You've made sacrifices. It may not seem like it, but I have noticed. And I know this can't be easy for you, either. Lund's a snake."

"He really is, isn't he? I'm worried that—" Her throat closed up. She smoothed an invisible crease on her pants.

"Whatever it is, you can say it. I promised I'd help you, Temp. I'm on your side."

It was the first time he'd ever called her that. *Temp.* That small liberty, a tiny sign they were on familiar terms, maybe even friendly ones, touched her more than anything else he'd said. It gave her the courage to keep going. "I'm worried that I'm outmatched."

Roar nodded. "He won't go down without a fight, that's for sure. But I'd choose you over him any day. Frankly, I almost feel sorry for him. I've seen what you can do to your foes."

Tempest winced, her gaze dropping to his chest. She didn't think she'd ever be able to joke about the hurt she'd caused him.

"Come on." He play-punched her knee. "It was a *little* funny." He glanced down. "Besides, this is growing on me. I think I finally know my left and right."

She laughed. Apparently, she could find humor in it. "Shame it's an X instead of an L."

"It's uncanny, isn't it? A perfect X, like in old maps."

"I guess if you get lost, you'll always be able to find your way back to yourself."

He looked up. "I guess so," he said, his eyes becoming so direct her pulse skipped.

"Thank you, Roar," she said, making herself hold his gaze. "For forgiving me."

"Thank *you*, Tempest," he returned earnestly. An unfinished note hung in the air. She thought he might fill it by mirroring her words. *For . . . something.*

But he didn't.

Roar disappeared into the bathroom and emerged a short while later, washed and dressed in fawn-colored pants, a black shirt, and black boots. She'd taken his clothes to be laundered earlier, but it was Lerra who had thought to provide these. *I eyeballed his measurements,* she'd said, *but we'll get him set up proper right away.*

"You think I could trouble your aunt for a belt?" Roar asked. "Maybe a bigger shirt?"

The pants were a bit loose, sitting low on his hips. The shirt was a bit snug, stretching over him in all the right places. "Sure," she said, though she wouldn't have changed a single thing. "I'll ask her."

"Thanks." He looked around the chamber. "At dinner, you told Lerra that last night was going to be our first together in private, as husband and wife."

She nodded. "I did." Was she imagining it, or was her face growing warm? "I told her our journey began right after our vows. It seemed like a good idea to stick as close to the truth as possible."

"I agree, it is. I'm only wondering if it's customary for people in your circles to expect proof?"

"Proof?"

His mouth tugged up to one side. "Of consummation."

"Oh, *that*." A nervous giggle burbled out of her. "This just got personal, didn't it?"

A dark eyebrow ticked higher. "I think it's been personal since the day we met."

"Oh, because we . . . when we . . . Right. I honestly have no idea if, um, *proof* is needed. For Night tribe, absolutely. But here? I don't know. I was seven when I left."

"No problem. We'll play it safe and fake it. Won't be hard to do."

"Good thinking," she said, but she didn't have a clue what he had in mind.

"First, tell me these aren't your brother's clothes." He raked his hair back into a knot, exposing a turn of muscle where his lower abdomen swooped down. "I don't think I can wear them if they are."

Great, now you really are blushing, she thought. *What's next, drool?* "They're not," she replied. "They're new. My Aunt Lerra's doing. It's what she does. Beautifies anything she can get her hands on. Food, living spaces, gardens. Parties are her specialty. All my memories of her feature cake. She is most definitely going overboard tonight for our ceremony, by the way. I think she had people working through the night. I wouldn't be surprised if she got no sleep at all."

"That's exactly the look we're going for here." He went to the bed and started throwing pillows off, tossing them on the rug and chucking them around the chamber. Then he yanked the linens back, twisting and rumpling them like he was braiding rope.

"Isn't that a bit much?" Her cheeks were legitimately *searing* now.

"What?" He looked at her in mock offense. "Not even close." He abandoned the linens and went to one of the curtains. With a small yank, one side came off the rod with a soft ripping sound. "Don't worry, I'll mend it later."

"You sew?"

"You don't?"

"No." She blinked. "Roar, a *curtain?*"

"Yes, a curtain. Where's your imagination? I can think of plenty of ways to make it fun and I'm not even trying." He plucked up a white rose from a vase and started peeling off petals, scattering them around on the rug, the bed. When he scattered them on the horns of a marble ram bust, she had to laugh.

"A bit on the nose, don't you think?" she asked.

He sent her a waggish smile. "We want people talking about our rock-solid marriage, right?"

"Oh, they will be. They'll be talking about rock-solid other things, too."

He laughed, and something changed in his eyes, a warmth lighting in them. "What are you doing still sitting there? This was *our* big night. Don't you want any say in it?"

"You know what? I do." She stood and then pushed the upholstered chair she'd been sitting on over. When she looked up, Roar's eyebrows were arched in pure fascination. "What? You said to use my imagination, didn't you?"

"I did. I think you just broke mine." He looked around, his hands coming to his lean hips. "All right. Maybe we are overdoing this," he said, like it was just occurring to him.

"Nonsense!" she said cheerfully. "You find me irresistible!" She was having fun now. She poured a splash of wine into a goblet and set it down next to Roar's bed by the fireplace.

"Oh, good save," he said. "That's a must."

"Agreed." She grabbed a pillow, opened the balcony doors, and tossed it down on the flagstones. "I'd say this is—"

Turning, she saw Roar inside. He stood as still as a statue, his eyes flared. He snapped out of his trance with a shake of his head and strode to the sideboard.

Damn, she thought, shutting the doors and coming back inside. He stood with his back to her, his hands braced on the counter. For a long moment, she had no idea what to do. The easy—and cowardly—route would be to ignore the tension. To let it smooth away in a long silence, but they were *just* starting to be comfortable with each other. It was a victory she wasn't ready to relinquish. She walked over, joining him at the sideboard. "I wasn't thinking, Roar. I'm sorry."

"You know?" he asked, peering at her. "How it happened?"

"Yes. The main things." Through a complicated network of conversations during their trek to Rim (Straggler to Cal to Daisy to her), Tempest had learned some of the circumstances surrounding Liv's death. Liv, shot by her brother with a crossbow. Roar and a girl named Aria escaping the fortress by plunging into the Snake River. *Balcony.* It had happened on one of the many balconies in this very fortress. "Are you angry that I know?"

He straightened off the sideboard. "No," he said, shaking his head. "No. I'm glad you know—and that I didn't have to tell you." He picked up the water pitcher and poured two glasses. He gave one to her and drained the other in two tilts, the lean muscles in his neck rolling like waves. "I don't think I can talk about Liv with you, Tempest," he said, setting the glass down.

"That's okay."

He looked at her. "Is it?"

"Yes."

He gave her a soft, grateful smile. Grief was so potent in his temper just then, so bleak and smoky, that she almost reached out and squeezed his hand.

Her thoughts ran to *her* losses. Ventus and her brother. Her parents, who were mere shadows in her memory. When people passed away, they left holes in your life. You could carry on with things, but when you fell through one of them, you went right back to aching for them, the pain as fresh as ever. She took a sip of her water, needing a moment to gather herself.

"So, was I your first?"

By some miracle, she didn't spew water everywhere. She did end up swallowing some of it the wrong way, though. As she coughed, Roar crossed his arms and waited, his expression unreadable. Not amused, but something close.

"No, actually," she said once she recovered. "You weren't."

She thought of Ash of the Night tribe. Like her, he'd been raised as a hostage—albeit with Rose tribe—for a long stretch. When they'd reunited after spending six years apart, everything between them had been different. He'd gone away a funny and annoying cousin-like figure with ears that stuck out and a passion for putting snakes in her bed, or her shoes, or her pockets. But when he'd returned, he'd been almost unrecognizable. He was calmer. He had an air of mystery. He had *shoulders*. It had long been Banyan's plan to see her and Ash married and, in some ways, their brief flirtation had been curiosity. Putting that plan to the test. They'd only been intimate twice during those few weeks together. The first time, disastrous. The second, less disastrous but still a confirmation they were better off as friends. "Thank goodness," she added, under her breath.

Roar's eyebrows drew inward. "Why 'thank goodness'?"

"Because it was awkward and unpleasant and just generally awful."

"Sorry to hear that," he said sincerely. "If it's any comfort, I don't think the first time's ever great."

He went to the fireplace, leaving her with questions she couldn't ask. They'd just agreed that Olivia was off limits, after all. "I think there's one thing missing here." He picked up a dagger resting by the hearth, giving it a quick, expert spin. "We should probably give them what they'll really be looking for."

"I'll do it, Roar."

"No offense, Tempest. But you almost cut your hand in half during our vows." He nicked the pad of his thumb and went to the bed. Kneeling, he grabbed the sheets on the floor into a fist. "Done," he said, but he didn't rise right away. "You know," he said after a moment, "we're creating a story together. That means we can make it whatever we want." He turned, looking at her over his shoulder. "Our first night wasn't awkward or unpleasant. I would've made sure of it. I would've treated you right."

"Do you like it, Tempest?" Aunt Lerra asked, a short while later. "It was your mother's. It's unconventional for a wedding, I'll admit. But I thought it would be lovely for you to wear the Horn crimson, and all the floral arrangements will match. If you think it's too much, though . . . ?"

They were in one of the rooms that opened to the large center courtyard. Through glass doors, Tempest saw servants pruning climbing vines and sweeping flagstones. Others were hauling out tables and chairs, and unfurling banners from the second-story arcade.

"It's not too much, Aunt Lerra. It's perfect." Tempest smoothed her hands over the red silk. In truth, she'd almost asked for an alternative when she'd first stepped into the simple, strapless sheath with chiffon ruffles at the bottom. It was a dress to stop hearts, nothing bridal or innocent about it. But Daisy had shaken her head, giving her a *don't say no yet* look, and sent for a floor-length mirror. When it arrived, Tempest had been fascinated by her own reflection.

It'd been a year since she'd really seen herself. In the Pod, the only mirrors had been small, warped ones above the sinks. She'd had a mental image of herself as a boyish, knock-kneed girl whose auburn hair was the most interesting thing about her. The girl in the mirror looked slightly lost and overwhelmed, but more than either of those, she looked determined. She had nice gray eyes. Thoughtful eyes. And she most definitely didn't look *boyish* anymore.

As for the dress . . . well, only a woman centered in her own power would wear such a thing. That was precisely the image she wanted to project. Besides, it wasn't a real wedding. Who cared it if it was a vehement cardinal red?

Not that it mattered, but would *Roar* care?

Images spun through her mind: scattered rose petals, a toppled chair. That earnest look over his shoulder. *I would've treated you right.*

What would it be like to be in a true relationship with him? High passion and laughter, or chivalry and tenderness? She shivered, sending her reflection a glare. *It would be like nothing, Tempest, and that's an idiotic thing to waste time wondering.* He'd be gone as soon as he could. And he resented her. *And* his heart was still Liv's.

"Are you cold, dear?" Aunt Lerra asked, and had the maidservant build up the fire.

Daisy, whose cheeks were pink in the stuffy room, sent her a questioning look. "Are you all right, Temp?"

"I'm fine," she chirped. She *would* be fine once she got the ceremony behind her. She understood the need for a political gesture. A formal appearance before the powerful families. But she had an uneasy feeling that Lund might have something up his sleeve. Maybe instead of giving a toast, he'd roast her or find some other way to minimize her.

After the ceremony and dinner tonight at the fortress, Lerra had coordinated an evening parade through the city. *A quick and comfortable carriage ride. You'll both look resplendent, and I insist on showing you off.* Tempest was much more excited about *that* than about trying to convince strangers she wasn't the little girl they remembered anymore.

Cal arrived as the fitting was ending. She leaned against Daisy's chair with the air of a bored lioness and waited until the chattering trio of Lerra, the dressmaker, and the dressmaker's apprentice left before she spoke. "Your aunt is an adorable featherbrain," she said, "but your uncle's a cad. A more dangerous version of Aldred. He's been planning for your return, Temp. It looks like he—"

"Hold on a sec." Tempest pulled the shirt over her head, tucking it into her pants, then she dropped on the edge of the fitting platform to lace up her boots. "Is it safe to talk here?" Lund would surely have Auds planted around the fortress, digging for dirt.

Cal nodded. "Of course. I had the whole corridor cleared out. Hyde's standing guard at the end."

Tempest nodded; she'd only wanted to be sure. "Daisy, can you take notes?"

Daisy was already searching for paper and pen in the secretary's desk. They knew her. They knew the way she worked. "Go ahead, Cal," Daisy said, sitting down.

"It seems Lund was anticipating your return," Cal continued, "or if not yours, then Sable's. Point is, he's been preparing to have his seat challenged."

No surprise there. "How?"

Cal glanced at the door. "Bribery, mainly," she said, lowering her voice in spite of the precautions. "He's been using the heavy taxes he's levied on the citizenry to pay off the seven families. He's buying their loyalty. Mattock thinks he has a few in his back pocket. Three, maybe four. As you know, each of the families has a small corps of soldiers for personal defense. Fifty trained fighters on average. Add them up and you've got a problem."

Tempest's heart had begun to pound like a drum. "Because?"

"Because Sable wiped out the standing army when he went after the Still Blue. He took most of the soldiers and he took the best. Left you with a meager force just over two hundred strong. And I say *strong* loosely. For the most part, what you've got are aging fighters, or fighters who are young and inexperienced. You might be able to raise another hundred in auxiliaries, if you needed to, but it's been harder going than usual. People are still trying to rebuild their lives after the Burning Year—that's what they're calling the year of Aether storms here—and Lund's tax policy isn't helping."

Tempest took a moment to absorb that. "So my brother depleted our forces and my uncle's paying for a private army."

"Correct."

"The two hundred you say are mine, are they actually mine?"

"Good question. Mattock seems to think so. The chain is yours by right of blood—that's the traditional way and we military types like tradition, so in theory they *should* be loyal to you. Also, it's no secret Lund is buying the big families. Even within the Horn army, he plays favorites and dispenses justice arbitrarily. He blurs lines and that's not good for a commander. It creates resentment and uncertainty in the ranks. I don't think he's well-liked."

"But?"

Cal crossed her arms. "But he's the known quantity in this situation. He's greedy and backhanded, but he's not a tyrant. He's the devil they know. You're the devil they don't know. And you've got added challenges to overcome he doesn't."

"Such as?"

Cal and Daisy exchanged one of their looks.

"I think I already know what you're going to say, Cal. But I want it on paper. I want to make sure I'm seeing it all clearly. I can plan better if I'm organized."

Cal sighed. "You're female. You're young and you're pretty and none of that should matter, but it does. Also, they remember a child. A lot of people will still see you that way."

"What else?"

"You have no experience with command they'll value."

"And?"

"Roar. Apparently, the servants who cleaned your chamber this morning are convinced it's . . . shall we say a *love match*. The rumors are flying. By the end of the day, there won't be a person in this city who will doubt that you two are in a legitimate union." Her eyes narrowed. "You didn't really . . . ?"

"We staged it."

Cal looked up at the ceiling. "Praise heaven," she said, but Daisy looked disappointed. "Smart idea."

"It was Roar's."

Cal grimaced. "I like it less now. So, the good news is you two are very much in love," she went on, "but there's some fallout to that. There are a few rumblings that he seduced you so he could claim the chain for himself. Or that he wants to turn you into a puppet ruler and rule through you. People around here just saw that happen with Lund and Lerra and, let me tell you, they *do not* want to see that again. Worse than a greedy Lund is a greedy unknown from the Tides."

"Makes sense. Anything else?"

Daisy cringed. "Please say no."

Cal smiled at her. "Yes. One more." She turned back to Tempest. "Nightrose. Mattock and a few other people I talked to expect that Banyan and Scar will still come for you. And I agree. We may be inside these walls, but that business isn't over yet."

"You think they'd lay siege on Rim to get to me?"

"I don't know. It's possible. Yes."

Tempest frowned. "That means I'm a liability to this place." Lund's machinations were significant problems. But so was this. Except she'd brought this trouble with her. "By being here, I'm endangering my people."

"No. And you're not a *liability*, Tempest," Daisy said. "You're valuable to two tribes."

That was a kinder way to see it. And not totally wrong, she had to admit. Tempest looked from Cal to Daisy, her heart swelling with love and gratitude. "Thank you. Both of you. Cal, this was great work."

Cal shrugged, her eyes smiling. "We're fortunate Mattock's with us."

Tempest was starting to see that. "Any other counsel?"

"No," Cal said. "But I should probably mention I'm not letting you out of my sight."

"I'm afraid you'll have to in a little while," Tempest said, standing. There was one person whose advice she needed, and their conversation had to be conducted in private. "Come on. I have to find Perry."

It was going to hurt to ask for his confidence, but she had no choice.

She was simply up against too much.

21

ROAR

Roar needed to move.

He needed to give his mind space to consider the past day. Or better yet *not* consider it.

Things were moving too quickly these days. He felt like he was blurring past huge milestones too fast to even see them. Even more unsettling, he couldn't shake the feeling he was rushing headlong into even bigger life turns.

He left the fortress to explore the city and the surrounding farmlands. There'd be a certain amount of danger in going out alone like this, but when they'd arrived late last night, the focus had been on Tempest. He figured he had a few days before anyone knew who he was.

Rim was the largest city he'd ever been to, and he relaxed as he meandered through avenues, passing shops and markets. The streets were bustling, and there was a cheerfulness in the air; the name "Tempest of the Horns" hummed in his ears. Everyone wanted to know what she'd be like, if she'd be like Sable, if she was smart and pretty, and whether she'd depose Lund—and who was the fellow she married? Had she really chosen a *Tider?*

No, he'd thought wryly. *She hadn't chosen him at all.*

On the south side of the city lay neighborhoods with stores selling finer goods than any he'd ever seen. He saw antiques from before the Unity hundreds of years earlier, modern goods manufactured without the electrical power that only Dweller Pods dared to use nowadays, as it seemed to draw the Aether. There were stores for textiles. Pottery, furniture, clothing. Weapons. Gourmet foods of all kinds. None seemed particularly busy, though. The city appeared to be in something of a slump.

He ducked into a bookstore on a whim, remembering the stack in Tempest's room in Resolute. He hadn't bothered to see what sorts of books they were, but he was certain she read widely. He'd only known her for a little over a week, but she was no stranger anymore. He walked through the bookshelves, surprised by all the small things he knew about her now: She wound her hair around her finger when she was deep in thought; she could recite long passages verbatim from the books she'd read; she despised onions and apples, but apparently the latter had once been her favorite; she had a particular smile for Daisy and Cal, and quite another for him and Perry.

She could make him *laugh*.

"That's a classic, sir."

Roar blinked out of his thoughts and turned to the voice, a little chagrined. How long had he been smiling at the shelf of books in front of him? When had he picked up the volume in his hand?

"I don't recognize you from around here." The woman behind the counter was smiling at him tentatively. She had a round, pleasant face and wore thick glasses. "Are you by chance . . . ?"

He shrugged, not sure why he felt sheepish. "I think so?"

Her smile broadened. "Well, welcome to Rim, if so. The entire city's going inside out about it all. I haven't seen people in such good spirits in a very long time."

"Oh," he said, eloquently.

"*Meditations*, is it?" She motioned to the book in his hand. "An excellent choice for anyone who wants to guide their life by ethical principles and clear thought."

"Not right for me, then." He wasn't sure why he said it. Often, joking with strangers was disappointing, but the woman chuckled.

"Young man," she said, a twinkle flashing behind her lenses, "I *sincerely* doubt that."

Roar smiled. Though he was still there, he was already looking forward to coming back. He looked at the book in his hand. *Meditations* by Marcus Aurelius. During his months in Delphi with Aria, he had leafed through a copy. He'd bring money next time he came by—he'd wrangle some up somehow—and buy it as a wedding gift to Tempest. He set it back on the shelf.

"No, no. Take it, please. Go on. Consider it a wedding gift." She opened a hand in the direction of the window. "From your new city to the two of you."

He couldn't refuse now, could he? Roar thanked her, and promised he'd be back.

For a while after, he roamed the streets in a glow of optimism, his faith in all of humanity boosted by her kindness. But at some point, his instincts prickled with warning. His good mood disappeared as he became aware that someone was following him.

Roar kept on walking casually as he considered his situation. He had returned the dagger to the guard that morning and planned to find himself a weapon as soon as possible. Judging by the light, purposeful footfall that was gaining on him, he hadn't done that soon enough.

Briefly, he entertained the idea of running it out. He was faster than most, but he didn't know his way around yet and might wind up in a dead end. And though his wound was healing, he didn't think he could sustain an all-out sprint for very long.

That left one option.

As soon as he saw a chance, he ducked into the next alley and turned, spreading his arms wide. "I'm unarmed. I have no weapon." He was, in fact, holding a *book* in his hands. Hardly threatening, though some might argue it *was* a weapon. Knowledge and all that.

A slender figure in a brown cloak stopped at the top of the alley. "So I've noticed," he replied coolly, settling into an easy fighter's stance. He had a young man's voice, surprisingly deep and sonorous. Like Perry's, but crisper. Between the triangle of shadow thrown by the building and the hood, his face was totally concealed in a dark void.

Roar lowered his arms. "Armed or not, I'll still destroy you if you come for me."

"I'm not here to kill you. I'm here to warn you. Tempest of the Horns is in danger, as are you."

"Do you think that's news to me?"

"No. But are you aware your murders are being planned at this very moment?" The young man took a step closer. "Are you aware that those plans will be put into action *tonight?*"

Roar's pulse was suddenly charging. "Tell me what you know *now.*"

The man tensed, an infinitesimal shift of light and shadow along his cloak. He was not unafraid. "Just be ready for anything. That's all I can tell you without risking my family's safety."

My family. Was he a member of one of the five dynasties in Rim? Before Roar could ask, the stranger whirled and plunged into the crowded road, his brown cloak disappearing into the fray.

22

TEMPEST

As Tempest knocked on Peregrine's door, a voice began to scream inside her:

Skies, what are you doing! He murdered your brother! You almost killed his best friend!

He opened the door and frowned down at her, just as perplexed by her visit as she was.

"Hello, Peregrine," she said, in a voice that sounded much too calm to be hers. "Can I come in? I was hoping to ask you a few questions."

He stepped aside to let her pass, though he didn't look thrilled about it.

His chamber was much smaller than hers, with a bed and fireplace. Cozy. Perry had readied himself for the wedding festivities. The smell of sandalwood soap wafted off him. He had shaved and his ropy hair was pulled back. Roar normally wore black, but apparently Aunt Lerra had wanted to try a similar look on Peregrine. Gone were his patched leather pants and tired shirt, replaced by finer versions in deep midnight blue. Against his green eyes and his streaky locks, the effect was unsettling. The pulled-together look made him seem even more fierce and untamed, like a living version of a painting she'd once seen in a book. *Starry Night*, it was called.

"I'm as surprised as you are that I'm here," she said. There was a scorched red scent in his temper. She imagined it wouldn't be very different from her own.

"Must be important." Perry propped an elbow on the mantle and watched her with preternatural calm. "If this is about Roar—"

"It's not—not directly. What I want to know is . . ." She fiddled with the hem of her sleeve, trying to locate the courage that had gotten her there. "What I'm trying to figure out is . . ." *Come on, Tempest.* She looked up. "How do I do this? How do I lead people who don't know me? How do I prove I deserve their trust? How did you bring the Tides to order? How did you keep them together through transition and turmoil? I need to know all of that, please. In specifics, and in a hurry. Now would be great."

"Aren't you getting married again in less than an hour?" he asked.

"Yes. Fine—just tell me generally, then. And when you answer, try to imagine that you're not, you know, seven feet of pure intimidation."

"Seven feet? Is that what it seems like from down there?"

He was joking with her. A good sign. She released a shaky breath. "From these lower altitudes, yes."

"It's not always the advantage you'd expect. A lot of people are put off by the way I look. Or by what they've heard about me. They assume I'm going to make demands. Impose my will."

"I'd take that over people assuming I'm a sweet girl with fluff for a brain any day."

He shrugged. "That's fair. But it's their problem if they underestimate you."

"That's not true, though. It's *my* problem. If they write me off right away, I won't even get a chance to show them who I am or what I can do. How do I prove I'm worthy?"

"By being worthy. People will judge you by your deeds and by the people who are loyal to you." He tipped his chin toward the door. "You've done well there." Tempest looked down at her boots, unexpectedly moved to learn he respected Cal and Daisy. "I was never a good leader," he continued, "but I managed. Partly on luck and instinct, but mostly because I relied on people who had the strengths I lacked. You don't have to do this alone. And you asked for specifics, but I can't give you any without knowing the specifics of your situation."

Here it was. A crossroads. Up till now, his advice had been helpful but broad. To really get his insight, she was going to have to decide: Was *he* going to be one of the people she trusted?

Not that long ago, they were screaming murder at each other. Flinging threats at the top of their lungs. She'd never yelled at anyone like that before. But to reclaim the Horns, she was going to have to push beyond her comfort. She reminded herself that he wanted the Tides back—so he *did* have a stake in seeing her succeed, didn't he?

She cleared her throat. "Specifically, my uncle is scheming to discredit my claim to power probably as we speak."

He dipped his chin. "No question about it. The smartest thing Lund can do is act quickly. People want you here and Lund can't let that sentiment take root. He'll come for you and Roar—that's a given. If he hasn't already, he'll move to secure control of your military, your armory, and your treasury. Your winter stores. He'll grab everything."

Her heart lurched; she let out a bark of laugher. "Is that all?" But he was obviously right. Lund had already shown foresight and deception by bribing the families.

"What's the worst he could do?" Perry's broad shoulders lifted. "Whatever the answer to that is, that's what you have to anticipate."

Cold fear shot down her spine. "*Roar.* He went into the city alone today."

Perry stared at her. "Roar can take care of himself."

"You're worried, though."

"As are you."

For a second, they stood in that space known only to Scires, understanding the shape of each other's fears. "I'll send people for him," she said.

He shook his head. "Better to not look panicked." The fire snapped, drawing his gaze. "I'll find him."

"Wait, before you go—" She knew he wanted to leave immediately, but she wasn't done yet. She had the attention of Peregrine of the Tides. He claimed he wasn't a good leader, but she'd seen the way he spoke to the brothers. To Soren and Rune and Roar. She'd seen the way they looked to him when they needed assurance or direction. "My uncle's been bribing the territory's powerful families," she confided. "Cal thinks he's raised a private militia."

Perry thought for a moment. The sound of music drifted in from the corridor, a joyful melody played by string instruments. "He won't use them unless he has to," he said. "It would mean pitting friends and neighbors against each other. It would damage the very prize he wants and create enemies he'd rather not have. He'll try other means first."

"Other means." The sound of that made her dizzy. "I have to tell Cal."

"*You* have to be at the ceremony. You're the one everyone's here to see. I'll talk to Cal and we'll come up with something. We'll do all we can."

"Thank you," she said, her voice wobbling. "I can't tell you how much that would mean to me."

A smile kindled in his jade eyes. "You don't have to. Before you go—" he went to his satchel, pulling something from its depths, "I think this belongs to you." He held out a thick chain loaded with gemstones that winked like colorful stars in the twilit room.

Tempest stared at it, feeling a swell of emotions that made her dizzy. Her brother had worn that chain. Perry had killed him and taken it. But that was *their* story and this wasn't.

"Thank you for offering it to me," she said. "But that's not mine. I'm going to do this my own way."

~ 23 ~

ROAR

The first guests were already arriving for the ceremony when Roar got back to the fortress. He pulled his hood up as he made his way through the corridors. Twice in the past hour, people had recognized him. He had no idea how that was possible; he hadn't even been there a full day.

He made for Perry's chamber. If there was truly a plan to kill him and Tempest tonight, he needed help defending against it. From the moment he realized he was being pursued, a kind of wild power had spilled through his limbs. He felt weightless, all his senses needle-sharp.

He found Cal outside Perry's door.

"Tempest is speaking with him," she said, her arms crossed forbiddingly.

"Great. She should hear this, too."

"You're misunderstanding. They're meeting in private."

"*In private?*" He laughed, a white-hot anger igniting in him. "That's my best friend in there, Calista. And my wife."

"Wife." She scoffed. "Aren't you ashamed to use that term only when it suits you?"

"We are *married* only because it suits us. Step aside, Cal. I have urgent information that I need to share with both of them."

She stared at him. "And you can do that as soon as they're done. *Goodbye*."

"You're being a fool right now. Do you know that?" He shook his head and strode away.

"Well, you're *always* an idiot," she muttered.

"I can still hear you, Cal," he called over his shoulder.

"Can you? In that case—" She proceeded to tell him exactly what she thought of him—*bitter, selfish, opportunistic*—continuing long after he'd turned the corner. His feelings for her weren't much sunnier—she guarded Tempest like a rabid, snarling hound—but he grudgingly respected her loyalty, and Daisy's. Such devotion was rare.

Cal had denied him entry, but he was not giving up.

He turned another corner and strode to the end of the hall, then ducked into a vacant chamber, tossing his cloak and the book on a chair. His heart began to beat painfully as he opened the balcony doors and stepped out into the dusky light. A storm was coming in, big dark thunderheads blocking out the Aether in the distance.

This wasn't the room where Liv had been murdered, but the vista was similar—endless sky and sharp mountains ahead, the Snake River far below, undulating and silky black—and he had a surprising moment's wobble as he hopped onto the stone balustrade. It passed quickly, though, his strong sense of hearing linked with his strong sense of balance.

He crept out onto the ledge that ran from balcony to balcony, circling the fortress's girth. The stone lip wasn't more than a few inches wide, and stretches were covered in pigeon droppings or in slippery green mold, but he was undeterred. He made his way along, sidestepping in the direction of Perry's chamber, gripping the creases between huge stone blocks with his fingers so he wouldn't take a dive into the writhing black water below as he had a little over a year ago.

Soon enough, he realized this wasn't his best-ever idea. Afternoon gusts were kicking at his back and whipping his hair into his eyes—and Perry's room wasn't exactly close. A smarter course of action would've been to get ready for the wedding he was expected to attend, as the groom, in less than an hour and talk to Perry later.

He didn't for a second consider turning back, though. In his mind it was simple: He was either going to get to that chamber, or he was going to die trying.

To pass the time—it was going to be awhile—he began to sing a duet his parents had been fond of. The theme was love, and the lyrics were metaphors that likened it to various forms of devastation: a plague, a fire, a snakebite. An amputated limb.

An abominable song, really. A nightmare in lyrics.

He found himself smirking as he sang, his beautiful mother's unhappy face alternating in his memory with his father's distracted, brooding stare. Gradually, as he sidestepped and sang, he became aware that he was furious. The closer he edged to Perry's chamber, the greater the pressure was in his chest. When he felt like someone was standing on him, he pressed flat against the fortress, his breath ragged.

"What?" he said. "*What?*"

And then it dawned on him that what he was feeling was jealousy.

No . . . *jealousy?* He tested the word out in his mind, comparing it to the pressure on his chest, which now felt like a fist, punching savagely.

Yep. That was it. Jealousy. The moment Cal had told him that Perry and Tempest were talking *in private,* it had started.

He pressed his face against the cool stone until it hurt.

"Yes," he whispered. "*Yes,*" he said again, louder, and for a few seconds, the world blurred under the power of his relief. Then a laugh shook out of the tension in his chest, like an animal startling out of the brush, and raced up his throat. He let it go.

He clung to the fortress and laughed like a maniac, his calves cramping, his forearms throbbing, his fingers shaking. Death was only a free fall away—one *twitch* away—but it hadn't felt so far away in ages. He was *burning* with life. Levitating with it.

It had been so long since he'd *burned* this way.

The feeling itself was ludicrous. He trusted Perry with his life—and he realized he trusted Tempest, too, surprisingly. What had cropped up in front of Cal just now was illogical, some primitive reflex peering out of his murky subconscious—was there any surprise with parents who'd flung their affairs in each other's faces?

No. There wasn't a shred of legitimate suspicion in him.

The critical thing was that he had to *care* to feel jealousy. He had to *want* something—or someone—to feel possessive. The fact that he felt vulnerable meant it *mattered*.

He *cared*. He *wanted*. It *mattered*.

She did.

He closed his eyes and stood, hanging on the edge of everything and feeling the vastness all around him. All the space above and below and behind him—and now inside him, too.

I'm alive again, he thought. *I'm alive.*

24

TEMPEST

Tempest left Perry and rushed back to get ready for the party. She was late, *incredibly* late. It wouldn't look good if she kept people waiting for long, and after all her aunt had done, she didn't want to disappoint her.

She flew into her chamber, frazzled and worried, and froze as a dozen women swung to look at her and broke into applause.

"She's here, she's here!" Lerra cried raising a glass of champagne and rushing over to her.

"I am, I am," Tempest said, her mouth twitching into something she hoped resembled a smile.

Lerra pressed a flute into her hand and introduced her to the smiling strangers. Tempest did her best to remember their names and to play the giddy bride, but her head was spinning. This was her life now: from discussing military coups to making small talk in minutes. Thankfully, Daisy saved her before long, sweeping her away from the women and into a steaming tub.

"Are you alright, Temp?" she whispered, as the merriment continued in the room. Tempest looked at her and shivered. "Oh, dear. You're not. All right. Deep breath, then talk quickly."

In between washing her hair and a quick overall scrub, Tempest filled her in on the conversation she'd just had with Perry.

Daisy held out a robe for her as she stepped out. "So Lund is plotting something, maybe as soon as tonight, and no one's seen Roar?"

'Yes." Tempest tied the belt, surprised by the shakiness in her hands. "But Roar's probably back by now, right?"

"Easy, Temp. I'm sure he is." Daisy gently moved her hands aside and tied the belt for her. "It's probably just superstition keeping him away. Bad luck for the groom to see the bride before the wedding."

"This is our second wedding."

"Double bad luck."

"I saw him this morning."

"He'll turn up." Daisy turned her by the shoulders and gave her a gentle push. "Get moving. There's an army waiting for you out there."

That was precisely her fear: an army, ready to challenge her.

Tempest sat in front of the fire as a team moved around her. Her nails were buffed to a shine. Her hair was perfumed and hot-ironed into waves. Her face was dusted with light powder, and rouge was applied to her cheekbones. She had a habit of sucking on her lower lip, so a stain "that won't budge" was dabbed over them.

"Are you sure that color won't budge?" asked one of the women. They were everywhere. Perched on her bed, sitting in the chairs, admiring the red gown that awaited her on the dress form. The seamstress had spent the past hours making alterations. "It *is* her wedding night."

This produced a round of laughter and got a blush from Tempest.

She forced herself to smile and joke, but she couldn't get her mind off Roar's whereabouts or the problems that Lund would surely lob at her. On top of all that, being surrounded by strangers, as kind and cheerful and well-meaning as they all were, was having an odd effect on her.

She felt *lonely*. None of these women knew her, and though she was genuinely grateful for Lerra's efforts, she ached for a truer connection based in history and loyalty and love. That got her thinking about Sable. In spite of everything, she missed him. And she loathed him. It was all so complicated, so messy. Shouldn't loving and being loved be simple?

Finally, as the seamstress Oleandra sewed her into the red gown, Daisy took pity on her.

She pressed a fresh glass of champagne into Tempest's hand and winked. "I just remembered I have to take care of something important. Any message for your groom if I should *happen* to see him?"

"Tell him I'm never letting him out of my sight again," Tempest replied, and she half-meant it—she hated this agonizing worry—but the women only saw a bride smitten beyond repair.

Aunt Lerra clapped. "She can't bear being parted from him for even a few hours!"

"Well, have you seen him?" Oleandra murmured through the pins pressed between her lips.

"I'd lock him up if he were mine," said one of the women on the balcony.

"Too much champagne for this group," Aunt Lerra said cheerfully. "Tempest, are you sure you're well, dear? You're sewn so tightly into the dress. What about dancing, Oleandra? Will that be a problem? Perhaps let it out some?"

"I do love dancing," Tempest said, running a hand over her encased ribs. The dress couldn't have possibly hugged her any tighter. "I also really enjoy breathing."

Lerra beamed. "Does Roar love dancing also?"

"Very much," she replied, and wondered if that was true. A dozen pairs of eyes stared at her expectantly, waiting for her to say more. "Well, he's quite coordinated." That *was* true, and after a few ribald jokes, the women were asking for more.

"Tell us all about him, dear."

"Yes! Tell us everything! We never had a chance to meet him the last time he was here."

A few awkward glances flew around the chamber. Tempest rifled around for something to say. Real wedding or fake, she didn't want Olivia's memory hanging over her wedding. Any other night, fine. Just not tonight.

"Um, he's a good hunter," she offered brightly, steering them back on track. "And he's musical." She'd heard the brothers mention he played guitar. "And he has a beautiful voice." That she knew firsthand.

"Will he sing to you tonight, darling?" asked a close friend of Tempest's aunt.

"I don't know. I hope."

At some point, they began peppering her with questions. She made up answers, no idea if she was even close to right. *Yes, he wants children. No, he doesn't have siblings. Favorite food? Strawberries. Best quality? His passion. Best feature? Impossible to choose just one.*

This last answer was roundly agreed to by all.

"And what of his Naming Marking?" asked Ivy, a pretty woman with a black braid that fell to her waist. "Does he have one?"

The image of that gorgeous panther that wove down his muscular arm came to mind. "Yes." She took a gulp of champagne. Life had been rather boring not so long ago. Now this. "Yes, he has a fantastic one, actually. It runs all the way down his left arm."

"Like *yours?*" said a woman with a tiny squeal. "They were made for each other!"

Tempest looked at her reflection in the standing mirror. Only a small percentage of people were Auds, Scires, or Seers, and it was customary, even compulsory, for them to have an inked pattern around their right bicep specific to their Sense. A person with a Sense who *wasn't* Marked could be ostracized by society for hiding their gift—or worse. She'd heard that some had even been killed for not abiding by this unwritten law. But Naming Markings weren't nearly as fixed a custom; most Sensed had them, but some didn't and that was fine. They could be inked anywhere on the body and drew inspiration, obviously, from the person's name.

In the sleeveless dress, *her* Naming Marking—a pattern of storm clouds that blended into waves at the bottom—was plain to see, beginning at her shoulder and tumbling down. Though hers was drawn in more delicate lines, she couldn't deny the similarity. She wondered what Roar would think when he saw it, then wondered for the hundredth time if he'd made it back safely.

Oleandra was finishing the last adjustment when the room swayed a little, and she realized she'd overdone it on the champagne. She seldom drank more than a glass of anything, but for the past hour, a fresh glass had appeared in her hand before she could even finish the previous one. Now, the bubbles were fizzing right up to her head. She felt buoyant, giddy, but she never forgot the tense undercurrents; she might be bobbing happily, but she was still in a sea of troubles.

Just let him he safe, she prayed. She could bear anything, anything at all, as long as he wasn't hurt because of her.

Never, she thought. *Never again.*

25

ROAR

Roar was still edging toward Perry's room when he heard Lund's voice.

He climbed over the balustrade, dropped onto a balcony, and crept toward the glass doors. A sliver of light poured through the drawn curtains, out to the darkness where he crouched.

Leaning close to the glass, he peered inside.

Lund stood behind a desk, swirling a glass of spirits in one hand. He was dressed for the ceremony: in an ostentatious wine-colored suit covered in gold embroidery.

A soldier, who appeared to have just entered, stood inside the chamber door.

"You look like you're going to give me a report I won't like, Sylvan," Lund said. Though the doors were shut, his voice came to Roar as clear as sunlight through water. "Out with it."

"It's concerning Roar of the Tides, sir," Sylvan said. "He went into the city earlier. I had a man in plain clothes follow him, as you requested. But he lost him almost right away."

Roar's heart was drumming hard. Had Lund sent someone to beat him? To *kill* him?

Lund stopped swirling his glass. "Are you telling me one of our men couldn't follow a stranger through our own city?"

"That's correct, sir. Because he was attacked, sir. Someone must have known we'd be following him—or at least suspected it. Our man took a pummeling, but he made it back. He didn't see his assailant and reported only that he wore a dark brown cloak."

Lund stared at his glass angrily, then he tipped it back and drained the amber liquid. "Wonderful," he said sarcastically. "A brown cloak. I'm sure he'll be easy to find. It was probably the Valders, those nostalgic fools." He looked up sharply. "Or Peregrine—where was he today?"

"He was here, sir. It wasn't him. He never left the fortress."

Lund swore. He moved to a table and popped a grape into his mouth, chewing angrily. "Is Roar back?" He poured another generous glass of spirits.

"Yes." The soldier watched him with worried eyes. "The gate guards reported that he returned a little under an hour ago. Perhaps we could try again, sir?"

Lund lifted the glass to his lips. "No—forget him. He's nothing without her. Tempest is the priority tonight." He took the drink back in one tilt and set the glass down with a crack. "Is the wine prepared?"

"Yes, sir," Sylvan continued. "It will be at their table, as you requested. We'll do it quietly. Mattock has no idea. He's preoccupied with his part of the plan."

"Good." Lund's smile came and went like a snarl. "She's a strong Scire. Be prepared to change plans if she scents the poison."

"Yes, sir. We'll be ready and awaiting your signal."

"Peregrine is to be kept alive. There's value in him."

"Of course, sir. Our best men are ready. Mattock chose them personally. We won't fail."

"Mattock won't like it, but it would be better if the wine works," Lund said. "Neater. But if blood has to spill, so be it. I don't care how it happens, so long as it gets done tonight."

Roar eased back into the darkness and stood. Cool rage filled him. Poison *and* an attack? He shook his head. "You want blood to spill tonight, you bastard?" he whispered. "No problem."

"Relax, Roar," Perry said quietly. "You're making me jumpy."

"This may surprise you, Peregrine, but I'm not capable of *relaxing* right now."

"Actually, neither can I."

They were seated at the head table in the main courtyard, which had been transformed for the party. Floral arrangements and lanterns sat on every table. Doors all around were thrown wide open to the fortress's glowing inner corridors and chambers. Banners streamed down from the second story. Musicians played in a corner and servants circled with trays of food and wine. Lerra really had gone overboard. And she'd done it all in *under a day*.

His gaze roamed to the stunning crystal decanter inches away from his hand. It wasn't filled with poisoned wine anymore—Perry had seen to that—but the sight still made his blood boil.

Perry's green eyes darted over. "The good news is you already married her. She can't turn back now."

Roar dredged up a smile. "True."

This exchange was for the benefit of the partygoers who were watching them closely and, if they were Auds, probably eavesdropping. He had to appear eager to see his bride, not worried that her life was in danger.

He glanced at the only closed doors in the courtyard. Where was she?

Earlier, he'd had a short window to exchange information with Perry. The situation was grim. Poison. A secret militia ready to act and, they deduced, probably dressed as guests. Perhaps also Horn soldiers who'd been bribed to do Lund's bidding. Mattock behind the treachery as well. The odds were stacked against them.

Not for the first time, Roar wondered why they were still going through with this. Why not avoid this ceremony altogether? Remove Tempest to someplace safe? But the answer was in all the eyes that were fixed on him.

This was pageantry. A presentation. He'd never felt so *seen* in all his life. If they hadn't shown, he could only imagine the message it would send, the gossip it would generate. It would smack of cowardice. Flightiness.

Tempest's first impression in Rim couldn't be a canceled event.

"Was it like this for you, Per?" he said tightly. "All the blatant staring? They don't even try to play it off."

"Yes." A bowl of olives sat on the table. Perry popped another one into his mouth. "Welcome to politics."

Roar sighed and sat back. He sifted through the evening's sounds—the string quartet, the babble of fountains, the chattering guests, and the commotion in the kitchens—and picked out spirited discussions about him and Tempest. Some harmless, even amusing. Others not.

"It's not even a full day they're here," said a nasally male voice. "Shouldn't we give them a chance? I hear they're a charming pair, and the city loves them. Every tavern was full last night."

"We don't need charming. We need capable."

"They think I'm an imbecile," Roar muttered.

Perry smiled. "Observant of them."

Roar looked at the brother he'd chosen. "I think I understand what's happening. This is a nightmare. I have become you in it, the surly young leader who's in way over his head, and you have become me, the witty and loyal friend everyone secretly prefers. If you're really going to be me, though, you need to work on your humor."

"You're not that funny."

"Hah. Better already." He listened to the courtyard again, hearing the gripes about Tempest.

"Bloodline or not, she's no Horn."

"How can she be? She hasn't been here in ages."

He was even less worthy. Their marriage was questioned. Rumors abounded. Sable's marriage to Olivia had been cursed; would his younger sister's be as well?

When Lund arrived, a silence fell over the courtyard so abruptly that the musicians faltered their tune before picking it up again.

Lund was wearing a Blood Lord chain, the links even gaudier than Sable's, but he was also wearing a headpiece that was technically a hat but, symbolically and visually, a crown. The black velvet cap blended into his hair, leaving only a lower headband of gilt studded with rubies visible. It was somehow both subtle and blatant.

He had a lot of supporters, Roar noticed. People swamped him. They showered him with flatteries and pumped his hand. He remained the center of attention until the great doors to the main hall opened and Tempest and Lerra stepped out, arm in arm.

Seeing Tempest, Roar lost his place in the world. Forgot everything. Poison. Bribed soldiers. Even his ears shut off, leaving him in rare silence. He couldn't reconcile Tempest with the goddess in the red dress. Her hair cascaded over one shoulder in shining curls. Down the other shoulder, a Marking wove down her skin in spellbinding tumbles. And that dress. It was the devil's creation. The shape of her in it was hypnotic, like she'd been hewn by wind. Every bit of her seemed somehow *more*, and yet, she had always been this Tempest.

As he stared at her, he began to see the difference in his perception was as much within himself as anything. The feeling he'd had while hanging on the edge of the fortress was still with him, sunken deep now, like rain into desert. He felt supple and keen. Dangerous.

He felt his name, through and through.

Tempest stopped and looked around the courtyard. She saw him and smiled, and he felt a stab to his heart not of pain but the opposite. *Can this really be happening?* The question rumbled through the deepest part of his mind.

Yes, came the answer. It *could* be. It *was*.

He was falling for her.

Perry jabbed him in the ribs, jarring him out of his reverie. "*Move*, you fool," he said. "She's waiting for you."

He went to her and bent to her ear, and whispered, "You are a perfect terror in that dress."

She laughed, her cold fingers gripping tight to his. "Is that a good thing?"

"Not for me." Her springtime scent enveloped him, making his pulse hammer. Her eyes were the soft gray that bordered clouds. He swallowed and reminded himself they had work to do tonight. They had to sell the story of their marriage and show her for all she was: capable, intelligent, dedicated. Most importantly, they had to survive the night. "You heard?"

"The wine?" she whispered and nodded.

That sounded incomplete. Lund's plan encompassed a lot more than wine. But maybe Cal hadn't had time to share the full extent of it. Or maybe Cal hadn't wanted to alarm her. Or maybe it was something else entirely. This was all unfolding minute by minute, and in layers of spectacle and subterfuge. Regardless, there was no time to get into it now.

He became aware of two things then: All eyes were on them, and he was holding her hands. And just like that, he heard her thoughts.

Incredible. He actually takes my breath away.

Some instinct for self-preservation kicked in—this wasn't helping him focus—so he let go of her abruptly and took a step back. Then he realized how that must have looked to the hundreds of staring eyes around them—not good—so he stepped in again and kissed her.

26

TEMPEST

Tempest stopped in her tracks the instant she saw Roar, the relief like a breath of air after a long, long dive. She dragged in another gulp and exhaled, the tension loosening in her shoulders.

"He's here," she said, still breathless.

"Of course he is," Lerra said, smiling.

Her aunt was oblivious to political schemes, but she wasn't. *He's safe,* she reassured herself again. *And he is unfairly, staggeringly gorgeous.*

How did he do that? She'd had *a team* working on her for the past hour, and there he was in a black shirt and pants, his hair in a tousled knot, looking effortlessly and utterly dashing.

He strode over to her, his eyes hooded and intent. Taking her hands, he bent to her ear. "You are a perfect terror in that dress."

His warm breath on her neck sent gooseflesh prickling over her arms. Her gaze raced down his lean build, so expertly showcased in the garments her aunt had arranged. "Is that a good thing?"

"Not for me."

That sounded suspiciously like flirting, but it couldn't be. Surely, she was missing something. Just last night, after all, the kindest thing he'd said to her was, *I don't hate you.*

He shifted back slightly. Serious brown eyes rimmed with thick lashes filled her vision. "You heard?"

Her mind lurched back to her quick exchange with Daisy just before she'd stepped out there. *It's bad, Temp*, Daisy had whispered, her eyes scared and shifting everywhere. Servants had been around, Lerra had been right there. *Do* not *drink the wine.*

"The wine?" she whispered to Roar and nodded. And for a split second, under his gaze and in his hands, the depthless loneliness inside her vanished. A feeling passed through her like she'd swallowed the sun and all her fears disappeared in pure blazing light.

Incredible, she thought. *He actually takes my breath away.*

Roar dropped her hands and stepped back. A tiny frown creased his brow, then he stepped in again and surprised her with a chaste kiss, a soft brush of his lips.

As he was leaning away, Tempest came up on her toes and kissed him again, not about to let the opportunity go so quickly. Because of his height and because her heeled shoes made balancing a challenge, she looped her arms around his neck. His hands came to her lower back, big and warm and firm. And before she knew what was happening, their tongues were sweeping in wild-hearted strokes, deftly and together, with a kind of thrilled abandon, liked they'd joined hands and were making a mad dash through a sudden downpour. It felt endless and instantaneous, time wrapping around them like a bubble, but it probably only lasted a second.

Tempest was so stunned when they parted, she wobbled. Roar caught her elbow, sending a hot glance down her arm. People were clapping all around them, but she felt like she was in another world.

"What . . . was that?" The questions slipped through her lips in spite of her. They had roles to play tonight, but that had *not* felt like a performance and his temper proved it. A heady scent swirled around her, alluring as woodsmoke on a cold winter night.

Roar's gaze was piercing.

"Seems pretty clear to me."

He guided her to the head table and held a chair for her. She sat and tried to look dignified, though she was pretty sure her face matched the color of her dress. The music began again and the party resumed, the hum of conversation rising like a tide in the courtyard.

Roar settled in the chair beside her. "That's safe," he said, gesturing to the wine decanter on the table. "Would you like some? Or maybe water's a better idea? I couldn't help noticing just now that you—"

She looked at him, her anger flaring. "I know what I did, Roar, and it didn't seem like you minded." Sure, she'd had more champagne than she should've, and maybe she'd been the one who'd nudged that peck into something more, but she wasn't about to be shamed for it, or controlled by him.

His eyebrows drew together almost imperceptibly. "I was going to say I saw your balance falter, but if you mean what I think, then no. I didn't mind at all."

"Oh." People were watching; she tried to put on a happy face. "I misunderstood."

"Seems to happen a lot with us." His eyes were soft, thoughtful, his blink slow. "We never have any trouble when we're kissing, though."

Their communication was usually such a delicate tiptoe around Liv and Sable and Ventus, around their first kiss and the pain she'd caused him, that this direct acknowledgement almost made her gape. "I guess it's better than nothing," she said dumbly.

Humor winked in his eyes. "It's *a lot* better than nothing."

Roar poured wine and water for her. She needed time to recenter and to absorb the last head-spinning moments. She turned to Daisy and managed to carry on a conversation even though her mind felt like it was flying apart.

Lund had meant to *poison* her. She had stepped out into this courtyard enraged by that, and terrified for Roar's safety. She'd also been anxious to make a good first impression on the families whose support she needed. But now there was yet another element working on her attention.

Something was very different with Roar. She'd begun to notice it that morning, but now it was undeniable. He seemed bolder. Charged. Like whatever force animated him had been dialed up to high. The shift even came through in his temper. He'd been all billowing, smoky darkness when she'd first met him. An unsettling and distant presence. He was still darkness, but there was clarity in it. The hazy smokiness in him was entirely tempting now, warm as cedar and hickory. He didn't feel *distant* anymore, either. His proximity made her skin buzz. She may as well have been sitting beside a lightning bolt, one splitting through a winter night.

Cal came over, looking tense, and set her hand on Daisy's shoulder. "Temp, can I borrow her for a little while?"

Roar dropped off talking to Perry in mid-sentence and looked over. She could tell he wanted to ask what was wrong, but he didn't.

"Sure," she replied, and watched Cal and Daisy hurry inside.

"How are you doing?" Roar said.

"Overall, fine." She'd noticed how often he asked her that. "And thank you. For asking."

He smiled. "You're welcome."

He draped his arm over her chair, his sleeve brushing past her nape. She stared ahead, her heartbeat lurching as his scent wafted over her.

"What about you?" Her voice sounded thin. "How are you doing?'

"I feel better than I have in ages," he replied.

She badly wanted to ask why, but couldn't seem to make herself. "That's great."

From the corner of her eyes, she saw him smile. "It is indeed."

More guests were arriving by the moment and the courtyard thrummed with good spirit. Mattock was roaming the perimeter, keeping a close watch. Lund was unquestionably popular, but everything seemed to be going fine. In a little while, she was going to have to exchange wedding vows with Roar again. She was dreading it and she wasn't sure why. They'd be just as false as before, and it should be easier the second time, right?

"Something interesting about my hand?" Roar asked.

She'd been staring at it because he was so *close*. With the tiniest shift, she could've slipped her hand inside of his, or leaned against his cheek. "Yes," she answered. "You have so many little scars. How did you—" She looked up, the question dying on her lips.

His eyes were soulful as they roamed over her face. Candlelight glowed on the tips of his eyelashes and shone on the scruff over his jaw. "Tempest . . ." His hand came to her shoulder, his fingers drifting in warm circles over her skin. She felt like she was floating, like he was carrying her away on a tide. "I know we've had a complicated go of it so far, but what if we let—" He turned suddenly, like he'd heard something crash to the floor.

"What?" She'd heard nothing out of the ordinary.

"It's starting." He took her hand and pulled her up. "Time to go."

Terror and confusion sliced through her gauzy mood. She looked around frantically as she followed him. "Roar, what's happening?"

"Lund," he said over his shoulder.

Shouting broke out in the far corner. People were scattering, knocking over chairs. Soldiers poured into the courtyard through open doors. Lund had tried to poison her. After her conversation with Perry, she was expecting other quiet, underhanded moves. Whatever this was, it wasn't *quiet*.

"Hurry, Tempest" Roar said.

She opened her mouth to explain that she couldn't hurry—that in her dress and shoes even walking was a nightmare—when Roar spun and dove at her.

She flew back and hit the ground. Her teeth slammed together; her shoulders scraped the flagstones. She heard a loud *crack* and saw the blur of an arrow, then heard it crack off the vine-covered wall above them. Right where she'd been.

Roar was everywhere. His hand cupped the back of her head; his body covered her like a cloak. He leaned up. "Are you hurt?" He looked utterly calm, but she knew he wasn't.

"N-no," she stammered.

"I don't like this party anymore," he said, springing up and pulling her with him. Then they were moving again, weaving around chairs and tables. Toward the doors. Inside. *Away*. Chaos was spreading around the courtyard. People screamed and arrows whizzed through the air. "You have to move faster, Tempest," he said.

"I *can't*," she croaked, her throat tight with fear.

He turned, his gaze falling to her feet. "I've got you." He wrapped his arm around her and hoisted her to his side, half-carrying her as they hurried on. All around, people were pushing and shoving, glomming into panic-stricken groups. No one seemed to know what was happening, herself included. Finally, they reached a set of closed doors.

Roar tried the handle and cursed. "Locked."

"Can you kick them open?" she asked.

"Worth a try." He stepped back and sprang forward, throwing all his weight behind a kick. The thick doors hardly trembled.

Tempest looked around. People were trying other doors; they *all* seemed to be locked. Fighting had broken out in earnest. Men in Horn uniforms were fighting each other. An appallingly wrong sight.

This can't happen, she thought. She felt cold and furious. At Lund. At herself, for not having prevented this.

"We have to try something else." Roar swept two knives off a table. *Dinner* knives, she thought, aghast. There were *swords* clashing all around them.

Her expression must've betrayed her thoughts. He winked and made them spin prettily in his hands. "It's not the weapon but who wields it. Hold on to the back of my belt and don't let go."

They'd barely taken three steps when Cal bounded up. "Tempest!" she shouted. "I've got her, Roar. I've got her."

"No," he returned coolly. "She stays with me, Cal."

"Don't be stupid!" Cal spat. "Separate! Give them two targets instead of one!"

Targets? The word hit home. But of course Lund would want to kill Roar, too. He was her husband, after all. Why would Lund keep a heartbroken young widower around who might come after him for revenge? "Roar, listen to me," she said. "Cal's right. They'll have to work harder if we're not together."

Pain slid behind his eyes, quick as a thief in the night. "If that's what you want," he said, then he turned to Cal. "Don't leave her alone—not for anything."

He was off before Cal could reply, taking three long strides, then ducking under the arm of a man who swung a massive sword, like an executioner's ax. Tempest's heart stopped. *Now,* she thought. *Right now is when I shatter.* But Roar seemed to dance past, moving twice as fast as the lumbering attacker. He was a blur as he dodged in and stabbed the man in the armpit, then moved on, diving into the fray beyond. The huge sword fell with a clatter and the man's expression turned pensive for a split moment, then he clamped a hand over the blood gushing from under his arm and collapsed.

It was the work of an instant, horrible and masterful.

"Move!" Cal pushed her, propelling her toward the next door like an irate human wave.

The mayhem in the courtyard only seemed to be intensifying. People screamed in panic and pounded on the doors. Soldiers fought across toppled chairs, spilled food, and trampled flowers. The fear in the air sparked deep in her nose, roiling and acrid.

Movement on the second-story arcade drew her eyes up. There, she saw four figures, one at each corner. Even though it was darker up there, she recognized them. Knew their blond hair, their broad shoulders and immense bows. She'd spent the past week walking with those figures, day and night, dusk to dawn. It was Perry and the brothers: Hayden, Hyde, and Haven, better known as Straggler. From protected perches behind columns, they fired arrows with precision and eerie calm. Tempest's heart soared. Her mind flew back to earlier. Perry saying, *We'll do all we can.*

All we can, she now saw, was high ground. Archers—the best she'd ever seen—in shielded, elevated positions. A strategy that took their slim advantages and turned them into undeniable strengths. Nothing short of genius, considering they'd had no time to prepare.

But would it be enough against Lund's militia?

Cal lurched to a stop and pushed her down to the ground. For the second time that night, Tempest crashed against the flagstones. This time, the skin scraped off her elbows. Steel clanged above her, Cal's sword colliding with another.

Tempest rolled and looked up. A huge, rust-bearded man glanced murderously down at her even as he fought Cal. Then another came, a bald man with a terrifying, snaggle-toothed leer, and Cal's effort had to split in two, but that wasn't all. Everywhere Tempest looked, she locked eyes with predators. They seemed to scent her like hunting hounds and closed in from all directions. Against so many, Cal wouldn't stand a chance and *she* was who they wanted—not Cal. Not the dozens upon dozens of innocent guests who were trapped all around her. She had to act before Cal was swamped.

Still on the ground, she kicked her heels away and rolled under a table, then she began to crawl, pushing aside the chairs and debris that blocked her way.

"No!" Cal yelled. "Tempest, *no!*"

Yes, Cal, she thought back. *This is how it has to be.*

When she saw a clear path to a set of doors a short distance off, she scrambled to her feet and ran. Only a few strides later, pain of the brightest kind exploded in her foot. Something sharp, slicing deep into her sole. She cried out, but didn't stop. She had to get out of there. They wanted her and Roar.

Where was Roar?

She looked around. Didn't see him.

"Run, lady! Run!" yelled the young boy who had started the fire in her chamber—Elias. He dumped a bucket of water on table linens that had caught fire with the oil of smashed lamps. If the fires spread inside, or up to the second story, this nightmare would become worse. It would become horrific.

She reached the doors and tried them. Cried out again in sheer despair as they didn't budge. What now? She spun, and her foot slipped. There was a dark red puddle beneath her. Blood, flowing from the cut on her foot.

"There!" Her uncle pointed at her from across an obstacle course of furniture and fighting soldiers. "Get her! She's there!" His crested hat had been knocked forward, giving him a ram-like intensity. Around him, she saw a concentration of men in the Horn's battle uniform: black tunics and vests over gray pants.

Nice touch, Uncle, she thought, seething. By putting his hired force in battle dress, he'd made them appear serious, imposing. It made the other soldiers, those she presumed were loyal to her, look fanciful, like storybook illustrations in their red and gold-trim ceremonial uniforms.

Lund's henchmen came after her, shoving people and objects aside. She ran. There was nowhere to go to avoid them because they were everywhere. Tears pushed into her eyes, rage and fear colliding, lodging in her throat like a scream. There was no way out. This was it. Failure. *Death*. And it was coming how she most feared, practically lifted from her nightmares: *alone*.

"Tempest!" shouted a male voice. She froze and waited for a sword to find her back. An arrow. "Tempest, over here!"

She whirled and saw Mattock. He ran toward her, the light of the fires reflecting in his intense, worried eyes. She hobbled to meet him, collapsing in her final steps as another sharp object found the cut that already opened in her foot.

"Are you hurt?" he asked, catching her under the arms.

"Where's Roar?" she gasped.

"I don't know. Come. I've found a way out." He took a firm grip of her arm and they made for a set of doors. They opened—a miracle. She stepped through and spun, wanting to see Cal, Daisy, Roar. Her aunt. Instead seeing only rabid fighters. Bodies slumped and motionless on the floor.

"Stand back," Mattock said. He yanked her back, then shut and relocked the doors.

"No!" she yelled. "You can't leave them out there!" She'd been running for her life only an instant ago; now that struck her as cowardly and wrong. These were *her* people. She couldn't abandon them. "Mattock, we have to do something!"

"I *am* doing something. Your safety takes precedence over any of theirs."

A cold chill raced down her neck. Through the small glass panes in the door, she locked eyes with Cal in the courtyard.

Cal was yelling; she looked more terrified than Tempest had ever seen her. Then at the edges of her vision, there was a sharp movement—powerful and close—as the haft of Mattock's sword slammed down on her skull.

~ 27 ~

ROAR

There was only one way to stop this: He had to find Lund. Roar saw him across the courtyard, past burning linens and scattered chairs. Lund had his back to a wall and nearly a dozen soldiers surrounding him in a perfect protection formation.

Roar cursed under his breath. There was no way to get to him—*yet*.

He looked up and let out a series of whistles. Old hunting calls he and Perry had developed as kids. Above, mostly concealed behind a pillar, Perry paused in delivering his barrage of arrows and peered down.

"Lund!" Roar shouted.

Perry's chin dipped and he shouted at the brothers to concentrate their volleys on the men surrounding Lund. Several of the soldiers fell as arrows impaled them, but some had shields.

"Wall!" one of them yelled. "Shield wall!"

They moved swiftly, gathering around Lund and raising their shields with a unified snap.

Roar cursed again. Lund was even more unreachable now; he'd only made his problem worse. As their arrows stuck in the soldiers' shields like porcupine quills, Perry and the brothers stopped firing. It was four of them against dozens, and there was no room to waste arrows.

Roar had to think of something else—but not now.

A massive man was charging for him, swinging a chain mace in a circle overhead.

Roar spun the knife in his hands to gauge the balance, then hurled it. He hated throwing blades and wasn't particularly good at it, either. The knife, which had a dull point as it was made for cutting roasted chicken and not combat, glanced off the man's shoulder.

He laughed as he pounded up, the mace still whizzing above him.

In that split second, Roar was down, swiping another knife off the floor as he rolled. He came up beside the man and buried the steel in his kidney.

Lund. Lund was yelling. "Find Tempest! Find her!"

Roar wanted nothing more than to do that himself, but she was safe with Cal and this had to end. As two men broke away from the shield wall to follow Lund's orders, he saw his chance. He sprinted and barreled through the brief gap left by the two vacating men. He fell on Lund like a panther, taking him to the ground in an instant and feeling nothing as they crashed down.

Ten stunned soldiers spun, lowering their shields and staring, agape.

"One step, and this knife goes into his brain," Roar told them.

Lund lay in front of him like a drowning man Roar was rescuing. Roar had yet another dinner knife in his hand, pressed to Lund's ear. Dull, but it would still do the job.

"Listen to him!" Lund cried. "Don't move!"

A rustling sound drew Roar's attention away. Hayden was scaling the vines and coming down from the second story, his great bow slung over his back. He jumped down, landing with a clatter of arrows. "I've got him, Roar! Go!"

Roar released Lund and swept to his feet. "We're not done, Lund."

Lund laughed. "You think this matters? She's dead by now. Tempest is *dead*."

Roar spun and took off, fear blazing through his veins.

28

TEMPEST

Tempest's life was on the line.

Even as she emerged from the depths of unconsciousness, she knew this. She had to gather herself, marshal her wits and her strength, or she wasn't going to survive.

Awareness came back in pieces. She was being carried. By Mattock. Along empty corridors. Then he was ducking through a door into a dim room that was small, cold, and reeked of wine.

A cellar.

Mattock shut the door. Darkness clamped down, heavy and thick. "Can you stand?" he asked.

"Yes," she replied, though she wasn't sure.

He set her down. Pain bit deep as she put weight on her right foot, but there was a wall behind her. She slumped back against its cold rough surface and felt hot tears slide down her cheek. No—those weren't tears. She was bleeding.

Mattock had struck her.

She couldn't see anything. The darkness of the small room was blinding. Sounds seemed especially loud. Mattock's hard breathing. The shouts outside. Her pulse.

"I'm sorry I had to do that," he said with a sigh. "I had to get you out of there." His tone was more explanation than apology. "We'll stay here until things settle down. Don't worry. You're safe now. As long as you don't scream or do anything stupid."

Nausea rolled through her. She forced herself to draw a few slow breaths. In and out. Breathing was all she could handle at the moment, but that was all right. It was vitally important, breathing. It deserved her attention.

"I'm going to check your head. Don't be scared." He probed it with blunt fingers, finding the spot from where the pain radiated. Her nausea intensified, churning in her stomach. "You've got a decent lump. That's to be expected. The cut's small, though. Doubt it will even need stitches." He paused. She had the horrifying sense that he might be waiting for her to *thank* him. "I know it might be difficult for you to understand," he continued, "but I was careful. And I didn't want to do it, but you were going to argue. You left me no choice. You'll have a headache for a few days, that's all. I'll take a look at your foot later. How did you hurt it?"

"I don't know." She couldn't remember. Her mind felt so thick and slow, but she had to come up with something. She was trapped. Mattock was nearly twice her size. A trained killer. She was only getting out of this with courage. "I have to go back. Cal and Daisy are out there. Roar."

He wouldn't agree, of course. She only wanted to see how he'd react and buy herself time.

"Cal is where she should be. My men will take care of her. Daisy is important to you. I made sure she was out of harm's way. You'll see her when this is over."

He sounded so calm. She wrapped her arms around herself as she began to shake. "And Roar?"

"He'll be handled. He won't be an impediment to you anymore."

A bolt of ice speared through her. "What have you done?"

"Nothing more than fix your problems for you." He gripped her under the jaw with a hand, anchoring her in place. "Isn't this what you want? The Horns? I've given them to you."

"All you've given me," she said through her clenched teeth, "is a reason to destroy you."

He chuckled, an awful, smug sound. "You do remind me of Sable sometimes. But you can stop the lies now. A messenger arrived from Aldred this morning. I know you married Roar because you had to. That barely moments later, he was calling himself a king. He's an unknown Tider, Tempest. How does that not infuriate you?"

She cringed inwardly, thinking back on that bright morning in the Tides' clearing. Her hand, bleeding. Roar's meaningless comment as they'd stalled for time. But Aldred had taken it seriously. And now Mattock, too. "You've got it all wrong."

"I know I don't. And I know it's unpleasant to think about now, but soon you'll see. This is for the best. All the obstacles are gone. The army is loyal to me. The people are loyal to you. The territory belongs to *us*. We'll rule together, side by side."

A fresh surge of terror washed over her. "You . . . think I want to *be* with you?"

"Not now. But in time, yes." He released her, but the place where his fingers had dug in still ached. "You'll warm to the idea. We can learn to care for each other."

It was too much, too sickening. She had to go back to breathing. In and out. *Good.* That wasn't so hard, was it? Again: Deep breath in and—she froze, catching an unusual scent amid the wood and fermented grape of the cellar. Hope came, bright as a flare in the night.

Was that *nightshade?* Was the poisoned wine that had been meant for her *here?*

"What if I don't want that?" she asked.

"You will."

The hair on her arms lifted at his certain tone, but she had to keep him talking. Her goal now was to get him to let down his guard. The way to do that, she knew, would be to play to his ego. "I thought this was all Lund's doing. That he had contracted a secret militia. You helped put it together, didn't you? Then you turned on him?"

"I prefer to see it otherwise. I was already planning his demise when he came to me to secure a force for him. I gladly obliged and used his coin to outfit and supply men who were already loyal to me. I was in on all his plans. He really couldn't have made it easier for me to bring him down and to protect you."

"Protect me? Mattock, how can I believe that? You don't even know me."

"I know who you used to be. I knew your brother." He shifted closer, his voice going softer. "Tempest, I just *knew.*

When you arrived yesterday, it was like a sign from the gods. Everything came together. What I feel is real. I know we'll be great together one day. This is what your brother would have wanted. Me and you, ruling together."

He was relaxing; she just had to keep coaxing him in the right direction. "I don't know. You could've told me before this all happened. I trusted you, but you didn't trust me. You kept me in the dark."

"*There was no time*," he said gruffly. "You've not even been here two days." She took a chance and didn't reply, instead letting a silence curl out and surround the ugliness in his tone. In the distance, she could hear people screaming. Good people were being cut down because of this man. "I'm sorry," he said, after a moment. "I *would* have come to you. But there was too much to coordinate and I couldn't risk Lund's suspicion. You'll learn to trust me again. I do know what I'm doing. I've been a soldier longer than you've been alive. I promise you, all your worries are behind you. No one will take better care of you than I will."

She let that comment hover in the darkness as well, cementing into a promise. His temper had a strident edge, desire and pride and impatience coalescing into a green, torn-grass odor. He was actually desperate for her to capitulate, to fold neatly into his plans.

"I want to believe that," she said. "But I may need some time to think." She had to be careful. He'd become suspicious if she threw in the towel too easily. "This has all happened so—so—" She let her voice crack. "Mattock, I think

I screamed my throat raw. If you really want to take care of me, I could use something to drink."

He chuckled. "We're in the right place for that."

The air shifted as he stepped back. Immediately, she bent and groped through the darkness at her feet. Her fingers brushed the slats of a wood crate, the glass bottles inside. The crate wasn't full; she felt only three bottles. She grabbed one and pulled the cork out as silently as she could, then lifted it to her nose. *Wrong one!* Quickly, she put it back and grabbed another. *Wrong again!*

Her heart stopped at the sound of wood splintering. "These crates are nailed shut, but I've almost got one open."

"It's all right," she said, grabbing the last bottle and straightening. It was either this or nothing. "I found one by my feet."

The rummaging stopped. "Well done." He came back and took the bottle out of her hand. He stood closer now, an arm propped on the wall somewhere by her head, the smell of his breath and his sweat inescapable. "Shall we make a toast?"

"S—sure," she replied. "To what?"

"To the long-lived success of the Horns." She heard him yank the cork out with his teeth and spit it aside. Then the dark, burnt-clove smell of poison wafted into her nose and tears of relief stung the back of her eyes. "And to their new lord and lady, Mattock and Tempest."

Tempest counted slowly to five so he would think she was deliberating. To accept this toast was to accept *him*. She was positive he'd view this as a small first step that would ripple into the future like a pebble splashing into a pond. A shared sip. A shared bed. A shared territory and life. When she finished counting, she fumbled for the bottle, her fingers brushing the wiry hairs on the back of his hand. "To the Horns," she croaked. "And to us."

She managed to get it out and pretended to take a sip, tilting back the bottle and swallowing nothing. Mattock was a Seer and enough light came beneath the door, she imagined, for him to see rough shapes where she saw nothing. She lowered the bottle, sighed softly, and waited. She'd done all she could.

"My turn." He took the bottle from her. "To the Horns. And to us."

She listened to the wet sound of him drinking. "Good stuff. Your brother always knew how to find the best wine." The scent of nightshade, hemlock, and serpent's venom wafted on his breath, as heavy to her sensitive nose as a cloying purple stream flowing through the still air.

"Did he?" she heard herself say. This was a dream. A nightmare. She had to see it through. "I like to think I can recognize a good vintage myself. Most Scires have a strong sense of taste."

"Hmm." He cleared his throat. "Yes. I want to hear more about this discerning tongue of yours," he said, the innuendo plain in his voice. She heard him tip the bottle back again, taking another long pull.

Then for an interminable stretch, nothing happened, and she thought she'd failed. That in her desperation, she'd smelled something that wasn't there. That she was going to remain here, trapped in the darkness, as Cal and Roar were killed, and as innocent people were slaughtered. That she was going to have to live with the aftermath: Mattock, forcing her to be someone she wasn't. Day by day, breaking her down. Bleeding her of her hopes and dreams. Forcing her to live a life she hadn't chosen.

Again, Mattock cleared his throat. Once, twice. He coughed. Coughed harder. Then the bottle smashed against the floor in a shockingly loud *pop*. Liquid exploded all over her shins and feet.

"*Bitch*," he said, and took a few messy steps, crashing into crates. "What did you do?"

Her head whipped to the side suddenly, her teeth punching into her bottom lip. She fell over and grasped for an anchor, but there was only rough granite sheering the skin of her palms. Her shins barked against a crate and she went flying. She landed on her hip, crates and bottles smashing all around her. An avalanche, sharp, pummeling her limbs. After what seemed like an hour, the tumbling stopped. All around her, she heard the glug of broken bottles pouring out their contents.

Mattock was somewhere a few feet away, choking and sputtering. Cursing her and begging. He had punched her—she was only just understanding that that was why she'd fallen over.

She lay in an awkward heap, like a doll thrown haphazardly in a toy trunk, and listened to him struggle ferociously as the poison tore him apart inside.

"Tempest, *help me*—help me—you *bitch*—should've killed you—why—why did you—help me—*please*—"

She felt sorry—for him and for herself. For all the days and nights in her future that would be plagued by the questions that found her now. Could she have done anything else?

Should she try to go get help? She knew this moment, trapped in the darkness with evil she'd endured and committed, was going to haunt her forever.

Mattock's struggle seemed unending. When silence came—loud, final—a sob burst through her lips. And then, bizarrely, a teary laugh.

I guess I am a bitch when I need to be, she thought.

Small waterfalls of glass and wine rained down on her. The liquid soaked her dress and hair. It slithered all over her skin and stung her eyes, and the dozen cuts and scrapes she couldn't see but felt. She had to get back to the courtyard, to stop the massacre happening there.

She tried to shift. Mistake. There was more toppling, more glass explosions. Cries of pain from a dozen different places in her body. Her hip was on solid ground. She bent her leg and tried to get a foot beneath her, but her bleeding sole wailed, and the cellar's blackness spun. Vomit crept up the back of her throat, a mystery. She couldn't remember when she'd last eaten.

She slumped back down and spit out the blood that had pooled in her mouth. Her bottom lip already felt enormously swollen and she was suddenly immensely tired. Sleep was an urgent necessity. Right here, in this bed of shards and splinters and spilled wine.

It came fast, her mind shutting as crisply as a book.

Time passed. When she stirred again, she had no idea how long. She had no idea where she was, either, nor why she was pinned down and aching everywhere.

All she knew for sure was: *light.*

Someone had just swung open a door, letting a bright shaft of lamplight into the darkness that had held her down. The shape in the door resolved into the blurry figure of a woman, indistinct as a cloud. Tempest blinked hard but couldn't get her eyes to adjust anymore.

"Help!" the woman screamed. "*Help!*" And then she was gone.

More time passed, then Peregrine was there. Also a figure but a very large one with a pale head of hair and a scent she knew. He crouched down, setting a lamp on the floor. Tempest felt his attention settle on her for a long beat, then move to Mattock's body briefly.

"Tempest," he said, softly. "It's Perry. Will you let me get you out of here?"

She was afraid to move; it seemed like everything was going to come down on her. But anything was better than spending another moment in there. She managed a small nod.

He stood and began to move things. She held her breath as the sharp weights pinning her shins and her shoulder lifted. With those gone, she couldn't stop the tears leaking from her eyes. She saw other figures gather in the door. There were shouts outside now, too, in the corridor. The sounds of people running.

Perry knelt again. "I'm going to put a blanket over you, then I'm going to pick you up. If I hurt you, let me know and I'll stop. Okay?"

She nodded again. The scent of wool struck her nose as he lay the blanket over her, but she didn't feel it or its warmth. She couldn't feel anything at all.

Perry gathered her up like she weighed no more than the blanket itself and brought her into the corridor. She tried to clear her eyes again, but she was beginning to understand that blinking wasn't going to change anything. Deep inside her skull, a hammer worked on a stubborn nail. Pounding and pounding. Though she saw nothing clearly, she could make out people everywhere, gathering around her. Down the halls, voices were still shouting.

"We found her!"

"She's alive!"

"Get the doctor!"

She winced.

"Quieter, everyone," Perry said. Then, "Find Roar. Tell him I've got her." He shifted, gathering her more securely, and began to walk.

"Whe-uh?" Tempest said. "Whe-uh taken me?" Her mouth wasn't working right.

"Your room."

"Caw? Dizzy?"

"They're fine. Looking for you. They'll be here any second."

She asked if Roar was all right. It came out a string of R's, but Perry understood.

"He's unharmed, but I wouldn't say he's all right." He peered down at her. "We lost you, Tempest. I'm so sorry."

She shut her eyes. A week ago, she'd hated no one more than this person. Now she was in the basket of his arms, and she felt safe. Sometimes life simply astonished.

As Perry reached the stairs to the second story, familiar figures converged on her. Aunt Lerra, Cal, Daisy. Perry stopped and all was suddenly confusion, tears, and conflicting directives: bed, a doctor, a bath.

"No," Tempest said, silencing them. She formed her next word carefully, so they'd understand. "Parade." The city was expecting it. And everyone would hear of tonight's disastrous celebration. If she disappeared now, it would only feed rumors she was fragile, flighty. She had to do this. She had to see the Aether, the night. Remind herself that not all darkness was a deadly trap. Remind herself that she was here to serve, not cower. More than anything, she needed to remind herself that she was strong and free. That *she* held the reins to her life. "*Parade*," she said again, more clearly.

"Hell no," Cal growled. "No chance. She's not going anywhere."

"Tempest, sweetheart," Daisy said, "you're injured. You need to be seen by a doctor."

A woman separated from the crowd and came forward. She was introducing herself as a doctor when the corridor stirred. People stepped aside, making way for the dark figure who strode up.

Roar. She knew that quiet wolf-stride.

When he reached her, he said nothing, but there was a howling quality in his temper, as intense and blind as rage. Scenting it made her own heart beat painfully.

"She wants to do the parade," Perry said.

After a beat, Roar's head came up. "Then that's what we're doing. Bring her, Perry." He strode for the main doors.

Perry followed, carrying her. *Everyone* followed, the clatter of footsteps and din of their anxious voices thickening in her ears. Movement was making her nauseous. She tried to concentrate on Roar's voice.

"Hyde, Hayden, Strag," he said, "load your quivers and Perry's. Daisy, can you find a heavy cloak? Anything warmer than that blanket. Cal, get orders ahead to lose the carriage and ready horses."

"She can't ride, Roar," Daisy said. "Look at her."

"A carriage offers comfort, but it's a slow and large target. We don't know what else Mattock and Lund had planned. She'll ride with me."

It was strange to hear them speak like she wasn't present.

Then again, she didn't feel completely there.

In moments, she was under the Aether, grateful for the gentle luminous flows. It was so at odds with all she felt, but seeing it reminded her that terror could change. Dissipate. She would not always feel as she did now.

Roar mounted a black horse, all but blending into it. Then Perry was lifting her up. She tried to throw a leg over the saddle, the habit ingrained from years of riding when she'd lived with Night tribe. She heard a rip, some tear in her dress widening but not enough. She was going to incinerate the thing, she decided, as soon she got the chance.

"Sidesaddle might work better," Roar suggested. He swept her across his lap, gathering her into a heavy cloak. Without so much as a thought, she melted against his chest.

Daisy handed up a towel. "For your mouth."

Tempest nodded gratefully. Her body felt like a world of hurt, but her mouth and foot were like magnetic north and south, drawing most of her energy. She took the towel and pressed it to her bottom lip, her eyes watering. Oddly, that brought the world into better focus for a few moments.

"Just another second here," said the doctor with the soft voice. She slathered something on Tempest's foot that immediately muted the pain, then deftly wrapped it in a bandage. "It'll work for now. Stay off it if you can."

Roar shifted so he could look into her eyes. "Need anything else before we do this?" The ferocity in his eyes couldn't have been more at odds with his casual tone. She shifted, trying to burrow closer. In spite of the heavy cloak, she was beginning to shake. The unsteadiness seemed to come from deep inside, like an earthquake in her bones. "Stay or go, Temp?" Roar said quietly, the horse dancing beneath them. "Either way is fine. Your call."

"Tighter," she said. Then, "Arms." And then, finally, "Go." Every word was a struggle. Her lip throbbed and stung; it felt as big as a banana.

"I've got you. I'm not going to let go." He paused, staring at her for a long moment. "Whenever you need to tell me something, touch my hand and think it. I'll be able to hear you. Do you understand?"

She didn't. She couldn't begin to puzzle that out right now, or to consider the implications. But she accepted it wholesale, feeling only relief. To test it out, she fumbled through the folds of the cloak and found his hand. *I'm going to want to talk about this later.*

That almost got him to smile. "I'm looking forward to it." He gathered up the reins in one hand and wrapped his other arm around her, pulling her snug against him. "You're incredible, by the way. I've never known anyone braver." Then he looked up and addressed the escort assembled around them. "Come on. Let's introduce this girl to her city."

~ 29 ~

ROAR

Unlike the previous night, Rim was *not* in a state of celebration. People crowded in the streets, but the mood was tense. Roar looked into their faces as he rode past and didn't see happiness. He saw fear. Anger. Betrayal. He saw people who didn't know how to feel.

The slightest spark of provocation, he thought, *will turn them into a rioting mob.*

It took everything in him not to turn around and take Tempest back to shelter.

In spite of the heavy cloak, and no matter how tightly he held her, she shook in his arms. She had every reason. She was concussed. Bloodied all over from scrapes and cuts. Some of them—like the one on her lip and on the sole of her foot—were bad. She was soaked in wine. She'd just been attacked, had just been forced to murder and, adding insult to injury, it had just started to rain.

The hour he'd spent searching for her had pummeled him emotionally. When he'd finally seen her—small, battered, and every inch a hero—he couldn't think. The need to make her world right again, safe again, had come over him like a madness. It had nearly turned him inside out, and this so-called *parade* was yet another test to his self-control.

She wanted this. She wouldn't be out here if it weren't important to her. But he wasn't sure how much more he could take. But then, if he did what he wanted and got her the hell out of there, he'd fail her—and that he wasn't doing ever again.

"Slow down, Roar," she rasped.

"Do you need to be sick?" He'd felt a lump on her head when he'd brushed her hair away from her face. He could only imagine the headache she must be feeling. He shifted the cloak, creating some slack. "I'll turn back, but if you can't wait, just go for it and I'll cover you."

Her hand settled over his, cold and small and shaky. *No, it's not that. This doesn't feel right. Just slow down, please. Better yet, stop.*

Hearing her voice in his head sent a quick shock through him; he'd forgotten the intimacy of this. He brought the stallion to a halt, garnering puzzled looks from Perry, the brothers, and a few of the Horn soldiers riding escort under Cal's command.

"What can I do?" Every time he saw her swollen bottom lip, his heart fell off a cliff.

"Help me down please?"

She wanted to *get down?* Already, he was questioning the wisdom of parading her around. Who faced their followers like this, bloodied and bruised?

Answer: Kings did. Generals did.

She did.

"Sure." He dismounted and carefully helped her down to the cobblestones. Rain sluiced past her bandaged foot, blood seeping through. Her lip was starting to bleed again, too.

Their party adjusted to the improvisation, dismounting around them before a squat little tavern with windows that glowed amber with firelight. The front door was open, and people stood out front holding tankards and cups like they'd only just come outside to see the parade ride past. Spectators who'd lined the street came closer and an expectant murmur lifted above the drone of the rain. There had to be a couple of hundred people there, he thought, and still more were coming. Every last one of them had eyes only for Tempest, who was practically swallowed by the soldier's cloak Cal had found for her.

Instinctively, Roar took a step back. Perry appeared at his shoulder then, a quiet pillar, doing the opposite of what he'd just done. Life, playing out in solos and harmonies.

"Hello, everyone," Tempest said, her voice surprisingly clear. "Thank you for being here out in this rain. I'm glad to see you. I'm so glad to see every one of you." She drew a breath, her exhale fogging in the air. "You might have heard what happened tonight. If you haven't, give it a few seconds." Burbles of laughter swept down the street. "There's a lot I'll need to figure out over the coming days and weeks, but I want you to know I will hear you. I will be just. I will be yours. I *am* yours."

No one moved. People were holding their breath. Roar heard it. Rain. Rain and a silent crowd of hundreds. She was in pain, exhausted, and dazed—and the message to the Horns couldn't possibly have been clearer: No matter what, I'll show up for you.

Tempest turned, catching his eye. He stepped forward and she immediately sagged against him, Roar wrapping his arm around her. Though it must've looked like affection, he was the only thing keeping her upright.

"This is my husband," she went on. "That's probably obvious." More ripples of laughter. She was good at this, at putting people at ease. "Roar and I didn't have a chance to celebrate the way we wanted to earlier—that's also probably pretty obvious—but we're not giving up yet. I hope you'll help us do that now. I can't say the night is young, but we are. And I think we have time for a drink, don't you?"

She looked up at him. Her eyes were very much like a sea storm then, a tempest, swirling with all the emotions of the past day. The past weeks. Looking into them, he felt something give deep within himself, an old anchor finally pulling up, freed.

"Yes" he replied. "I'd say we have time for one or two."

"Then let's have some fun," she said.

Cheers erupted all around them and continued as they entered the tavern.

Someone called out, "Welcome home, Tempest!"

Someone else yelled, "Congratulations!"

It was warmer inside, and nearly empty, everyone having spilled into the street to see them. The proprietress, a portly red-haired woman, rushed over, wiping her hands on her apron. "Oh, goodness. Oh my. Come in, come in. Over here, by the fire." She guided them to a sitting area before a hearth. "What can I bring you, lady? Roast chicken? Carrot soup? Bread and cheeses?"

"Yes." Perry dropped into a chair and kicked his feet up on a low table. "Bring it all. I'm famished."

The woman almost broke into a run to do his bidding. Roar settled into a wood bench with Tempest. "Are you cold?" She shook her head, but she was still trembling when she nestled against him. Roar looked at Hyde, who nodded and clapped a tavern worker on the shoulder.

"Fresh wood for that fire there, fellow," he said, waving at the anemic glow in the hearth. "Get it snapping hot. And bring ale, for god's sakes."

"And wine," Straggler added.

"*Wine?*" Hayden shot him a glare as he dragged over two chairs.

Straggler shrugged. "Tempest likes it."

"Not anymore," she said, a sparkle of humor in her eye.

"Ale, then." Hayden fell into one chair, kicking the other over to Straggler. "Tell him, Hyde."

"He's got it. Don't you, friend?" Hyde gave the tavern man another amicable shove. "Go on, then. And be quick, eh?"

"Wait," Roar said. The man turned back. "Whatever food and drink you bring to us, bring it to everyone in here." People were streaming in from outside, shaking rain from their hair and their coats and staring wide-eyed at their group. He had no coin, but he'd figure it out somehow. Tempest wanted a celebration; if he had to sell his soul to give it to her, then so be it.

"Yes," she said. *Keep going, Roar,* she added privately, slipping her hand into his. *Let's have a real party.*

"And feed those out in the street as well," he told the man. "Turn out your kitchen and your cellar until there's nothing left in either. And get a message to the seven nearest taverns to do the same. Tonight, all of Rim will celebrate. Tempest of the Horns has come home."

The tavern keeper didn't need to send any message. A roar went up, shaking the walls of the tavern, and kept going. Roar heard it tumble out into the streets, gaining momentum.

"Great thinking," Daisy said as she squeezed in on Tempest's other side. "This is what they'll all talk about. Not what happened earlier, but that you were here, and that you gave them a night of celebration."

At the mention of earlier, Roar looked at Cal. She stood a short distance away, still vigilant, scanning the rapidly crowding tavern. She looked tense, the set of her mouth brittle. Tempest had been under her protection when Mattock took her. He had expected to feel furious at her, but he could tell she was already punishing herself.

He wasn't calm, either. He wouldn't be until he was back in the chamber with Tempest, the door barred, the entire world shut out.

People kept pouring in from outside, drenched and murmuring excitedly. Not long ago, the gawping of the guests at the wedding ceremony had unnerved him, but these open stares were more tolerable. Maybe because they seemed more innocent and welcoming. Or maybe because he was too focused on Tempest to care.

In some unseen corner of the tavern, a band struck up a tune. Food and drink arrived quickly and in plenty. Soon, the tension shifted into a sense of normalcy as Perry and the brothers attacked loaves of bread and bowls of stew. While the others feasted, he and Tempest pretended to share ale. He had no appetite or thirst.

As the night spun into a true celebration, he forced himself to dip into conversations here and there. Tempest slumped against his shoulder, her eyes heavy as she fought sleep. Inside, he was calculating: *How much longer? When can I take her away?*

When she dozed off, he looked at Cal and Daisy. They nodded. Breathing a sigh of relief, he gathered Tempest up carefully and stood. It had been his plan to make a stealthy exit, leaving the others to their fun, but that didn't happen.

Somewhere in the back, a voice yelled, "Stop the music! She's leaving!"

Then others shouted: "Shut up, everyone! And make way!"

When he walked out with her in his arms, he could've heard a feather drop. Despite the hushed tavern and the crowds outside, it *did* seem like a parade now. People were packed in the street. The rain had stopped and their faces were flushed, their joy, palpable.

They'd been dancing, he realized.

He glanced down at the sleeping girl in his arms; he couldn't wait to tell her about this later.

Someone—Daisy, probably—had thought to send for the carriage. He climbed into it and settled her in his lap. As Daisy was shutting the carriage door, he saw Perry swing onto a horse. Then the carriage gave a lurch and trundled off. Tempest was relaxed in his arms, deeply asleep.

Roar sat back and felt his life change in ways he couldn't begin to fathom.

Sometime later, he paced around the chamber as he listened to Daisy and Cal tend to Tempest in the bathroom. His ears were so attuned, he could see the scene on the other side of the door. Tempest in the tub, drooping with exhaustion. The two people she trusted most, hovering over her. Caring for her.

"Is it morning?" Tempest asked.

"No, darling," Daisy replied. "But it will be soon. Your foot's already looking a bit better."

"My head?" Tempest asked. "My mouth?" A little while ago, the doctor had treated the cut on her sole with binding spray. The woman, Ivy, had reassured Roar as she left. *She'll be fine in a few days.* That wasn't fast enough. "Do I look horrible, Daisy?"

Roar stopped before the door, holding himself there. *Tell her no, Daisy. Tell her she looks like a warrior who's won a battle.*

"You've looked better, Temp," Daisy said. "But you'll heal."

And that was the end of his self-control. He opened the door, and three heads swung his way. He received two expected glares. But Tempest, in her bathrobe, gave him a soft smile from the small stool where she sat as Daisy combed out her hair. "Hi."

"You don't look horrible," he said. "At all. You look fierce."

"Liar," she said. But she, of all people, would know he spoke the truth.

Cal, who'd been uncharacteristically quiet all night, helped her into the high bed, then she and Daisy bid her goodnight and left.

Roar went over and jabbed the fire with the poker a few times. After all that had happened, the stillness was unsettling. He realized he was listening for danger that wasn't there anymore.

"Roar," Tempest said. He turned. She looked so small in the enormous bed. "Can you stay here with me? And . . . be close? Like in the tavern?"

"Anything you want." He set the poker aside and settled beside her in the bed.

Tempest scooted in and rested her head on his chest. "Is this all right? Your chest . . . ?"

"Better than all right." It was exactly what he needed.

"Can you hear what I'm thinking?"

"No." He had taken care not to rest anywhere against her skin. He tried to explain his ability, likening sound to waves and wind, and how it was just energy, no different to him. How *thoughts* were like this, too, and how garments weren't conducive to sound—the same principle that made bare spaces echo, but not rooms with a lot of fabrics. He had no idea if he was making any sense, but she listened quietly, occasionally nodding her head. "I haven't been abusing your privacy, by the way. Maybe that first day in Resolute, when the flashlight went out. It didn't seem like a good time to tell you. But not since. At least, I've been trying not to."

"I know you haven't."

A silence lengthened. Roar found himself holding his breath, waiting for her to say more. His thoughts skated to

Liv and how she'd hated this ability. He'd never understood why she'd felt it was an invasion of privacy when *she* could scent every shift of his emotions. And he couldn't change it about himself any more than she could've stopped being a Scire. Tempest still hadn't spoken, so he decided to ask the question himself. "Does it bother you?"

"*Bother* me?" She rested her hand on his. *Roar, I think it's incredible! I guess I'll have to keep it in mind, though. If I'm thinking about things I want to keep to myself. But that's not a big deal. Being able to think right into your mind seems more than worth it. This will expedite my plan to brainwash you.*

He smiled. "Trust me. You already have."

She moved her hand away then. A casual, no-fuss movement that left him breathing through a swell of emotion. *It's unnatural*, Liv had said. Maybe he'd believed it. Not just that his ability was, but that *he* was. What a thing, he thought, to simply be accepted. To feel . . . well, *natural*.

Tempest had gone quiet, but he knew she wasn't asleep. "You want to talk about what happened tonight?" he asked.

"No. Well, maybe. Actually, yes. Roar . . . I killed Mattock."

"I know. You did it to protect yourself. What you did was brave. Necessary."

"Then why do I feel guilty? Why am I still so scared?"

"You feel guilty because you're a good person. And you're scared because fear is irrational." He swallowed thickly and watched firelight dance on the intricate woodwork on the ceiling. He should've been with her. "I wish I could take it away."

"You can't. I have to live with it. With myself. How do you stand it? Knowing you've taken someone's life?"

He wasn't expecting that turn and needed a moment to adjust. "You find a way." Memories flashed before his eyes. Ventus. The faces of men he'd slain on that night, and on others. In the Komodo, when he, Perry, Aria, and Soren had been captured by Sable. When other tribes had attacked the Tides. He didn't keep a count, though he knew people who did. He couldn't even recall all their faces perfectly. But each life he had taken did weigh on him. Every single one. "You find any way at all."

"Maybe if you give me something else to think about. Tell me about your family."

He pursed his lips. "I'm not trying to avoid answering you, but that won't exactly lighten the mood." In the beat of quiet that followed, he sensed he was disappointing her. That wasn't going to work. "I didn't have a happy childhood, Temp. My parents weren't meant to be parents. They left me alone a lot." The more he said, the easier it became to say more. She was a great listener, he realized. Her attention was so complete, it made him feel safe. Wrapped in a sort of cocoon. "They died when I was still young and my grandmother raised me for a while. When she died, I took care of myself. I found Perry's family and I made them mine. Of course, they had their own troubles. But if you're as alone as I was, anything's better."

"I'm sorry, Roar. I know what it's like to grow up without family. I was sent away when I was young. My brother used me as a political pawn."

His heart was suddenly in a vise. He did *not* want to talk about Sable right now, but fair was fair. "That must have been difficult."

"It wasn't terrible, actually. Banyan and his wife treated me like a daughter when they were in the right mood. When they weren't, they just ignored me. Pretended I wasn't there."

"Still pretty painful." He swallowed the lump in his throat. "You were neglected because of your importance. I, because of my unimportance."

"No. We were children and children are always important. We were mistreated because of other people's flaws. We didn't deserve what happened to us."

He felt that burn again behind his eyes. "You keep that up and I may start to like you."

"Oh no, anything but that." In spite of her joking tone, she was clinging to him like they were falling through the air together. "I think you do like me. You know how I know? You've called me 'Temp' a few times now."

"Nah, that's just laziness."

She laughed softly, and just like that, desire woke in him, the feeling stronger than he could ever remember feeling. Since that moment on the side of the fortress, life was roaring inside him, a hibernating beast awakening to a clawing hunger. He remembered earlier when she'd arrived at the courtyard. The way she'd looked in that dress. Their kiss.

He cleared his throat. "I could go if you want to rest. Just say the word." She didn't need to deal with his desire now—or even to be aware of it.

Her arms tightened around him. "Don't you dare. We'll sort it out some other time. For now, I'm glad to know I'm not the only one."

He shouldn't ask, but he had to ask. "By *it* you mean . . . ?"

"Us. You want me and I want you."

"Right." He pressed his eyes shut. "Does that mean my temper . . . ?"

"Is speaking loud and clear, and it's amazing. You smell *amazing*. Your usual scent is smoky and woodsy and cool. Like a nighttime bonfire by a crashing sea. But right now, there's a muskiness, like rich earth and warm amber and something spicy and clean. Not citrus and not bergamot but, like, some perfect mix of the two."

"Weird. That's exactly what I thought you were going to say."

She laughed again, a small husky sound.

He smiled. "Sleep now, Temp. You need it." He pressed a kiss to her hair, careful to avoid the lump Mattock had given her, and tried to ignore the soft curves wrapped around one side of him. She smelled of flowers and other sweet things his average nose couldn't parse out.

Gods. And he'd given Perry so much grief about violets.

"I wish I could sleep," she said. "I hurt everywhere and I'm so tired." He sensed her mood shifting. "But I don't want to sleep. I may never do it again. Every time I close my eyes, I'm in that dark cellar again with—with—"

"It's all right. You're safe now." He turned toward her and gathered her closer, tracing the shape of her shoulder blade, following the line of her spine, sinking his fingers into the soft silk of her damp hair. "I promise you're safe. I'm going to watch over you tonight. I'll stay awake until Cal shows up, then she'll watch over you." Knowing Cal, that was probably going to be in about five minutes, but he wasn't leaving anytime soon. He couldn't imagine a time when it would feel right.

"You don't have to do that."

"Actually, I do." He nuzzled her forehead with his nose. "Sleep now, little duckling."

"I'll try, kitten."

If he could've, he would've purred to make her laugh—he was officially addicted to the sound. Instead, he started singing. It seemed the only possible thing to do at the moment, and it had helped him as a child. Of course, he'd had to sing *himself* to sleep then, but it had helped nevertheless.

He sang the "Hunter's Return," which hadn't passed his lips in more than a year. It belonged to this land, the song did. To the Aether. To steely blues and cold seas. It had never felt right for Cinder. But it was about great bravery and homecomings, and if that wasn't right for now, then nothing was.

His voice was unsteady at first. A surprise. But he soon found his way, and not just to perfect pitch. He found his way to truth. He found his way to the part of him that wasn't bound to past wounds or future uncertainties, but just was.

He stopped when he felt damp seep through the fabric of his shirt. "Tempest?" He peered down. Her eyes were watery with tears. "What's wrong?"

"Nothing. When you sing, Roar, absolutely nothing in this world is wrong."

"Really?" He smiled. "Too bad I only know this one song."

"I won't get tired of it. Ever."

"I was kidding."

"I wasn't. Sing, please?"

He sang.

— 30 —

TEMPEST

Tempest pushed aside stacks of papers and arched her aching back. Her eyes burned from another long day of sifting through the territory's official records.

A week had passed since Lund and Mattock's insurrection. While her body healed, she'd made use of the time learning everything she could about Rim's economic situation. She'd studied the archives and learned that, through negligence and over-spending, Lund had wreaked havoc on the careful systems her brother had created. It was going to take time, effort, and good people to put things right. She knew she had two of those.

Time, though. That was in limited supply.

How much longer until Nightrose tribe reappeared in her life? How much damage could Banyan and Scar cause? Though she'd only met Scar of the Rose a few times, she knew Banyan well, having spent nearly a decade under his roof. He was unbending and intractable and proud—and she had wronged him when she'd fled. It wasn't a question of *if* they came for her, but *when*. Like Aldred, they would see her as an opportunity. A hook they could use to lure the Horns into their control.

Daisy looked up from her desk on the other side of the room. "Please tell me you're exhausted, because I'm exhausted."

Tempest smiled. "I'm exhausted. Let's get out of here." She blew out the lamp on Sable's desk—her desk now, really and truly *hers*. Then she took Daisy's offered arm and made her way back to her chamber. The cut on her foot, like the one on her lip, still bothered her a bit, and lately she found physical contact a comfort.

In the most random moments, the memory of being in that cellar with Mattock could slam into her. She could be halfway through a report on taxes when, with no warning, she'd suddenly feel herself being struck and falling onto crates and broken glass. It happened less when she was near Daisy or Cal, though.

Or Roar.

Since that night, he'd been the picture of gallantry, handling her with extreme tenderness. Not like a bird with a broken wing—he never made her feel fragile or weak—but more like an eagle that needed some time to heal up. Beneath his solicitude, she continued to see signs that he was changing. There was a straightness in the way he stood now, a steadiness in his eyes. When he entered rooms, he seemed to make the air sharper and brighter. Of course, it *was* possible her perceptions were colored by her feelings, which she'd finally accepted she had for him.

Somehow over the past days, they'd become as in tune as if they were rendered Scires. She could look at him during dinner, and he'd know she was tired and ready to head off to sleep. With a glance, he'd know to pull her into his lap and sing to her. One roll of her neck and he'd come over and massage the throbbing knot out of her shoulders. If he didn't sing her to sleep, he'd read to her from *Meditations*, a book he'd gifted her, and what a surprising pleasure *that* was. She could listen to his voice for hours.

She had no idea what to make of things. She was still desperately attracted to him—more than ever—and it didn't help that she could scent it was mutual. But that part of their relationship had stalled after that night of the attack. It sat like a ripe vine: lush and sweet and unharvested. She simply didn't understand it—if it was temporary, or if he'd decided it best to not complicate their situation—and she was too cowardly to ask, or to take a risk and push things forward. Already she felt like the two times they'd kissed, in Resolute and at their failed wedding, she'd been the one who lit the spark, and a girl had to have a little pride.

As she and Daisy wove through the corridors, dusky Aetherlight pouring in soft blue beams through the windows, she was amazed by how little evidence remained of the revolt that night. Servants bustled about contentedly, lighting the lamps and smiling as they passed her, and the courtyard was being restored to order.

She stopped on the second-story arcade and looked down. By the light of a few torches, masons were busy chiseling the names of the twenty-six people who'd died into the stone pediment of a fountain, their tools clanging softly.

After she'd requested the monument, there'd been questions. Didn't she want to forget what had happened? Well, yes. Of course she did. She wished they could *all* forget. But that was never going to happen.

Every night since, she'd been plagued by nightmares of Mattock. Overnight, her fear of the dark seemed to become public knowledge. Wherever she went at night, there were candles, lamps, snapping hearths. But forgetting that night wasn't just impossible—it wasn't the right thing to do. People had *died*. They had drawn their last breaths here, and no matter what role they'd played or hadn't played in Lund or Mattock's schemes, they were citizens. It had been a tragic night for everyone.

She thought briefly of Lund, who'd been captured while she'd been in the cellar with Mattock. Her aunt's traitorous husband was a matter of some controversy. Plenty of people wanted him exiled—or killed—but she wouldn't accept either of those.

She had yet to decide what to do with him. She needed time to think. For now, he was being held captive in a suite within the fortress, where Aunt Lerra could see him as often as she wished. That was the important thing. Tempest wanted the foundation of her rule to be justice, and Lerra was innocent; she didn't deserve to be punished for her husband's treachery.

She had so many ideas in her mind, big and small, for the changes she wanted to make in Rim and throughout the territory. They were rough, but she knew she could shape them, especially with Daisy helping her stay organized.

She just needed time.

Daisy drew a bath for her. She climbed in and soaked in the steaming water, letting her aches melt away. Water always cleared her mind and helped her think.

Sable had kept meticulous records, unsurprisingly. Attention to detail was a family trait. She had few memories of her parents, but they included her mother's orderly jewelry cases and her father's tidy desk. Going over the records this past week, a picture had crystallized in her mind of Rim's strengths and weaknesses. She considered it as she watched the steam rise around her.

What Rim needed more than anything, besides hope and good leadership, was defense. This had been true even before she'd arrived, but with the tenuous situation between her and Nightrose tribe, it was even more so.

Given the recent divisiveness Lund had caused within Rim's soldiery, she couldn't count on the numbers she had. Too many of her soldiers had proven themselves traitors. They'd participated in a plot to *assassinate* her. It still sent a shiver down her spine. Even if she *could* trust them, Rim was still vulnerable against an attack from Banyan and Scar. There was only one solution to the problem.

She slipped under the water. Breath held, she made the decision: She would go to the Nightrose tribe to negotiate an agreement with the two Blood Lords. She'd take pre-emptive action before they launched an offensive that would only devastate Rim. Twenty-six people had died less than a week ago, nine of them civilians. She wouldn't let that happen again. She would go to Delphi to see them, and the sooner the better. She'd needed this week to heal. But the real rebuilding of Rim couldn't begin until Nightrose was no longer a threat. To begin her future here, she had to face the mess in her past and stop running once and for all. She decided she'd tell everyone at dinner tonight.

By midday tomorrow, she'd be on her way there.

Her pulse quickened when she thought of leaving Roar. But she was a ruler now, responsible for thousands upon thousands. That role was firm and real. Her marriage? She didn't know what it was anymore. And regardless, she couldn't let her heart interfere.

31

ROAR

While Tempest spent her days healing and poring over records, Roar roamed the city, letting his curiosity lead him. Sometimes Perry went with him, sometimes he went alone.

Having glimpsed the solid character of Rim's people that night in the tavern, he had a genuine interest in learning more about this place. Yes, this was where he'd experienced the worst days of his life, but it was becoming easier to look past them. To see today and imagine tomorrows.

He went where the wind blew him. More than once, he'd been back to the bookseller, Lilly, to bring home more books for Tempest. Aldred had kept his father's knives, so Tempest had hired a weaponsmith to make him new ones as a wedding present. Roar had spent a full afternoon with the man discussing weight and balance, testing the samples he had in his shop, then drawing out exactly what he wanted. He visited other shops in the city or wandered to the outskirts and talked to shepherds or farmers, or lumberjacks or fishermen. He asked what they loved about Rim, what they'd see changed. He inquired about weather patterns, the best hunting grounds, the last crop yields and expectations for the coming one.

Sometimes, people accompanied him for stretches and he'd have a guide introducing him around, shelling plump peas and dropping them in his hand, offering him a wriggling shepherd puppy as a wedding gift, which he'd declined after serious deliberation. A dog required commitment, and he was already fumbling enough with a marriage.

On that particular day, he and Perry were talking with a city engineer, who was giving them a tour of the aqueducts.

"We have always been great builders," the man said. "The infrastructure of the city and surrounding farmland was planned to provide clean water and shunt sewage far downriver to an unused tributary. These aqueducts feed fresh water in every direction. A decade ago, they were in such bad shape they barely put out any water. It was a priority of Sable's to repair them."

"This mattered to him?" Roar pushed his hair behind his ears, wishing he had tied it back. It was windy, and it kept whipping into his face. "He was committed to keeping the city clean?"

Mark, the stonemason, nodded. "Yes. He had the streets cleaned regularly and passed rules about rubbish disposal—things like that. But he also organized public celebrations, like the day of Rim's founding, the Feast of the Horns, and the Day of the Aether. When the storms got worse, of course, his priorities changed. He had to think about the Still Blue.

Things around here suffered, but it wasn't for anything he did. It was just—" he made a general gesture upwards, "*that.*"

Roar shared a look with Perry. No matter who you were, Blood Lord, farmer or stonemason, the Aether commanded them all.

Thinking of the Aether got Roar wondering about Soren and Rune. Had Soren gotten sidetracked? Instead of going to Cinder, had he gone east to try to get answers about the change in the Aether? Soren didn't talk about it often, but he had scars far deeper than the one on his jaw. His father, Consul Hess, had perpetrated true evil and kept secrets within secrets. In some ways, he was very much like Tempest: raised on lies.

As Roar saw more evidence of other public works Sable had overseen, he begrudgingly recognized the good his archenemy had done. He'd only witnessed Sable's leadership through manipulation and coercion, but Sable *had* taken care of his city and people. Moreover, Roar was beginning to see that the Horns were more than any single leader. Blood Lords came and went but this place, this land, its waterfalls and people—they endured.

They were the Horns.

"I think I'm finally starting to understand what the Tides really means to you," he said to Perry as they headed back to the fortress, the sun setting behind them. A culture was inseparable from its land. History and meaning came from the soil, the sky, the rivers. In the Tides' case, the sea. Roar felt like he'd had horse blinders removed. There was a vastness and interconnectedness to life he'd never appreciated before. Why not? Why had he kept his world so small, confined to a few people he loved almost obsessively? In a flash, he saw himself sitting under the window alone in his tiny childhood house, too small to even look outside. The world had never been his as a boy. Why want the thing that took his parents away? That made them miserable? Maybe he'd even been jealous of it. His parents had certainly loved the world more than him.

Perry nodded. "I was just thinking about the Tides. Regardless of what Talon says, I've decided I need to get it back. I just . . . I have to."

Roar froze, relief sweeping over him. "And Aria?" he asked, recalling Perry's comment about not being reckless with his life anymore because of her and Talon.

"She'll understand." Perry looked away for a second, frowning. "Right?"

"No doubt."

Perry nodded, shifting his weight. Roar waved hello at a few staring people in the street, pretending he didn't see how hard it was for his friend to be hundreds of miles, and an Aether barrier, away from the girl who owned his heart.

"Roar, I might need Tempest to do it. Everyone's in Cinder. They've moved on. I can't bring them back to fight for a place they left behind."

"You won't have to. Tempest will help. She gave her word."

Perry looked as though he might say something more, but he didn't.

As they walked on, Roar's thoughts held on Tempest, as they often seemed to nowadays. He didn't spend his days away from the fortress just to indulge his newfound interest in Rim; he did it to give her space to immerse herself in her new role—and because he was confused as hell about what they were now.

Not enemies anymore, no doubt about that. Not a married couple, either.

Friends? Well, sort of. Friends who slept in the same bed every night. Who touched and cuddled and even kissed—not on the lips or with any heat, but still. He didn't cuddle and kiss Soren, did he? Or even Aria, for that matter.

It all *felt* natural with Tempest, but he couldn't help wondering if she was just playing the role they'd laid out in the woods that day when a pine needle had spun down and landed on his shoulder. Then again, he also kept remembering the conversation they'd had at the end of that horrible night a week ago.

Sort it out. By it you mean . . . ?

Us, she'd said. *You want me and I want you.*

She *had* said those words, he was sure. But it still might not mean anything. Or it might mean that she was attracted to him, but that didn't mean she liked him. Or it might mean that she was attracted to him *and* liked him, but it still didn't mean she'd want to do anything about it. *Or* it might mean—

"*Grrr, enough,*" he muttered, as he and Perry stepped into the fortress. "Perry, when a person is concussed—"

"Welcome back, sir," said one of the guards. "How was your outing today?"

"Good, Devlin. I learned all about aqueducts. Any trouble here?"

"None, sir. Not a stir."

"Because you're terrifying." The man actually made Perry look small.

"Thank you, sir."

"Back at you, Devlin." Roar clapped the big guard on the shoulder as he walked past. "Stop looking at me like that, Peregrine."

"Who are you?" Perry asked. "Is that you, King Roar?"

"Yes. In the flesh," he replied dryly, a strange shiver passing through his shoulders. The truth was that he *liked* who he was becoming. He *liked* it here.

But did he really want this life? A life with Tempest? The Horns? These jagged mountains with their waterfalls, this sprawling northern city?

Yes. Yes, he did. Very, very much. Tempest far and above any of the rest of it.

If he could've, he'd have wrapped it all up in burlap, thrown it over his shoulder, and made off like a bandit in the night, but that wasn't how it worked. Everything hinged on Tempest—on what *she* wanted—which brought him back to his question.

"As I was saying, when a person is concussed, and terrified, and perhaps still in shock, is it possible they might say something they don't mean? Roar heard sputtering to his right. "Really? Now you're going to laugh at me? Your sovereign?"

Perry kept walking, shaking his head. "I wish Aria was here to see this."

Roar wished she was, too. He could've used some solid advice.

32

TEMPEST

That night at dinner, Roar draped his hand over the back of Tempest's chair. "Are you sure you're feeling well?" he whispered by her ear, his breath sending a shiver down her spine.

Across the dinner table, Daisy's mouth curved in a knowing smile.

"I'm fine," Tempest replied. "Just a little preoccupied."

Roar frowned, candlelight dancing in his brown eyes. He looked concerned and a little confused. And *tired*. She'd told him a dozen times he didn't need to stay awake while she slept, but whenever nightmares woke her, there he was. Awake and ready to pull her into his arms. "I know you've got a lot on your mind, Temp, but I wish you'd . . ."

He trailed off, and the noise of dinner conversation swirled up. Hayden, Hyde, and Straggler were talking over each other, trying to outdo each other in their impersonations of Perry as they recounted some story that, by all evidence, was the funniest thing anyone at the table had ever heard. Something about a threat he'd delivered in the midst of vomiting.

"You wish I'd?" she prompted.

His frown deepened. "Tell me when you're cold," he said, shrugging off his coat and draping it over her shoulders.

She pulled the fine wool around her. "That's not what you were going to say, but thank you." She had been a little cold, actually, and she didn't at all mind wrapping herself up in his scent.

"You're welcome," he said. "And I'll tell you what I was going to say later, in private. When I can be appropriately rude and horrible to you."

She smiled. "I quiver in fear."

His eyes flashed her way. He picked up his water glass and drained the rest of it.

Tempest pushed food around on her plate, trying to make herself eat. Again, she wondered how in the span of a few days, they'd gone from loathing each other to *this.* Whatever *this* was. What he'd just started to say, she was positive, was that he wished she'd trust him. But how could you trust someone you knew would walk away someday? She'd been through that already with her brother. She wasn't going to go through it again.

She ate gingerly, working around her healing cut, and enjoying the laughter that filled the dining room. Tonight's dinner—roasted chicken, medallioned potatoes with thyme, a salad of fresh greens and toasted almonds—was delicious, as every dinner had been. According to Lerra, the head cook had been inspired since her arrival.

When the food was cleared away, servants came by with fruit and hot drinks—tea and coffee and hot mulled wine, for those who wanted it. The weather was cooling. In a few weeks, the dramatic peaks around Rim would be dressed in white.

"Honey, sir?" the woman with the tea tray asked Roar.

"Thank you," he replied. "That would be great."

Tempest hid a smile, watching him from the corner of her eye.

It never failed. To every servant, and in every situation, he was the picture of courtesy. And not just *please* and *thank you*, either. *How are you tonight?* he'd ask. And *this stew is incredible—who made this?* He was so unaccustomed to luxury, so easily impressed and effortlessly thankful. Most of the time she loved it, but it could also break her heart a little, too. She knew his gratefulness stemmed from a childhood of neglect. At times, part of her wanted to shake him by the shoulders and say: *You deserve nice things, don't you know that?*

He caught her peering at him. "What did I do?"

"Nothing," she replied.

The smile disappeared from his eyes and he turned away, rejoining a conversation with Hayden and Cal. Too late, she realized she'd dodged another one of his questions.

Tempest mentally shook *herself* by the shoulders. She was distracted tonight; the decision to go to Nightrose was weighing on her. She had to tell everyone and she was dreading it. Once she spoke her piece, everything would change again and she didn't want that. She'd loved these past days. She wanted to cling to them for as long as she could.

Even as her cuts scabbed and her bruises faded, even as she'd struggled to sleep, to comprehend the scope of her new responsibilities, to make sense of what she and Roar were, she'd loved the promise in them, the path they unfurled into the future like an endless, plush carpet. Days of hard work with—and for—people who appreciated and respected her. Nights with a beautiful boy who could make her laugh, who could drive her crazy with desire, who could bring tears to her eyes when he sang. Who—and here was the real shock—now seemed to *like* the place he'd come to against his will, inwardly kicking and cursing.

By every account that came to her ears, he was doing a *great* job of pretending to be Blood Lord. People were seeing what she saw. He wasn't some reclusive and scheming dictator like Lund. Nor was he harsh and obsessive like Sable. Roar walked with the citizenry. He talked to them on their level. Joked with them. Sympathized with them. Learned from them.

And his creative solutions were undeniable.

She thought of what he'd said yesterday as he'd leaned over his sink, following the planes of his face with a blade: *Did you know there are massive herds of rams on the western foothills? They're so large, they're coming down to the farms to find food and destroying crops. I was thinking that if we could arrange a group of hunters to cull them down to sustainable numbers, we'd have meat and fur for winter and help the farmers there. I'd be glad to set it up and lead it, if you think it's a good idea.*

And when she'd sat down to dinner tonight, he'd told her: *I was talking with an apothecary in the city today and she mentioned our doctors and medicines are so widely respected that people travel weeks to get access to them. What do you think if we established a medical school so our skills could be taught?*

There were more, and they were all wonderful. Simple enough to implement and they'd make an unquestionable impact. While she tended to think in numbers and trends—it was utterly daunting to be responsible for *thousands*—he reminded her daily that the reports spoke of individuals, that her job wasn't much different than when she'd looked after Cal and Daisy and Ventus. Or, at least, that it was the same job multiplied by the hundreds.

But now, tomorrow, she was leaving. She was going to Nightrose in Delphi, and what would that mean? Would everything that was just starting to be good change? Collapse? Vanish?

She shook herself out of her thoughts and decided it was time to break her news. When there was a lull in the conversation, she jumped in.

"I wanted to share a decision I've made with all of you." It'd been quiet before, but now silence fell over the table; she could hear the sputter of a guttering candle. Clearing her throat, she told them about her history with Nightrose, her concerns they'd attack Rim, and the solution she'd come up with. "I'll take a small escort to go see them. Daisy and Cal. A half dozen soldiers. It's only precautionary. Banyan won't want to hurt me, and that'll leave more to help with defense here. Roar will stay." She couldn't look him in the eyes, so she looked at his hands. "It would be too dangerous for you to go to Nightrose, obviously, and it's me they want.

I'll negotiate a truce with them. I've already got some ideas. Then I'll come home."

She thought she laid it out rather well, so the protracted silence that followed surprised her. Then she picked up the molten iron of Roar's temper and her stomach dropped. His angry stare bored into space. No—he wasn't angry, he was *incandescent.*

"Can we have the room, please?" he said.

In seconds, they were alone—and her heart was bumping crazily in her chest.

"Roar, I—" She knew where she'd gone wrong, or thought she knew. "I know I probably should've told you first—"

"*Probably?*" He pushed out of his chair, strode to the other end of the table, and swung around. "Tempest, I don't even know where to start. Have you gone mad? You want to go to the men who've been *hunting* you for the past year? Who've threatened your life? *That's* who you want to pay a visit to?"

"Yes." Exhaustion suddenly washed over her. "I explained why it's the right decision."

"I know that!" he boomed. "I heard! I'm not disagreeing! It *is* the right decision, but you're not even healed yet! Am I supposed to be okay with you throwing your life in peril again? How do I stand by and let you do this?"

"I don't need your permission."

"I know that, too! You don't need anything from me!" He jammed his hands into his hair. "You certainly don't need to consider what I think! That would just muck up your plans! You just tell me along with everyone else. By the way, I'm leaving tomorrow. Off to see my old enemies, but you just stay here fearing the worst, Roar, because you're no longer useful."

"What? No." She came to her feet and went to him. "That's not what I think."

His hands came up. "No—don't." Pain radiated from his voice, his temper, his body. "Just go, Tempest," he said, bitterly. "Do what you need to do."

"Can't we talk about this? I'm sorry I didn't tell you before. This has been a lot for me. I'm overwhelmed, you know that. And I wasn't sure you'd care."

He gave a humorless bark of laughter. "*You weren't sure I'd care?*"

"Well . . . yes." It was the truth, albeit a clumsy way to put it. She knew he'd care, but she had no idea *how much*. A little? A lot? There was just no road map for being temporarily married to someone you'd almost had killed, who turned out to be an astonishingly excellent person you shared a bed with. Platonically.

"Right. Got it." The bone in his neck bobbed. "I do know this has been hard for you. I do. And I'm sorry I yelled. I shouldn't have." He seemed calmer, but her panic only ramped up. "You've given your orders. Is there anything else?"

She winced. Thinking back, it did seem like she'd given orders. The silence thickened, cementing them in a standstill. All she wanted to do was wrap her arms around him, feel his heartbeat against her cheek.

He sighed. "Fine. I guess I'll go."

"Go?" Something sharp twisted in her chest. "Where?" He didn't mean *really* go, did he?

He shrugged. "No idea. Somewhere."

"Roar, don't." Her vision blurred; she blinked it clear. "I'll follow you. I'll hobble right after you." A lame attempt at levity, but she was desperate.

His gaze fell to the table. When he looked up again, his eyes had the sheen of unshed tears. "So when *you* go, I'm supposed to stay like a dog, but when I do, you get to follow me?" He shook his head slowly. "Who's moving pawns around now? Tempest . . . is it possible you think you're a worthier human than me?"

"No! Roar, this isn't even about you!"

"My point exactly."

"That's not what I meant! It's not about me, either! I have to do this for the Horns. How can you act so hurt when you're only in this marriage because you have to be? You didn't want any of this, remember?"

"Yes. I remember," he said, his expression icing over. "Seems you've got things under control, though, so we can stop the charade. I'll leave tonight so I don't interfere with your plans. Please don't follow me." A breeze swept in, making the candlelight shimmer in his eyes. "Goodbye forever, Tempest."

33

TEMPEST

Tempest made it into bed before the tears spilled over. She poured them into her pillow, aching in ways she'd never known.

For the past nights, Roar's shoulder had been her pillow, his voice and scent like magic spells, erasing her troubles and pains. It was an especially cruel twist that she most wanted his comfort now when she couldn't have it—and *because* she couldn't.

She cried until her head throbbed. Then she got up and sat before the fire and stared into the flames, missing her brother, of all things. But Sable would've known what to do. In spite of his horrible flaws, he had always given sound advice. Was it terrible that she missed him? He'd been a killer, but wasn't she that now, too?

She felt like she was a child again. Lost, alone, scared. She kept feeding kindling to the fire. One by one, she watched the flames consume the slivers of bark as her forehead and cheeks went scalding hot.

Roar was leaving and it shouldn't be a shock. This was never going to last. They'd agreed. Temporary. A temporary arrangement. That's what it had been. A few weeks. Was it even a month yet? No. Not even a month yet.

So why did it feel like her heart was dying?

A knock on her door had her leaping up to answer it. She threw it open, hope winging in her chest. It was Daisy—and Tempest didn't have it in her to hide her disappointment.

"I know, sweetie. I know." Daisy wrapped her into a hug.

"What happened tonight, Daisy? I made such a stupid mistake." The tears were flowing again. "I should have talked to him before, but I was afraid because I can't tell what we are, or if he even likes me."

Daisy snorted. "I don't know how *you* can't tell, but it's obvious to everyone else."

Tempest stepped back. "It is? And who's everyone?"

"All of us. Me, Cal, Perry, the brothers. Your Aunt Lerra even showed up. We've all had a long discussion and the consensus is you're terrified of each other."

Tempest couldn't think about so many people discussing her private life right now, so she set that aside and concentrated on the rest. "Terrified of each other?"

That had a ring of truth; she felt it hum over her skin. As close as she and Roar had been for the past week, it'd felt like they were edging up to something thrilling and frightening. Like they stood at the top of a waterfall, afraid to leap into the pool below. Afraid of getting swept away. Afraid one decision—a real one not made in haste or under duress—could change them forever.

"Yes. And we all agreed you should go to him tonight."

Tempest felt something hot pop in her chest, like an ember. "He's still here?"

"Yes."

She went back to the hearth. She wasn't cold, but she needed its warmth, was drawing on it like strength. "He told me not to go after him."

"I know."

Tempest turned. "How do you *know* that?"

"It came up. Roar told Perry and Perry told us."

"This is unbelievable." She heard herself laugh. "So what did the council decide?"

"The council decided you need to try anyway. From what Perry shared, part of what's happening has to do with Liv."

"Liv. Because she left him and came here?"

"That's right. Apparently, she made the decision without any thought to his feelings. Left him without so much as a goodbye. That's a harsh way to treat the person who's supposedly the love of your life. And though Perry didn't say, I get the feeling she wasn't the only one who's made him feel discarded. I think he has some deep scars, Temp."

This part, she knew. "His parents. They were monsters. They left him alone for weeks on end. He told me he used to be afraid to wake up because they often disappeared overnight without telling him." Why hadn't she seen this pattern? He'd practically spelled it out for her. A memory flashed before her eyes. Two nights ago. She'd been braiding a lock of his hair as he'd lain in bed—an excuse to touch the earthy-black waves he usually kept tied back.

I hate braids, he'd said. *I don't know why I'm letting you do this.*

She'd laughed. *You* hate *braids? How is that even possible?*

They were one of the signs, he'd replied. *When my mother asked me to braid her hair, I knew they'd be leaving soon.*

Tempest jammed the heels of her hands into her swollen eyes. "No, no, no. Tell me I didn't just do the most insensitive, horrible thing I could've done to him."

"You didn't. Ordering Ventus to scar him was worse."

Tempest gasped, looking up. Daisy was laughing. "Daisy! That's a horrible joke!" But she was laughing now, too.

"Sweetheart," Daisy said, coming to her side. "It's not been an easy stretch for you. Maybe instead of punishing yourself for an honest mistake, one you regret, you could concentrate on fixing it? He's still here, Tempest. He hasn't gone yet. And though I know he's starting to like this place, that's not what's holding him back."

Tempest grabbed her by the elbows. "You're right! I'm going to talk to him. Tell the council good work but mind their own business in the future or heads will roll!"

Daisy laughed. "That's the spirit! Wait! Slippers, or that gash will open up again!" She swept them up. Tempest stepped into them and hugged her. "I love you."

"Well, I adore you." She spun Tempest by the shoulders and shoved her toward the door. "Now, go get that boy back."

"I'm going! I'll break his door down if I have to!" She flung herself into the corridor and would've smashed into Roar if he hadn't stepped back and caught her arms. "Roar!"

He let her go and took another step back. Daisy slid past them and was down the corridor faster than Tempest had ever seen her move.

"Hello," he said. His hair was in a ragged knot and his eyes were bloodshot. He seemed hollowed, like he'd been through a hundred nightmares. "You don't have to break my door down. I wasn't eavesdropping, I just—" He pointed generally at his ear.

"I know."

He nodded. "Tempest, I behaved terribly earlier and I—"

"Wait. Will you come inside?"

He exhaled. "Sure."

As he stepped past her, a thousand different thoughts crashed through her mind. She was trying to figure out where to start, how to avoid more misunderstanding, what she most wanted to say. But then a strong whiff of saltwater swept into her nose. She looked down and saw the damp at his sleeve, and something in her crumbled. She shut the door and threw herself at him, wrapping her arms around his neck.

He staggered back, a breath shuddering out of him as his arms cinched around her, hard as stone. "Tell me if I hurt you."

She shut her eyes and pressed her cheek against his. "You're not," she said, and heard her slippers thump to the floor. They were both breathing strangely, like their lungs had forgotten how to keep a rhythm. She leaned back and looked into his eyes. "I have so much to say, but the main thing is I'm sorry. I'm sorry if I made you feel unimportant or disrespected and unwanted. You're important to me and I respect you and you are very much wanted. By me."

He laughed; it was the best sound she'd ever heard. "Thank you for being specific." He set her down gently and framed her face with his hands. "And I'm sorry I lost my head. I *hate* yelling and I—"

"You were frustrated because I keep everything inside."

"Because you think you've got to do this all alone. You don't, Temp. I'm here for you."

"I know." She *had* known, she realized. She'd just been afraid to believe it. "And I really am so sorry about earlier."

"I'm sorrier."

"I'm sorriest."

"Well, you should be."

"Well, I am."

"Well, I was kidding."

"Roar . . ." She smoothed her hands up his back. He was all tightly wired strength. "You're beyond worth."

His eyes turned vulnerable again, clouding. "So you're not going to get another fake husband?"

"I have no plans to."

"Let me go with you to Delphi, then."

"They'd kill you. Banyan and Scar are no different than Aldred. Actually, they're worse."

"They'd kill your husband. I don't need to go as that. I'll go as one of your guards. They won't know. They have no idea who I am or what I look like."

He stroked her cheek with his thumb. She couldn't resist leaning into it. "You've been thinking about this."

"All I've been thinking about since we parted ways was how to avoid having to do it again. I know the territory is your priority. I won't get in the way of that. But I have to go with you. I'll stay out of your way if that's what you want. But I can't stay here while you're in danger. I can't do that."

"You don't want to let me go?"

"I can't. It's different." He leaned down and brushed a kiss over her lips. "Was that all right? Your lip . . ."

The intensity she saw in his eyes made it hard to breathe. "Very all right. And a persuasive addition to your argument."

He pulled in his bottom lip like he wanted to taste their kiss again. "I can be much more persuasive than that, Tempest. If you give me the chance."

The question couldn't have been clearer. She felt the answer like a shimmer throughout her entire body. "Chance granted." Before she'd finished speaking, she was off her feet and in his arms. She let out a yelp, her heart leaping.

In three strides, he was in front of the bed. "Damn. I'm going to have to throw you up there. Not very seductive."

"Depends. If you throw yourself onto me after, I think it might work."

His eyebrows arched. "I like this challenge. Here goes."

Somehow, he did it. He managed to gracefully heave her onto the bed, then follow immediately after, landing over her. She sank into the pillows, laughing. Most of his weight was on his elbows, but some wasn't and the feeling of him heavy and big and everywhere made her head spin. "Roar?"

"Here," he replied, as he kissed a trail down her neck.

"Are we sure about this? Everything's been so complicated with us."

He popped up, the dreamy look in his eyes sharpening. "It's never been us. Everything else has made us complicated. And I am *very* sure. But it doesn't mean a thing unless you are."

She wanted this. *Him*. In the back of her mind, she was afraid she might want him too much, and that if they did this, it would only hurt more when he walked away. But it wasn't reason enough to deter her. No matter what happened in the future, she knew she would never regret being with him tonight. "I'm sure."

"Okay, then." His smile was hooded. Utterly seductive. He bent to her lips again, kissing her slowly and deeply until her limbs felt like butter under a hot summer sun. Her mind was still racing, though. Filled with stupid thoughts. *Is this really happening? How can lips possibly be this soft? How can I make this keep going forever and ever? Is he hearing this?*

"Yes. And forever and ever sounds good." He leaned on one arm and slipped her robe off one shoulder, then moved to the other. The fire was still burning and throwing light, but when he looked down at her, his eyes were lost in shadow. No more than a second passed, but it was long enough for gooseflesh to break out over her skin and for her self-consciousness to flare up.

"What—what are you thinking?" she stammered. "You get to know my thoughts. But what about yours?"

"Honestly?" His eyes flicked up. "I wasn't thinking until you asked that question. But now . . . I don't know. I'm thinking that I feel like I've finally found my way home."

It was a gorgeous sentiment, and it felt like an embrace to the heart. She couldn't think of anything nearly as lovely to say back. "Are you saying I look like a *house?* Are you attracted to houses?"

He grinned. "I'm pretty sure the answer's obvious, but yes. You're a *beautiful* house, perfect in every way, and why are we talking about this—it's so odd—and I'm going to die if we don't—" his knuckles skated past her belly button and drifted lower, "if we don't—"

"Come here, then, and let's do." She pulled him into a hungry kiss that spun on and out, to his jaw, to the divot at the base of his neck. She paused only to pull off his shirt and toss it aside. She had already seen him shirtless that first morning in this room and knew he was stunning—sculpted and spare and smooth—but it was an altogether different thing to be able to touch him, to feel his fire-lit skin.

Her lips and her hands developed a sudden raging appetite. Every hard curve along his arms, every ridge of rib and knob of hip bone, every shivering breath she could coax out of him only made her hungrier. Then her attention came to the raised pink skin of his scar and her heart stopped.

"Hey." He took her hand and pressed a kiss to the center of her palm. "Let's leave the past where it belongs. We're here now. Let's make a new memory. One bright enough to outshine the bad ones."

She nodded, her eyes stinging. "Why, Roar? Just tell me once and for all. Why are you so beautiful?"

His mouth lifted wryly, but his eyes were deeply sincere. "For a long time, for no reason at all. But I guess I am for you now."

I am for you. She loved the sound of that.

She touched the X on his chest again, thinking briefly that it was the mark at the end of a long long journey, where treasures awaited. *You*, she thought to him, *are a treasure beyond compare*. Then she surrendered to her hunger, to the need to bring him as close as he could possibly be, devoured, consumed, part of her, aching with her, thrown out of the world and cast into the stars with her, then melting back into it together. Breathless and still wrapped in each other's arms.

34

ROAR

"It'll take a week to get there and to get back, plus a few days in Delphi, I'm guessing," Roar said early the following morning. "Probably three, four days." The sky above the courtyard was just beginning to brighten. He brushed away the sweat on his temple with a sleeve. "So, accounting for surprises, three weeks round trip. You'll be okay here without me?"

"*Yes*," Perry grumbled. "*Yes*, Roar." They were wrestling in the courtyard, like they used to as boys. The flagstones were far less forgiving than beach sand, though. Perry's elbow was bleeding. He didn't look happy about it. "We could've had this conversation as a conversation," he said gruffly. "And it could've waited until the sun came up. What are we doing out here? I thought you said things went well with Tempest."

"It went great." That was, perhaps, the biggest understatement of his life. "That's why we're out here. Good things never last for me."

"Idiot." Perry lunged for him, Roar dodged a few times until he was cornered, then they locked up and began another round.

Some time later when they stopped, Roar noticed they'd gathered an audience. About two dozen servants whose names he was finally learning were watching from around the courtyard and the upper arcade. Roar swept his sweaty hair back. "Morning, everyone." He jerked a thumb at Perry. "I usually dominate him."

"He does not," Perry said.

"Yes, I do. Look at his elbow."

Perry laughed. "Okay, sure. He's right. He usually wins."

Roar glared at him. "I *hate* it when you yield."

Perry made a bizarre face, presumably trying to look innocent. "Who's the winner now?"

The boy who tended to the hearth in his room, Elias, darted over with cups of water. "For you, sirs," he said, his wide eyes bouncing between Roar to Perry.

"Roar, Elias." Roar's hair fell into his eyes again. He swept it behind his ear and took the water. This had to be the fifth time he'd told the kid to call him by name. "*Roar.*"

The boy looked utterly puzzled. Then he roared. He actually *roared*.

Perry choked on his water. Roar clenched his jaw until he felt like his teeth might crack. "Wow, Elias. That was something. But it wasn't a command. Roar is my name."

The boy went red as a holly berry. "Well, I—I know that, but we never call our lords *by name*."

"Well, you do now. You can even roar it if you like. You are terrifying." The kid actually went even redder. "I'm kidding.

Hasn't anyone ever . . . ? Never mind. Meet me in Peregrine's chamber in ten minutes with shears."

"Shears?"

Roar made a cutting motion with his fingers. "Shears."

"Yes, Roar!" The boy ran off, his feet barely touching the ground.

Roar watched him go. "Is this what power feels like?"

"Intense, isn't it?" Perry took Roar's water and drank half, then poured the rest over his elbow.

Roar's attention moved more fully to his hearing. A group of serving girls were on the arcade above, whispering brazenly about Perry. None of them knew about Aria, which reminded him. "How long's it been since Soren left for Cinder?"

"Just over two weeks," Perry replied without missing a beat.

"Seems like longer."

Perry nodded tightly. "We'll hear something soon." It sounded like he was trying to convince himself. "You just concentrate on getting to Delphi and back."

An hour later, Roar stood outside the front gates of the fortress, where the escort party was gathered and waiting for Tempest. It had been decided that Cal should stay behind in Rim. She was respected amongst the soldiers there and would provide a stabilizing presence, which was needed after the recent upheaval. Though she didn't say it, Roar wondered if her staying back was also a symbolic gesture of sorts. A silent acknowledgment that she was officially ready to start sharing her Tempest-guarding duties with him.

She personally picked five of the best soldiers in the territory for the escort party. A good group, Roar had to agree after meeting them. Also joining them—as a late addition at Perry's request—was Hayden, the eldest of the Seer brothers but otherwise a clone to his siblings: funny, enormous, blond and blue-eyed archers. Like disciples of Perry.

Roar cut a glance his way. "I know you're not Perry. I *can* tell."

Hayden patted his black gelding on the neck. "What gave it away?"

"Just a gut feeling." Roar looked at Perry, who held the bridle of his horse. "Relax, Per. We're only going to visit our worst enemies. What could possibly go wrong?" He looked up as Tempest arrived with Daisy. Her smile sent heat rolling through him. A dozen versions of that smile, seen overnight, flashed through his memory. All stunning. She was wearing riding clothes, fitted black pants that hugged her curves and almost made him fall out of his saddle.

"Your hair," she said, walking over to her paint mare.

"Yeah, shorter." He scrubbed a hand over his head. He'd thought it might look more guardly, and he'd been craving a change—a lighter, lither feeling. He probably wouldn't have done it, though, if he'd remembered how it coiled into ludicrous baby curls when it was this short. "If it looks bad, blame Elias." He tipped his head at the boy, who stood with Daisy, and who promptly flushed with embarrassment. "Come on, Elias. We've been working on this."

"Oh—a joke!" Elias forced a laugh and smacked his knee to drive the hilarity home.

"I like that kid," Hayden said, seriously.

"You did an excellent job, Elias," Tempest said as Cal helped her into the saddle. She sent Roar a wicked smile. "Especially considering what you had to work with." She spurred her horse and set off, and the rest of the party followed.

For a long time afterward, Roar was still fighting a smile.

Roar's new role as one of Tempest's guards began immediately. From the moment they left Rim, they had to assume they were being watched. More than likely, Nightrose had spies in the borderlands, and that wouldn't change all the way to Delphi.

Cal had arranged a uniform for him. He was dressed like the other elite guards: black pants, boots, and under-tunic, black coat with the red Horn insignia and detail on the sleeves. He didn't much like his new get-up—he felt too conspicuous—but far more difficult was having to stay at an "appropriate distance" away from Tempest.

They'd just crossed the border between friendship and something more. He wanted nothing more than to hold her and kiss her, to say things to make her laugh and blush. To have to suppress the urge quietly drove him mad.

They rode during the days. At night, after everyone shared a meal around a campfire, Tempest and Daisy slept in a tent while he slept under the Aether with the others. He liked the crew Cal had assembled, and Hayden was always good for a laugh, but he missed his late-night talks with Tempest. He ached to feel her next to him as she told him about her day.

She cared so deeply about her people that it was infectious. She could make conversations about *granaries* interesting.

Forced to keep a distance from her, he savored every private smile and every casual touch. When he took her hand to help her into the saddle, he'd hear her voice in his mind telling him, *I miss you.* And that would carry him for hours, until he could find an excuse to be near her again.

But in the back of his mind, Nightrose was always there.

In the short time he'd known her, they had escaped Aldred's maniacal plan and Lund's revolt. Tempest had prevailed against Mattock, though it'd been close and come at a steep cost. None of those adversaries would compare with Banyan of the Night and Scar of the Rose—two ruthless and seasoned Blood Lords with thousands under their command—but he trusted her instincts. If she wanted to head right for the lion's den, then they'd do it.

Somehow, they'd make this mission succeed.

35

TEMPEST

As they approached Delphi, Tempest's stomach tied up in knots. A week in the saddle had given her plenty of time to think about the proposal she'd make to Scar and Banyan. She would strike a deal with them, some arrangement that would stop them coming to Rim. In spite of her plan, she was terrified.

"Roar," she said.

He was riding ahead of her, abreast of Hayden. He drew back immediately, bringing his horse even with hers. "What is it?"

There was a cold intensity in his gaze. Tempest knew he'd been to Delphi before, when it had belonged to its previous owner Marron, who'd been ousted by Banyan and Scar. She stopped her horse. Roar stopped with her. The others rode on, leaving them alone on the dirt road.

Along with her strategies for dealing with Banyan and Scar, she was thinking about how she and Roar would get through the next days. After making the decision to come to Delphi without consulting him, she was determined to be more open with him.

"What's going on, Temp?" Roar said.

"I've told you I grew up with Banyan's family. His daughter, Raven, and his son, Ash?"

"You have," he said carefully.

"Ash and I have a . . . a past."

"Ah, so he's the one." Humor lit in his eyes. "You worried I won't approve of your taste?"

"Oh, I think you will." Everyone approved of Ash. He was like Roar that way. He was actually like Roar in *a lot* of ways. A slipperier Roar with a mercurial, wicked streak.

Roar's eyebrows rose. "Interesting. Thanks for telling me, Temp. I mean it." He winked at her, and they pushed on.

As they made the final approach, her hands were sweating in spite of the cold. Delphi, like Rim, sat on a mountainside. Unlike Rim, here the slope was gradual and covered with thick evergreens. There was no Snake River, no sheer granite walls. The settlement itself was entirely encircled by a stone wall.

At the entrance gates, she announced herself to the guards, both of whom she recognized—and who didn't even bother to disguise their surprise at seeing her there.

They were led inside along a paved road through a broad yard. To the left, it branched into streets busy with people buying and selling goods. To the right, there were animal paddocks and stables, as well as what appeared to be a forge, a tannery, and a lumberyard. Directly ahead was an enormous structure—a cement box at odds with the quaint timber and stone structures everywhere else. Over the past week, she'd learned the history of this place. Originally, it'd been a mine. Then it became a bomb shelter. In spite of the ivy on the walls, it still looked grim and intimidating.

In front of this looming square structure, in an island where the path divided, there was a large fountain with a rusting iron sculpture centerpiece—a moon with a rose twisting around it. The symbols for the Night and Rose tribes.

Inside the cement structure, they were escorted through wide corridors with shining tile floors to a large dual-level room. In the central lower square, both Blood Lords lounged on furniture. People sat in tables along the elevated perimeter. They all fell quiet as she arrived.

Tempest felt an unexpected wave of emotion when she saw Banyan and his wife, Ivy, rise from their seats. They weren't her parents, but they had raised her from the age of seven. Though they'd only done so to fulfill a contract, she'd made a lot of good memories with them.

Her feelings toward Scar of the Rose—who didn't budge from where he sprawled—were very different. She'd only met the man a few times. He'd terrified her every time. Apparently, he still had that same power.

Tempest made herself keep walking. She'd been so sure about this idea, but doubts flooded her now in wave after wave.

"Tempest!" A girl jumped off a couch with a squeal and ran over. "I've missed you!"

"Raven!" Tempest laughed, catching the girl in her arms. "Let me see you! I didn't even recognize you!" Her relationship with Banyan and Ivy had always had invisible boundaries, but she'd never felt that with Raven or Ash. "You're so tall now!"

"You're so short!" Raven wasn't just taller—she'd gone from girl to young woman. She was almost fifteen now. Tempest had missed an important year of her life. She wore color on her lips and her eyes now, defining their elongated, poetic shape. Her hair was the same as ever, though: a black shining waterfall. "Temp, people are saying you're married! Is it true?"

"It is," she replied, keenly aware of Roar behind her.

Raven hopped up and down excitedly. "Is he here, is he here?"

"No, actually. He stayed in Rim."

"Oh." Raven looked crestfallen for a half a second. "Well, what's he like? Tell me everything!"

"Enough, Raven. Step aside, or I'm knocking you over."

Raven bounced away and there was Ash, with that mischievous smile and those beautiful ebony eyes. "Hello, you wily fugitive," he said, wickedly.

Ash had been a hostage just like her, part of his youth split in half, but his situation was even stranger. He effectively had three parents and all were present: his biological parents, Banyan and his wife Ivy; and Scar, who'd raised him until two years ago, when he'd returned to Night tribe at eighteen.

"Hello, you problematic ne'er do well," she teased back.

He swept her up in an embrace, popping a kiss on her cheek. "Marriage suits you. I'm so glad you're here," he said, but he was clearly in the minority.

An undeniable tension had fallen over the large room. Even if she hadn't scented it, she didn't miss the shifty looks people exchanged.

Ash stepped aside for his father. Banyan came forward leaning on a cane. That was new. So were the deep wrinkles around his eyes and the paleness of his skin. He was dealing with some kind of illness, she suspected. "You do know how to hide, don't you?"

Tempest's mouth twitched. *Or you don't know how to seek*, she wanted to say. But her goal was to negotiate and that would be easier if they kept things civil. "I'm here now. Hello, Banyan."

"Your husband stayed away?" he said, glowering at her. "It sounds to me like you married a coward." Despite being obviously unwell, he was still a handsome man like his son. The entire family—Ash, Raven, and Ivy, too—had ink-black hair, flawless skin, delicate bones and a natural elegance, like they were painted in watercolor.

"I married a responsible servant of the people. Roar stayed behind to supervise some important projects."

"*Or* you married a coward," Banyan said. "What would your brother have thought?"

That landed like a punch to the gut. No *sorry to hear of your brother's passing*. Tempest swallowed, reminding herself she'd hurt his pride by leaving the way she had. This was just his wounded ego speaking. She looked to Ivy, who stood beside him smiling mildly. She'd either been instructed to remain aloof or was choosing to. But even at her best, Banyan's wife was a withdrawn, morose woman. Tempest had always thought it a wonder that she'd given birth to such luminous, life-loving children.

Scar chuckled, plunking his feet on a table. He hadn't moved from where he sat. "She'd already be a widow," he said, in his deep, growling voice. "That's what Sable would've thought."

Tempest's heart slammed in her ribs. She remembered him as a big, foul-smelling, rumpled man with a quick temper and a violent streak a mile wide. He was more frightening than she recalled. Behind his bloodshot blue eyes there seemed to be an endless supply of rage.

Thoughts bounced crazily in her mind. Was she a fool to have let Roar come here? She could scent the anger in his temper—would he blow up under the insults? And though Scar was a good distance off, he was a strong Scire. Could he scent Roar's temper? What if he became suspicious?

"Well, welcome," Banyan said finally, without a trace of warmth. "Get yourself settled. We'll talk at dinner."

They were given chambers inside the main complex several flights underground, in the area that had been a bomb shelter.

"Not very subtle, are they?" Daisy said, as they entered the room the two of them would share. Tempest's guards were given the room next door—all seven of them, packed into bunks. "I mean . . ." Daisy brushed her shoe through the thick layer of dust on the cement floor, then plopped down on one of the hard cots. "Surely they have something a *little* better than this?"

"They do." She shivered. The room was frigid. "This is strategy. They're making sure I know my value—or lack thereof." She wasn't surprised. They'd have other tactics up their sleeve, too.

"I had forgotten how passive-aggressive Banyan is," Daisy said, whispering.

The only good thing about being in a windowless underground chamber was that they'd have some measure of sound protection. The first thing Roar had done was determine that if they kept their voices low, they could speak in relative privacy.

"I hadn't." Tempest sat down on her cot, flopping back. The mattress was musty and thin, but it would be better than sleeping on dirt and rocks. "And I'd take passive aggression over active aggression any day."

"Scar?"

Tempest stared at the electrical wires stapled to the ceiling that powered the flickering fluorescent light. "Scar."

She was tired and intimidated, and wanted to stay right where she was, but she made herself get ready for dinner. Though the room was sparse, dingy, and dark, it had a bathroom that adjoined the room next door. Tempest locked herself inside and took a quick shower, washing away the road dust, then Daisy pulled her hair into a circlet braid. While she'd studied Rim's account books and records, Aunt Lerra had crafted an entire wardrobe for her. Tempest had brought along a few items. She chose an emerald silk shift, adding her mother's gold earrings.

Roar was waiting with Hayden in the corridor to escort her to dinner. She tried to catch his eye, but he stared straight ahead all the way to the dining room. *And that's a* good *thing*, she reminded herself. The more focused both of them stayed on the mission, the better.

Like her room, the dining room also had no windows. Two of the walls were lined in rich red fabric. The other two walls were floor-to-ceiling telescreens, behind Scar and Banyan on either side of the room. These projected images of a forest at night from the point of view of someone walking through it. Almost immediately, Tempest found them disorienting—not only because of her fear of the dark but because it felt like walking in two opposing directions at the same time.

"Delphi has treated us well for the past year, but we have too many mouths to feed here," Banyan said, jumping right into politics. "We do have a long-term plan, however."

"I'm not surprised." Tempest had just started on her salad. Reluctantly, she set her fork down. She hadn't eaten a bite all day. "And what would that be?"

Down the table, Ash made a face at her, trying to get her to laugh. She sent him a quick head-shake. He was bored already—the price of being brilliant. He had probably thought through this dinner and already seen it to its inevitable end in his mind. She'd been placed at the middle of the table between strangers, away from him, Raven, and Ivy. This was no doubt another tactic meant to wrong-foot her.

"We'll do what we do well," Banyan replied, oblivious to his son's antics. "About four hundred miles to the northeast, there's a Dweller Pod that hasn't been raided, or destroyed by the Aether yet. It's the largest one, apparently. The heart of all the Dweller operations. We'll infiltrate it in the spring and make it ours. We deserve it, after all. The harsh state of the world, the Aether. Everything is all their fault." He waved a hand. "A subject for another dinner. Our concern for the present time is making it through the coming winter. I'll say this plainly. We don't have the food stores to accommodate our tribe. Going by our sources, you have your own shortage in defense. We know Sable took hundreds of your best fighters when he went to seek the Still Blue. So we'd like to propose a trade that will benefit us both.

"We have an excess of warriors. We can provide a supplemental force for you—two hundred of our best fighters. These are lean times, and you'll need them to protect your city against any threats. You have a surplus of food, which we will accept as compensation. We've enumerated our needs for grain, rice, spices, and salted meats. It's really a straightforward trade."

Tempest smiled. "I'm glad you've started us off. I'm also here to make a bargain that will benefit all of us. But I don't think what you've laid out will work."

Banyan scoffed. "*You don't think it'll work*," he repeated, mockingly. "They're good terms. Be reasonable, Tempest. Or it'll be *him* you have to deal with." He tipped his chin to Scar, who watched her like a hawk from the other end of the table.

"I don't think I'm being *un*reasonable," she said, holding on tight to her temper. "All I said was that what you've proposed won't work for the Horns. I'm sure we can come up with something that will, though."

"And how do you know it won't work? Because of your infinite experience as a ruler?"

Tempest took a sip of water, imagining she was quenching the inferno inside of her. "I suggest we leave the personal attacks out of this discussion."

"I *raised* you. This *is* personal. I'd hoped you might show some loyalty, or at least a little respect."

Tempest stared at him. *She* hadn't been disrespectful in the least. On the edge of her peripheral vision, she noticed Roar shift his weight.

"My turn," Scar said from the other end of the table, his voice a deep venomous drawl. Leather squeaked as he sat up. "Banyan has a point. You may be married, but you're still a mere girl, probably haven't even had your first blood yet. *Everything* you have done so far has been a mistake." His mouth curled into a sneer. "You are a *Horn.* A *Scire.* Yet you marry an unknown Tider who brings no strategic value. The Tides are gone. Their territory is in our hands. Did you not look ahead? How did you think you'd protect your tribe? How did you plan to unify them when you haven't been to Rim in years? You're an outsider who's brought them another outsider. They may think you're their savior now, but they'll soon see that you know nothing. Take our offer." He sat back. "Or live to regret it."

Tempest's fingers were trembling in her lap, but she'd been through this before with Lund. Roar had saved her then. This time, she was prepared. She drew a slow breath, holding the gaze of the enormous man across the table. "You've made many good points, Scar. As have you, Banyan. I'll try to respond to them all.

"You mentioned our weakened defense. I won't deny it. We are compromised in that regard. All the more reason why I won't allow a single one of your warriors inside my city. Offering 'help' to a vulnerable tribe to gain an inside position from which to betray them is a siege tactic that's been successful for you before, Scar. I've read the record of your extermination of Ghost tribe a few times. It was an impressive accomplishment. Not a single casualty to your warriors, yet you annihilated all of theirs in a day. Now *that* is an efficient ambuscade. I'm sure you understand why I'm declining your offer of *help*, given your history.

"As for the Horns' morale. Yes, it is low for us, as it is for everyone in these hard times—your people included—but it's heading in the right direction." She tapped her nose. "Thanks to this, I always know how the people around me are feeling.

"What else? Oh—you said I know nothing about ruling. It's true, I'm only on my second week at the helm of the Horns. Nevertheless, I do know a few things about political strategy, leadership, and government, which I've learned from the greatest minds in history. Thucydides, Herodotus, Kant, Machiavelli, Sun Tzu, Rousseau, Marx, Aquinas. I could really go on, but I can't forget my favorite—well, *one* of my favorites—Maimonedes who wrote, 'you must accept the truth from whatever source it comes.'

"In this particular case, the truth is that, in spite of your petty efforts to make me feel diminished, I am not afraid of either one of you, even though, yes, I am just a girl—who *has* bled, by the way. Though I fail to see how that's relevant. If you were feeling the effects of your age, for example, like stiff joints or diminished bowel control, or say you just weren't as virile anymore, that wouldn't be material to these negotiations, either. Don't you agree?

"Oh, I almost forgot. Roar. There you've got me. He *is* an outsider who brings no strategic advantage. To speak bluntly, he's not a born leader, either. But he is a natural one. From what I've seen so far, he's not turning the Horns into his followers. He's turning them into leaders themselves—a rather awesome thing to see. Fortunately, they've been giving him their fealty regardless. I think it's because they can sense, as I can, that his commitment to the Horns is genuine and deeply felt." She paused, realizing she felt utterly calm now. "Did I miss anything, Daisy?" She glanced over at her brilliant friend and assistant, who stood with Roar and Hayden against the wall, waiting, should she need them.

Daisy straightened. "No. That was everything."

Tempest smiled. "Good."

"Your own people tried to *kill you*," Banyan snapped.

Tempest hid her reaction. They either had a spy in Rim, or the news had come in another manner. She could only pray they hadn't been tipped off about Roar being there. "My aunt's husband tried. It didn't work. Has that never happened to either of you?" She looked from one end of the table to the other. Neither man said anything. "Interesting. I'd chalked it up to a consequence of having power. Listen, I feel for your situation. I do. No one should have to go hungry. When you're ready to have a civil negotiation, I'd be glad to discuss the ways I can help." She stood and went to the door, stopping there. "Banyan, have I ever told you that Tempest is actually a nickname? My brother gave it to me." She smiled. "He used to say that's what I turn into when someone pushes me far enough."

36

ROAR

"That was incredible!" Daisy whispered excitedly, squeezing Tempest's hands. They were in the chamber Tempest and Daisy shared, the entire escort party of seven crammed on the cots and standing against the wall. Daisy had just explained what had happened to those who hadn't been in the dining room.

"Beyond incredible." Hayden shook his head, grinning. "Beyond."

"Was it?" Tempest asked. "I can't even remember what I said."

"Don't worry, I've got every word locked in here." Roar tapped his temple. He thought he'd seen her at her best the night of the revolt when she'd stood in the rain, battered and bleeding, and addressed her people. But verbally slaying two Blood Lords with casual ease—*that* he wasn't ever going to get over. Who was this girl? What was she doing to him? Standing there in green silk, she looked like a goddess—even though she also looked exhausted.

Roar had lost track of the conversation. Daisy was describing the looks on the Blood Lords' faces.

"Banyan puckered up, but Scar—Scar looked like he'd been eviscerated." She laughed and looked at Tempest, finally noticing her dazed mood. "You okay?"

Tempest nodded. "My stomach's just a little quivery."

"Come on, Jons. Let's hunt down some tea." Daisy laughed. "Or champagne!"

When they left, Roar looked at the men who remained in the room. "Talk amongst yourselves for a minute?" They obliged immediately. Roar took Tempest's hand and pulled her aside. "Are you really all right?"

She looked like was she going to speak, but then she stepped forward and all but fell against him. He pulled her in closer. One week without this. He wasn't sure how he'd survived it. They stood like that for a long time, then she giggled against his chest. "This should be more awkward."

He knew what she meant. In the corner, Hayden was loudly leading a discussion on Delphi's access trails, while River, Lorelei, Beck, and Gavin loudly asked obvious questions.

Tempest looked up. "Scar is terrifying."

Roar wasn't going to disagree. There were few people in the world who actually gave him pause. Scar was one of them. "You know who was *really* terrifying?" He ducked down. "*You.* That was so brave. You amazed me. I almost gave myself away. I wanted to start throwing things around the room. Chairs and things."

She laughed. "You wanted to *throw* things?"

He shrugged. "Yes. Don't ask me to explain 'cause I can't." She was so small and soft. She felt like heaven through the thin silk. "All those books you mentioned—that was so sexy."

She smiled. "My brother used to send them to me, then make me send him reports about what I learned. I had to pare them down to three essential points and they had to be organized, clear, and brief."

He frowned. "That seems harsh."

"Maybe." She shrugged. "Maybe not. It did help me tonight. What about you?"

"Me? I think I've written zero book reports." Roar told himself to step back. A hug for moral support was one thing. He was crossing over into desire territory now and that wasn't going to help them. He bargained with himself. *One more second.*

Her expression softened. "There's so much we don't know about each other." Her gaze moved to his mouth.

"It's been hectic," he said. "And I really like where your thoughts are right now, but we better not." If they kissed, he knew he'd shatter whatever barrier he'd built around his focus. If he was going to protect her, intimacy was a line he couldn't cross. In this place, within these walls, it would only complicate their situation. He touched his forehead to hers and stepped back, strands of her hair getting caught on his scruff.

Daisy and Jons returned soon after, each hefting bottles of champagne. The group in the corner disbanded and came over.

"Low on grains, rice, beans . . . low on everything, but the cellar is *stocked*," Jons said.

Roar took one of the bottles. "Marron knows how to live." He slipped out one of his knives and popped the cork with a swipe. "To our fearsome ruler, Tempest." He held the fizzing bottle out to her. "Or whatever your name is."

She smiled. "Wouldn't you like to know?"

"Oh, I will. Some day."

They stayed awake late into the night, draped on chairs and sitting on the floor, passing the bottles around and telling stories. After a week together, day and night, a strong sense of camaraderie had developed between them. Roar had always been on the outside of such situations. Perry was the one who drew people in. Roar had always just come along for the ride, remaining on the periphery. But tonight he was right in the middle of things, laughing right along with Tempest and the others. And it felt good. Better than good. It felt right.

It was late when they all parted ways. Instead of going to sleep, Roar and Hayden went for a walk along Delphi's perimeter, following the wall. Noting everything that might matter—the layout, the height, the guards. The loose timbers and places a person might squeeze through. If things went south with Scar and Banyan, he wanted them to be able to make a fast getaway.

"You know, I've known you some time now," Hayden said, without preamble, "but it's only now it actually feels like I do. I'm not totally disappointed."

Roar looked at the tall figure loping beside him in the pre-dawn light. "I'm genuinely glad to hear that. Thanks, Perry."

Hayden laughed. "You're welcome."

37

TEMPEST

Tempest spent the following morning with Ash and Raven walking Delphi. She wanted to see—up close—the true state of the people of Nightrose.

Were they gaunt from going hungry? How was their morale?

If she was going to strike a good bargain with Scar and Banyan, she needed to see these things with her own eyes.

As it happened, there were plenty of signs that food was genuinely running low. The morning marketplace offered anemic stalks of kale, leeks, and carrots. There was little by way of meat for sale—only salted and smoked goods and small local game—and simple dairy products like milk, cheese, and butter were fetching high prices.

"Not much to sell or buy right now," Ash said, as they strolled together. He was handsomer than she remembered. But he was appealing the same way *anything* was: a sunset, a roaring fire, a blooming rose. He had never taken her breath away. "For the most part, we're on rations. My father's sent out scouting parties to find food for us. I think they're heading to the Pod where you were. Ironic, isn't it?" he continued. Raven had bounced ahead to a vendor selling bushels of asters and goldenrod. "We probably just missed finding you there."

"You have no idea how close it was," she said.

Ash made a funny face that got her wondering if maybe he did know. This was a quality she hadn't forgotten about him. He was mercurial. Enigmatic. Probably a defense mechanism from being raised as a hostage. Whereas she'd retreated behind a wall, learning to be independent, he'd learned to shift. To dart away from anything that might trap him. To think not *two* steps ahead but *ten*.

As they left the market behind, Tempest continued to see signs that Nightrose was in trouble. Delphi had never been built to shelter thousands upon thousands. The land was too rocky for good farming, and it wasn't near a healthy water source like a river, either. There was also an obvious tension between the people who were formerly of Night tribe and Rose. Rather than melding into a single cohesive society, the two groups seemed to coexist proximally, but separately. They hadn't really merged at all.

Members of Rose tribe appeared to have taken the eastern side of the settlement, with more outside the walls and camped along the upper slopes. Night tribe was primarily on the west inside the walled compound, and on the lower slopes outside. Many of the homes she saw were rickety lean-tos made of wood, canvas, metal sheeting. Anything that could be found. She knew it grew cold here in winter and shuddered to think of what it would be like for them when the weather turned cold in earnest.

They came to an overlook on the edge of the mountain. A cool wind chilled her cheeks and she shivered. Ash dropped an arm around her shoulders. "So are you going to help us?"

"I want to. But I can't sacrifice the Horns' health and safety. We're in better shape than this, but we're still suffering, too. There's so much that needs to be done."

"I know you're up to it. Is your new husband?"

"Yes."

Ash peered at her. "Just like that, yes?"

"Just like that, yes."

The sun was setting, the temperature dropping quickly as winds kicked up.

"So what's he like?" Ash wandered to the edge of the trail and crossed his arms. "He can't possibly be as handsome as me."

"Well, who could be? But, yes. He is handsome."

Ash looked surprised. "My god, Tempest. You're blushing!"

"I am not."

"You are so. Damn. I'm happy for you," Ash said seriously. "Strange. I've never been the jilted one before. It's not pleasant."

"We were never going to work out." There'd always been discussion about them marrying. Night and Horn tribes would've been a better union than Night and Rose. Sable had written to her about it. Both Banyan and Ivy had mentioned it to her often. Raven had even taken to calling her "sister" for a while. Everyone had known about their brief tryst, not because she and Ash had been obvious about it, but because they'd been hoping for it. Waiting for it.

"I know," he said. "But we could have been content together."

The note of disappointment in his voice surprised her. Ash had brief and passionate love affairs. He loved beauty and playfulness and freedom. Had they married, he'd have suffered the loss of that. What they had was much better. They loved each other as family.

"Now I'll have to marry some shrew who won't understand me," he said, broodingly.

"Maybe not. Maybe there's a way you can become Blood Lord and still be who you are."

"Our succession is hereditary. Eventually, I'll need a wife."

"No, Ash. What you'll need eventually is an heir. It's different."

He stared at her for a long moment. Then he came over and hugged her. "Thank you for giving me false hope."

"Anytime."

He stepped back, leaning against the tree beside her. Tempest waited for the pain to wash out of his temper before she spoke again. "Ash, there's no need to stay here anymore. The Aether is gentle again. Night tribe can return south. Rose, too. Going home might be possible. If not now, then soon." She recalled the textures of Night's territory. Good farmland, fertile hills for grazing animals. Olive groves and citrus. The four low hills that surrounded the main part of the city, providing a natural defense. Such a beautiful region. Some of it had to be recoverable, didn't it? Certainly, it would be better than this. "Don't you want to go home?"

He laughed humorlessly. "That's *all* I want. We sent scouts down there a few weeks ago. The report is that it's damaged, but recoverable. Actually," his head lolled to the side, "the report is that it's much more damaged than your land. To bring it back to functioning would take a year of repair and rebuilding, in addition to the logistical nightmare of moving thousands of people back safely. Your land is in much better condition. It's also seven days away over forgiving terrain, offering fresh water and places to shelter along the way. Night lands would take twice that long to reach and be four times as risky—and ultimately can't accommodate what we are now. Not six, but twelve thousand people." His mouth pressed into a grim line. "My father can't make decisions freely anymore."

She thought of the years Ash was hostage with Scar, knowing all too well the strangeness of the arrangement. "Don't you feel the slightest bit of loyalty to him?" She didn't need to name Scar for Ash to know who she meant.

In response, Ash just stared at her.

She nodded, understanding. She'd asked a question he couldn't answer.

"Turning to more important matters," he said, lowering his voice. "Who's your guard with the godlike looks?"

She almost burst out laughing. "Which one do you mean?"

"Tempest. How is it not obvious?"

"Oh, I think I know. But don't waste your time. He's duller than a wall."

"I'm not looking for scintillating conversation."

"Well, in that case, by all means. Give it a go."

"You don't mind?"

"Of course not. Why would I?" she returned.

"Thank you," Ash said, with a glint in his eyes.

As they headed back, she wondered: Did he know the truth about Roar?

If so, was Roar in danger?

That night, Tempest attended another dinner with Scar and Banyan. This time there was entertainment—a musical troupe that made talking with anyone beyond her close neighbors impossible. Tempest had been seated between Ash and Raven. *On purpose*, she thought. They were subtly manipulating her. Getting her to relax, have fun. Replace last night's tension with candlelight and wine, good food and good company.

They probably hoped she would go to sleep feeling aglow. That as she dreamt, that glow would seep into the place where her feelings for them resided, and that by morning, she'd have reconsidered their offer. Softened to their plight.

It was probably going to work, too.

She *did* feel more relaxed than the previous night, thanks to her day with Ash and Raven. She didn't want to be in an antagonistic relationship with Banyan, and especially not with Scar. She allowed herself a glass of wine. That relaxed her even more, so she let her gaze drift Roar's way.

It had occurred to her that if she solved her problem with Nightrose tribe, then her territory would be safe. And that would mean that her deal with Roar, to pretend to be married until the Horns were secure, would be fulfilled. Bizarrely, she felt like she was simultaneously working toward and against herself.

What would come after this? Anything?

As she ate fresh whitefish and roasted vegetables, she and Raven had a deep conversation about books while Ash interjected insightful commentary. He hadn't actually *read* any of the books they discussed, but he was frequently spot-on anyway. Their debate felt familiar, a well-worn pattern, and she realized just how much she had missed them. The truth was, she was closer to Ash and Raven than to her own aunt—or her husband.

But was that really still true?

Tempest sipped her wine and stole another glance at Roar. Candlelight swayed over his face, and he looked mysterious and dangerous, fitting the part of a watchful guard. Except she'd never seen a guard like him. Desire wove through her like hot ribbons, curling around her limbs. She wanted to kiss his elegant nose. The graceful bones of his jaw and high cheekbones.

Roar turned slightly, his eyes sending a clear message. *You are being incredibly obvious.*

All she wanted was to be even *more* obvious.

"Do you miss your husband?" Raven asked, dropping her chin on her hand.

"Constantly," Tempest replied.

Raven giggled, a light blush coloring her cheeks. She whispered, "Is he a good lover?"

"Oh." A nervous laugh tumbled out of her. "Well, with all that's happened, we've only had one night together. But the word *good* doesn't begin to approach it."

Raven squealed. "Tell me everything!"

"Yes," Ash said. "Tell us everything."

"Sorry. All I'll say is that reality, with him, is better than any fantasy." This produced an uproar between the siblings. Tempest stole another glance at Roar while they were distracted. He was glaring at the opposite wall with the oddest expression—part smug confidence, part inner torment.

She smiled and took another sip of her wine.

Later, she lay in bed regretting that second glass. The room was spinning and the cold seemed to have settled inside her bones. She lay, shivering and uncomfortable, staring through the darkness at the wires on the ceiling. Like last night, she was in a sweater over a long-sleeved nightgown, and wearing a second pair of socks—but they didn't help. Also not helping were the fears that seemed to always lurk in the deeper shadows. She could almost smell that midnight carriage. That apple orchard, and the wine cellar. She eyed Daisy's sleeping form on the bed next to hers and considered climbing in with her, but she'd only disturb Daisy's sleep.

She turned to her strengths for comfort. For a while, she ran through the events of the day. All that she saw. She made calculations in her mind, thinking through crop yields, the potential effects of the Aether, the Horn's population, the numbers Banyan and Scar had given her for Rose and Night. She adjusted those down slightly after making some estimates based on what she'd seen on her walk with Ash. At the end of it, she knew what food stores she could spare—what was generous—and she would be that. But she would also be smart.

She let out a big breath and ran through the exercise again to be sure, and to account for any errors caused by the wine. She'd just confirmed her decision when she saw a shift in the darkness. She shot up, cracking her forehead against something hard. There was a muffled curse, the voice deeply resonant and familiar.

"Sorry!" she blurted.

"It's me. Didn't mean to scare you," Roar said. "I've been listening to your teeth chatter. I brought you a blanket." He lifted a shape in the darkness.

"Oh, thank you. I'm freezing. Are you all right?"

"My nose might be broken."

"Tragedy! Let me see!" She fumbled through the dark and found his hand, pushing it—and his objections—aside. She ran her finger down the bridge a few times. "Still straight. Oh, *relief!* Such a good nose. Why do I feel like crying? That was a close call."

Roar was silent, his dark eyes glinting softly. "I'm going to get you some water."

"No—stay." She pulled him down next to her. "I'm so cold, you're better than a blanket."

"I preferred being better than a fantasy," he said, a smile in his voice. The cot creaked as he settled in. "I'm not staying long."

"Yes, you are."

"No, I'm not."

She ducked under his arm, burrowing into his chest. "Have I lost you to Ash?"

"Temp, lower your voice a bit," he whispered. "I'm not the only Aud in the world, you know. And no, you haven't. But not for his lack of trying. Great guy, but you're more my type."

She giggled. "*More* your type. How fortunate for me." She slipped her hand under the hem of his shirt, splaying it on his smooth stomach. "You're exactly my type."

He tensed, his abdomen ridging with muscle. "You. Same," he said, breath held.

The musky, amber scent of his longing was heady and strong, and there were notes of the outside on him. Trees and grass. Autumn on the edge of winter. He smelled like survival. Like proven strength.

She suddenly remembered. "Roar?" She turned her question inward. *Did you get that?*

He exhaled. "I did." He kissed the top of her head. "Thank you. I've never been complimented much. Not for things that matter. Not like that."

That seemed a crime. She knew about his parents, but she was wondering why Liv hadn't complimented him when she realized she hadn't moved her hand away.

"No—it's all right," he said. "Really. That's something I've wondered myself for years. I think it had to do with her father. When he drank, he became violent. With Perry, not her. But Liv was his protector. I think growing up like that hurt her. Collateral damage, you could say." He shook his head. "I shouldn't be saying these things. Disparaging her memory like this."

Tempest turned and looked him in the eyes. "You can still love someone and honor their memory even though they're flawed. I have to believe that."

"Because of your brother." The way he said it was more a statement than a question.

"Yes. And because none of us is perfect."

He swept her hair over her shoulder. "Debatable," he murmured against her nape. "What about you, Temp? Am I dishonoring you by talking about her? She shouldn't be here with us. I don't want her to be."

"We can't ignore them. Not Liv or my brother. They're part of our past. But a clever fellow told me recently that it's possible to make new memories bright enough to outshine the bad ones."

"Sometimes when I look at you, I wonder if I'm in a dream."

She kissed him then, unable to stop herself.

"We can't, Temp," he said between kisses. "The plan. And Daisy. Right there. Awake."

"No, I'm not," Daisy said.

This is torture, Tempest thought to him. *Why did you join me on this mission?* She slid her hand lower, down to his belt.

Roar caught her wrist. "*Whoa*-kay," he said, rolling soundlessly to his feet. "I'm going to go now." Tempest watched him shift his shoulders in the darkness, drawing a hissing breath. "Oh—almost forgot. I didn't just come here to give you blanket. I came to say I may be onto something. While you were out today with Ash and Raven, I spent the day eavesdropping on any conversation I could hear—which was a lot. There's trouble between Night and Rose."

"Yes. I picked up on that, too."

"Of course you did. I'll keep listening in. Maybe it'll give us something to work with. Goodnight, Daisy."

"Goodnight, Roar," Daisy returned.

"Goodnight, Autumn?" Roar said.

Tempest giggled. "No."

"Goodnight, Hazel?"

"No again."

"Goodnight, Wren?"

"Still no."

Tempest heard a soft sigh of disappointment. "All right, then. Good night, little duckling." The door opened and closed. She rolled onto her side, hugging the pillow close. It was a pathetic replacement.

~ 38 ~

ROAR

In the morning, Roar went to the dirt pen where the Nightrose guards drilled. Hayden and Jons were already there as planned, draped over the wood rails that surrounded the pen, which appeared to have been for livestock at some point.

At the center, two pairs of guards engaged in sword combat. Off to the right, in a clearing backed by the woods, archers practiced shooting at straw men. The clang of steel rang into the crisp mountain air.

"Anything?" he asked, propping his boot on a slat.

"Nothing new," Hayden said. "There's no love lost between them, though. No doubt about that."

Roar watched the guards in the pit. One of the pairs out there was Night men, sparring together. The other was a Rose guard against a Night. There was an obvious difference between them, the mismatched pair far more aggressive, well beyond what was typical for simple drill.

Along the perimeter, he noticed very little co-mingling between the two uniforms. The guards in the gray tunics with the rose embroidered at the shoulder kept to themselves, as did the guards in the black tunics with the moon symbol. Since he arrived, he'd been hearing jibes and insults pass between them. Nightrose was *not* a stable tribe.

"Morning." Ash appeared at his side, propping his elbows on the fence. "Thinking about going in there?"

"Depends," Roar replied. "If I saw an opponent who might challenge me, maybe."

Hayden and Jons casually moved away.

Ash smiled. "What's your weapon, Rush?"

Roar was using his father's name as his false name. "Whatever's handy. But knives are my preference."

"Ah. Bows for me. Once again, we're not aligned," Ash replied good-naturedly. Yesterday, he had not been subtle about making a pass at Roar. Self-confidence was not a problem for Ash of the Night. Banyan's son was charismatic, smart, and handsome. While most of those qualities were lost on Roar, Jons was another story.

"Alas," Roar said. "But you might have better luck elsewhere." He tipped his chin in Jons' direction. Jons was laughing at something Hayden said with extra gusto, like he knew he was being watched.

Ash's gaze narrowed. "The blond tree, or the shorter fellow with the braids?"

"The latter. Jons is his name."

Ash was quiet for a moment. Then he returned his attention to the pit.

Roar rested his elbows on the fence. "Are your fighters always this zealous in training?"

"No. Things changed when we merged with Rose. My father and Scar have tried a number of things to bring the tribes together. That ridiculous fountain with the moon and roses, for example. Scar's idea. He was damn proud of it, too. 'The Fountain of Unity,' he called it. He's big on symbols. Appearances. But it didn't work. Nothing really has. They were our enemies for generations. That sort of enmity doesn't disappear overnight."

"I can imagine. But it's been more than a year, hasn't it?"

"Yes, but barely. Food shortages have kept tensions high. My father does what he can. Doesn't always work. I lived with Scar for a while. They're . . . different men."

This was all great information. Going on pure instinct, Roar decided to take a chance. Ash was being rather forthcoming. "Has the merger been beneficial overall?"

Ash smiled without looking away from the men fighting in the training pit. "In the past? Yes."

"I see."

"Sometimes you solve one problem, but create others."

Roar nodded. "As I well know. Hold on a sec—hey!" he shouted at a Rose soldier—a woman who was wrestling with a Night soldier nearly twice her size. "Reverse it! Pull his arm *back*, not across!"

The woman did as he'd said, folding the man's arm behind him and yanking just to the point of dislocation. Her opponent swore viciously and tapped out. She tossed him a nod in thanks, and for a while, as another pair entered the pit, Roar felt Ash's attention on him.

It was an intense thing. Like being dissected. "Are you trying to see into the workings of my mind?" he finally asked.

"No. That part I've got."

Roar didn't doubt it. When he was around Tempest, he could feel the sharpness of her intellect, but Ash was something else. "Care to share some insight? Spare me some mistakes down the line?"

"Sure." Ash turned his attention back to the fighting. "Know when to bend."

"Sorry?"

"Do the thing you just advised. Know when to modify a tactic. Some people are unable to change their minds once it's set. Scar, for example. If he decides he wants blood, he gets blood, no matter what. That's just how he is."

Roar's pulse was thudding hard. "Seems like the type who wants it often," he said quietly.

"Not often." Ash looked at him again. "He *always* does."

Roar watched him walk away, absorbing the tip he'd just received wrapped in the guise of advice. No matter the negotiations, no matter what Tempest or Banyan wanted, Scar's mind was set. He was going to attack Rim.

As Tempest had gone on a long ride with Raven that day, Roar had to wait until evening to talk to her, but it gave him a chance to confirm what he'd learned. It was easier to overhear things if he knew what he was listening for. He did, in fact, confirm that Scar was quietly preparing his soldiers for an attack on Rim, gathering provisions and taking meetings behind closed doors.

Finally, that night, Roar caught Tempest alone in her chamber. Somewhat alone. Daisy was in the adjoining bathroom showering. He told her everything. After, she fell into one of her long, "I'm thinking" silences. Roar could almost see her sorting through the information like she was tidying stacks of paper. *This goes here. This goes there.*

"Ash," she said finally, shaking her head. "He's given it all to us. Everything we need to know. Yesterday, he took me where I'd see their weakness—the same thing you picked up on, too. Their tribe isn't cohesive. It's not Nightrose, so much as Night *and* Rose. Today, he made sure we're motivated by telling us that Scar is preparing to attack." She laughed. "It's so obvious. He's probably been waiting for it to click. I bet he thinks we're thick-headed dopes."

Roar nodded. "Right. But if, say, you knew a thick-headed dope, how would you explain the obvious conclusion?"

Her grin went wider. "We divide them. We can't survive an attack from Nightrose. There's just too many of them. But if the tribe disbanded into two again, if it was just Rose, we'd have a chance to stand against them in Rim. I think we'd even have the advantage. And if we split them, there'd be the added benefit of helping Ash get what's best for the Night tribe. They'd be free of Scar."

"Yes, brilliant," Roar said, seeing it. "How do we do that?"

"We give what's already starting to happen a little nudge."

That night, Tempest flattered Banyan relentlessly at dinner. With every compliment, Scar's mood darkened like a coming storm. Roar stood in the shadows of the dining room and watched Scar carefully. More and more, he saw that the big man did *not* like sharing power. His mouth curled into a snarl every time Banyan spoke. When Banyan's wife spoke, Scar talked over her like she didn't exist.

Earlier that afternoon, Roar had spent some time in the kitchens with the serving staff, flirting when needed. Singing a song or two. For his trouble, he was rewarded by seeing Banyan's wine refilled more often. The meat served to Scar was tougher, the bread staler, the vegetables wilted. Every little thing contributed to their objective: to drive a stake between the two men who, they now knew, would attack the Horns regardless of Tempest's diplomatic efforts.

Dinner was only the first part of Tempest's plan: when they'd plant the seeds. The second part, sowing them, would come later. Roar couldn't wait to find out what she had in mind.

"You two *do* impress me," Tempest said, raising her glass to her lips. Last night, she'd been genuinely tipsy, but tonight she was only pretending to be. "It's *remarkable* how well you share power. Like a marriage, almost. Without some of the other rather enjoyable aspects."

Ash let out bark of laughter. Beside him, Raven giggled.

Tempest continued. "How does it work? Do you take turns making decisions? Who gets the final say in things? Or do you negotiate? Roar and I negotiate until we're both satisfied."

"You must disagree often," Ash said, with a mischievous smile.

"A girl never shares her secrets," Tempest said, demurely. "But as you said recently, Scar, Roar brought little to our union, and he recognizes it. He hasn't got the pride nor the expectations of someone raised to power. It's refreshing. It makes him reasonable in discussions. He's not one of those bellicose types who have to throw their weight around to prove their superiority."

Scar stared daggers at her. "Some *bellicose types*, as you call them, *are* superior."

Roar watched as Banyan and his wife exchanged a knowing look.

"I suppose," Tempest replied innocently. "Seems to me like most aren't, but what do I know? Everything I learned about power, I learned from either books or my brother. He wasn't bellicose."

The dining hall was already quiet, but Roar heard the silence deepen now. This was Sable's power. Even in his grave, he commanded respect. Awe.

"And what did your *beloved* brother teach you?" Scar asked, his voice laced with sarcasm.

"Oh, a lot. So much."

"Weren't you raised away from him?" Scar was practically spitting venom.

"Yes, but we wrote often." Banyan nodded, knowing this to be true. "My stack of letters was this thick." She held her hands apart about the width of a brick. It wasn't even a lie. "It was almost better, in a way, getting his lessons written down. I read them over and over. I've got them all memorized." She tapped her temple. "They're all right in here."

"Well, go on. Tell us one," Ash said.

"Now?"

Ash shrugged. "Now."

"All right. Well, there's this one lesson that's more of a story." She stared up at the ceiling for a second. "'Tempest' he wrote, 'say you're lost in a dark wood and you come to a crossroads. To one side of the road stands a traveler with a great sword, fresh blood still dripping down the blade. To the other stands a man in a heavy cloak, which he removes and offers to you. Both of them promise they can take you to shelter. Which one do you trust?'"

The entire hall was listening, Roar noticed. Even the servants had frozen in place, trays and pitchers balanced in their hands.

"Who, who?" Raven pleaded, like an owl. "Tell us!"

"Neither, of course," Tempest said. "You trust no one on sight."

"But what were you supposed to do?" the younger girl cried. "Where's the lesson in that?"

"Oh, there's a lesson." Tempest popped a blackberry in her mouth, then tapped Raven's nose with a finger. "Never get lost!"

Laughter ran through the hall.

"Have you taken that to heart, Temp?" Ash asked. "Trust no one? Do you not even trust your new husband?"

Tempest frowned like she hadn't ever considered this, but every word she chose was deliberate. Intentional. Like a script that Ash seemed to know by heart, too. He had instigated the drama that was unfolding. Like a puppet master.

"I think I do trust him," Tempest said at last. "But only up to a point."

Banyan, who'd been silent for some time, stirred in his seat. "Only to a point? Is that possible? Can it be called trust if it's not given fully?"

Again, Tempest pretended to think. "No, actually. You're right. If you can't trust someone completely, then you can't trust them at all. You always need to be on the lookout. You always have to anticipate that they might turn on you or fail you in some terrible way. That's not trust."

This time, it was Scar who exchanged a loaded glance with his first in command, a hulking figure by the door.

Tempest smiled, looking between the two Blood Lords. "I just realized you never answered earlier. How do you two decide who's right?"

Roar had to drop his head to hide his smile.

My fake wife, he thought, *is a damn genius.*

Later, by roaming the halls ostensibly in search of Hayden—who was actually sleeping in their room—Roar overheard Banyan yelling at Ash, and Scar yelling at over a dozen people. As planned, tensions were running high.

At the heart of their disagreements was Tempest. They debated whether to make a hostile push for the Horns or not. Was it worth it? Banyan was on the fence. Scar was not.

If they did attack Rim, whose men would lead the fight? If Rose tribe took Rim, could they be trusted to admit Night tribe? If they lost and suffered mass casualties, would that create an imbalance with Night tribe? If they sent equal numbers of troops, half Rose and half Night, who would lead? Could the soldiers be trusted to fight alongside one another, considering the simmering discord between them?

It was all music to Roar's ears.

Now, in the deepest part of the night, he slipped into Tempest's chamber. It was time for the second part of the plan—sowing the seeds. He was about to find out what that meant.

Tempest immediately rose from the bed, like she'd been waiting for him. She was dressed in black from head to toe, which set off a warning in his mind. He promptly forgot it when she folded her arms around him.

"You're good?" she asked.

"Yes. It couldn't have gone more perfectly. Remind me never to get on your bad side."

She smirked. "You've been there already. I regret it every day."

Roar peered down at her. "We're going to have to work on that."

"Later. We'd better get moving. We only have a few hours until daylight."

Roar looked at her, the feeling of unease building within him. "What are we doing, Temp?"

Her smile was downright wicked. "Just a little vandalism, is all."

39

TEMPEST

Tempest wasn't sure if she loved that Roar was going along with her plan or if it terrified her—but he *was* going along with it. He firmed his grip on her hand and pulled her through the corridors, pausing every so often when he heard things she didn't before continuing on.

He'd spent months here a couple of years ago and it showed. He seemed to know every shadowy corner to hide, every closet to duck into whenever guards passed by.

There was an intensity in him she'd never seen before, predatory and cool. Not long ago he'd told her that, because of his parents, he'd learned to disappear. While her heart ached that that was true, she was grateful for this skill now. If they were discovered, they'd undoubtedly be killed for what they were about to attempt.

They made it to a stairwell in the distant reaches of the main building, slipping into the cool space. It smelled strongly of urine and she couldn't see anything at all. Fear edged in. Images of Mattock. The damp smell of that wine cellar.

Roar squeezed her hand, then brought it to his shoulder. "Can't turn the lights on," he whispered. "The doors have small windows. So just take it slow. The steps are evenly spaced. You'll find a rhythm. And I'm right in front of you."

"How many flights do we have to climb?"

"Seven."

It felt like ten, but she managed it. They left the stairwell behind, exiting to the roof—a broad stretch of cement, bordered by a low wall. On the far end, a sentry paced alongside it, singing to himself. Aether flowed in gauzy threads against the night sky.

Roar, no bloodshed, she thought to him, touching his hand.

He nodded once. "See that pail against the wall? When I say so, run to it. Go five feet past it and climb over. There's ivy on the other side. It's sturdy—supported by an iron frame. It'll hold you, I promise. I'll be right behind you."

She nodded, her heart beating furiously. The guard had settled with a boot on the wall and lit a cigarette. Tempest had only ever smelled them once before in her life, but Marron kept extravagantly old items here, and it must have been amongst his archives.

He smoked it with his back turned to them. It seemed like the perfect time to go, but Roar held still, waiting, waiting. Finally, a stiff breeze swept across the evergreens all around the compound, making the leaves hiss. "Now," he whispered. "Go."

She darted across the roof, trying to stay as light on her feet as possible. The pail was much farther than it had appeared. Roar stuck close to her side, silent and fluid. Finally, she passed it, counted five feet, and didn't hesitate.

She swung her leg over the low wall and climbed over. The ivy was there, and she felt the firmness of the iron grate beneath. What he had neglected to tell her, however, was that they were easily five stories above ground. She flattened herself against the ivy, her body locking up.

"It's all right," Roar whispered into her ear. "It's okay. Breathe, Temp. Take a breath."

He was behind her, his chin right over her shoulder, his chest against her back. His cheek rested against hers, so she let herself yell into his mind.

You didn't tell me it was this high up!

"Cause I didn't think you'd like it," he whispered. Was he *smiling?* "But I also knew you'd be able to handle it. You wanted to be part of this, didn't you?"

Yes. She had insisted. This was her idea. Roar had only come in with the logistics—the how and when.

"Well, this is what it takes. I'm going to move away now, but you're fine. Just don't look down. Trust me. I won't let anything happen to you." He popped a kiss on her cheek. "This is fun, isn't it?"

Fun? She glared at him. "*You are a fool!*" she whispered.

"Why, because I did this?" He planted another kiss on her temple. "All right, let's climb. This is dangerous as hell."

It was actually those two kisses that got her down that wall. They got her thinking about how very *alive* he seemed. How danger seemed to suit him, to elevate his charisma and confidence. Apart from those first few seconds during the night of the revolt, she hadn't seen this side of him. She felt like everything suddenly made sense. Like she had the full picture now. *This is who he is*, she thought. Next thing she knew, she was stepping off the grate and onto the gravelly ground. She was out of breath, but Roar didn't look the least bit tired.

"Okay?" he said.

She brushed away the sweat from her temple. "I don't know." Her muscles were quivering. Even her gut felt like it was quaking.

His grin flashed in the darkness. "You did great. Come on. It's this way."

He led her past the main streets toward the animal pens. With the walls to one side, and the main building at the center, the shadows that pooled within Delphi were especially deep, and she was glad that he was so familiar with it—and glad for his hearing. Once again, they moved in stops and starts, Roar gauging any presence of random night wanderers.

She had recovered her steadiness by the time they arrived at the paddocks to the north of the complex. All manner of livestock slumbered in enclosures. There were larger paddocks outside the wall, but these were the ones that kept the animals awaiting slaughter.

The smell here was almost too much for her. It wasn't just the scent of manure—which was unpleasant, but natural. This area had the rancid odor of neglect, festering and sick. From what she'd seen, Delphi's previous ruler Marron had run a tight ship, but Banyan and Scar had let things slip badly.

"Pig, sheep, or goat?" Roar asked.

"Um . . ." She was suddenly having second thoughts, even though this was her idea.

"Better this than human lives, Temp. And these animals are marked, anyway. It's either me tonight or someone else tomorrow."

He was right. "Sheep. Wait, no. Goat. No—pig!"

"Do you have something against pigs?"

"*Roar.*"

"Kidding. Pig it is." He climbed into the enclosure, landing on the other side with a squelch. "I'll do it fast. It won't hurt, but look away if you'd rather." Roar turned and approached a large round figure in the recesses of the pen. He was usually so quiet, but every step sucked in the mud. "Hello there, big fellow. How would you like to be a hero?" he murmured. He paused, bending to grab something outside the fence post. A carrot? Tempest watched as he knelt before the massive pig and offered up the stub. She heard chomping, and Roar cooing softly. "I promise you, friend, your life'll mean much more this way than it would've filling the stomachs of thankless men."

Tempest was holding her breath, cringing and waiting.

"Good boy," Roar said. "It's done."

"You mean . . . done-done?" She hadn't heard a squeal or grunt. She hadn't even heard the animal topple to the mud.

"Done-done. Still all right over there?"

She was actually feeling unsteady. "Fresh blood is not a smell I particularly like." The hot coppery smell leaking into the air was making her stomach roil. On top of that, the darkness was starting to press in on her, making her heart race. Though it would only make the smell worse, she climbed over the fence and moved closer.

From her new vantage point, she watched Roar work with the efficiency of a lifelong hunter.

First, he hung the animal, which wasn't nearly as large as she'd thought, on a hook and filled two huge pails with its blood. Then he removed the entrails. Finally, he disappeared for a minute and came back with a horse blanket, covering the carcass. There was no practical purpose for this last step, she discovered, but to keep scavengers and birds off the meat. "That's a lot of good meat," Roar said. "No sense wasting it." With the pails of blood and entrails loaded onto a small wheelbarrow, he picked up the handles and said, "Ready."

"I thought I said no bloodshed," she whispered, as they headed for the Fountain of Unity.

"You did," Roar replied. His face and hands were both darkened with blood. "Funny, right?"

"Hilarious."

They reached the fountain. Tempest stood for a moment, looking at the sculpture at the center: an iron crescent moon with winding roses. Ash had told Roar this fountain meant something to Scar. So far, she'd sent subliminal messages of trouble in Nightrose's union. Time to be more obvious. If this worked, Scar would surely be rattled.

Roar hefted up one of the pails and looked at her. "Yes?"

"Yes," she said. "Do it."

Bracing the pail on the cement lip of the fountain, he tipped it over, pouring out the dark liquid into the shallow pool. The blood gurgled and ballooned outward, staining the water deep, deep crimson under the Aetherlight. He went back for the other pail and did the same. This time, the water turned almost black.

"Roar, wait," she said, when he hoisted up one of the pails with entrails. "If we're doing this—"

"Which we are—"

"Yes—which we are—then this part has to be good." She stepped over the edge, climbing into the shallow water. For a moment, nausea reared up in her—she was standing knee-deep in a pool of blood—but she found her composure. This mattered. What they did here could have significant ramifications. Twenty-six people had died in Rim right before her eyes. It haunted her. If Banyan and Scar attacked, it could be a hundred times worse.

"Up here," she said, sloshing to the central sculpture. "Put it all over the moon."

Roar shook his head. "You have a dark and twisted mind. I like it."

She watched in admiring horror as he artfully wrapped the twisting intestines around the sculpture that was intended to represent the health and harmony of the united Rose and Night tribes. At some point, she found herself helping to adjust the draping in the places she could reach, swept up in the drama, in the effect she wanted to create, a little of her aunt's influence percolating up. It was disgusting and horrible—really and truly horrible—but this was about sparing the lives of innocent people. Her people.

When they were done, she admired their ghastly handiwork, whispering a quick prayer of thanks to their pig martyr, while Roar returned the pails and wheelbarrow.

"Crazy night, huh?" he said, jogging back to meet her. He sounded like he did this sort of thing all the time. Then he whistled low, shaking his head as he took in the fountain. "You really do have a great mind. We've got a problem, though. We can't go back like this, or we'll track blood everywhere. Won't take them long to guess whose work this was."

She looked down. She was covered in blood just like he was. She couldn't even imagine what they looked like as a pair. "What do we do?"

"I think I've got a solution." He crossed his arms. "But first, tell me your real name."

"*Now?*"

He shrugged. "I can't think of a more romantic moment to learn my wife's name."

She snorted. "Fine. It's Opal."

A grin broke over his face. "I knew it."

She laughed. "You did not."

"Sure did. I knew I'd love it. Come on." He swept her hand up. "Let's keep moving. Daylight's coming soon."

He led her through narrow streets to a darkened cottage with an open front. Tempest smelled iron ore, coals, leather and sweat, and put it together before she saw the glowing seams of the forge. A blacksmith's smithy.

Roar led her inside, where it was darker and warmer. "I'll be right back."

He disappeared. Tempest moved closer to the forge, a large, elevated hearth made of mortar and fieldstones. Its iron doors were almost closed, but it still put off plenty of heat, which she soaked in greedily. She was drenched and sticky with blood, and the cold had found her now that the adrenaline was wearing off. She had no idea what Roar meant to do, but when she saw a well pump just a few paces off that fed a trough, she jumped into action and stripped out of her rancid garments.

"Never say I didn't court y—" Roar froze as he ducked inside, fabric bundles tucked under both arms.

Tempest stood, totally bare. Her clothes were soaking in the trough, most of the blood already wrung out of them. "This was the idea, right?"

"What? Yes."

"Well, don't just stand there."

"Okay," he said. He piled the bundles—linens he'd stolen from a clothesline—on an anvil, then joined her by the trough and shucked off his clothes, setting his knife belt aside.

As she pumped in fresh water, he sloshed their clothes around. Under the glint of his eyes, the pale line of his teeth appeared in the gloom. "Ahh, domestic bliss."

"Great, isn't it? Why do people say marriage is dull?"

"Beats me." He dunked his head and scrubbed his hair. That seemed like a good idea—she'd somehow gotten blood in hers, too—so she did the same. As she righted, ice-cold water sluiced down her back. "Ack!" she cried, shuddering. "One shock after another tonight."

"Not really," Roar said grimly as he washed his arms. "Some things are happening pretty predictably. And please don't do that again."

"Do what?" She wrang the water out of her hair.

"What you just—what you're—" He huffed. "Can you just try to act like you're not naked?"

She'd been trying not to notice the very same about him, but she couldn't help it now. She turned to him, letting her eyes sift through the darkness, pulling him out of it. There was some kind of magic in the lines that made him. In the barely-there light cast by the forge, that magic was especially potent. He was breathtaking. She shivered again, her skin rippling with gooseflesh. This time, not from cold.

"Not helping," he grumbled, bracing a forearm on the trough to wash his face.

"Roar," she said, helplessly under his spell now.

He looked over at her. She could just see deep lines of concentration between his eyebrows, the hard set of his mouth. "What?" he said sharply.

"I just had an idea. It's probably not a good one, though."

She could've counted off five seconds before she saw his Adam's apple bob. "Does it involve me touching you?" he said finally.

"Yes. And vice-vers—"

A tiny yelp left her as he pulled her against him, crushing her lips with his, his mouth skirting some line between hard and soft. One of his hands plunged into her wet hair. The other flattened on her lower back and yanked her in. Tempest's breath caught, and guttural sound rolled through his lips. "Temp?" he said. She saw his brown eyes up close, full of emotion. She nodded, then his mouth was on hers again, their tongues dancing even as he swept her up.

Tempest wove her legs around his waist and linked her arms around his neck, the feeling of his body stealing her breath away. He was slick and warm, all bewitching, hard muscle. Desire radiated from every part of him, stoking the heat that spun through her.

In a far corner of her mind, a voice of reason piped up, asking *here? Now? Was she mad?*

She was, very much so. He drove her wild. He made her feel greedy and reckless and free—and those weren't feelings she ever allowed herself.

The answer, then, was yes. Resoundingly yes.

"I like you greedy and reckless and free," he murmured. He carried her to the forge, sweeping up a bundle of linens and placing it at her back, then bracing her against the hot stones. He bowed his head and kissed her skin, his hands unerring, knowing exactly what she wanted, the pads of his fingers somehow rough and tender. The combination too much.

"How do you do this to me?" he whispered.

She didn't know what he meant by *this*, and, anyway, she was beyond thought. The entirety of her being was focused on one thing—her consuming need for him—and he surely heard that thought, too, for he shifted her slightly and answered.

Earlier when they'd crept across the roof—and when they'd climbed down the wall—he had promised that he would be right with her, in tune with her, and now was no different. She dug her fingers into his back, holding on. He was everything she needed, the only answer that mattered. She'd known this for some time now. This wounded, charming soul she'd been forced to pledge her life to was worth it—the best of her and the worst of her. *All* of her. She gave him that—herself—and reveled in the feeling of getting all of him back in return. All the strength under her hands. All the heart and wit, all the honor and kindness.

When it was over and she was discovering the world again, it didn't feel like the same world at all. He made everything seem better. Every moment. It was all better with him.

He set her down gently and took her face in his hands, placing kisses on her cheek, her nose, her forehead, then pulling her against his chest. "Tempest—Opal?"

"Whichever you prefer."

"Let's go with 'my heart' for now."

"My heart?" She traced her fingers over the scar on his chest.

"Yes." He drew back, looking into her eyes. "You've given it back to me. I didn't feel anything for the longest time, but now I feel so much. For you. For everything, but for you. Tempest, I *am* for *you*."

She smiled, her eyes stinging with tears. "That's what I feel, too."

"What are we saying to each other?" he whispered, stroking her cheek.

"What are we not saying to each other?" she returned.

He laughed, then straightened sharply, like he'd heard something. "We're going to have to pick this up later. For the record, though, that was an unbelievably good idea that I will *always* agree with."

They dried off with the linens and tossed them in the forge, then wrung out their wet-but-clean garments and tugged them back on. Within minutes, they were climbing the ivy again.

It was much tougher to go up the wall cold and with soaked clothes, a true test to her muscles. But whenever tiredness or fear edged in, she only needed to glance at Roar to feel a jolt of fresh energy.

The sky was just beginning to brighten as they finally came to the top.

"Can you hang on for a minute longer?" Roar asked.

"Yes," she said, wondering if he could hear the uncertainty in her voice. Her hands and legs were shuddering. He peered over the low wall, then vaulted over it and was gone.

Tempest counted while she waited. She came to thirty-two before Roar reappeared above her and helped her onto the roof. Her gaze went to the prone figure on the far side.

"He's alive—just knocked out," Roar said.

They hurried to the stairwell and flew down the steps they'd climbed only a couple of hours ago. Absurdly, Tempest felt a giggle come up. She smothered it, but the urge to laugh only grew more powerful. She made it to her room, collapsed on her cot, and finally allowed the pent-up gales to tumble out of her.

"You're back!" Daisy was dressed and wide awake, her expression quickly transforming from surprise to confusion. "And you're *laughing.* And you're *soaked?*" She looked at Roar. "Did you do it?"

"With flair," he replied with a grin. "Any trouble here?"

"No," Daisy replied. "It all went well."

As part of her plan, Daisy had made two trips to the kitchen while they were gone to lay the groundwork for an alibi for Tempest. Her cycle was often painful, which Banyan would've likely heard about in the time she'd spent under his care. In the kitchen, Daisy made sure to casually mention that she was fetching hot compresses and tea to ease her discomfort. She also made a crack about the poor guard she'd left with Tempest (you know, the handsome one?) who was totally out of his depth. She'd go back down soon to reinforce the story again, and, if there was any reaction to their scheme, she'd hear about it and help fan the early flames of scandal.

Tempest's laughter was finally abating. "That was terrifying. And the most fun I've ever had in my life. Now what?"

"Dry clothes," Roar said. He paused at the door to the adjoining bathroom. "Pack a bag, Temp. We need to be ready if things go sideways."

Daisy shut the door behind him. "The most fun you've ever had in your life?"

"Easily."

"You're in love with him."

Tempest's mouth curved with a smile. She was, totally and completely. But she knew Roar might be listening—that even in the other room, he might've heard Daisy's question. If she decided to share that huge truth with him, she was going to do it while she looked him in the eye.

For now, she nodded in reply.

40

ROAR

"Someone's unusually quiet," Hayden said.

Roar looked up from the knife he was twirling in his hand, reversing the grip over and over. The others were all there as well, waiting for Delphi to wake up. Waiting to find out if the fountain ploy worked. The sun would rise in under an hour. Any moment now, someone would walk by it and Nightrose would begin to disintegrate.

In theory.

He had showered and dressed in black pants and a plain black shirt, eschewing the Horn uniform tunic. He needed to be himself right now for reasons he didn't quite understand.

Somewhere between pig entrails and a blacksmith's shop, he'd fallen for Tempest. *Really* fallen for her. He had no idea what that meant, or where it would lead. He wanted her, but life had taught him it wasn't that simple. *Liv* had. Sometimes love wasn't enough.

You could want someone with every fiber of your being, and think they wanted you back just as much, but be totally wrong. Or tragedy could strike. A murderous bastard could fire a crossbow and stop a heart. There were thousands upon thousands of reasons why love could not be enough. If that even was what Tempest felt for him.

Why hadn't she answered Daisy?

"Roar, seriously. Are you all right, man?" Hayden asked.

Roar shook off his thoughts. "Never been better."

Jons snorted. "That's exactly what it seems like."

Roar turned back to his knife, trying his tougher tricks. Tricks that demanded presence, his full attention. He didn't look up again until Daisy and Tempest stormed in, both of them flustered. He sheathed his knives neatly and stood.

"It's bad," Daisy said, a scarlet patch creeping up her neck. "I mean, it's good, but it's *bad.*"

Tempest's head bobbed. "She's right. It worked too well. Scar is in a monstrous rage. He's barefoot in the courtyard and mindless with anger. I thought he'd ask questions, that he'd demand an inquiry, threaten Banyan—something like that. But he's lost all reason. He killed two of Banyan's men with his *bare hands*, Roar. He's mustering his soldiers. Nightrose is over. We destroyed it. I just hope we didn't doom Raven and Ash."

"We didn't," he said. "They're fine. I haven't had a chance to tell you, but I took the liberty of making some moves where they're concerned. I thought it would be what you'd want." He looked at Jons. "Tell her."

"Yes, sir," Jons said, switching instantly into a formal address. This was something Roar had noticed happened between Tempest and Cal and Daisy. More and more, he was experiencing it himself. "I was given leave, by Roar, to go on a diplomatic mission earlier tonight to see Ash about . . . diplomatic matters. I may have mentioned to him, upon leaving, that it would be wise to be prepared for anything. He seemed to know we were up to something already."

Tempest nodded. "Good. Hopefully, they'll be safe."

"Ready, Temp?" Roar's only concern was her. "We need to go. This place is about to erupt."

"Wait," Daisy said. "I've been thinking that you two should go alone. If I'm here—if *most* of us are here—they'll think Tempest is still here. We can buy you time. It'll be easier for you to go unnoticed. To stay hidden in the woods."

Hayden scratched his jaw. "I don't like it, but it is the best option. We can catch up to you."

Roar nodded. His ears were feeding him information now, corroborating what Daisy had learned. He could hear the drumming of footsteps, shouting, doors slamming.

Delphi was waking up to a firestorm.

As Daisy and Tempest stepped out to get her bag, Roar described the trail he'd take to the others. He knew these mountains well, and designated a primary route and a secondary one, in case they had to abandon the first.

Tempest returned and they bid quick farewells. Twice, Daisy asked Roar to promise he'd protect Tempest. When he sensed a third time coming, he took her by the elbows. "I'll die before anything happens to her, Daisy, and I'm not easy to kill."

She tried to smile. "There's always a first time, you know."

He did, all too well. Liv had died as they'd tried to get away from Rim. A beautiful future could vanish in an instant. But he couldn't think about that now. He nodded at the guards who were his peers, his subjects, and above all, his friends. Then they left.

They took the lift to the ground floor; for the moment, speed was more important than stealth. Roar could hear shouting echoing from all parts of the complex and beyond.

"Did we make a mistake?" Tempest whispered. She looked pale, stunned.

"No. All you've done is the right thing. Just coming here after they've been hunting you for a year took incredible courage. You offered them peaceful solutions several times, *generous* ones, and they were still going to attack us. You gave them more respect than they deserved—far more than they ever gave you. You did everything you could."

"You just said they were going to attack *us*." The corner of her mouth lifted. "You were speaking like you're part of the Horns."

Roar realized that was true. "Is that all right?"

"Very all right."

The elevator chimed and the doors opened. Immediately, all was chaos. The corridor ahead of them was crowded with shouting people slamming into each other, hurrying off with terror and rage in their eyes.

He grabbed Tempest's hand and they muscled through that corridor, then another, weaving toward the main doors. Finally, they exited the complex, stepping out into a cool morning, and flowed into the commotion in the courtyard.

People were gathering around the fountain to see what the uproar was about. Scar's voice boomed from somewhere at the center, ranting about breaches of respect and failures of honor that had to be punished. "Blood for blood!" he yelled. "Blood for blood!"

In moments, the angry chant was picked up by his followers.

Roar kept his eyes forward and pressed on. His heart was crashing against his chest. In minutes—or less—there'd be bodies falling. He knew it. He could feel it. He'd been in enough situations like this—fury thick in the air, clogging it like smoke—to know the pressure had to release soon. He wanted Tempest nowhere near when it happened.

As they left the fountain behind, he saw Night tribe members gathering in clumps around the yard, but they were fewer, roaming directionless in search of answers or orders.

"Where is everyone?" he heard one of them asking another.

"*Gone,*" came the desperate reply. "They're all *gone!*"

Roar stopped, grabbing the man's shoulder. "You should get gone, too, if you want to live."

"Ash," Tempest said, as they hurried on.

"Yes," he agreed. Ash had probably started evacuating Night in the predawn hours.

On Scar's orders, which were shouted forward, the main gate began to shut ahead of them. Roar had anticipated this and they adjusted their course smoothly, heading for the smaller south gate. It was the farthest away, but if Scar was locking Delphi down, it would take longer for his orders to get there.

As they hurried through the same streets they'd crept through hours ago in darkness, people emerged from their homes and hastened toward the fountain, curious about the trouble. It forced them to move against the flow of traffic, which was getting them noticed, but there was nothing to be done about it. The streets began to thin as they reached the outskirts of the settlement, nearing the south wall. The sun was up, bleeding through the treetops. Soon it would rise above them.

Rounding a street corner, they saw the wall across a muddy clearing. Roar swore inwardly. The south gate was manned by two guards in Rose uniforms. They looked alert. Alarmed. They were clearly aware that something was amiss. Making matters worse, another guard was jogging along the wall to meet them, obviously bringing news or orders—or both.

Tempest's mind had been quiet, but he heard her now. *What do we do?*

"Keep walking." He firmed his grip on her hand. "Temp, whatever happens, keep going. You leave here. There's a trail just to the south of this gate. Take it for at least a mile, then hide. The others will know where to find you. Understand?"

Her gray eyes met his. "*No,*" she said. "*No*, Roar. I will never leave you."

A wave of nausea rolled through him as the words echoed in his memory. Liv had said similar words to him once. Then she *had* left him. Forever.

Tempest's hand slipped out of his as they reached the guards, who were watching them with fearsome glowers.

"I'm Tempest of the Horns," she said. "And I demand you let us through that gate. If you do not, I will consider my detainment an act of war."

None of them seemed surprised; not by who she was, nor by her command.

"Right, right. I've seen you around," the shortest guard said. He took a step forward, drawing his half sword and laying the point under Roar's chin. "And who's this?"

"No!" Tempest gasped, stepping in front of him.

The man adjusted, bringing the blade to her throat. Then everything seemed to stop, tension thickening in the air. In Roar's veins. To his horror, he found his eyes blurring. *The same. Too much the same.* His hands, hovering over the knives sheathed at his hips, began to tremble. A first. Never in his life had it happened, but it was happening now, in the worst possible moment. *Lower your sword*, he wanted to say, *or you're a dead man*. But he couldn't find his voice.

The guard addressed Tempest, his cold stare holding on Roar. "Can't let you pass. We've orders from Scar."

"You can and *will* let us pass," she returned. "Or I'll see you're all punished severely."

"I don't take orders from you," he said. The other two guards were drawing closer, building a human wall before the gate behind them. "My orders were to bring you—alone—to Scar."

Roar assessed the men before him, trying to gauge whether *he* was a dead man. They looked well-trained. Big, strong, capable. Even the shorter man was thick with muscle and looked like he could move. He saw the next moments unfolding in his mind. He could put down two, but the third would likely kill him, and Tempest would be trapped, taken to Scar, and that was as far as he allowed himself to think. This was not a survivable situation for him, but maybe he could save her.

He had just made the decision when Tempest's voice bloomed in his mind, her hand brushing briefly against his. *Pull me behind you, Roar! Please! Trust me!*

He didn't give himself a chance to question. He grabbed her wrist and yanked her back, saying the first words that came to mind. "I'll handle this."

As she slipped past him, he felt one of his knives slip out of its sheath.

"I don't think so! *I* give the orders!" she snapped, stepping forward again.

And then it began.

41

TEMPEST

For the past year, Tempest's sole focus had been protecting Cal, Daisy and Ventus. Then that had changed, and her tribe had taken precedence. Protecting Roar was just the newest outlet for the strongest instinct in her—the very force that gave her life meaning. And though he wielded knives with mastery, she knew three to one was unrealistic. A superhuman feat.

She had to do something. But *what?*

"I don't take orders from you," said the shorter guard. "My orders were to bring you—alone—to Scar."

Panic stopped her heart. Then an idea came, sharp as a whipcrack. She reached forward and touched Roar's hand. *Pull me behind you, Roar! Please! Trust me!*

Without missing a beat, he tugged her behind him. "I'll handle this," he said.

Tempest pretended to lose her footing. As she stumbled backward, brushing past Roar, she grasped the dagger sheathed at his hip and drew it.

“I don’t think so!” she cried out indignantly. As she stepped forward again, she kept the dagger low and behind her. “*I* give the orders!”

She took three steps—as quick as if she were running downhill—and was suddenly upon the guard, staring right into his shocked wide eyes. It didn’t feel quick, though. Time seemed to warp and slow, much as it had on the night of the revolt in Rim. In a way, she was going on pure, adrenaline-powered instinct. But she was also consciously thinking. Deciding. Where to stab him? She did *not* want to kill him. For what, following orders? For being a loyal subject? No. He didn’t deserve death for that. But then, she also had no experience with this. As many times as she’d watched Cal and Ventus spar—a hundred times, a thousand—she still had no idea where to drive the knife in her hand. Fortunately—or unfortunately (impossible to know), instinct made the decision for her.

She plunged the knife into his side, pushing all the way to the hilt.

Tempest let go and stepped back, appalled by herself. By the fragility and weakness of flesh against sharp steel.

The guard’s eyes flicked down. He grasped the hilt and screamed. Spittle flew from his mouth. His voice was an angry, broken wail.

As these moments unfolded crisply, one after another, like she was flipping through a stack of photographs, Roar became a blur of motion.

Before she knew what was happening, one of the other guards was down. His throat was flayed open. Blood coursed darkly from a horrific gash that he tried, in vain, to staunch with his hands. The last guard was ready for Roar's attack.

He drew his sword with a growl and swung it in a vicious arc. Roar leapt back, narrowly avoiding the point. The dying man with the slit throat was behind him, but Roar neatly stepped over him, like he was incapable of losing his balance. The knife in his hand flashed as it spun once, catching the morning sun.

"Only a matter of time," he said, a predatory glint in his eyes. "You either yield or you die."

"K—kill him!" stammered the guard Tempest had stabbed, who had crumpled to the dirt. "Kill the bastard!"

Roar's mouth tugged up. "Not going to happen. Last chance. Either—"

The guard lunged forward and thrust with his sword, trying to catch Roar unaware. Roar turned aside, his arm swinging out. The knife he held had reversed in his hand—she hadn't even seen it happen—the tip of blade facing his elbow. With ferocious speed and total economy of movement, he stabbed the guard in the hollow of his throat. The man was dead before he hit the ground.

Tempest turned away, suddenly feeling horribly sick. She bent over. She couldn't get any air into her lungs.

Roar's shadow fell over her. She looked up. She noticed the knife was resheathed at his belt, and that he stood so he blocked her view of the bodies. "We have to go, Tempest. Now." She nodded and made herself straighten. Roar jogged to the wall, unbarred the door and swung it open. He turned to her. "Come on. Let's get the hell out of here."

The next stretch passed in flashes of pine trees and treacherous roots. She ran. She stumbled and fell and got up and continued. The whole time, she felt like a wagon with loose wheels, like she might topple over or fall apart. Birds sang above without a care in the world. Sometimes there were patches of sky woven with gentle threads of Aether.

She kept going. It was the only thought in her mind.

Regardless of whether Scar and Banyan discovered what she and Roar had done, she was sure they'd be after her soon enough. Once again, she was being hunted. An old wound, reinjured. And this time, they'd catch her—and Roar.

What had she done?

Roar pulled her to a stop. They'd left the trail behind. There were less trees here, and she finally noticed the view. It was spectacular. Rolling hills below, covered in thick pelts of trees. A shining river weaving through them.

"Tempest." His hair was damp with sweat. He looked pale and haunted. "You all right?"

She nodded. "I will be." Her voice was a raspy whisper. "Is there anyone chasing us?"

"Yes, but they're not close. Can you—" He swallowed. "Can you wait here? I just—I just need a second." He jogged away, disappearing behind a crop of boulders. As she watched him go, the wind swept his temper to her. She scented the awful despair and grief that she'd picked up when they'd first met. It held the darkness of caves, the darkness of black smoke. Pain of the deepest bruising.

Her eyes moved back to the gorgeous valley below.

Can you wait here? he'd asked. No. She found she could not.

She scrambled over the rocks and found him doubled over and sobbing quietly into his hands. He'd been sick a little way off. She could smell that, too.

"Roar," she croaked and sank beside him. "What happened? Are you hurt?"

He shook his head and stammered something about her leaving, that he was disgusting. "Go," he said. "Please."

"No. Come here. Roar, *come here*." She took his shoulders and pulled him around forcibly, until he relented. He wrapped his arms around her, burying his face in her neck, and for a while she held him and rubbed his back as he trembled, and as his tears dampened her skin.

When he'd calmed down, he eased away and brushed his sleeve over his face. He looked destroyed. His eyes swollen, tears still threading his lashes together. He'd never looked dearer to her. "You were thinking earlier about being on the run again. How it was an old wound. I helped you up and I heard. I'm sorry—maybe I shouldn't have overheard that—"

"It's all right. Yes. I was thinking about that."

"I thought the same thing back there. It just felt so much like when Liv and I—when she and I were trying to leave Rim. I thought I was going to lose you. If you hadn't done what you did, I could've lost you. It almost happened. It was going to happen."

"But it didn't." She gave him a shaky smile. "It didn't happen, Roar. I'm right here. We are."

"I know." He scraped a hand down his face. "I don't know why this happened—why it hit me now." He shuddered. "Sorry. This fear, it's like something alive inside me."

"I understand. I do." She scooted against his side and leaned her head on his shoulder. "I'm not sure I'll ever stop having nightmares of Mattock. Maybe some fears are too big to overcome. Maybe the best thing we can do is find a way to live with them. Maybe that's how we beat them. We don't let them stop us. We live the life we want in spite of them."

He nodded. "Thank you for that."

She looked up. "You don't have to thank me. You're my fake husband, remember?"

"Fake thank you, then."

"Fake thank *you* for being honest with me. For trusting me."

"You're fake wel—no, that's enough. Temp, you're the best thing in my life. I love you. I'm sorry I'm saying it right now. Here, like this. But I need you to know it."

She smiled, her eyes blurring with tears. "I love you, too."

His mouth lifted to one side. "I was hoping you'd say that. So, will you be my girlfriend?"

"Whoa. No need to rush ahead. Let's just stay married for now."

"Works for me. You know, I feel it all now—my vows. All the things I said to you that day. I feel them." He touched his chest. "Right here."

She slipped her hand into his and thought, *so do I.*

They found a stream and quickly washed up, then continued working their way down into the valley. Thanks to Roar's hearing, they were able to keep a few hours ahead of the parties that were searching for them. Groups that followed different paths than those Roar had coordinated with Hayden and Daisy.

"Don't worry," he told her. "I'm good at this. I've spent a lot of time on the run."

As it happened, so had she. They were swift and silent together. A pair of owls slicing through the sky.

That night by a river, Roar caught a fish with his bare hands. They cooked it over a hot stone and ate, then clung to each other for warmth as the temperature dropped, and because they wanted to. They were both exhausted, but they stayed awake, whispering and discovering each other. To Tempest, every moment with him felt new and thrilling. Like unwrapping a gift.

They resumed their trek after only a short rest, needing to stay ahead of the parties that were after them. They had only been walking an hour when the hover appeared over the horizon, blurring in the red blaze of the rising sun.

"My queen," Roar said, breaking into a grin, "it appears our chariot's here to save us again."

Soren was the pilot, of course. Perry and Cal were with him. They had also picked up Daisy, Hayden, Jons, and the others a short while ago, after flying over Delphi and seeing the chaos unfolding. Amazingly, thankfully, everyone had made it out safely.

Tempest sat with Cal and Daisy in the main hold, talking a little, drinking water, but mostly drowsing on Cal's shoulder. She heard laughter in the cockpit.

Roar and Perry had a certain sense of humor together, dry and witty, but Roar and Soren took sarcasm to another level. She'd missed seeing them together.

It had taken a week of riding to reach Delphi from Rim. In the hover, flying at a leisurely speed, it took under two hours to get back. Soren asked for permission to land inside the main courtyard. She granted it, though she had no idea how he'd manage such a tight landing. He did it with ease, though, setting it down with hummingbird-like precision.

The hatch opened and the midday sun blazed in, cheerful and bright. Tempest climbed out first and was stunned to hear the swell of cheers and applause. The fortress staff—guards, kitchen helpers and chamber servants—stood around the yard and crowded the second-story arcade. Aunt Lerra rushed up, embracing her and gushing about how much she'd missed her. Tempest breathed a huge sigh of relief, feeling safe and nourished by the sturdy walls around her, the history and responsibility that settled comfortably in her bones.

I'm home, she thought. *This is home.*

Her attention pulled to Roar, who flew down the ramp and swept a girl into his arms. "Aria! Where've you been?" he shouted, spinning her around.

"Missing *you!*" she returned, laughing. "How did we survive?"

"I don't know," he said, setting her down. "Did we even?" He planted a kiss on her cheek. "God, I missed you! How long was that? A year? Two?"

"Too many miserable weeks." The girl, Aria, looked him up and down. "You look *good*, Roar."

"Not sure why you sound so surprised." He tipped his head. "Come here. I want you to meet someone."

Seeing them together, Tempest felt a twinge of jealousy, but it evaporated as they walked over. Perry looped an arm around Aria's shoulder and smiled, falling in step.

"Temp, this is Aria. Aria, Tempest," Roar said. Then he crossed his arms and smiled, mellow and utterly satisfied, like he was observing a gorgeous sunset. "You're going to love each other."

Aria came right in and hugged her. "I'm *so* happy to meet you." She stepped back. "When you're ready, I have a million questions."

She had the same, limby elegance as Roar and dark hair like his, too, but she was fairer. And very pretty, with a high forehead and a glimmer of curiosity in her eyes.

"I've got just as many for you," Tempest admitted with a smile.

Aria laughed, her eyes darting to Roar. "I bet."

Roar's brow furrowed. "What does that mean?"

"Come on," Daisy said, tucking Tempest into her side. "You need a bath, food, rest." As she swept Tempest off, Aria appeared on her other side like she'd been invited along.

"What have you done to him?" she asked.

"I can hear you," Roar said, behind them.

"Ignore him." Aria looped an arm through hers. "Seriously, though. He looks *really* happy."

"I am!" Roar called from the courtyard.

Aria's dark eyebrows lifted. "*Skies*," she whispered, "he's totally in love with you!"

"Now you're getting somewhere!" he shouted.

42

ROAR

"Thank you, sir," Elias said, his skinny arms trembling as he hefted the heavy glass pitcher and refilled Roar's water again. He was on pace to refill it with every single sip Roar took.

Roar was going to say something, but it'd become a matter of some entertainment for Hayden, Hyde and Straggler. The brothers, sitting on the far side of the dining table, were doing a poor job of hiding their laughter. They had even laid wagers on how long the boy would keep it up. Roar wondered if any of them had bet "infinity."

"Elias," Roar said, "I think I've told you a few times that you can call me, 'Roar.' And you're the one serving me. *I* should be thanking *you*."

"Yes, sir. Thank you, Roar." The boy grinned. "We're all so glad you're back, sir." He hustled out of the room, surely to refill the pitcher.

Roar shook his head as he watched him go. "He's determined to treat me like I'm someone important."

Perry, who'd been whispering things in Aria's ear that Roar had been trying hard not to overhear, looked up. "I think it's time you face it, Roar. You are."

Roar opened his mouth to reply. Closed it. He'd been kidding—he knew he was important, or at least not *un*important—and Perry's sincere answer caught him off guard.

Aria laughed. "He's speechless! So it *can* happen!" She reached across Perry, squeezing Roar's forearm. "I second that. You've always been important," she said, the humor fading out of her expression. "*Always*."

Again, he was caught wrong-footed. He cringed a little and looked at Tempest beside him for help, but she just smiled and gave him a little "you're on your own" shrug. Unable to come up with a joke to bandy back, he waved his hand and shook his head, and tried to appear interested in where Elias went, aware that he was being awkward because he *felt* awkward.

On Aria's other side, Soren yawned and raised his hand. "I third that. You're important to me." He batted his eyes.

To Roar's horror, he realized the laughter on the other side of the table stopped.

"I fourth it," said Straggler.

"Fifth it," Hyde said, raising his wine glass.

"I *guess* I'll sixth it," Hayden said, like it was a huge sacrifice.

"Seventh it," Daisy said brightly.

Cal rolled her eyes. "Oh, what the hell. Eighth it."

"Ninth it," said Aunt Lerra, with a proud smile.

He thought that was going to be the end of it—was already exhaling in relief—when the game changed. Or rather, expanded.

"Tenth it!" Elias practically screamed, water sloshing out of the pitcher as he rushed over.

Roar laughed. And from there, other staff felt comfortable jumping in.

"Eleventh it."

"Twelfth it."

It went on around the room, and continued out into the halls, with people chiming in who had no idea what they were doing.

Though he was laughing, and embarrassed, he couldn't help thinking back to that day on the beach with Perry and Talon. That day he'd first heard Tempest's voice crackling through that recording. His life had held no meaning then. No feeling. He had closed himself off to the world. Even the few attachments he'd had—with Perry and Aria, Soren and Talon—had been based on the false pretense that he was fine.

All he'd done in those days was serve that lie. Maintain it.

He shook his head, truly speechless now. It was amazing what a few weeks could do. What hope and friends and time could do. And a girl.

He cleared his throat and reached for his water to buy himself a moment. He'd barely set it down before thin little arms reached past him to refill it.

"Thank you, sir," Elias said, stepping back again.

"You're welcome, Elias," Roar muttered.

Across the table, laughter erupted.

When the normal rhythms of conversation returned to the table, he leaned toward Tempest. "I couldn't help but notice that you didn't chime in?"

She was wearing a flowing dress in a pale color, more gray than purple. Tonight it perfectly matched the color of her eyes. "Didn't I?"

"No. Do you not think me important?' He lowered his voice. "Please say yes so I can feel like I deserve you."

She was quiet for a long time. Then her cool hand settled over his. *You're more important to me than anything. I'm going to make sure you feel it every day.* He swallowed. Tonight, he couldn't seem to get the raw feeling out of his throat. *No—don't say thank you. Just accept it, Roar. Accept that you deserve it. All of this.*

Her hand came away. She tipped her chin slightly, indicating Elias.

He suddenly saw what she did: a boy who'd been through some trauma. Who was scared of the world and unsure of his place in it. Who didn't see his own worth.

Realizing he had Roar's full attention, Elias snapped to. "More water, sir?"

"Absolutely, Elias." He picked up his full glass and drained it. "Fill it up and keep it coming."

They all lingered at the table long after the meal was done. The conversation made the shift Roar had been anticipating all night, to matters that weren't fully resolved.

Aria, as usual, led the way. "After Soren arrived in Cinder and told me the Tides are under someone else's control, I had several long conversations about it with Talon. I wanted to be sure he wasn't reacting out of emotion. He's young, but so intuitive. So confident and sure about what he wants. He never once wavered. He wants it back." She reached over and took Perry's scarred hand. "He says if you don't get it back, he will."

Perry's smile was fleeting. Like a passing glow behind dark clouds. "I'll do it, of course."

"We will," Tempest said. "I made you a promise."

Perry looked up. "I'd be forever in your debt."

"You saved our asses," Cal said. "We save yours."

"That's true," Tempest said. "But this isn't just about some score that needs to be settled. I want to help. I will help."

For a long moment, they stared at each other. "Thank you," Perry said.

Soren scratched his jaw. "Well, don't pop the champagne yet. I took a little ride down to the Tides earlier with the hover." He sat up. "Guess who's moved into the Tide compound?"

Tempest grimaced. "It's either Rose or Night. I'm going with Rose."

Soren nodded. "I can't be totally sure, but it looked like it from a thousand feet up."

Roar had known it was a possibility, but it still filled him with anger to imagine Scar there, on land that was all but sacred to him. To Perry and Talon. He and Tempest had broken Nightrose apart, removing it as a threat to the Horns. But in doing so, they'd made matters worse for the Tides. "I'm sorry, Perry."

Perry smirked. "Don't be an idiot. How could you have known?"

"He can't help being an idiot," Soren said. "Anyway, whoever it was, there was a lot of them. We're talking *thousands* of people."

"It doesn't matter," Tempest said. "We'll find a way. You can all stay here indefinitely. You have the Horns' full support."

Aria smiled. "And Cinder's."

"Thank you," Perry said. "But before we start down that path, there's something I want to say." He stood, sweeping up his wine glass.

"A *toast*, Peregrine?" Roar laughed. "You've never done this!"

"And yet somehow I'm already regretting it." Perry straightened his shoulders and continued. "Roar, Tempest. Those first few days, you two were about as pleasant to be around as a pair of vipers. I've never seen a more miserable couple. But you found your way past anger and misunderstanding and proved something I've known for a few years now. Extraordinary people come into your life in extraordinary ways." He raised his glass, his eyes moving briefly to Aria. "Here's to life's beautiful surprises."

43

TEMPEST

"You make such a fine pair," the woman said, shifting the little girl on her hip. "May you have a long and happy life together."

Tempest thanked her, Roar gave the girl's braid a playful tug, and they continued on through Rim's streets. It had snowed overnight and there were still clumps of it in the shadows, but the first notes of spring were in the air. Tempest breathed in when a breeze swept past, smelling damp earth, green growth, and pollen.

Her afternoon walks with Roar were a daily habit now. Sometimes when she was in the throes of her responsibilities, she couldn't break away. But for the most part, Tempest joined him—and never regretted it.

They reminded her that Rim had a face. It had *thousands* of faces. Rim was that woman and her ginger-headed little girl. It was the two boys who ran past, shouting at the tops of their lungs about something. It was the dozens of other people in this street, and every other. These walks reminded her to take a deep breath, to pay attention to what it all ultimately meant.

"Tempest," Roar said, as they ambled past the tavern they'd taken over the night of the revolt, "if we weren't already married, would you still want to be with me?"

"Probably not."

He frowned. "Such a jokester."

She slid under his shoulder, wrapping her arm around his narrow waist and squeezing. "You know I would."

It was a question she frequently asked him, too. They'd been together almost five months now. They were stronger than ever, but she understood why it still came up. One of the biggest decisions of their lives had been forced, made under duress. To make up for it, they did this.

They chose each other often.

They walked on, returning smiles and greetings. Every week, it seemed more people were out on the streets at this hour or poking their heads out their windows to wave.

After a while, they left the city and took a dirt path that wove through an olive grove. All around her, leaves the color of verdigris swayed in crisp breezes. There was still so much work to do to return the Horns to prosperity. To recover the Tides for Perry and his nephew. And there was always the Aether to fear and to try to understand. But she let herself enjoy the good moments when they came. She glanced at Roar.

Lately, they came often.

It was almost an embarrassment of riches. Almost.

Roar was quiet, staring into the distance.

Tempest stopped. She knew that look. “Do you hear something?”

He turned to her, his eyes like liquid amber in the soft light. “Only the entire world.” He smiled. “It’s good music.” He swept up her hand and pressed a kissed to it.

And without another word, they headed home.

ACKNOWLEDGMENTS

This book turned out a lot longer than I expected, so I'll try to keep it brief here.

Thank you, readers! Thank you, thank you, thank you. You're the reason this book happened. To this day, I am moved when I hear from you. I am so honored that the trilogy earned a small place in your hearts. I wanted to give you this book for the ten-year anniversary of the publication of UTNS. Alas! It took longer than I expected. Part of the reason being that I've created this on my own. (If you encounter any typos, that's totaly on me—wink-wink.) As such, I'm at the mercy of a new economic model, which is not ideal for either of us, I promise you. That's out of my control. Anyway.

A special shout-out to my agent, Tina, for being the perfect advocate. Tulip, this world is better with you in it. Thanks also to Josh and Stephen. I appreciate all you do and have done for me. Michele and Ronda, thanks for making this process so easy and enjoyable.

I owe huge thanks to Talia Vance and Trish Doller, who read early versions of this story. Thank you also to Beth Hull, who's answered fifty-billion questions about self-pub with patience and extreme generosity. Thank you to my writing community: Donna, Kristen, Katy, Bret, Kim T., Kim L., Tamara, Henry, Lorin. And if you're name's not here, know that I'm thinking of you and just trying to keep this short. Finally, thanks to my family and friends. Michael, Rock, and Luca: you make me the luckiest.

Once again, thank you for taking this journey with me. Should we keep going!?

Soren's been tapping me on the shoulder . . .

ABOUT THE AUTHOR

VERONICA ROSSI is a New York Times and USA Today bestselling author of books for young adults. She was born in Rio de Janeiro, grew up in California, and graduated from UCLA. She lives in the San Francisco Bay Area with her husband, two sons, and her dog, Beckett.

Also by Veronica Rossi

Rebel Spy

From the Under the Never Sky Series

Under The Never Sky

Through The Ever Night

Into The Still Blue

Roar And Liv (novella)

Brooke (novella)

From the Riders Series

Riders

Seeker

~

www.ingramcontent.com/pod-product-compliance
Lightning Source LLC
Chambersburg PA
CBHW020556310726
48979CB00008B/1235/J

* 9 7 9 8 9 8 7 2 3 0 5 0 3 *